SNOW BOUND

EMMANUELLE

USA TODAY BESTSELLING AUTHOR

SNOW

Smart Lily
Publishing

BOARDING PASS

PENA / ABIGAIL

BOARDING PASS

FORD / ANDERSON

SILVERVILLE, PA

Emmanuelle Snow
emmanuellesnow.com

CARTER HILLS BAND UNIVERSE
(SUGGESTED READING ORDER)

Carter Hills Band series
False Promises

HEART SONG DUET
Blindsided
Forevermore

Whiskey Melody series
Sweet Agony

SECOND TEAR DUET
Cruel Destiny
Beautiful Salvation

BREATHLESS DUET
Wild Encounter
Brittle Scars

Upon A Star series
Last Hope

Midnight Sparks

Love Song For Two series
LONESOME HEART DUET
Fallen Legend
Rising Star

TWO OF US DUET
Snowbound

Wicked Love

All titles available at
emmanuellesnow.com

For the best experience, read in the order as shown above

Trust that the universe has your back.
Or cross your fingers and toes it does.

TRIGGER WARNINGS

Disclaimer

My books are realistic and emotional love stories.

I'm an advocate for mental health, and some topics could be sensitive for certain readers since they are portrayed as close to real life as possible.

I've listed the potential trigger warnings for each title on my website.

Be advised that those trigger warnings could potentially be spoiler alerts for the storylines.

Those sensitive topics have been written with the utmost care and respect. Please reach out if you have questions or comments.

All books contain sexuality, mature content, and language not intended for people under 18 years of age.
For other readers' sake, please avoid spoilers in your reviews.

Thank you and have a wonderful day!

Emmanuelle

emmanuellesnow.com

BECOME A VIP

TO NEVER MISS A THING

Snow's VIP

Join **Emmanuelle Snow's VIP newsletter**

Be the first to know about new releases, giveaways, sales, and special events. And step into a space where big emotions are celebrated, love is messy and beautiful, and stories linger long after the last page.

emmanuellesnow.com

Snow's Soulmates

Join Emmanuelle Snow's Facebook VIP group, **Snow's Soulmates**, to chat with her and other readers, get updates, and more bonus content.

facebook.com/groups/snowvip

THE WAY SHE MADE ME FEEL
THE SONG

No, it wasn't a typical Thursday
    night
The wind was blowing, and the
    snow was piling up outside
Sipping my black coffee, reminiscing
    about the lost days
I thought I could get through the
    night on my own
I thought I was well enough on
    my own

[chorus]
I felt helpless, but then you walked
    my way
With your smile and your conta-
    gious optimism
Soon I lost myself in your crystal-
    blue eyes
And there're so many things I wish I
    had told you

Starting with the way you made
    me feel

We found ourselves stranded in an
    airport
I had no intention of making a
    friend that night
Sipping my black coffee, I tried to
    block you out
I believed I would be better off all
    alone
I believed we weren't supposed to
    get along
(God, I've been wrong, so wrong)

[chorus]

You showed me how to seize the day
And I don't remember the last time
    I had that much fun
Sipping whiskey, I wanted to hold on
    to you forever
I should have asked for your number
    that night
I shouldn't have let you go in the
    morning light
(Oh, how I wished I'd asked for your
    full name)

[chorus]

We were strangers destined to meet
    in the night

We were soul mates drifting apart
    too soon
We were supposed to be together for
    longer
Forever, you and I, I will remember
From the way you made me feel to
    the sparks shining in your eyes
Abby, I wish I'd asked for your full
    name last night
Abby, I wish I could see you again
    tonight

Music and lyrics by Anderson Ford

Prologue
Abigail

My eyes hurt from the lack of sleep. I'd been up all night, searching the internet to find the one person on this Earth I didn't know the name of. I rubbed my heavy eyelids with the sleeve of my hoodie, hoping to clear my now cloudy vision. I swore my brain had decided to see everything in dual frames. A thick fog enveloped my mind, making it hard to think straight.

Every social media platform I could think of, I'd checked numerous times.

How many Andrews about my age lived in this country? Way too many. It was a lost cause. A conclusion I'd come to minutes ago. He could be anywhere around the world right now.

I sighed.

Soon, I would have to resign myself to my fate and go through this alone. *On. My. Own.* I scanned the space around me and took in the pile of boxes my best friend

Ellie and I had emptied last week, and my eyes brimmed with hot tears. A wave of sadness washed through me. Exhaustion settled in.

I had promised myself I would find him. And I had failed.

Rivulets of my sadness cascaded down my cheeks, and I let them flow freely, too tired to even patch the broken pieces of my heart and the dam that had ruptured.

How had I become such a failure at nineteen? I wasn't even out of my teen years, yet my life seemed all set to derail—in more ways than I could count—and I was all alone for the ride.

Ellie had left before dinner. She had taken a flight back to campus.

She didn't have to come all the way to Tennessee for me after I'd broken the news to my parents that I'd withdrawn from college. For now.

She didn't have to help me set my new life on track either. Or even fly here once more to unpack my things after I'd moved.

Three months ago, my parents gave me an ultimatum and threw me out without a second glance. For eleven weeks afterward, I'd been living someplace I never thought I'd consider home in this lifetime. But what other options did I have? Zero to none.

Deciding not to let life have the last word in my future, I worked double-time—even when exhaustion got the best of me—and so far, it had paid off, because now I had a place to call mine. A home. Or more like the only non-dump I could afford.

Ellie didn't have to fill the refrigerator of my new apartment with healthy options. And she didn't have to stop by the store to pick up colorful decor items to give this place a little character and make it lovelier than it was. I had told her I'd pay her back. Eventually. One day. She'd brushed the idea away with a flick of her wrist. "My treat," she had said. Something that she often repeated these days whenever it concerned me. Or my screwups.

No, Ellie didn't have to do any of those things. But she did them anyway, out of the selflessness of her heart. And I would forever be grateful that she'd stuck by my side, because no one else did.

To add misery to my already complicated existence, I was now failing at the promise I'd made to myself: to get hold of the one person I needed to talk to, to confide in about everything. Be honest. And tell the truth. And yet, he was the one who didn't seem to exist. As if my brain had created him one night. And he'd evaporated in the morning light.

Fresh tears blurred my vision.

Pulling the fluffy purple blanket Ellie had gotten me to cover the not-so-pretty brown couch that came with the apartment around my heaving shoulders, I curled up on the worn wooden floor that must have looked fancy in its earlier years. Now it just looked old. And sad. Like me.

Even though I tried, I had no more fight left in me.

These days, every effort felt harder than it really was. I was constantly exhausted, but I always tried to push a little more because I only had myself to rely on. And being tired wasn't an option.

My body let go first. But even in my dreams, my mind was restless.

Images of our time together waltzed behind my closed eyelids.

"I'm sorry," I murmured through the raw lining of my throat. "For everything."

That was when my brain lost the fight too.

I would be all right. I had to be. What else could I do?

His name fell from my lips as his handsome face, brightened with joy, formed in my mind, the sparks in his eyes aimed at me. He smiled and whispered, "I'll never forget you, Abby." The last words he had spoken to me.

How I wished it were true. The image dissolved, and there was nothing left of the man I'd been thinking about for months now.

I begged my mind to bring him back. Not a flicker. Nothing. Even the dream version of him had abandoned me.

For the first time, fear made me a prisoner, its steel claws digging into my heart.

I wouldn't let it win. I had to fight back. To make it work. Somehow.

Oblivion filled my head, my heart heavy with tears.

Chapter 1
Abigail

PRESENT

All my life, I'd been wanting to work in the music industry and after everything that happened, I never thought I'd see this day coming. Or that my dream could become tangible one day. For more than three years, I'd worked my ass off as a virtual assistant while juggling home, college, and all the other responsibilities a twenty-three-year-old woman shouldn't have had to deal with all by herself. But hey, I was now ready to prove to Mr. Burns I could be the assistant he was looking to hire.

Three months ago, I had finally graduated with a dual degree in business administration and music management. One I'd worked my ass off for. Days and nights. Literally. I was overqualified for this position, but I didn't care. I would be an assistant any day if it meant I could prove my value. Climb up that career ladder until I reach my ultimate goal. Yeah, anything to bring me closer to my dream job.

In the full-length mirror in the entryway, I glanced at my power outfit one last time—white blouse and red pencil skirt—my first impulsive buy and the most expensive one to date. Along with matching heels. Money had been scarce in the past few years. But I had always made it work somehow. I smoothed the fabric over my thighs with trembling fingers, doing my best to calm the jitters invading me.

Tears pooled in my eyes, and I felt a little pinch in my heart.

"I can do this. I will do this. I deserve this." I repeated my mantra over and over. Nothing like a little pep talk to put me in the right mindset.

I blinked hard to chase the moisture away. Now wasn't the time to think about every bump in the road, all the things that needed to be done to reach where I was today. Instead, I focused on Aisha Jones's country song "In Your Dreams" playing in the background. A reminder that the Holidays were seven weeks away. And a nod to the best night of my life.

Two weeks ago, I had celebrated my birthday with Mixchos—reinvented nachos—and the biggest mug of hot chocolate I could find. Ellie, my best friend, had sent me the new pair of heels I was wearing today as a present and told me they would bring me luck. I hoped she was right.

From my spot near the front door, I surveyed my small apartment, the single main room, two closet-sized bedrooms off to the side, and an open kitchen. My eyes caressed all the furniture and the mess around it lovingly. It had been hard, but totally worth it.

A hint of a smile peeked on my lips. If I'd come all this way, the interview would be easy-peasy. I crossed my fingers, hoping it wasn't wishful thinking on my part. I'd been learning all about CB Music for the last month, from the awards Mr. Burns had won over the years to each page of their corporate website. A girl couldn't be prepared enough. The guy was a household name on the international music scene. I wouldn't let his credentials and achievements intimidate me. I would be the professional he expected me to be. Even though, deep down, I was kind of amazed by his career and success.

Every day, I listened to each of his songs, just in case they quizzed me on them.

Back when I was nineteen, I used to be a music encyclopedia. I knew every artist, even the emerging ones, and could recite by heart every award they'd won in their careers and all their biggest hits. I could tell which songs would be chart-toppers and which ones would be misses. Over the last few years, I'd lost my magic touch, too busy with the numerous curveballs life had thrown at me. Now I was ready to take my power back—to get to the top of my game and dig up the version of me I had somehow lost along the way.

Looking in the mirror, I wiped the tears from my eyes with my fingers and swiped a hand through my hair. I was ready. I would get this job. I could feel it. Today was the day my life would change for the better. It was about time. I huffed. Yes, the stars would finally align themselves. It was my time to shine.

At the front door, with a hand around the doorknob, I closed my eyes. This job, this opportunity, would mean the world to me if I got it. I believed in the magical power of the holidays. A girl could always hope for the best. Growing up, my grandma had told me multiple times that all the best things happened around this time of year. I could tell she spoke the truth, because I had already experienced a Christmas miracle four years ago. Now I craved a second one. If it wasn't too much to ask.

Locking the door behind me, I exited the building with a pep in my step. All week, I'd been walking around my apartment in heels to get used to their feel and look confident wearing them.

On the sidewalk, I let a full breath out as I glanced at the sky. An immaculate blue canvas and glittering sunshine. Yes, today would be a good day. A great day. One to remember.

A prayer to the Gods above and I climbed into the backseat of the idling cab that would drive me to Nashville's tallest building where I would meet some of the most important music executives in the country.

Wish me luck. No, not luck. I knew I'd be the best at that job.

Go, get them, tiger. Yeah, much better.

I exhaled. This position was mine. I was ready to hustle for it. Whatever it took, I'd be the newest CB Music employee by the end of the day. I, Abigail Peña, would be a rising star on the Nashville music scene. One day, I would sign the biggest artists under my management and would become a household name in this industry.

———

One breath in. I passed though security, filled the logbook, hung the visitor pass around my neck, and made it to the twenty-sixth floor. Yes, I belonged here. I could feel it deep in my bones. Goose bumps spread on my arms, and excited flutters danced around in my stomach. This was my chance. And I wouldn't miss it.

I checked my outfit and makeup one last time and smoothed a hand over my hair in the mirrored wall of the elevator. Satisfied, I rubbed my clammy hands on my skirt discretely and steeled my shoulders.

A woman in her fifties with a businesslike demeanor gave me a not-so-subtle once-over when I exited the elevator.

I cleared my throat softly before approaching her, hoping my voice wouldn't squeak.

"Welcome to CB Music. May I help you?" she asked, lifting a dark eyebrow.

I breathed out. "Yes, I'm here for the interview. For the assistant's position. I'm meeting with Mr. Burns and Mr. Jacobson at ten."

The woman tapped something on her computer before bringing her attention back to me. "Ms. Peña. You're early. That's good. Just take a seat. I'll call out your name when they are ready for you."

I nodded and sat on a white leather chair in the small waiting room, crossing my feet at the ankles.

To avoid freaking out, I grabbed a magazine and pretended to glance through it.

I had an interview with Curtis Burns, one of Nashville's most famous country music stars turned record label owner slash manager.

If he were as good a manager as his son Riley, this was promising. Riley Burns had signed many upcoming country rock stars over the years. He was as famous as his dad, even though they chose different career paths. One day, I'd play in the big leagues. Just like him.

The receptionist called out my name, and I jumped to my feet, adjusting my top before following her to the conference room. My breath hitched when I took in the view. The room had a floor-to-ceiling glass wall, offering the best view of the Cumberland River and the football stadium on the opposite shore.

Curtis Burns and Gregory Jacobson rose to their feet to shake my hand as I entered, and I took the seat they pointed me to, a genuine smile plastered on my lips. I finally had my chance to shine.

Deep down, I urged my throbbing heart to take a rest.

Confidence spread through me. It spurred me to talk slowly and show them I was the real deal. That I was the perfect—no, the only—valuable choice for this position.

The interview passed in a blur.

If someone had requested me to write down the questions they'd asked, I couldn't have done it. The words had flown out of me with ease before I could think them through. Every time the men exchanged nods and took notes, I high-fived myself in my head. I could do this. Excel and take the first step toward making my dreams a reality.

"Before you go, Ms. Peña, I want you to meet the first artist we've signed under our label," Mr. Jacobson said. "Being Mr. Burns's assistant means you'll work closely with our artists." He pressed a button on the speaker set in the middle of the table. "Laura, please send Mr. Ford in. We're ready for him."

Laura said a few words and hung up as we waited.

Moments later, a discrete knock resonated through the room, and the door opened to let the man in. I moved to my feet, ready to greet him and introduce myself. Longish brown hair, dark enigmatic eyes, nonchalant gait.

Our eyes met, and air froze in my lungs.

"Ms. Peña, this is Anderson Ford," said someone in the background.

I tried to speak, but words refused to make their way up, my feet glued to the floor and my arms hanging at my sides.

Then a rush of air along with a single word. "You?"

The man's jaw fell open and he blinked, an expression I couldn't decipher crossing his eyes.

Mr. Burns harrumphed. "You two know each other?"

I nodded, still unable to speak.

"Well, let's all sit and discuss, shall we?"

Neither of us moved, unable to break eye contact as my insides burned and melted, hurting me until I couldn't seem to breathe.

As I closed in on myself, I heard for the first time the faint strain of country Christmas music playing on a speaker somewhere in the ceiling. Ironic, right?

Santa had mixed my wishes—or was late delivering them—because it had been two years since I had last wished for this man, the one whose full name I hadn't known until today, to walk back into my life.

Anderson.

Not Andrew.

And now that he was here, I had no clue what to do.

Chapter 2
Anderson

Four years ago

"This was good, man. If you don't make it big one day, you could become a country music Santa for older ladies," my best friend Joe remarked.

"Yeah, right. That's what I want out of life. To be Santa." I couldn't help chuckling at Joe's teasing. He did this every time I finished a Christmas gig.

"Just saying, man. Those cougars were drooling whenever you strummed the chords. And when you sang, I'm pretty sure they soaked their panties. You'd be rich and famous entertaining them. I can picture it in my head." He raised both hands before him as if unveiling a banner. "Anderson Ford, singing Santa in retirement homes." I grimaced as he continued further. "Man, I think it sounds very…very promising."

"Forget it. You can't even convince yourself." I let out a

sigh followed by a deep laugh. "I'd choose dive bars over office holiday parties anytime. But thank your dad for hiring me tonight. It means a lot."

"He's happy to help. And you know he loves your stuff. He talks about how good you are to all his friends. Anyway, I need to go back. Those ladies are generous when they're tipsy. No way am I letting Jess cash in on all the extra money tonight. Are you gonna make it home in time for Christmas?" Joe, aka the bartender at his father's office party, asked.

"Yes. My plane is leaving at midnight. I must head to the airport now. We'll talk in a couple of days."

"Sure. Say hi to your mom for me. Tell her she can send a gallon of her special eggnog my way anytime."

"Will do." A loud chuckle left my mouth. "Merry Christmas, man." I grabbed my guitar case and made my way outside, relishing the cold winter air as it filled my lungs.

I had bigger dreams than singing in bars and office parties for a living, but, for now, it paid the bills and got my name out there. One day, it would be my turn to headline a world tour. I could feel it deep in my soul.

Snowflakes swirled over my head, and already I could see two inches of snow on the sidewalk. The wind picked up, and I buttoned my jacket, hailing a cab before shoving my other hand into my pocket. Damn it. They said the storm would start the next morning. Not tonight. I couldn't afford to miss Christmas. Ma would be all by herself if I didn't make it home in time.

"Where to?" the cab driver asked once I hauled myself onto the backseat, sweeping the snow from my shoulders and hair.

"Airport."

"Oh, you didn't hear, did you?"

I shook my head when our eyes met in the rearview mirror.

"Most flights have been delayed tonight. There's a blizzard coming our way. I hope you're going to Florida because unless you are, there's a big chance you won't board a plane tonight."

I dragged a hand over my face. This couldn't be happening. I was supposed to leave two days ago, but when Joe's father booked me as the main event at his office Christmas party, I switched my flight to make a pit stop in Silverville, to fit in the new engagement.

"Let's pray it calms down before midnight," I said, hopefully—or rather, trying to be. Holiday miracles existed, right?

With the snow falling, the streets were mostly empty at this late hour. People rarely ventured out when the weather was this bad.

An hour later, I was sitting in one of the airport cafés, my face buried in my hands. My flight had been rescheduled for the next morning. I could have made it back to Joe's parents' for a few hours, but in this weather, I risked not coming back in time if the snow kept piling up all night in this small Pennsylvania town.

The waitress, a woman dressed in a Santa hat and apron, neared me and refilled my coffee cup. "Feeling down, son?"

I grunted in response.

She sashayed down to her counter and turned up the volume of the Christmas song playing through the café speakers.

I quirked an eyebrow up as to say *Really* when she shrugged and went on to welcome a new customer.

A girl. Jet black hair, crystal-blue eyes, and a shy,

lopsided smile. Our gazes met when she sat at the table next to mine.

"I'll be right back with your order," the waitress told her, disappearing behind a door.

"Hey," the girl said. "Delayed flight?"

"Nah. I just enjoy whiling my time in airport cafés during the holidays. What kind of question is that?" My piss-poor attitude didn't seem to faze her because she smiled at me as if I'd just complimented her.

"Where are you heading?" she asked.

"Memphis."

"Oh, I'm going to Nashville."

I nodded and returned my focus to my coffee, shutting her out.

"Why are you in Pennsylvania?"

I blocked her voice, doing my best to ignore her. It didn't do shit because she kept asking questions as if we were buddies and having a back-and-forth conversation when in reality, I was staying quiet.

"I love it here, but the weather can be harsh during this time of the year."

Nope. Minding my own business. Not engaging with her.

Silence fell upon us. Until she decided she wasn't done annoying me. "Is it a connecting flight, or do you live around here?"

Would she just shut up for a second? Couldn't she read the sign plastered across my face that said I wasn't in the mood to chitchat with a stranger?

"Music gig." The words left my mouth before I could stop them. There was nothing friendly about the way I uttered them. Still, my broodiness didn't deter her.

"Oh, you're a musician?"

I nodded, sipping my coffee, while she droned on. "I'm

attending Silverville School of Business, also known as SSB. Want to be a music executive. I guess we share a common passion for music then. What about you? Are you a college student?"

"Yep." *One-word answers, lady. Read between the lines.*

"In Silverville?"

No such luck. Wouldn't she let go? Why did she keep making conversation with me? I was good on my own, wallowing about my upcoming night, before she came along. "Some art school in New York."

The girl clasped her hands, her pretty face brightening with a smile. "Wow, that's amazing. I wish I could be an artist. But no, I'm more into business. But I wanna work in the music industry. Growing up in Nashville can do that to you."

The waitress came back with a sandwich and a cup of what smelled like hot chocolate and placed them before her on the table. "Here you go, darling. Let me know if you need anything else." She lowered her voice to a fake whisper. "And if I were you, I'd stay away from this grumpy fellow right here. He's not really the friendly type." She winked and disappeared through the same door she'd come through.

I huffed an annoyed breath out, and the girl giggled. Everything inside me stilled, then slowly came back to life. My insides quivered at the sound, the storm deep within me beginning to fade. It was the most beautiful sound I'd ever heard. Clear and soothing. Warm and addictive.

My lips bent a little. I hated being in a bad mood, but somehow, I couldn't shake the situation I was in tonight.

"Oh, you smiled," she exclaimed. "You should do it more often. It lights up your face."

"Whatever."

"Why are you being such a grouch? It's Christmas Eve tomorrow. You should be happy. And festive."

I grunted. Why couldn't she stop trying to psychoanalyze me? I had my reasons, and they didn't concern her.

"Well, you have nothing to say in your defense?" she probed.

"I'm not brooding. Just tired."

The girl snorted. "Oh, come on. You're full of crap." She pointed to my face. "You are in a funk. That face of yours is not good at lying."

"Funk? You know nothing about my face, and we're not friends, are we?"

"Believe what you want. I'm the one seeing it right now. And we'll be friends. Give it some time."

Gosh, why couldn't she let it go? Deciding to prove her wrong, I straightened my features.

"Well tried. Not working, though. I can still see those wrinkles around your eyes."

"No, you're not."

She watched me, waiting for my explanation. I debated telling her the truth, but the intensity of her gaze broke through my reservations.

"My mother… If I don't make it home in time, she'll spend Christmas all alone. I'd promised I'd be there."

"But it's not your fault. It's the weather. It's not like you're doing this on purpose."

I shrugged. "I had a flight home, booked two days ago, then got a gig, so halted here. That pushed my flight to tonight. Totally my fault. I changed the plans."

The girl leaned over and pressed her hand over mine. Electricity traveled from her fingers to my spine.

"Don't blame yourself, okay? I'm sure your mother will understand. And Christmas Eve is just a number on the calendar. You can celebrate it in two days or a week from now. Who will care?"

I relaxed my jaw. "I guess you're right but still, I hate doing that to her. I'm all she's got."

The girl squeezed my hand. "It will be all right."

She removed her hand, and I missed the warmth of her touch.

Remaining silent, she gulped down her food as if she hadn't eaten all day.

I watched her throat work with every bite of her sandwich, and it turned me on.

Oh fuck. What's happening to me?

———

The girl's phone rang, and she stared at it with a frown, oblivious to the effect watching her awakened in me. She took a deep breath and straightened her back as she swiped the screen to answer. Right now, the curious side of me was dying to know who was on the other end of the line. From the way she twirled the string of her sweater around her finger and chewed on her bottom lip, I could tell she was nervous about answering.

An array of emotions crossed her face when she said, "Hello?" Something resembling fear and discomfort—or maybe annoyance—tinted her voice. She blinked fast, sank her teeth into her bottom lip, and her shoulders sagged.

I tried to focus on my coffee but couldn't help watching her because she looked to be part in pain, part hesitant.

"No… It's not my fault there's a snowstorm on the East Coast." A long pause. "I'm not being arrogant, but I have no control over the weather."

She bit on her thumbnail, nodding as she listened. Was she being faulted for the weather?

"No, I couldn't leave yesterday. I had stuff to deal with before winter break."

She sighed, casting a glance down. Whatever the other person was telling her, he or she was trying to guilt-trip her for something she had no power over. What a jerk.

Some of the tension that had knotted my back since I'd learned my flight had been rescheduled melted away—and so did my annoyance. My reasons for being upset sounded silly right now. At least I didn't have someone calling to make me feel bad about things I couldn't control.

Her voice quivered, snapping me out of my thoughts. "I understand my life here is not meaningful to you and doesn't fit into your plans, but it is to me." A pause. "I'll be there in time for the banquet. The flights are delayed until the morning." Another pause. "Yes, I know how important it is to you."

The girl who'd asked me twenty questions earlier shut down right before my eyes. She lost her spark. Gone were her animated features and extrovert persona. I only saw a husk of her sitting in front of me. Staring down, she kept bobbing her head over and over, as if she'd done something wrong. It angered me to witness how someone could fuck with her mind and steal her light without a second thought.

"Yes, I had my hair trimmed last month." She shook her head and stifled a sigh.

Seriously, what was that with all the questions?

"No, I have no dark circles under my eyes." She idly traced patterns on the table with her fingertip, suddenly looking exhausted.

Was it a prank? If not, who the hell asked things like that?

"I'll make you proud, I swear. I can tell how much—"

The other person interrupted her, and the girl continued gnawing on her nail.

How could they make her feel like she had no right to speak in a situation that clearly made her uncomfortable? For an unknown reason, I wanted to grab the device from her grip and tell that sucker to leave her alone and go annoy somebody else. It made no sense I wanted to defend a stranger, but I hated seeing her light being dimmed when it had radiated so strongly minutes ago.

"Do I really have to pretend to tolerate him?" A dark flush colored her cheeks. "You…you know what he did last time... It was inappropriate and—" A long pause. "I'm aware his father is a well-respected businessman, but it doesn't excuse his son's behavior…" A fat tear rolled down her cheek, and she wiped it off with the heel of her hand. "I'm not complaining. I'm just stating facts. It's just…I would feel more comfortable going with someone else."

Her throat worked on a swallow. Not the sexy kind, but the painful one.

"He's the one who did this to me. Why are you still not believing me? Why are you taking his side?"

My fists clenched under the table. I wasn't even pretending not to eavesdrop on her conversation anymore. Fury bubbled up in my core. Whoever that dickwad was, he or she didn't deserve someone like her. I bet this girl couldn't even kill a fly. She had innocence written all over her pretty face. Why would she try to make small talk with me otherwise? Even though I kept pushing her away, she kept trying to start conversations I could engage in.

"No… I won't cause trouble. Huh…I'll wear that gown and smile whenever you tell me to. By now, I know the drill and how these events work." Another pause. "I under-stand. What?" Disgust shadowed her face. "No. No hickeys or cold sores that would look bad in pictures and need to be covered with makeup." Her face blushed darker. "I-I'll see you tomorrow."

She pinched the bridge of her nose, annoyance flickering across her features. Within seconds, she turned into a bolder version of herself, her tone now clipped and decisive. "This situation is out of my control. I've already told you. I will—" She got interrupted again. She transformed right before my eyes, firming her back and tipping her chin up. "Listen to me. I'll be there as soon as I can." A pause. "Yeah, I get it." She ran a palm over her face. "No need to put him on the phone. I understand everything you said already. I won't—oh, o-okay."

She tore the phone from her ear, lifting the screen to her face as her nose scrunched in disbelief. The line had gone dead. It was obvious the other person had hung up on her. With a shake of her head, she wiped the dismay from her face and dried the remaining tears in her blue eyes with her sleeve.

Closing her eyes, she took a deep breath and relaxed her shoulders. When she reopened them, her gaze found me, all traces of pain gone. "So, where were we?"

Chapter 3
Abigail

"What was that about?" the guy on my left asked, watching me with a raised eyebrow and a *don't fuck with me* expression. With disheveled dark hair—I wished I could run my fingers through the locks—a square jaw, and dark eyes that could suck me in if I let them, he was both intriguing and very cute. He had a set of broad shoulders, and even sitting down, he appeared tall enough that people probably would never mess with him. Next to him, I felt petite and delicate. Not that I was a tiny girl, but still, his build made me seem smaller than I really was.

His gaze locked on mine as he waited for me to answer, and I shrugged, trying to play innocent. Deep down, I was still queasy about the conversation with my mother. She had a way of inserting herself into my life and making me feel like I was always in the wrong. My parents would attend their annual Christmas benefit tomorrow night, and my presence was mandatory. Somehow, they liked to show me off as if I were a prize. A well-mannered, shiny trophy to parade around. Like they had done for the last three years, they set me up with Troy, whose father, a wealthy businessman, always made generous donations. Needless to say, my parents used me to get their way all the time.

Troy had tried to force himself on me last year, his mouth aiming for mine and his hands roaming over my front even after I said no. Seconds later, he stopped and doubled over in pain after I kneed him in the balls and headbutted his nose, resulting in a bloody mess all over his white shirt. My mother accused me of trying to seduce him. My father said he was disappointed in my behavior. Neither of them took my side or listened to my version of the story. In their minds, my behavior was at fault, just like it always had been.

No matter how much I had stood up for myself and denied any wrongdoing, Troy, with his future-politician charisma, succeeded in walking away from a situation that could have ended badly—for me and me alone.

For weeks afterward, my parents blamed me to save face with Troy's father. They even forced me to apologize and say I had overreacted.

Troy said I'd been sending him mixed signals all night, and he'd tried to kiss me because I had begged him to. They all believed him, and now they wanted to preserve their fake dignity again and had promised his father I had gotten over our little disagreement and would happily accompany him once more. Without ever asking me what I thought about it.

I was so used to this kind of behavior it didn't surprise me anymore.

"No idea what you're talking about," I said with a shrug.

"C'mon. That phone call. It upset you. Who was it?"

I flicked my wrist, doing my best to hide the messy feelings still simmering inside me from him. "Nobody. Not important."

"It didn't sound like nothing."

I turned to face him. "Were you eavesdropping on my conversation?" I lifted one eyebrow to accentuate my words.

"Huh…not really. It's just, I couldn't help hearing some of it since you're like sitting two feet away from me."

A soft blush took over his face, and he looked adorable with rosy cheeks. *Busted.*

"Anyway, you should never do anything you're uncomfortable doing. Just sayin'. No matter who's asking you."

"Oh, so you're all philosophical now. Surprising," I said with a way-too-wide smile.

"What's surprising? That I can reflect on stuff?"

"You were all moody before, and now you're giving me free advice based on something you've only partly heard and have no idea what it's all about. Isn't it a bit presumptuous?"

"Not really." He gave me a half-shrug. "Take it or leave it."

"Well, I'm glad to know my standing up for myself is important to you." His gaze drilled holes through my skull, and my fake confidence crumbled. "Family stuff. It's hard to please people sometimes… Mostly when it goes against your own values and dreams."

"Yeah. I get it. I'm attending college to please my mother. She insisted I get a degree before pursuing my dreams." His shoulders slouched forward. "It is what it is."

"You don't look happy about it. How can it be bad? I would have given anything for my parents' encouragement to get my degree. So far, they haven't been my biggest supporters."

"I'm sorry. My mother is not a fan of my pursuing music as a career, but she wouldn't want me to do anything other than what excites me. Getting a degree in music is my idea of meeting her halfway."

My lips tilted at the corner. "You are lucky to have her rooting for you. It's precious."

"I guess. She's important to me. It's only been the two of us all my life. She sacrificed a lot for me so I could get the best…and still does. It hasn't always been easy growing up with a single parent. She loves me, but I can't imagine what she's had to go through to make it all work."

"My parents are still together, so I can't tell. Sometimes, though, I feel like I don't fit in. I'm the outsider. Either they don't get me…or they're not interested in trying…" I sighed. "Enough with parental drama, please." I pointed to his empty cup. "Want another one?"

"Huh…sure. Black and no—"

I lifted a hand to call the server before he had time to finish. "I'd like two hot chocolates, extra whipped cream, candy cane sparkles from your holidays menu, and chocolate cookie straws."

"Gimme a few minutes," the waitress said before returning to the counter, a pep in her step, joy pouring out from her.

The airport café was small. White tables, black chairs, and maple-colored floors. Single black-iron pendant lights hung above each table. The counter was pale wood and sat in front of a black-and-white tiled wall. It looked chic and vintage all at once.

A song I knew by heart played on the speakers embedded in the ceiling, and I lost myself in the melody until a grumpy voice interrupted the moment. "I never asked for hot chocolate. I thought you meant another coffee."

I rolled my eyes as dramatically as I could muster and shook my head. "You, my friend, need some Christmas spirit in your life. You could loosen up a bit too. It would do you good."

His eyes turned to dark slits as he watched me without uttering a word.

I motioned at him with a flick of my hand and decided playing with him could be a nice way to pass the time while being stuck in here with nothing to do and nowhere to go.

There was something about this boy that appealed to me. He looked like an old treasure chest. Sturdy and severe from the outside, with hints of mystery peeking from underneath. And he looked hot. If the smile I'd spotted earlier was an indication of what he hid inside, opening him up would turn out to be a nice surprise.

Somehow, I couldn't resist sitting at the table next to his when I'd walked in earlier. Sadness had been etched into his handsome features, and it called out to me to fix it.

"I'm perfectly fine with coffee. Black, if you were wondering." He flashed a fake smile at me, but that didn't deter me. Instead, it made him even more attractive in my eyes.

"Nah. Chocolate will cheer you from the inside. It will bring magic to your night. You don't need coffee when you can have winter nectar instead."

He snorted. "Winter nectar? Are you on drugs? It's just plain, boring hot chocolate. Don't sugarcoat a simple beverage with fancy words."

My fist hit my chest with a soft thud. "Oh God, you're hurting me with your nonsense. Try it the way I like it, and then you'll be allowed to judge my taste."

The waitress placed both mugs on the table before me. "Good luck," she whispered with a wink before retreating.

I took in the snowflake-shaped sugar confetti, red and green sparkles, and the mountain of whipped cream atop. It looked delicious. And perfect for what I had in mind.

The guy pointed to the steamy delicacies in front of me. "This is your big plan to seduce me?"

"I-I wasn't… I'm not trying to seduce you."

"If you say so." His eyes sparkled at the challenge, and for a second, I lost myself in the amber hue. When he leaned toward me and extended his arm to grab a mug, I snapped out of it and pushed his hand away.

"Not yet. Don't you dare touch it before I say so."

His eyes rounded, and he studied me with bunched eyebrows. "Aren't you bossy?" He brought his forefinger and thumb closer and tilted his lips into a blinding smile, showing too many teeth. "You *almost* scare me."

I chuckled despite myself. "Nah. I'm on a mission. Don't disrupt it. Even your charming ways won't work on me."

He stared at me but added nothing.

"Close your eyes," I said.

"No." He crossed his arms over his chest, the fabric of his shirt tightening around his biceps and catching my attention for an instant.

"Don't be a baby. I'll prove to you that hot chocolate isn't some boring beverage."

"I'm not closing my eyes."

"C'mon. You blink, and it'll be over. I won't steal your innocence during those ten point three seconds." I lifted three fingers of my right hand, holding my pinky down with my thumb, and saluted him. "Scout's Honor."

"Wait, are you a Scout?"

"No."

"Have you ever been?" he asked.

"No."

"Then your promise means nothing because you can't use the Scout's Honor."

"Are you always so by-the-book, Mr. Self-Righteous?"

"Nah. But you can't use the Scout's Honor. That I'm sure of."

"Fine. I promise not to hurt you, take advantage of you, run away, or injure you. Are we good now?"

"I suppose."

I sighed. *This guy.* "Then close your eyes."

"The answer is still no."

"You sound like a two-year-old." I sighed. "Please trust me for ten seconds."

"Ten point three you said earlier. I prefer to know what I'm saying yes to. In this case, you haven't overshared the details of your plan."

"Are you being impossible on purpose?"

He smirked, and I wanted to scratch it off his handsome face. Or kiss it away.

"Reel that in. And stop being difficult. It will be fun. The unknown is kinda thrilling."

"Says who?" he asked with one quirked brow.

"Me. Stop with the questions and play along."

"You love the control? Is that it? Dominating makes you wet?"

I felt a warm flush spreading across my cheeks. "No. It's not like that. I just—" I inhaled in a weak attempt to calm the rush of both attraction and shyness surging through me. "You're missing the point. Stop trying to change the topic. Close your eyes, and we'll be done quickly."

"The girl prefers quickies. Noted."

"What? Not what I said." I buried my face in my hands

and took a deep breath in. "Can't you just do as I tell you for a few seconds?"

"Anyone ever told you that you're stubborn?"

I rolled my eyes again, unable to stop myself. "I like it when you recognize your own flaws."

We engaged in a staring contest, neither of us backing down.

The guy huffed and shook his head. "Ten point three seconds. Not a millisecond longer."

I pumped my fist. "Great. Now let's hurry before the whipped cream melts away."

He closed his eyes, his posture so rigid, I almost reached behind him to massage the tension away. Instead, I focused on my mission and stood between our tables.

"Have you ever caught a snowflake on your tongue?" I asked.

"Sure."

"Then let's try my version of it. Stick your tongue out."

"Why?"

"Because. Geez, trust the process."

He executed himself.

With a spoon, I put a tiny bit of confetti on the tip of his tongue. "Pretend this is a real snowflake. Wait for the aftertaste to kick in as it melts." With the same spoon, I dropped a mixture of hot chocolate, whipped cream, and sprinkles on his tongue. "It's melting now. Taste it."

He closed his mouth and swallowed. A low growl formed in his throat. Surprise and delight played on his face. For a long second, I failed to look away. When his tongue swept across his lips, I got entranced and wondered how soft they would feel on mine.

I wiped the corner of his mouth with my thumb. "You missed a spot." My finger hovered in the space between us.

His eyelids fluttered open, and he caught my gaze. A

slow smile curled his lips. When his broodiness dissipated, he looked pretty irresistible. My treasure chest assessment earlier was on point. Underneath his shadowy exterior, he wasn't as dark or moody as he pretended to be.

Without thinking it through, I licked the tip of my digit, and he sucked in a breath. A zing filled my stomach as he captured my eyes. The air kindled between us. Instead of watching his eyes, I returned to my mission. "See? I told you hot chocolate could be magic. You just have to believe it is. And you loved this little game. Your smile is a tell-all sign."

He set his lips in a poorly executed pout. "I'm not smiling. And it wasn't so bad."

I scoffed. "So bad? You liked it. You might not be aware, but I saw it. Your face betrayed you. By the way, you're welcome." I folded my arms, giving him my most satisfied expression. "If you're honest with me, I'll give it to you now." I returned to my seat and took a sip of my hot chocolate. Deciding I liked how he'd reacted a minute ago and wanting to test him further, I dipped my finger into the whipped cream and licked it clean, taking my time as I watched the guy whose name I still ignored squirm in his seat.

His pupils dilated, and he blinked. Yeah, I hadn't dreamed his reaction.

"Fuck. You play dirty," he said after a moment, a low rumble caught deep in his throat.

"Nah. I'm just enjoying a little sweetness. It tastes better like that." I shot him a playful look, and he groaned.

Lifting both hands between us in surrender, he sighed. "Fine. You win."

"I win? Awesome. Where's the prize?" I perused the space around us as if searching for something.

"The drink."

"What about it?" I asked.

"Are you gonna make me spell it?"

I nodded quickly, smiling.

"It was *kinda* good," he quipped.

"Oh wow, you're impossible. Do better."

He shook his head, then stared at me. "Okay, I liked it. Happy?"

I grinned so big my cheeks hurt. "I knew it." I placed the mug before him plus a handful of cookie straws.

His lips twitched into a smile behind the mug as he brought it to his mouth, but it didn't escape me. My pulse kicked up a notch, and my body temperature soared. Why did he make it so hard to look anywhere else?

"Enjoy. My treat," I said as I bit into a chocolate straw, trying to rein in the desire building inside me and keep my hormones in check.

———

My phone rang, disrupting the moment. My father's face filled the screen, and my insides knotted as I anticipated the conversation. My playful mood evaporated. It was late, and my parents were usually in bed by nine every night. Only one thing could keep them awake at this hour. The thought of my not being ready in time for their stupid Christmas Eve event tomorrow night. One I didn't care about because it was all fake and just for show, and I didn't fit into their plastic world. Just the thought of having to go with Troy was enough to send cold chills down my back. That jerk had no class and no spine, and I was well aware I should stay as far away from him as possible. After he'd blamed me last year in front of our families for his lack of self-control, I got lectured by my parents at least a dozen times about my inappropriate actions, as if I were the one who had tried to assault him.

With a big inhale, I pressed the accept button. No matter whether I turned my phone off or pretended the battery had died, if my father decided to get a hold of me, he'd make it his mission to call the airport and have my name announced over the speakers. He had connections. And not a lot of people denied him anything.

"Father," I said when I answered the call. All the cells inside me tightened. I knew the blame would come. I just had no idea what form it'd take this time. "Everything okay?"

"Abigail. I'm really disappointed in you right now. Your mother had to sip herbal tea due to all the stress you're causing her."

"It's a snowstorm. No one died. How am I responsible for Mother Nature's onslaught? I should already have been home by now. She's the one you should be angry at."

"Abigail, watch your tone. Your actions have consequences for those around you. You can't just do whatever pleases you without thinking it through. You are nineteen years old. When are you gonna prove to us you're responsible enough to be treated as an adult? Your mother and I were almost married at your age. It's time you grow up."

I pinched my lips together to avoid saying something I might regret. My parents were delusional. They were disconnected from reality, so convinced their world was a picture-perfect ideal everyone envied.

"I already told Mother I'd be home by noon tomorrow, which means I'll have more than enough time to be ready by five o'clock."

"You've never tried the gown. How can we be sure it fits?"

What my parents called a gown was a demure boatneck maxi dress with long sleeves, showing the bare minimum of skin and curves, in a not-so-lovely shade of pickle and reddish-brown. Not flattering. Not holiday-ish. Not meant for a girl my age. I would look like I'd escaped from the pages of a bad fashion magazine from the nineteen-twenties. Not my greatest moment.

"The tailor made it for me, and I confirmed my measurements a month ago. It will fit just fine. Everything is set. I'll be home in time. Overreacting won't fix the situation."

My father sighed, the proof I exhausted him. "Again, watch your tone, young lady. Abigail, this night is important to me. Don't mess it up. And no repeat of last year. Troy Burgundy is a gentleman; don't try to portray him otherwise. You've already done enough damage to his reputation for a lifetime as it is. No more acting out. And stop stressing out your mother with all the nonsense. It's about time you learn to behave yourself. Don't be late. Good night."

Before I could reciprocate, he hung up on me. Great, I'd talked more to my parents in the last hour than in the last three months, and all I had received from them were warnings and disappointment.

"Who was that?" a voice asked from my left, and for a moment, I had forgotten I had company. "Your dad?"

I folded and unfolded the paper napkin on the table, avoiding the gaze I could feel weighing on me. "Yep." Emotions swirled inside me. I hated that my parents would have preferred me to be a different person. It stung. A lot. Even when I pretended I didn't care, it still hurt. "They're not happy about the fact I'm stranded here. They had assumed I'd land tonight, and I seem to have deceived them and fucked with their planning or expectations of me. Whatever."

"How is it your fault?"

"Exactly." I slumped in my seat, looking up, tired of trying to please them and never succeeding. "It always ends up being my fault somehow. I'm used to taking the blame."

"You shouldn't have to."

I straightened my stance, not wanting to take shit for actions that weren't mine anymore. "You're right. My degree, it's my ticket toward independence. Toward the life I have dreamed for myself. If I don't attend college, they'll try to coerce me into becoming a trophy-wife. No, thank you. That is not the life I have pictured for myself."

"I'm glad you're holding your own. Don't let anyone turn you into something you're not."

"Not my intention." At his words, my happiness returned. Yeah, I would follow my own beat and break free of the chains my parents had tried for so many years to bind me with. I'd be my own star. Bright and shiny. One day I'd prove to them I was destined to become someone I valued and make it the way I intended to. My lips curled up of their own volition. I could see it all in my head—my dreams, my successes, my achievements. I'd be a rock star in my field. Passion would lead my actions and take me where my heart belonged. All because of me. All because I was following my gut. "I think I have an idea. Are you in?"

He watched me with a funny expression. "Will it be safe for me?"

I shrugged and snickered. "It depends."

Chapter 4

Anderson

Once we were done with our hot chocolate, the girl, whose name I hadn't asked yet, angled her body to face me. "You wanna get out of here? Have some fun instead of being miserable."

I scrunched up my face. "Don't think so. I'm good. I'll order more coffee and maybe hot chocolate, who knows? I'll be fine. Knock yourself out, though. I'll stay glued to my chair."

She jumped to her feet. "Come on, it will be fun. The airport will be our playground. Sulking about the weather, our parents, or the circumstances won't do us any good."

I fixed my gaze on her for a long moment. Her eyes, the color of a waterfall on a summer day, brightened. Gone were the clouds I'd seen there minutes ago. Once again, she glowed from within, and it mesmerized me.

She held out her hand, and a sigh later—a long one for good measure to show my level of exasperation—I slipped my hand into hers but didn't get up. Instead, I just gave it a quick shake.

"Andy. I'm done calling you the coffee shop girl in my head."

A contagious grin stretched her lips. "Coffee shop girl, huh? That's a first. It sounds nice, but I actually have a name. I'm Abby." She flashed me the biggest smile. "See? Our names rhyme. We already have something in common. We'll get along just fine, *Aaandy*."

The way she said my name sent signals to every part of my body. Even though she was too perky for my broodiness, she was hot—and her energy contagious. I had to admit that. Our gazes fixated on each other. There was something about her. A strong yet vulnerable side that appealed to all my senses.

"So, Abby…you have a last name?"

She shook her head. "Nah."

I cocked one brow and waited.

"Well, I do, but it's more interesting if we keep the anonymity, don't you think? Two strangers who meet during a snowstorm, stranded in an airport. They never exchange their full names and spend a night to remember together. One night of magic with no tomorrow. It sounds like a movie plot."

"A night to remember? Is there something I should know?"

Abby snickered, the sound fucking with my mind once again, and picked up my guitar case along with her bag. "You'll see."

"Hey, what are you doing?" I asked, rushing after her. "Give it back."

"Relax already." She shook her head, her smile never faltering. "I'm only asking the nice lady to keep our stuff while we explore the airport. Stop making assumptions about my intentions, *Aaandy*."

"I'm not." I closed my eyes. That guitar was my most precious possession. A gift from my dad on my twelfth birthday, one I knew nothing about because he had chosen his other family over us.

For a reason I couldn't explain, the instrument had more sentimental value than anything else in my life. Maybe because it was the only thing I possessed, linking me to him, other than my genes. Deep down, I wished he had chosen us. That we had been enough for him and that he had loved us enough to stay and be a part of my life. These days, I thought about him a lot. And how my life would have been different if he had stuck by us. Maybe it was because of our common love for music—the only piece of information Ma had revealed about him. Or maybe I just missed the idea of having a father. Locking my emotions down, I swallowed the lump forming in my throat and followed Abby.

"You can get up. See? I knew it." She mocked me with her eyes, and I groaned. "Your guitar is safe here, Andy. Trust me."

Why did I trust her? I had no idea. But after the conversations I'd overheard and the hot chocolate episode, everything about Abby screamed sincerity. I refused to give in too easily though because a part of me took pleasure in messing with her on purpose.

I kept a straight face when I asked, "And I'm supposed to believe you because…?"

She sighed and halted until we faced each other.

I pinched my lips together, trying not to laugh at her serious expression.

"Do I look like I'm about to murder you?" She tipped a hip forward and lifted one eyebrow. "C'mon, answer me."

Oh, she meant business, and it somehow made her even more attractive.

"Huh…no. But that's not the point."

"Well, do I look like a thief?"

"What? No. Who knows, though. What do thieves look like anyway? When you're a crook, the whole idea is to avoid looking like one."

She shrugged. "Maybe. No idea. Anyway, if I wanted to rob someone, I'd go for something super expensive, not something with sentimental value. Be realistic."

"Okay, you have a point."

"Also, did I attack you when you closed your eyes for a grand total of ten point three seconds?"

"Nah. I survived."

"So? Are we good?" she asked, her blue eyes full of sparks.

I squeezed the nape of my neck with one hand, casting a glance down at my feet. "Guess so," I said, exhaling a long breath before meeting her expectant gaze.

"Then let's go. Follow me."

After we dropped our pieces of baggage behind the café counter, we walked side by side for a moment. I broke the silence, wanting to make sure Abby had heard me loud and clear. "I'm not taking part in your airport fun, you know. Already told you."

She sighed and entered an empty room that resembled an office or an interrogation room.

"You can't go in there."

She glanced at me over her shoulder with an expression that said *watch me*. Seconds later, she wheeled herself out on a desk chair.

"What are you—?"

"Since you're not being a great sport and I have no

intention of spending the night alone in here, I'm going to give you a tour of the airport."

"You won't. I'm not—"

"Oh yes, you are. Now sit, won't you?"

I shook my head but did as she said. Why? Again, no idea. Maybe I loved the company. And her energy. Or the idea that somebody cared enough not to leave me behind.

Whatever.

She stood in front of me, a serious demeanor painting her beautiful features. "Now the rules. Listen carefully. You and I, we're playing Santa's challenge."

I watched her and blinked. "Santa's challenge? Are you fucking with me?"

She rested her fists on her hips, her don't-argue expression firmly in place. "Do you think you're too cool for some fun, *Aaandy*?"

"No. You said Santa's challenge. I interpreted it as a childish game. And I'm not in the mood for some stupid dares or whatever waste-of-time activities you've got planned. If we're playing games, I'm out."

Abby continued, ignoring me. "Santa's challenge means I can do whatever I want to you as long as you sit on that chair."

"Forget it. Already told you I'm not a willing participant."

She shook her head. "Stop arguing. Now you're the one wasting *my* time. As I said, as long as you sit on that chair, you're at my mercy. I can challenge you as I see fit, and you're not allowed to refuse, or you lose."

"Are you messing with me right now? Who came up with this idea?"

"I did. Just now. Thought you liked being challenged. I saw that smile you tried to conceal earlier during my snowflake experiment."

At the sound of her voice, now low and gravelly, and the memory of her licking a whipped-cream-coated finger, a tightness grew between my thighs.

She quirked an eyebrow, and my insides clenched.

I kept a neutral face. "I do." I cleared my throat in an attempt to shake off the effect she had on me. "Not tonight, though."

With her hands resting on the armrests, Abby leaned forward, her crystal-blue irises drawing me in. "Get used to it. I love games. And this will be fun."

Did she even hear a word I'd just said?

"You can't stand. That's the first rule. You can move your upper body, but…"

"But what?"

She pointed to my crotch—no, my legs—she pointed to my legs.

"But not the lower part because you'll be disqualified. I'll come up with Christmassy challenges, and you must play along."

"Or else?"

"No gifts for you."

"This is ridiculous. Not doing it." I argued just for the sake of it. She was breaking down my walls, but I refused to acknowledge it or give her any power over me.

The glint in her eyes magnified.

"I won't be naughty, I promise. Your honor is safe." She quirked an eyebrow, her grin full of mischief. "Anyway, I'm always on Santa's nice list."

"Tell me, what's my present if I win?" Even though I acted as if her little game didn't appeal to me, deep inside I was curious to know what she would come up with.

Abby smirked. "Don't worry. I'll figure it out. I already have ideas."

"And if you win? What will you get?"

She shrugged. "I'll think of something." Her voice dripped with lust as her eyes blazed. Just for a second.

I ran a hand over my face. It was late. I was now imagining things that weren't real. Great.

I tried to find reasons to walk away from Abby's silly challenge, but my curiosity got the better of me—and that ass of hers too if I were being honest. Sitting on the chair, I had a perfect view of how her jeans hugged her curves. No, I wouldn't complain. I huffed when I realized how weak I was around her. Like she had a way of making all my reservations vanish—and we didn't even know each other.

An hour ago, I still believed I would spend the night here all by myself. And now I'd had the most unexpected encounter I could have ever imagined—and someone to call a partner in crime. Maybe I could let go for a couple of hours and just savor the moment. I had nothing else to do anyway. Abby was turning out to be quite entertaining. And very gorgeous without even trying to be.

I studied her features, how she nipped at her bottom lip, waiting for me to agree to her rules. Once again, I tried to come up with dozens of reasons why I should refuse and stay away from her but found none.

Perhaps this could be entertaining. Her energy could rub off on me. I needed to add spice to my life. Joe would agree. He always complained I was too serious and obsessed with my goals and had forfeited the fun side of me and that he missed it.

This was my chance. To prove to myself I still could let loose sometimes. And forget about everything for a night.

I rubbed my stubbled jaw with my fingers, then raised my hands in front of me.

"Okay, girl. This is my offer to you. I'm all yours. Do what you want to me. All of me. For tonight only."

A red flush spread across Abby's cheeks. She didn't miss the innuendo. My words affected her, and I kinda relished the fact. That small detail alone made me like the challenge a lot more. From the looks of her—adorable and flustered—Abby was right. This would be a fun night. Or at least an interesting one.

"This chair is my throne. Show me what you've got. I'm pretty sure you'll give up first. The real question you should ask yourself is, are *you* ready for the night to come, Abby?" I teased her with a wink, using the huskiest voice I could muster.

Sparks returned to her eyes. They shone brighter than before. Her lips stretched into the widest smile I'd ever witnessed. Her cheeks blushed darker. "Oh, don't worry about me. I'm a tough girl. Be prepared to be amazed. I'd like to see the day I surrender, *Aaandy*."

She held out her hand, and we shook on it. Tingles awoke where our skin connected. My heart skipped a beat, but I put my best poker face on, not willing to reveal her touch had aroused me.

"Game on," I said with a nod.

"First stop." Abby entered a gift shop and came back minutes later with a Santa hat, a pair of elf ears on a headband, and a bag.

She placed the hat on my head, but I removed it as fast. "Not in the mood to wear this," I said, pushing it into her hand once she finished adjusting her fake ears on her head. "Don't push your luck. I agreed to your little games, but this is a firm *no*."

"*Aaandy*, are you forfeiting?"

My dick twitched at the way she rolled my name on her tongue and watched me. I cursed under my breath and put the hat back on. "No, I'm not. Happy now?"

She giggled and gestured to the length of me. "You're

dressed in all black. That doesn't say Christmassy. A little color would add magic to your life. You'll thank me later." She tilted the hat on my head, giving me a rakish look. I lifted my eyebrow, and she giggled. Again. Her closeness, the sweet smell of her—peach and spice—her laughter, they all did funny things to me. I was doomed. I should forfeit before this thing between us got out of control because I could feel my resistance slipping away with every passing minute.

Abby wheeled me toward a Christmas display and removed a bright pink and silver garland from one of the trees. She wrapped the tinsel snake around my neck like a scarf, stepped back, and grinned. "Now you almost look the part. You're like my own personal Christmas tree. That's a good look on you." She opened the bag hanging from the crook of her elbow and presented me with a bottle of whiskey. "Oh, and I bought a booze bribe in case you were tempted to walk away."

"How did you get away with this? I'm pretty sure you're not twenty-one. Didn't the cashier ask for your driver's license or something?"

She gave me a smile that suggested mischief and innocence. "I told her I was an assistant to a big country music star and that you were throwing a tantrum about not getting your whiskey. I begged her to give me the bottle as I wanted to keep my job. She was more annoyed about your childish attitude than my age." With that, a loud laugh escaped her, and her cheeks reddened.

Wow, I couldn't believe she had used me like that, but I had to admit, this girl was more innovative and a lot more fun than I'd initially pictured her to be. I admired her.

This night should be interesting.

"Oh." My lips curled, unable not to join her in her humor. "Gimme some," I demanded, giving her my best puppy dog eyes. "Since it was bought for me, I deserve a sip."

"Only if you are nice to me. And stop trying to charm me, it won't work." She nudged me playfully and reached for my hand.

Her palm fit perfectly in mine. Without even realizing it, I interlaced our fingers for a moment before she let go. I shivered. The simple gesture had awakened something in me.

I was hooked. Abby possessed some sort of power over me—raw and intoxicating. Even my body agreed.

Deep down, I had one certainty: I was screwed, because I'd never be able to walk away from her silly game.

Chapter 5
Abigail

Andy stared at me with a mix of amusement and interest. Yep, I didn't miss it. I could have sworn there was a spark of lust too. Could it really be, or was I reading him wrong? My heart cartwheeled in my chest at the realization we shared a deep connection.

There was an aura of magnetism around him. From the moment I'd walked into that coffee shop and laid eyes on him, something about him had drawn me in. By now, I'd concluded he was the kind of guy whose sulking attitude only added to his charm.

I wouldn't lie to myself. I was attracted to him. To the mystery surrounding him and the energy he did his best to suppress. I could tell something about tonight was weighing heavily on his shoulders, even though, right now, he was failing to keep a straight face. He wasn't fooling me, and I intended to discover the other side of him.—the one he tried so hard to conceal—and remove every brick from his walls. I loved the idea of solving the puzzle he was. And freeing his soul from its makeshift prison.

A zing traveled along my spine when he spoke. "Pass it to me. Since it was bought for me, I deserve it." Glad to know I'd sized him right when I chose the liquor. With the strong country-boy vibe he gave off, I assumed it was a safe choice. I high-fived myself mentally. For a reason that seemed foolish, I liked being right about him. Also, I believed the bribe would help appease his doubtful side. I crossed my fingers, hoping it would work.

I grabbed his hand and offered him a blinding smile. "Only if you are nice to me."

Andy's fingers closed around mine, and flutters invaded my chest. How could his touch have this much effect on me —and every inch of my body? Tingles ran up my arm from where our skin touched. It sounded crazy. The guy was hot, sure, but we were strangers who had just met. Not longtime acquaintances. The way my insides heated up every time my hand grazed his made absolutely no sense. Perhaps the idea of being stuck in this airport for the night, or the snowstorm raging outside, was to blame. It disturbed my body's chemical balance. Or my hormones.

All semester, I'd been so caught up with school that I didn't take the time to go on dates and avoided most parties, too busy aiming for perfect grades. Perhaps a few hours of harmless banter would bring back the fun side of me. The one I'd missed a lot lately.

Unable to process all the sensations swirling inside me, I let go of his hand and swallowed hard, averting my eyes after his turned darker, liquid amber that could have a lot of pull on me if I let them.

"What's next?" Andy asked.

His words didn't register.

"Abby?"

This time, my eyes met his, and I could see the flames banking low. Could he see the same in mine? Read my inner thoughts? The attraction I was trying hard to cover up? I hoped not.

"I'm sure you can do better than a Santa hat."

Oh, I was right about him. He enjoyed being challenged. He was just too stubborn earlier to admit it.

My lips stretched at the realization. "Ready for phase two?"

Andy gave me a heavy-lidded stare, then looked away and cleared his throat. "What's phase two?" he asked, bringing his attention back to me.

"Let's get to know each other better."

"Explain."

"I'll tell you three truths and one lie about myself, and you gotta guess which one is the lie." I pushed his chair toward a corner and sat on a bench facing him.

"And?"

"Then you'll do the same. It'll break the ice, and we'll feel less like strangers." I fidgeted with my hands, wondering what I was ready to reveal about myself. "One. Huh…I've never skinny-dipped. Two. Let's see… I have two sisters named Chloe and Shana. Three…" I paused, thinking about my next two statements. "I'm not always as confident as I pretend to be. Four. I was voted 'Most Likely To Live Out My Passion When I Grow Up' in high school."

Andy tapped the side of his chin. "Easy. Two."

I blinked and leaned back. "Wait? How?"

"Your nose twitches when you lie."

"No, it does not."

His clear laughter vibrated through every fiber of my being. "Yes, it does. So, you never skinny-dipped?"

"No." I folded my arms, upset he could figure me out so easily. "Have you?"

"Once. But it's not about me. Do you want to?"

I looked away. "Maybe. Growing up, I-I didn't have a lot of freedom. I like to experiment with new things. Skinny-dipping seems like the ultimate definition of being free."

He appeared to think for a moment before he said, "My turn."

"O-okay." I was glad the conversation had shifted away from me.

"One. I've been in love once. Two. I'm an awesome cook. Three. I hate watermelon. Four. This night is more interesting than I anticipated."

I felt my face warming up at his last statement and the way he watched me when the words left his mouth.

His eyes locked on mine, and a flock of butterflies filled my stomach. For a long beat, I forgot what we were doing.

"So, what is it?" Andy asked.

"What?"

He frowned. "Huh, my lie?"

"Oh, yes. Sorry. I think it's… Well, I'm not sure someone can really dislike watermelon, but why would you have picked it up otherwise…?" I paused, thinking it through. "You look like the kind of guy who *can* fall in love. So, now I'm confused."

He studied my face but said nothing for the longest minute of my life. "What makes you say *I look like the kind of guy who can fall in love?*"

I shrugged. "My gut."

"Well, even though I had a girlfriend in the past, I'm not sure I was *in* love. Like the head-over-heels feeling people describe. This is my lie."

"Interesting." I moved back to my feet. "See? We don't

feel like complete strangers anymore. Let's keep playing." I wheeled him forward but halted mere feet away. "You really hate watermelon?"

"Yep. Hate with a capital H. It's gross. Even flavored watermelon stuff tastes awful."

I couldn't help the chuckle that passed my lips. "Andy, you'll forever be the guy who thinks watermelon is gross to me."

"Well, you'll forever be the airport café girl."

We exchanged a smile.

"Since you've been playing nice enough so far and you haven't thrown a tantrum, you've earned yourself a treat."

"A kiss?" he asked, his face unreadable when his eyes searched mine and stayed there.

I didn't have to look in a mirror to know my cheeks must have turned bright pink as his words registered. My face warmed as he arched an eyebrow. Liquid heat pooled in my belly. Why did he have to look so hot when he said it? My jaw slackened at the mischievous curl forming on his lips, but I regained my composure before doing something I wasn't ready for and instead rummaged through the bag resting on his lap. "No, silly. Whiskey. You want some?"

Andy's hand skimmed mine as I presented him with the bottle. Shivers lined my spine, and my heart flipped in my chest. I was feeling things. Things I had no reason to feel.

"Yes, please." His husky voice caused my insides to melt. Every cell in my body pulsed with need. He took a hefty swig and passed the bottle to me.

I brought it to my mouth, desperate for the fake sense of courage it would provide.

The liquid burned the lining of my throat as it went

down, and I grimaced. And coughed. Then blinked away the tears filling my eyes.

"You okay?" Andy asked.

"Mm-hmm," I replied, fighting a shiver and using the back of my hand to wipe my mouth. "Not used to drinking booze straight from the bottle."

He burst out into a fit of laughter. "Ah, so you're a virgin."

I crossed my arms over my chest. "I. AM. NOT."

His snicker wrapped around me in tight ribbons. "Thanks for the info, but I didn't mean it *that* way. I meant a virgin to whiskey, a virgin to reckless actions and wild nights."

"Nah, you're wrong. I know how to have fun. And I can hold my booze. I just prefer pink cocktails with umbrellas to Neanderthal's liquor. A woman is allowed to have her own indulgences, you know. I can be wild when I want to be."

How could a guy I'd only met a few hours ago read me so well? I hated parties and only drank on special occasions. Honestly, I was the worst drinker. And a bit of a homebody when given the choice.

Tonight, a piece of me wanted to live without fear for once. Be free. And another piece of me wanted to cheer up the boy I'd met a couple of hours ago for a reason I refused to acknowledge other than I hated the sadness etched in his gaze. Bringing him joy, even if only for a short time, felt meaningful to me.

"Prove it," he said, snapping me out of my thoughts.

I offered him a pointed look.

"Prove to me you can get out of your comfort zone. Here and now."

"How?"

A cocky smile stretched Andy's lips. "Kiss me."

"No. Forget it."

"See? I *am* right. You're a good girl, Abby. And predictable. I knew it. You can't lie for shit. And there's nothing wrong with it. But I also like this other version of you tonight. The one where you let go and live a little. The freedom. It suits you. Your eyes glisten. You look happy. Here and now, no one expects anything from you. Be whoever you wanna be. This is your chance."

"Andy, you're wrong. Also…you know nothing about me."

"Oh, I think I do. Much more than you can imagine."

Was I that obvious? I huffed. "Whatever. I can be wild."

"Keep telling yourself that. I'd like to experience your wild side." He drowned his words with more booze. "I'm sure I'd be impressed by the sight of you getting frisky."

I tried to play it cool, but I'd heard him all right.

The tension growing between us suffocated me. Why did every word coming out of his mouth feel like sensuous foreplay? Damn it…not sensuous…hot and smoldering? No… What was I thinking? Geez…something was wrong with me. Very, very wrong.

With my best poker face in place, I made an effort not to show how much his words had stirred unknown sensations inside me. With my chin up and my back straight, I stared at him when I said, "Oh, I can do a lot better. This is just the appetizer. Are you ready to play, *Aaandy*?" Right then, I prayed my face wasn't scarlet as more heat pooled in my cheeks.

Andy grinned and nodded. "The right question is, Abby, are *you* ready to play with me? You know this works both ways, don't you? Truth be told, I'm an amazing player. The best."

"Wh-what do you mean?"

"If you challenge me and I complete the dare, I get to challenge you as well. Isn't that how it works?"

"No, I object. That was not in the rules. You're the sulking type, and I get to dare you, not the other way around."

He offered me a crooked smile, his expression full of teasing, and I blinked, scared of what was about to leave his full lips. "Well, it is now, Abby baby. When I play, I play hard. Play hard and love harder. Roll with the dice. Rock and roll."

I blushed when I heard his words. "What? That doesn't even make sense."

"It will. Gimme a minute to think."

"Huh, if I remember correctly, minutes ago, you didn't want to play."

"That was before. This is now. Got it? Since you are not a virgin, let me see the wild side of you. Get up and get naked."

My eyebrows probably leaped to my hairline. "*Whaaat?*"

"Hahaha, I am just joking. Not about the *get up* part, though."

"I'm already on my feet. You speak nonsense." What happened to the broody guy I'd met earlier?

"Let me explain. Your challenge is to stand on a chair of my choice at the departure lounge and dance to the song I play on my phone."

"What? No. *No, no, no.* I can't do that." I chewed on my bottom lip, unsure of how to get out of this one.

"Are you backing down? What about the untamed side of your personality you've bragged about? The girl who doesn't shy away from a good time? I'm more than ready for her. Bring her on." Andy leaned back and smirked at me. "This is like skinny-dipping. Nothing to hide behind if you chickenshit in the middle of it."

Fire rushed through my blood at the expression in his eyes. Nope. Not giving in. Still, I loved the adrenaline rush his dare shot through me. "Nah, of course. I mean, yes, of course, I *am* doing it… I-I think." I sucked in a breath and climbed on the chair behind me.

"Oh Abby, didn't I say the departure lounge?"

I winced. "But there are people there."

He raised a single eyebrow as if to say *So what?*

The ass. *Huh, okay.*

I wheeled his chair forward, all the while hoping he would change his mind and come up with another challenge. Or choose a nice ballad I could sway to if he went on with it. Or maybe a Christmas carol that would get people to join me and sing along, so I'd feel less awkward about being up there. But the look in his eyes and the way he was grinning like a maniac told me that I was in for the most embarrassing episode of my life.

Oh Abby, where have you landed? You were playing with fire. Weren't you aware you could get burned?

I cursed at myself. I chose the absolute worst player to partake in this dare game with.

Without my realizing it, Andy had twisted the rules— *my rules*—to his advantage using his charming ways. I bet he knew how to get the upper hand in his everyday life. I was screwed, but some sick part of me reveled in his attention and felt proud he'd agreed to this silly challenge with me and cared enough to include me in whatever we were doing tonight.

He was right earlier when he said stuff about me. In life, I usually played it safe.

For once, I wished this untamed side of me would

reveal itself, the one that needed to take the lead and say *Screw it* to the consequences. Once I arrived at my parents' place for winter break, I'd have to hold my own, keep my chin up, and not let them berate me for voicing my feelings, since obedience was what they expected of me instead. I hated fights, but agreeing to my parents' rules had always felt easier than going against their will. Damn loyalty. It was both my most enticing quality and my worst fault. It was about time I stood up for myself. In every area of my life.

My insides tightened as we neared the lounge, as I had no idea what to expect.

Andy sank back into the chair and laced his fingers behind his neck, his arms folded wide as I pushed him forward, looking far too smug for his own good. "Ready?" he asked after a beat.

The word "Sure" passed my quivering lips, and even I wasn't convinced by the weight of it.

He turned his head to stare at me over his shoulder. Something passed between us, but I couldn't name it.

Warmth spread through me, but I stayed silent.

"You'll do great." His lips tilted up. "I have faith in you."

I nodded once. "We'll see."

One of Andy's hands enveloped mine. "Believe in yourself. Always."

With a roll of my shoulders, I nodded again, as if trying to convince myself I was brave enough to go through with it. "Okay. I can do this."

"I know you can."

Minutes later, we reached the lounge that was packed with people who had been left stranded, away from their families, looking frustrated and tired. Some were spread over multiple seats or on the carpeted floor, using backpacks and folded jackets as pillows, while others busied themselves scrolling on their phones. A young mother was pacing back and forth, rocking a fussy baby in her arms. Three teenagers about my age were playing cards, sprawled on the floor. A faint scent of pizza lingered in the air. Empty to-go coffee and soda cups, along with other food wrappers, were scattered across the low tables. These people looked bored as hell. And not very *entertainable*, if it were even a word.

Ohmygod. I just realized they'd be my audience. For a second, I had forgotten about the challenge, too busy taking the scene in.

"We can find something else," I offered. "Or…huh… or someplace else."

Andy smirked when our gazes met. "Nope. Here is perfect. These people need a distraction. Something to take their minds off the predicament they're in."

"Oh, okay." I fisted my hands, trying to shoot some courage through me. And wondered what song Andy would come up with. When I had suggested this game tonight, I hadn't anticipated I'd be a participant. My only goal was to get him out of whatever funk he was drowning in.

Jitters filled my belly as I waited, and I pinched my lips together to hide their tremors. A million reasons to flee the scene passed through my mind. My heart lodged in my throat. I couldn't do this. All these people. Watching me. Analyzing me. Judging me. What if I fell and made a fool of myself? Air got stuck midway through my lungs, and I choked on my own breath.

I could feel knots forming in my stomach, tightening one by one.

My feet weighed tons. And my head spun.

"Abby, get ready." Andy's voice brought me out of my mental breakdown.

"W-wait… I need a few minutes. To…to get in the right state of mind. I'm not *ready* ready yet."

He smiled, his gaze softening and his eyes conveying reassurance. "Take your time. Nobody is going anywhere. I need to put some things in motion first. Relax. You'll be fine."

Feeling dizzy, I sat down on a chair, hung my head low, and closed my eyes. How did I end up here? What was I thinking when I'd roped Andy into this game tonight? It was a bad idea. Now I could tell. Refusing to open my eyes just yet, I took a few deep breaths in.

I could do it. Let go for once. Be wild. Go with the flow. Forget about right and wrong. Live as if there was no tomorrow. No expectations, no rules, no nothing to stand in my way or dictate my next move.

No parents to make me feel like I didn't fit in because I was too much. Too optimistic. Too jovial. Too opinionated.

I only had one shot at this, to let the wildest parts of me shine without having to think about the consequences. Or how people would perceive me. To just be without my brain analyzing my actions. Or my parents blaming me. It was harmless fun, right? Nothing to worry too much about.

Andy had agreed to play with me, and I had to show him I wasn't afraid of a little challenge if I wanted to keep the game running all night.

With a long exhale that fortified my resolve, I decided to go along with the dare. I'd climb on that chair and give Andy the show of his life. And then I would call the next dare. The idea of getting even encouraged me to agree. A big part of me yearned to prove to him I wasn't afraid, that I *was* fearless. Even if it meant dancing in front of all these strangers, standing on a stupid chair.

When I reopened my eyes, Andy was nowhere to be

seen. Sitting in that office chair, he couldn't have gotten too far away.

Behind me, probably on a speaker, the beginning of the raunchiest song I had ever heard started playing. My heart dipped in my chest and tried to leave the premises and never return. All my previous pep talks dissolved. Was he kidding me? I clenched my fists to keep my hands from shaking and turned around, only to lock eyes with Andy, who gestured to me with a finger to start dancing.

I glared at him. The nerve. Did he have a death wish? The more I tried to kill him with my eyes, the wider his smirk grew.

Uneasiness coiled around my stomach.

What did I get myself into?

I shook my head, and he bobbed his in return, his smirk turning into a blinding smile. His kissable lips didn't look so enticing anymore.

His throat worked as his gaze roamed over me. I eyed him from a distance, loving the way his eyes drank in every inch of me, as if he couldn't look anywhere else.

After a moment, he jutted his chin, silently encouraging me to go on with the challenge.

Adjusting my sweater with trembling fingers, I rolled my lips over my teeth to avoid chewing on them and stepped on the stupid chair.

Heads turned in my direction.

Eyes drifted to me.

A few people whispered, but I blocked them out.

Andy watched me with his arms folded over his chest, sparks blazing in his bewitching eyes. Seriously, I didn't think he knew how much power they held over me when he pointed them at me like that.

You can do this, I repeated in my head over and over

again. *Show him you're not scared easily.* Yes, I was Abigail Peña, and it would take more than a dance to break me.

Deciding to give Andy my best, I swayed my hips to the music, keeping my eyes on him. Only him.

The fire burning in his dark irises multiplied.

Heat rippled through me at the sight, and courage filled every inch of my being.

Was dancing in front of these people making me hot and bothered, or was it the Andy-effect? The way he undressed me with his eyes, his gaze caressing my body from head to toe, a sexy smirk lingering on his lips. My cheeks burned. My heart skipped a beat. Something in my chest swelled. I breathed easier. The game we were playing got me hooked. My movements were more assured now. Fear left me.

Without breaking eye contact with the guy who made me feel more powerful and alive than I had ever felt before, I slipped my sweater over my head. The hem of my shirt underneath lifted a little, giving the spectators a glimpse of my stomach.

Someone wolf-whistled.

Andy's jaw flexed.

The playfulness in his features vanished to give way to a scowl. Still, he couldn't hide the twinkle in his eye. From where I stood, I could see it clearly, and it gave me a surge of confidence.

To test—and play—with him, I unfastened the first button of my shirt. Then a second.

Tension rose in Andy's shoulders and neck. I noticed the subtle change in him, and my body overheated in response.

I nibbled my lower lip, then moistened it with a sweep of my tongue, trying to look in control—and make him lose his. If he wanted me to let loose tonight, I was not going to miss my chance to tempt him in any way I could. Two could play his little game. Wasn't that what he'd told me earlier?

His gaze now burned holes into my flesh. Soon, I'd combust. Still perched on that office chair, he rushed in my direction and tugged at my hand. From up close, I savored the blush coloring his cheeks and how his breath hitched on the way out. Another wave of heat washed through me. Yes, I was bothering him. Way more than I ever thought I could. This seductress version of me surprised me too. Never before had I been so bold, toying with a guy using my feminine power and charms to tempt him, and despite myself, I'd become addicted to the feeling. If someone had asked me if I could flirt, before now, I would have laughed it off. Yeah, I was usually the third wheel in my friends' dating lives. "Enough." His sharp tone surprised me, and I let out a gasp. "Get down. The show's over now."

Wait. What?

His eyes were like deep abysses, darker than I'd seen them all night. He raised an eyebrow and cocked his head to the side, as if to say, *Have you heard what I just said?*

Somehow, his reaction amused me. I pulled my hand away from his and wagged a finger in front of him. "Nah. You see? I'm not done. You wanted me wild and free, and you're getting exactly what you asked for. As you said, roll with it, baby. Now move back and enjoy the show. The song isn't over yet."

He growled and retreated without another word, watching me from a distance.

Without taking my eyes off his, I flipped my hair over my shoulder and, using my hand as a microphone, decided to up the stakes and started singing along to the song.

I pointed in his direction, and he shook his head, not even a hint of amusement on his face. We eyed each other, neither of us breaking contact first. I loved how powerful I felt in that instant. How he devoured me with his eyes, while I held all the control, able to make him lose his mind. Andy did that to me. He had unleashed the wild part of me and let it shine. This game turned out to be far more intoxicating and addictive than I would have thought.

People applauded, and my heart frizzled in my chest.

Freedom had my blood pumping.

I relaxed my stance.

All around me, men and women moved to their feet and started dancing. Little kids who weren't fast asleep did the same.

Right before our eyes, the lounge transformed into a makeshift dance floor.

Some angry passengers watched us with deep frowns, but I didn't care. I twirled around and jumped from the chair, sashaying toward a frozen and stunned Andy.

I pulled his chair forward, and he locked his hands on my swaying hips.

He stared at me, not a trace of a smile on his lips, his gaze hard enough to melt me to pieces.

"What?" I asked, using my most innocent voice. "Something wrong?"

He cleared his throat, and the wrinkle carving his forehead smoothed out. His entire demeanor shifted. "Abby." His voice sounded huskier than before. We fixed each other for a long moment, the intensity of the moment rendering me breathless. The muscle in his jaw ticked. Right now, I couldn't tell whether he was amused or upset at me.

Deciding to break the tension between us, I batted my eyelashes at him, and he sighed, his stance relaxing.

"You... I..." He paused, flicked his fingers, and said instead, "You made it. See? It wasn't so hard."

His words barely registered—only the heat and pressure of his fingers on my hipbones did—and I savored the feel of his hands on me.

"Dance with me?"

Andy shook his head.

"Please."

He watched me. "Permission to stand?"

I shook my head, struggling to breathe as the current of attraction zipped back and forth between us. "You can't," I whispered. "Or you'll lose."

"I don't wanna lose. Not with you."

What did he mean by that? Why were his words sending my heart into higher gears?

Before I could ask him, he said, "Why not? Let's dance. We'll figure it out."

There was some unspoken meaning lingering beneath the surface when he said those words. I could sense it.

Giving up the fight and letting go of me, Andy straightened in his seat as I spun his chair around. Lost in our little world, I held his hands as we twirled, as if he were standing up beside me. Both of us burst out laughing. "Can I drop the chair now?" he asked after a moment, his grip returning to my waist and tightening while his eyes sucked me in. "I wanna dance with you. For real. Hold you against me."

Air caught in my lungs at his words.

He said everything that, in any other circumstances, would have made me swoon. Tonight, though, it translated into alarm bells inside my head. A dangerous idea—for me. One that could end badly—for my heart. Pushing the attraction away, I shook my head. "Nah, I love it when you are at my mercy." The teasing in my voice couldn't be missed. Nor the notes of lust as my hushed tone betrayed me.

He tried to speak, but his voice came out rough, so he

coughed. "So, I was right, huh? You are a dominatrix when you want to be. Interesting."

Not reeling in my smile, I slapped his arm. "Oh gosh. You are terrible. Guess you like me zesty after all."

"The spicier, the better."

We both chuckled as the air between us grew charged with something hard to define, sending goose bumps across my arms.

Once my laughter died down, I asked, "Why do I sense this night will be one to remember?"

Andy eye-fucked me without shying away from it and remained silent for a long beat.

Heat crept up my spine as I waited for him to say something. Anything.

"Abby, you started this. Do you want to drop out?"

Okay, not what I expected him to say. Not that I knew what he would reply, but that certainly wasn't it.

His stare weighed heavy on me. I swallowed. "Never. I…huh…I never forfeit anything, *Aaandy*."

His eyes twinkled. "Awesome." He moved and broke the eye-contact. "What are you waiting for, then? Keep rolling."

I did just that and kept wheeling him around to the beat of the music, losing myself in the freedom of the night.

After a few more songs, we killed the music and moved to a corner of the airport where we could be alone. I went to get snacks and sodas and set up a picnic for the two of us.

"Thanks," I said when Andy's focus landed on me.

"What for?"

I scanned the space around us. "All this. And making me feel alive tonight." I shrugged. "I know it sounds lame, but I'm usually always in control. I enjoyed the liberty of just living tonight, even though it's for only a few hours. Anyway, thank you for pushing me to do things I wouldn't have attempted on my own. And for spending the night with me."

Andy bowed his head. "You're welcome. And thank you for getting me away from my brooding earlier. It's much more fun being with you than on my own, upset at the snow for ruining my plans. And for your information, I wouldn't want to spend the night with anyone else."

His stare stayed glued to mine, and I noticed the racing pulse point in his throat. Right now, I had no idea how to interpret his words. Something was clear, though. I loved his companionship and how he made me feel. For now, this was all that mattered.

In comfortable silence, we finished our food. When I moved to my feet to clean up our space, Andy circled my wrist with his long, musician's fingers and tugged me toward him until I landed onto his lap.

"Hey, what are you doing?"

"Relax." One of his palms connected with my knee, and electricity zipped through me. I blinked, trying to hide the effect just his single touch had on me. "I'm making sure you're not leaving me here because I haven't been allowed to get up from this chair yet."

His Adam's apple worked, and the movement mesmerized me. Sitting on him like that, I felt his hard chest and firm thighs pressed against me, his warm breath against my neck. Why was everything about this boy affecting me so much? Why was I so attuned to all he was?

Andy said nothing, watching me. Attraction took us hostage. Even if I wanted to deny that it was mutual, I couldn't anymore—dilated pupils, hastened breaths, pursed lips. All the signs were there. Still, I tried to convince myself I was reading him wrong. Maybe the whiskey I'd drunk earlier was to blame…or maybe not.

A million thoughts raced through my head.

My blood—now as hot as scorching lava—pumped through me at a dizzying speed, warming my entire body.

With a flimsy resolve, I locked all the sensations away when he looped one arm around my waist. A part of me wanted to just lean into his embrace and melt against him. But I knew better. This was a one-night deal, nothing more, and I wasn't about to start making up *what-if* scenarios in my head.

Looking for a way to tame the raging fire inside me and focus on anything other than the boy underneath me, I opened the bottle, downed a mouthful, and passed it to him.

It did nothing to dissolve the ache building in my lower belly. No, instead, it fueled it up. Yeah, alcohol and fire were a deadly duo, and I was paying the price.

An orchestra played a concerto deep within me, and I relished the feel of Andy. Every inch of his body brushing against mine overwhelmed my senses, even as it muddled my common sense.

I took another swig, determined to loosen up a little more, just as his fingers started drumming a beat against my thigh that vibrated through my entire being.

The liquor warmed my insides, and after another chug, some of my inhibitions slipped away. Feeling safe and relaxed, I pressed myself against his chest and took pleasure in the safety he provided me. His hand, which had been resting on my waist, slid to my hipbone, tracing lazy circles.

The simple gesture made me want to sink deeper into him. To spend the night in his arms. To bury my face in his chest and let his masculine, leather-and-whiskey scent envelop me, and never leave.

"You really want to be a music executive?" he asked, putting to rest all the wishful thoughts flickering through my mind.

I bobbed my head. "For as long as I can remember."

"I'm sure you'll be good. You have that drive. I would hire you for sure as my manager."

"Wow, thanks. I'm sure we'd make a great team." I brought the bottle to my lips. "I already know you play the guitar. Are you also a singer?"

Andy nodded.

"You write your own songs or play covers of other people's?"

He took a long pull of the alcohol. "My own. Most of the time... I started when I was a kid. Couldn't stop. I have books full of songs I wanna record."

I grinned. "Whoa. You must be talented."

He shrugged. "I think I am. We'll see in a few years. There's nothing else I wanna do in life than play music professionally. For now, I gotta finish my degree. My mother's only request before I focus on a musical career. One day, I'll find a way. No matter what it takes."

"I'm sure you will succeed."

Our gazes fixated on each other for a long minute. I darted my tongue out to lick the remnants of alcohol lingering on my lips. His eyes darkened as he studied me, and the orchestra inside me intensified.

A silence fell upon us, and all I could hear was my deafening heart. My attention drifted between his eyes and mouth. Each time his lips wrapped around the bottle neck, more surges of heat washed through me.

I asked the first question that popped into my head, wanting my focus to be anywhere else but on Andy's mouth. "Name three weird things you like. Don't overthink it. Just say the first items that come to your mind."

"Rain. Frogs. Candy apples. Why?"

I shrugged. "No reason." I paused, deciding on my next move. "Not sure we can find frogs and rain here, but I saw Christmas candy apples earlier in one of the shops. Let's get some." I turned to stand but thought better of it. "Frogs, really?"

"Had a few in the pond near my house when I was a kid. I even gave them names. You said weird things, so..." Andy angled his upper body to face me. "I'm still waiting for that badass side of yours to show up, Abby." One of his fingers traced patterns across my thigh, though I wasn't sure he knew he was doing it. "Change your mind about that kiss?"

Every time he talked about kissing each other, I pictured his lips on mine, soft and warm, and melted a little more inside. I held my breath. "Sorry. Huh...can't. Before we find treats, I have a question for you. A challenge that will determine if you deserve that candy apple."

"Spill it."

"Name the twelve reindeers," I said, doing my best to lead the conversation away from the kiss that had now taken permanent residence in the fantasy corner of my brain.

"Wait, they have names? I thought it was Rudolph and friends or something like that."

"Andy, tsk-tsk. They all have pretty names. You guess three of them, and you get your treat." I lifted a finger. "One hint. Many end with -er."

"Okay, let's see. Tumbler. Eleven. Chaser. Grace. How many chances before you call it quits?"

"Until I conclude you're a lost cause." I stared at him with a raised brow. "Grace? Really?"

"Shhh. I'm just warming up. Trust the process."

"Hey, those are my words," I said, backhanding his chest.

"One more reason to listen to them. Let me think. Huh, what about…what about Copper? Or Vixen?"

I clapped my hands. "Vixen. Yay. One right. Eleven to go."

"There is a theme here then. Easy-peasy. He named them Foxy, Racy, Teaser…"

"Ohmygod, stop. It sounds like a roll call at a strip club."

"Santa named one Vixen, what did you expect? He started this, not me. He says kids are on his naughty list, but we can easily guess who's the naughty one, no?"

We both laughed as we passed the whiskey bottle back and forth.

Tears from laughing too much formed in my eyes. "The day you have kids, promise me you won't be in charge of naming them. That would be a terrible idea."

"What, you don't like Tractor, Guitar, and Raptor?"

I shook my head, laughing so much I couldn't utter a word.

"I'm doing my best Santa impression," Andy said. "Going with a theme here. Would you prefer Kale, Raisin, and Basil?"

"Terrible. You're making fun of me. You know their names, don't you?"

He shrugged. "You'll never know."

He wrapped his arm tighter around me, and even if I tried to convince myself otherwise, I couldn't help but touch him. I traced an imaginary pattern along his forearm with my fingertip. He shifted in the chair but didn't lean away.

"You're ticklish?" It sounded more like a question than

an affirmation. I heard his sharp intake of air in response as I drew more figures on his bare skin. "I have an idea. Close your eyes."

"Not that again."

"Behave. For once. I'll write words on your forearm, and you gotta guess what they are."

He did as I asked and extended his right arm, the one not wound around me.

O-X-Y-G-E-N.

Goose bumps popped under the pad of my finger, and I savored the sensation.

"Oxygen," Andy murmured, not opening his eyes.

"One more."

W-H-I-S-K-E-Y.

"Are we playing Scrabble? What's with the high-point letters?"

"Spell it."

"Whiskey," he said, his lids still shut and his voice soft.

"Your turn."

His eyes flickered open and held mine for an infinite second. I'd bet we both stopped breathing, suspended there as we stared into each other's soul.

"Abby, close your eyes," he said after what felt like forever, holding my gaze without blinking away. His fingers sent delicious shivers all through me when he traced letters across my thigh.

For a second, I believed he spelled *kiss me*, and I held my breath, because at that moment it was the only thought looping through my mind, again and again. Until I replayed the movements of his fingers and realized what he really wrote. "K. I. S. M. E. T. Kismet?"

"Yeah. I think our meeting wasn't a fluke." He shrugged. "Let me try again." His fingertips returned to their task.

"K. A. R. A. O. K. E. Karaoke? Trying to score high? Are we still playing Scrabble?"

"It felt like something you might enjoy. Ever done it?"

"Once. I had a blast. Music is our common ground… our shared passion…"

"It's just a part of it," Andy said.

My heart jumped around inside my chest at his affirmation. In distracted motions, I kept my finger moving over his jean-clad thigh as he squirmed beneath me. "Wanna test something?"

He grinned. "With you? It always feels like a trap. Why is that?"

"*Nahhh.* Stop overthinking. Can you stay still if I do this?" I traced the contours of his jaw with my finger.

He closed his eyes.

"You move, you lose."

His entire body hardened, and his breathing hastened, but he stayed still.

I followed the column of his throat, the curve of his collarbones, the length of his arm. I felt each of the shivers running through him, but not once did Andy move—or open his eyes. His tongue brushed his lips. His eyelashes fluttered. A shiver ran through him.

One by one, I teased each of his fingers with the tip of mine.

My entire body ignited. This was a dangerous game we were playing. I wanted to feel his hands all over me. His soft touch. I wanted to hear him murmur my name. How long would it take before I shivered so badly that I'd beg him to stop because it felt too intense and brought me to the edge of a climax?

With a finger, I traced the side of his neck and his earlobe. "You're doing great," I whispered.

His Adam's apple bobbed in response.

Was this as much torture for him as it was for me?

No matter how much I knew I should stop, I just couldn't seem to find the will not to touch him. Keeping my gaze locked on him, I studied every one of his reactions —the tiny facial expressions I would miss if I dared to blink.

His lips parted on an exhale.

I couldn't look anywhere else. I was transfixed by the sight.

Was he serious, or was he joking earlier when he asked me to kiss him? A battle raged inside me. I had no idea what to do. Every part of me urged me to dive in and press my lips to his, but a small voice in my head told me I could be reading him wrong and making a fool of myself, so I held back.

Trying to get rid of the tension rising in the depths of me, I jumped to my feet and grabbed a scrunchie from my pocket and tied his wrists together. "Game over."

Andy's eyes sprang open, and he looked lost for a fraction of a second. "Hey, what's this for? What's going on? Did I lose? I haven't moved."

"Insurance policy. Not risking your hands traveling where they shouldn't."

"Why?" he asked.

"We're going somewhere."

"See? Now you're being bad. And kinky. I like it." He smirked, and I hesitated between kissing—for real—those full lips of his or slapping his cockiness away.

Either way, the sight of him, his masculine scent, and the tone of his voice messed with my senses. I wanted to kiss him. It would be Earth-shattering but would ruin me for all other men. That I knew. Because being so attracted to a stranger made no logical sense. But even though I tried, it was impossible for me to stay unaffected by Andy's closeness. It wasn't just lust, but him and all that he was. More like how things were between us. Easy and fun.

As if we'd known each other for a long time and were now reconnecting after being apart. Familiar and exciting.

My focus returned to his mouth. Why couldn't I stay indifferent?

His lips were a dark spell that kept me entranced.

I wasn't ready to let go completely. Not yet.

This night would be long. So damn long.

I had started this challenge, and I would see it through, even though, right now, I feared my heart would never recover.

Chapter 6
Anderson

Abby's gaze darkened as it swept the length of me and stopped on my mouth. Was she thinking about kissing me as much as I wanted to kiss her? Because right now, it was becoming almost impossible to resist stealing a taste of her. When her fingers were all over me moments ago, even my organs quivered beneath her touch. If I weren't afraid I'd read her wrong and that she would push me away, I would've already claimed her mouth. As soon as she started dancing on that chair earlier, my body had gone as tense as a bowstring, and the tension refused to melt away. I never should've dared her to do *that* challenge, because now I couldn't erase the images from my mind. All I could see whenever I closed my eyes was the way she swayed her hips, her eyes locked on mine the entire time, stealing not only my breath away, but my sanity too.

Abby wheeled me forward, and I couldn't decide

whether I was relieved she wasn't nestled in my arms anymore or annoyed by it.

How had this night become an exercise in pure torture?

Before I could get my act together and chase away the images infiltrating every corner of my mind, Abby halted, turned around to face me, and clasped her hands together. Her demeanor had changed. Gone was the lust in her eyes, and back was her cheerful demeanor. "*Aaandy*, I forgot I'm the one choosing the next challenge. Are you ready?"

Oh yeah, that. How did I forget about her Santa's challenge? I grimaced and braced myself for the words about to leave her lips. Red lips. Luscious red lips. The ones I wanted wrapped around me.

Cut it out, man. You need to stop dreaming about her mouth.

I rubbed the back of my neck, waiting for the sword to fall.

No doubt I had raised the bar when I'd asked her to dance earlier. To *that* song. Half of me hated myself for choosing something that was loaded with so much sexual tension. Every man in there had watched her sway those hips. Standing up there, lost in her own world, she was a spank-bank fantasy, looking innocent and sinful all at once, her gaze fixed on me as if she could read my filthy thoughts. I could tell the ones that filled these men's stupid brains. Because they filled mine too.

The rest of me—the lower half of my body—had definitely enjoyed the show. A bit too much. For once, I was glad to be glued to that chair or else I wouldn't have been able to hide the effect Abby had on me.

"What's wrong?" she asked. "Andy, are you okay? You look like you ate a sour grape."

I shook my head to erase the thoughts and images of

her that were fucking with my mind. "Yeah. Sure. Just waiting to know what I'm up against this time."

She giggled, and my body hardened. Every-fucking-where. I loved and hated how instinctively it reacted to her happiness. And her laughter—that addictive, clear, cheerful sound—always pulled at every thread of my composure.

"*Aaandy*, be patient. I need time. To come up with the perfect dare. A girl requires a moment to get in the mood sometimes. This is one of those times. I'll tell you when I'm ready, don't worry. Believe me, it will be *gooood*. So good you'll ask for more. A lot more. I never disappoint. One taste and you'll get addicted. You'll be blown away by my performance... Well, not performance, exactly, but my talent for dares, if I can call it that."

Why was she using *that* voice? Low and husky. The one I could only define as her sex voice. Deep down, I hoped I wasn't mistaken because whoa… It pulsed through me in agonizing waves that I reveled in. And her words were my ultimate demise. Gosh, had she said them on purpose? She had to have. Why else would she make it sound like she was about to go to town on me?

Heat crawled up my spine. Every bit of me tensed with desire I could barely contain. No one should be allowed to use that tone in a non-sexual context. Yeah, it should be voted as a law.

All night, I'd been entranced by her lips, but now I couldn't look away from her mouth, as if it could only spill dirty promises.

From the start, I'd pictured Abby wrong. She was the devil. A pretty she-devil, but still as evil. My own hell. And my biggest temptation.

I exhaled, trying to keep my composure and prevent

my body from betraying every thought invading my head —every scenario my very fertile mind was coming up with.

"Still waiting." I coughed, trying to relax my throat. And every other part of me.

"Chill out, Andy, and I'll show you just how good it'll be." She bit her forefinger and twisted it between her teeth, as if to think, but it sent all the wrong signals, flooding the sex center of my brain with brand-new filthy images instead. "Do you trust me?" That suggestive tone again. Her lips formed a pout, and she gave me puppy-dog eyes.

I was suffocating inside. With my hands still cuffed together with a scrunchie, I intertwined my fingers and pressed my palms together, my knuckles turning white. "Jesus, girl," I muttered through gritted teeth. My pants suddenly felt too tight. I shifted in my seat, but with my hands tied, easing the tension in my crotch wasn't something I could do subtly. Desperate for Abby to stop using *that* voice, I changed the subject. "You sure there are candy apples here? You promised me one. Haven't seen any so far."

"Mm-hmm. I swear." She grabbed two pairs of elf slippers as we passed a little shop and handed me one. "Wear these."

"No." I wished I could fold my arms over my chest to show her my refusal. "Not wearing those."

"Yes, you will."

"Is that my challenge?" I asked.

She shrugged. "Nah. Just a little Christmas bonus for not moving earlier. The candy apples will taste better if we look the part."

She kneeled in front of me, her hands on my thighs, and I almost died at the sight. Her soft touch, the heat from her palms transferring to me, her gorgeous face between my knees. It was a temptation I wasn't prepared for.

Fuck. *This*, right here, was the challenge. Resisting her. Not reacting to her closeness. Staying still when all I craved was to pull her up to me and kiss her senseless. This was insane. My dick throbbed. I swallowed hard. My body temperature rose to a feverish pitch.

Abby grinned at me as she removed my boots and slipped my feet into those silly shoes.

With both hands back to clutching my thighs, she moved to stand up. The innocent smile of hers returned. Fucking fuck. The night was taking a turn I'd never predicted. All the alarm bells inside me blasted at full intensity. I hadn't been this aroused in a long time. Horny. Abby made me horny. For her. For everything that she was. We were in an airport, and there was nothing I could do about it. Trying to tether my cravings and the chaos simmering inside me, I opened and closed my fists, needing something to distract me. Anything.

Abby cupped her heart with one hand as she watched me. "Perfect," she exclaimed before moving behind me to wheel the chair forward again. "Andy, this Christmas outfit suits you. It masks your broodiness. You look festive. And jolly."

"Jolly?" Why did my voice sound so rough? I cleared my throat and tried again. "Jolly?"

A joyful exclamation, resembling a moan, passed her lips. "It's a word, you know. And it fits you."

I swallowed, refusing to turn my head to meet her eyes. My breathing was less labored when I couldn't see her. I could still feel her warmth all around me, and smell her—and it was enough to mess with me. I couldn't risk a look over my shoulder, or I'd be done for.

Closing my eyelids, I counted to ten, chasing away the

images of Abby—red lips and big eyes—kneeling before me a minute ago.

Once my composure, or remnants of it, came back, I opened my eyes and lowered them to my *elf-ed* feet. I blew out a long breath and shook my head. The sight killed some of the desire invading my body. I couldn't believe this girl made me wear these. Whatever pull Abby had on me, I was too weak to resist it. The realization made me question my sanity.

Being tied-up was probably for my own good after all. Because I wasn't sure I could keep my hands in check and every part of my being if she set me free. Dirty images of her handcuffed to my bed, wearing little to no clothes and that sexy grin invaded my mind. My friend Joe was right. It'd been too long since the last time I let go and got laid… or even enjoyed myself on a date. Maybe that explained the pressure tensing each fiber of my body right now. Simple reasoning. My last serious relationship had ended over five months ago. We broke up when she moved to California, ditching her college plans to become an actress. All semester, I'd been so busy with music, school, and work that I'd barely had a minute to myself. And now I was the victim of my lack of social life. Damn it.

When I'd left the office party earlier tonight, I had no idea it would turn out to be the easy part. Joe would have a blast right now if he could see how pathetic I'd become in just a few hours. For a girl. A stranger girl. But a girl, nonetheless.

If he were here, I would never hear the end of it.

After Abby went to drop my shoes with my baggage at the café, we arrived in front of a little sweet shop, and she bought two candy apples. A red one decorated as Santa and a white one looking like a snowman with golden glitter. She studied both treats before offering me the red one.

"Sorry, I like sparkles. And everything that shines." She raised an eyebrow at me. "I can't resist a little white coating."

What the hell. What was that about?

I shut my eyes for a second, inhaled and exhaled, and thanked her with a smile.

Two could play this game. No way would I be the only one suffering in silence. Now I wanted to see that blush rising up her cheeks et engulfing her entire face.

"Oh, Abby, aren't you going to feed me? My hands are tied. I am *sooo* hungry." I lifted my *scrunchied* wrists, giving her my own version of puppy-dog eyes, filled with fake innocence. I could master that skill too.

Desire flared in her gaze before she looked down and bit her lower lip.

How I wanted to do that, lick her lips and suck on them. Just one taste. Just to satisfy some of my yearning for her.

She opened her mouth and closed it. Took a deep breath. This was going to be interesting. She lifted her chin up, a flicker in her expression, and used her sex-dripped, husky voice again. Seriously, she could make a fortune on those phone sex calls. "*Aaandy*, I'll feed you this big, juicy treat. Be careful, though. It's sweet and sticky." Her smile came back, filled with sensuous mischief, and my dick sprang wood in my jeans. Again.

The girl was good. And I savored the fact that she'd played along by agreeing to feed me instead of calling my bluff. Both of us knew I could get out of the scrunchie anytime if I chose to.

Had I opened a Pandora's box? My challenge seemed to have brought a sparkle in her. There was confidence in her stance, and each action was fluid. Feminine. This was bad. So bad…for me. But oh so tempting.

Before I realized her intentions, Abby straddled me, her knees on either side of me, and I startled, shifting in my seat, not ready for her to feel the hard part of me aching for her. Even though, deep down, all I wished was for her to acknowledge every inch of me and take control of the situation straining my pants. My thoughts and wishes were a complicated mess I couldn't seem to sort out. What I craved and what I shouldn't were at odds, screwing with every bit of me.

My dick pulsed every time her lips touched the white glaze, licking and sucking on pieces of it.

"This is so good," she moaned, her tongue licking her lips to capture the remnants of the sugar left behind.

Why did she have to pick the white one? Either she was clueless about everything or this was part of her master plan to fucking mess with me. This was no longer a silly challenge, but a test of my willpower. I had to regain control of the situation—and fast—otherwise I'd burn in flames…flames of repressed desire.

Not done teasing her, and deciding to play on the same field, I licked off the red coating, swirling my tongue, looking deep into her eyes.

Her jaw hung open, and her pupils dilated.

The air between us became electrified.

I emptied my lungs, trying to resume my normal breathing. "Abby, you have some white stuff at the corner of your lips."

She used her tongue to lick it off in a slow motion that got me lightheaded.

Fuck, this girl would kill me. I cleared my throat. "No, the other side." Like I was in a trance, I followed the movement of her tongue as it wiped the other side clean.

I dragged my joined hands over my face to calm down

for a moment. I exhaled and brought my hands back between us.

Holding both treats in one hand, Abby traced my bottom lip with a fingertip and brought it to her mouth. "Sorry, you had a little glaze there. And some at the corner of your mouth. Want me to wipe it clean, or you wanna lick it yourself?" She batted her eyelashes twice as she waited for me to say something.

What. The. Actual. Fuck.

My body overheated. This game had gone too far. I craved the woman as much as I craved some distance from her. My tone lowered. "Untie me. Please." I sounded desperate. And in fucking pain.

Let me kiss you, for God's sake. I give up. I can't take it anymore. Whatever the endgame is, you win.

She shook her head. "Not yet." She smiled, and it broke me a little more, destroying almost all the remaining self-restraint I had left. I was dying a slow death. I was sure of it now. All I could think about was capturing her mouth with mine. To feel her lips on mine. My hands tingled to touch her. To mold her body against mine. My heart pounded at the thought of being this close to her, of feeling her heartbeat.

The night was turning out nothing like I'd expected. Every cell in me was at war. How could I think straight when I was trapped, facing temptation for hours to come? Abby jumped to her feet and pushed my chair forward, and I snapped out of my racing thoughts, the ones drowning me and my flimsy self-control. Rolling my shoulders, I forced my angst down.

After what felt like seconds, she stopped and leaned down to whisper in my ear. "Oh *Aaandy*, I got your new challenge."

My voice sounded rough on its way out. "What is it?"

Her eyes shone like diamonds when I turned my head to look at her over my shoulder. "Surprise. You'll like it."

"No surprise. Tell me. Please." I'd beg if I had to—anything to get my mind focused on the game and shut down the rush of hormones flooding my body, or to brace myself for whatever might ruin me even more than she already had.

She waggled her finger and moved on to pick up my guitar from the café, then wheeled me toward the waiting area by gate seven. The same area where we would have waited to catch our respective flights.

She untwisted the scrunchie and stepped back before I could wrap my arms around her and hold her hostage—make her mine.

"What now?" I asked, my breath catching in a near gasp.

Abby clicked her tongue. "Gimme a minute." She walked to the counter and talked to one of the two attendants from the airline company. They exchanged smiles and nods. I frowned at the sight. There was far too much excitement flashing in her eyes, and a devilish glint when our gazes met from a distance.

She grabbed the microphone and started speaking to the other stranded passengers. "Ladies and gentlemen, this is your Santa representative talking to you. My good friend Andy right here, a very talented musician and rising rock star"—she gestured to me—"will give a concert to all y'all. It will be our Christmas gift to you tonight. To uplift your spirits."

We? I mouthed.

She shrugged and continued. "Please join us at gate seven. It will start shortly. Thank you and Merry Christmas."

Adrenaline raced in my blood at Abby's impromptu

concert announcement. It happened every time I was minutes away from walking onstage. I basked in this feeling. Music was my element, my passion, my calling. I was ready for whatever Abby threw my way if it meant I'd be able to perform. I rubbed my hands together as flutters stirred inside me. Yes, I loved this dare.

The girl, who had once again surprised me in all the right ways, sauntered toward me, and I mirrored her smile. "Did it cross your mind to ask first?" I inquired with a grin, pulling the instrument from its case, ready to feel the chords vibrating under the pads of my fingers.

"Nope. We'll see how well you perform on short notice. After all, you made me dance without any warning."

"Oh girl, you'd be surprised how well I can adapt to any situation, any setting. I'm always ready to go. I don't need foreplays. Bring it to me, and I'll deliver. Rock your world. And believe me when I say you'll beg for a repeat performance." I spoke the last few sentences with an edge to my voice, and a light flush colored her cheeks.

The fire that had been burning between us for hours turned into a blaze. The hair on my arms stood on end, and air struggled to reach my lungs.

Abby ran her tongue over her lips. Why was she always doing that? Couldn't she tell by now it fucked with me? On so many levels. Was she feeling the same pull I was feeling? She cleared her throat, and my eyes followed the ripple in her neck, the pulse throbbing between her collarbones.

She looked away, and air rushed back into my lungs. I could finally breathe.

"Can I ditch the chair?"

She shook her head. "Nah. Unless you forfeit."

"Yeah, not doing that." A new idea formed in my head. "Congrats, Abby, you've just earned yourself a job. You're on backing vocals. Unless you prefer we sing duets."

The thought of us singing together sent a zing of happiness to my heart. I loved that my girl was going to be up there with me. *My girl?* When did I start referring to a stranger as my girl? I was sick. Or perhaps it was all a dream. Or an alternate reality. Did I have an accident on my way to the airport and bump my head? This could explain so many of my actions and thoughts tonight. Was I still in that cab? Perhaps I was in a coma…

Or perhaps I was asleep, having the best dream of my life and not wanting to wake up.

She clapped her hands and grinned, stopping the influx of questions swirling in my mind. This all seemed so real. The entire night couldn't be some hallucination… could it? No. I wanted it to be real. I loved how a girl I would never see again after tonight had saved me from my funk and spiced up my existence, even if it was for just a few hours.

"You sure? I'd so excited. I've always wanted to do this."

I blinked, taken aback by her enthusiasm. "You sing?"

She scrunched up her face. "Yes. No. I'm not that good, but I like singing. Does it count? Nobody has ever complained that I burst their eardrums."

I stared at her, at a loss for words. How could everything coming out of her mouth never be what I expected? I thought she would freak out at the idea of our singing together. And here she was, ecstatic at the proposal. I scratched the back of my neck, confused.

"Andy, are you all right? You're looking at me in a weird way?"

I dragged myself back to reality.

She moved closer. "Are you always zoning out like this? You had me worried for a second."

Was my mind playing tricks on me, or did her voice get

even huskier than before? My body reacted—in a hundred different ways—again. Why was my dick having an opinion about everything Abby related?

I blinked, breaking the spell, when she took a seat next to me.

"Nah, it must be the late hour." I angled myself to face her. "Ready?"

It was her turn to study me. Her lips parted, but no words came out. After what felt like infinity, she exhaled and nodded.

She surveyed the little crowd that circled us, and a crimson shade tinted her cheeks. At least fifty people sat in the room, ready for us to begin.

"C'mon. You danced in front of people earlier. I'm sure you can get through a few songs. Forget all about them and look at me. We're alone and I'm right here. We're doing this together."

I strummed the first few chords and kept my eyes trained on the girl who, in the hours I'd known her, had added colors to my world and cheer to my existence just by being her charming self.

Thanks to her, my miserable night had turned into something I would remember for a long time. Maybe forever.

As we sang Christmas carols, I zoomed in on Abby's mouth. An indelible smile had taken root on her face. The crystalline sound of her voice sent shivers down my back. She couldn't reach every note, but she seemed content, and it made up for her lack of technique.

We sang our own version of Rudolph the Red-Nosed Reindeer, and I winked as I named every reindeer. Abby mouthed a *You dick* at me, and I couldn't help the smile curling my lips when she realized I'd been playing her earlier.

The next hour passed way too quickly. I could have sung with Abby for days, just for the pleasure of seeing those glitters dancing in her blue irises.

We finished our set, and my heart sank deeper into my chest. Our time together was coming to an end. For some reason, I wasn't so eager to go back home the next morning. I wanted this moment, here and now, to last much longer…maybe forever.

Abby moved to her feet and hugged me. The throbbing of her heart resonated through my chest, matching mine. I wrapped my arms around her, not sure I was strong enough to ever let go.

She leaned back, her face shining with glee, and I had to let her go, missing the contact as soon as we broke apart. "Thank you. It was epic. I can't believe I did that."

I held my guitar out of the way and wound my free arm around her waist, holding her close. We stayed like that for a long moment, neither of us seeming able to move apart. When she stepped back, I immediately missed the warmth of her body again.

"Andy, you're good. One day, you'll make it big. I can already tell. You have a rare talent. And your voice is something else. I still have goose bumps. You can trust me. I'm going to be a future music executive, so I know what I'm talking about."

"You are not so bad yourself, but thanks," I said, the ache to kiss those rosy lips of hers growing stronger deep in my core as she looked at me with stars in her eyes. Why did a compliment coming from her mean more than from any other person I'd ever met?

Maybe I had bumped my head after all, and I was still in that cab with a concussion. Still, I'd rather have a brain bleed than wake up from that dream.

———

In complete silence, we brought my guitar back to the café after Abby handcuffed my wrists to the armrests using pieces of garland from my neck.

"Hey, what are you doing? What's this for?"

"Nothing. I just like you tied up. It increases the kink factor." She flashed me a smile, and I cursed, in my head, at all the things I wished I could do to her. She wasn't some innocent girl earlier with all her innuendos. She'd known exactly what she was doing all along—playing with my willpower and my hormones on purpose.

Sitting on me, her legs slung over the armrest of the office chair, Abby fed me whiskey. After the concert, a dark flush had settled on her face. The liquor we drank did nothing to dull it. Her eyes shone brighter, and her smile grew with every sip of alcohol. Seeing her lips connect with the bottle's neck, I turned into a jealous motherfucker. Yeah, I was jealous of an inanimate object, wishing I could be the one tasting her innocence instead.

"I don't feel the burn anymore," she giggled, moving to stand and spinning around, her arms thrown wide open.

I lolled my head back and parted my lips as she poured more booze into my mouth. Some alcohol spilled all over my chin.

"Oopsy." Abby wiped the mess off with her small fingers, giggling as she surfed a drunken high. She looked adorable. I had no other word to describe Drunk Abby. "Open up." She poured another stream of whiskey between my lips, missing her intended target, and once again wiped the liquid running down my chin with her fingers. "Ugh." She winced, shaking her moist hand.

I watched her. "What's wrong?"

"Sorry. I hate it when I get soaked with fluids. My skin

gets all sticky." She scrunched up her beautiful face. "My fingers stick together." She squinted at her hand and separated her fingers, which were indeed stuck together. "See? It's not fun. I could maybe lick them." A cute grimace shaped her lips, as if she were debating the idea in her head. "Think this would solve the stickiness problem?" She brought a digit to her mouth, sucking on it. Fucking fuck, again, was she for real?

I blinked many times but said nothing, commanding my dick to stay put. I had to wonder again. Was she really that clueless about everything coming out of her mouth, or was it all on purpose? Earlier, I'd believed she was messing with my sanity for fun, but right now, I wasn't so sure anymore.

Abby moved behind me, wheeling my chair forward. I tilted my head to watch her. "Girl, you're crazier than I thought." But deep down, I kinda craved her craziness by now. It kept me on my toes. Well, not toes since I was sitting down, but still. I loved how unpredictable the night had been so far.

She tsk-tsked. "Make up your mind, *Aaandy*." Why was my name like a sex prayer every time she said it? Goddamn it. "I'm either crazy and fun, or good and nice."

"Why can't you be both?"

"Because. Sometimes I'm tired of being the nice girl. The one everyone expects something from. The one who's always there for everyone else and puts herself last. The one who says *Yes* even when she wants to say *No*. The loyal-to-a-fault person others exspect her to be. The pressure is real."

Her ocean-blue irises brimmed with tears, and an ache surrounded my heart.

"Hey, let's be bad then. I'm all in."

The flames grew back in her eyes, and she nodded.

"But just so you know, there's nothing wrong with being a good girl," I said, looking straight into her eyes.

"Thanks. For saying that." She tugged my Santa hat down over my eyes. "Let's go somewhere."

"Where? I can't see." Hating the idea I couldn't see a thing, I drummed my fingers against the armrests.

"That's the idea. Be patient."

She wheeled me forward, and I wished I could see where she was taking me.

"Hey, where are you taking me?" I shifted in my chair. "Your driving is making me dizzy."

"You'll see, *Aaandy*. Can you stop moving for a minute? Breathe, you'll be fine. Trust the process."

The humdrum of the airport had muffled.

I nodded, swallowing the lump forming in my throat. "Trying to. Anyway, I have nowhere else to go. I won't try to escape, I swear."

I heard some noises coming from behind me. Was she rummaging through the bag hanging from the chair? The sound of a door clicking made me nervous. My heartbeat deafened me when I felt her weight on my lap, her voice in my ear, her whiskey-and-mint breath filling my nostrils.

"No peeking," she said, her voice trembling. "No moving. You have to stay still. Do you promise?"

My Adam's apple worked. The darkness heightened all my senses.

"Yes. I do. I promise."

"I wanna play another game with you. It's different from what we've been doing all night. Can I get a free pass and challenge you again?"

I swallowed. Hard. My breathing accelerated. And so did my heart rate. "Yes."

"When I'm done, I'll be a good sport and take part in whatever you throw my way."

"Deal." My voice came out stilted.

"See? I'll let you taste something, and you have to guess what it is."

I gave a small nod, unsure what I was getting into.

"Do you like sweets?"

I nodded again.

The sound of plastic wrap being torn open reached my ears.

Something hard rubbed against my lips.

"Open your mouth, *Aaandy*."

I did. What tasted like candy cane caressed my tongue.

"Suck," she ordered.

I obeyed.

"Stop."

I stilled.

My breathing turned shallow.

I was a bomb about to explode.

Please. Make her stop.

No, I don't want her to ever stop.

Please. Keep going.

No, enough with the torture.

Yep, a ticking time bomb.

Chapter 7
Anderson

My mind was going haywire with all the sensations washing through me.

Right now, I wished I could jump to my feet, pace the room, and tug at my hair until the storm inside me calmed down.

Abby brought something else to my lips. It was soft and bitter.

"Open up," she said, her voice powerful and sensuous enough to make me come into my pants.

I took a deep breath, trying to calm my overactive hormones. Reining in the desire coursing through my body, I did as she asked.

She pushed something else into my mouth. "Lick it."

What tasted like a melted piece of mint and dark chocolate coated my tongue.

"You can take a bite now."

She slipped the remaining square between my lips, and

I heard the unmistakable sound of her sucking on her fingers.

This was it. The moment I would die. Or go to hell.

"You like this game?"

I nodded, wishing I could watch her right now and read her thoughts. See the expressions on her face. The sparkles in her eyes.

Moving closer, she pressed her hands to my chest. My heart drummed, and my breathing quickened. What was she doing? I could sense her deep in my soul. She drew a quick breath in, seconds before her mouth brushed against mine. "Taste this."

The contact of her soft lips electrified mine. The moment she leaned back, I darted my tongue out, easing the tingles.

In the darkness behind the hat covering my eyes, every movement of hers felt sharper, more intense. Magnified. With one hand, she fisted my hoodie just above my thundering heart. I held my breath when she pressed her mouth to mine again, claiming my lips with restraint. And a hint of curiosity.

The simple touch awoke something deep within me. My entire body frizzled. She parted her lips, and my tongue pushed inside her mouth, greedy and hungry for a girl, who I'd never seen coming into my life but who had succeeded in making an impact on me in the short amount of time we'd known each other.

Everything about kissing Abby felt as natural as breathing.

"That's my favorite taste," I spoke against her lips, returning to my mission of cherishing her mouth with every stroke of my tongue. I leaned back a little to watch her. "You're not so indifferent to my charming ways anymore." I raised my brows, teasing her.

She slapped my chest. "Don't be cocky. Shut up and kiss me."

She moaned, and my dick stiffened, threatening to drill a hole through my pants, desperate for attention—and a release. It pressed against her through our clothes, pulsing. This time, I didn't shy away from letting her know how she made me feel. How my body loved her company too.

"Andy, you're not allowed to move," she whispered in my ear, a smile tinting her husky voice.

A guttural groan tore from my throat. Abby's words had that effect on me. Even if I tried, she was right. I could no longer remain indifferent to her. All of her.

She looped her arms around my neck, deepening the kiss. My body heated up. Without thinking, I ripped the makeshift handcuffs and tugged her closer, my hands sliding under her shirt, enjoying the goose bumps spreading over her velvety skin.

"I thought you didn't want to kiss me?" I asked, my voice rough.

"I thought I ordered you to stay still?" she replied.

We both breathed hard.

"Wait, I tied you up. How did you—?"

I growled as I nipped her lower lip, smiling. "Girl, sure you did, but you're as strong as a hamster. What did you expect?"

She pushed back. "Hamster? Haven't you seen my muscles?"

I grinned and nodded in the dark, the hat still covering my eyes.

"Yep." I moved my hands further up her back. "But they are still puny. I love playing with you. Being dominated by you. I take pleasure in your being the boss. Taking control. And surprising me."

We kissed some more. Abby molded our bodies, not a

hair's breadth space remaining between us. Her inner thighs pressed against my erection, messing with me a little more each time she ground against me.

She lifted the hat, freeing my vision, and I blinked to adjust to the dim light. Seriousness had taken over her features. Her pupils were fully dilated and her cheeks, flushed. "Andy, I want my Christmas present now."

My attention drifted to her juicy lips swollen from my kisses. I forced the words out, my throat tight with the desire swirling inside me and toying with every string of my composure. "But I thought I had won the challenge." I licked and kissed the length of her jaw, her neck, her collarbone. Now that I'd had a taste, I knew I'd never be able to stop devouring her unless she asked me to.

"Nah. I did." Her voice quivered. "Which means you owe me a gift. That was the rule. And I'm requesting it now."

With keen hands, I unbuttoned her shirt and pushed it over her shoulders, my mouth following the trail of bare skin. "Anything," I murmured, busy sampling every delicious inch of her. "Abby, ask anything of me, and I will do it."

She paused, still hesitating.

I lifted her chin with a finger and looked into her eyes. "I'm all yours for the night. What do you want?"

"Love me. Like you mean it. I want to feel desired. And beautiful. And sexy. Just pretend I'm your girl, okay? I wanna know how it feels to be cherished on Christmas."

I leaned back, staring in her eyes. "You sure?"

She bobbed her head, her eyes trained on mine and her eyelids heavy with lust, not shying away from what she'd asked. "In my real life, I don't have much of a say. Tonight, with you, I can be myself. And I want you. I've been thinking about it all night."

"You have?"

"Yes. Haven't you?"

"Yeah. Ever since you danced on that stupid chair. I hated the idea of other guys watching you."

She quirked a brow. "You were jealous?"

"Nah."

She gave me a pointed look.

"Okay… Maybe a little."

"I gave the show for you, Andy. Nobody else existed at that moment."

I claimed her mouth in a bruising kiss. One that stole each molecule of oxygen from her. The air around us was charged with unsaid promises and anticipation. I swore the temperature of the room had soared.

"Want me to be honest?" I asked.

Abby watched me with quiet, unconcealed desire. Her bottom lip quivered. "Please."

"It's been torturing me… Not being able to touch… and kiss you." I scanned the area around me, noticing the unfamiliar room for the first time. "Where are we?"

"A VIP suite. To relax and stuff. My mom used to be a flight attendant. A long time ago. I've been here before and know all about the secret stuff. A customer left the airport after his flight got delayed due to the storm. He handed over his key to the nice lady working at the coffee shop. She gave it to me earlier… Thought I could use it…"

"You had the key all this time?" I asked.

"Yep. I…huh…I hadn't planned to use it until now."

"God, you're hotter by the minute." With a confident gesture, I unclasped her bra, slid one hand to her front, and cupped one perky breast, molding it to my palm. Abby purred, the sound sending all the right signals to my lower body, my erection bobbing in my pants. "And you are beautiful. Everything about you is."

For a long second, she watched me watching her, each of us captivated by the other.

With shaky fingers, Abby unzipped my hoodie and pushed it back. "I'm helping you."

I captured her lips with urgent hunger, seeking relief from the wildfire consuming me.

Still sitting on that chair, I yanked off my T-shirt.

Abby swallowed hard as her gaze traveled over my bare skin. In that instant, I found myself liking the power I held over her, and the way she admired me without shame. "Okay, you *are* very hot." Her gaze traveled down my torso, taking in every inch of my defined chest and the faint trail of hair leading downward. She chewed on her lower lip and lifted herself up when I reached for my belt. I lowered my jeans and pushed my boxer briefs down my hips, exposing all of myself beneath her unwavering attention.

With flushed cheeks and a look I would never forget, Abby watched at me as though I held all the keys to her heart.

She curled her small hand around my throbbing length, and I almost dissolved under her soft touch. Fuck, I didn't remember the last time I was this hard. This aroused. Maybe it was our hours-long foreplay. Or maybe it was all her. Abby had a way of getting under my skin. Of making me want to follow her anywhere and indulge all her crazy ideas. She had a pull on me I couldn't seem to escape, and I yearned for it. I had never felt anything so strong or addictive before. My airport fascination was everything I could easily get attached to…if we had more time together. She was a weakness I hadn't known about until she appeared in my life. A muse who could easily inspire my music and make me a better version of myself.

She leaned forward and peppered kisses all over the

planes of my chest, drawing patterns with her tongue. At a steady pace, she worked me over, and every cell in me sang for her. A glistening bead wet the head, and she spread it over with her thumb, her eyes locked on my hard-on as if it held magic power. "Told you I like shiny things."

"Geez, girl. Your smart mouth is like a powerful aphrodisiac. Permission to ditch the chair?"

Without waiting for her response, I lifted her in my arms and laid her on the couch, our tongues tangled in a heated kiss.

"Permission granted," she whispered against my hungry lips.

"Finally." Watching her, I asked, "You still wanna do it?" I leaned back, making sure I wasn't rushing her into something she was not ready for.

"Yes. Please. Don't stop." Her eyes had turned feral, and I was pretty sure they mirrored mine.

"Fuck, you're gorgeous. It's a shame we can only do this once."

"We have till the morning, *Aaandy*. Let's make the most of it. It's my Christmas present after all."

I plunged forward and captured her devilish mouth with mine, unable to go slow anymore. Our tongues swirled together. I stripped her of the rest of her clothing, driven by urgency.

I moved to my knees and lapped at her center once. Twice. Until she shivered. "Told you I like sweets." I moved over her, kissing her hard before plunging back between her legs and teasing her swollen clit with the tip of my tongue.

Abby entangled her fingers in my hair, pulling at the roots. She jerked her head back as a loud whimper broke free when she convulsed against my mouth the moment I pushed one finger inside her tight channel.

"You're fucking wet." I kissed her inner thighs and entered a second finger inside her, moving my digits back and forth at a slow and torturous pace that had her hips buckling off the couch.

"Andy… You… I… Don't stop."

"Never."

A loud cry pierced the silence, and she went rigid against me as waves of pleasure overtook her.

Never had I seen anything so beautiful as her then—vulnerable, trusting, and looking at me with a kind of reverence I would never forget—as she let go and came around my fingers.

With my free hand, I pushed my jeans and boxer briefs lower down my legs and kicked them off before fetching one of the five condoms from my wallet—a gift from Joe earlier tonight when I'd played at his father's office party. Right now, I loved my best friend something fierce.

I slid my fingers out of Abby to open the foil package. She propped herself up on her elbows and watched me with a glaze in her eyes. Her hair was tousled and her cheeks, a bright shade of pink. "Can I?" she asked, breathless.

"You want to?"

She nodded, taking the rubber from my hand and pinching the tip as she rolled it down my erection. Every caress of her fingertips woke up flutters inside me. My entire being shook under her delicate attention. She pumped me a few times, and I almost shot my load right there.

Through clenched teeth, I said, "Slow down, Abby, or it'll be over before it even begins."

She blinked her big blue eyes and watched me. "Andy, I've been a good girl all night. Can I get my present now?"

Fuck. When she used her sex voice on me, all my

control deserted me and I was at her mercy. Utterly and completely.

With one hand around her neck and the other busy kneading her breast, I lodged myself between her open legs, admiring every inch of her and burning every detail to my memory.

She frowned as she studied me. "You all right?"

I groaned an answer before pushing inside her in one slow stroke.

Clutching my shoulders and keeping me close to her, Abby trembled in my arms.

"Are you okay?"

She bobbed her head while nibbling at her lower lip. "Never been better."

I kissed her as my hips pounded into her of their own volition. I couldn't get enough of her.

Abby's hands pressed against my chest, and I increased the pace.

"What are you doing to me?" I parted her lips with my tongue and kissed her with everything I possessed. We lost ourselves in a tango, and I lost all notion of space and time.

My world shattered at that instant.

My vision blurred.

Everything I had ever known vanished.

Abby would be the end of me. She owned me—body, heart, and soul—as I was consumed by her. She had become my sole purpose, my salvation in a night that had started off all wrong before she decided I was worth her time. And her affection.

Our gazes met, and something intense passed between us. We froze, lost in each other's eyes, neither of us breathing nor moving.

"Abby," I said, after a long minute, breaking the lust-heavy silence, "if you were my girl, I would love you every day."

She gasped and I plunged forward to kiss her. Fast and steady, slow and consuming. Until we couldn't break apart. Until my body translated what my words couldn't say out loud.

"Fuck me." Her voice was a pleading murmur.

I shook my head. "Nah. I would never be able to just fuck you. You are too precious. You deserve love. And the whole nine yards. I'm sorry I can't offer you more than tonight."

"Shh, don't. We agreed it was for the best." She fastened her legs around me, deepening the connection of our bodies. "Andy, it's perfect. *You* are perfect. This… It's everything I've been yearning for. Love me and stop overthinking everything."

I stole a kiss before ramming into her with abandon. Her fingertips dug into my ribcage as she anchored herself to me.

Her eyes stayed fixed on mine. A whimper escaped her reddened lips. "More. Please, Andy."

I leaned over her and captured both her hands in one of mine and locked them over her head. My mouth found hers, and I flicked my tongue around hers. At the same time, I sank into her balls deep, relishing the rise and fall of her soft chest against mine. The beating of her heart enticing mine.

Life outside of this room stopped existing.

Her moans and my grunts transformed into a melody I was dying to record.

I clutched her ass cheek with my other hand.

Her tight walls drew me deeper, tightening all around me. Abby's back arched, offering her breasts to my starving mouth. I circled the pebbled tips, laved them with my tongue. The whimper-symphony escaping her luscious lips got me even harder—as if that were possible.

I wanted more. Needed more.

No matter what we'd agreed on, one night would never be enough.

Leaning back just a bit, I molded my palms to her hipbones. Her eyes opened beneath hooded lids, and the pleasure I read there rendered me speechless.

Angling her hips up to get a better grip, I dived into her in rhythmic thrusts.

Our eyes never broke apart. But something in my chest did. A piece of my heart hung loose. I was trying to hold on to every second of us, but I knew it would soon be over, leaving only a memory of one incredible night shared with a stranger.

Abby cradled my cheek with her small palm, and I focused on her pleading gaze, shaking my head to push away the thoughts that had flooded me seconds earlier. "Andy? You are far away. Come back here. Come back to me."

My attention returned to the girl spread beneath me, watching me with something I'd never experienced before. Something that would have looked a lot like love on any other occasion. Something that made my heart tremble and my lips curl.

"I'm here, baby." I held my weight on my arms, my mouth seeking hers. "With you. All of you."

I rammed into her faster.

With my thumb, I rubbed her mound of throbbing flesh where our bodies connected. Abby detonated under the caress, her body tensing against mine, pleasure softening her features. My mouth captured hers, needing to etch her taste into my memory one more time.

Once she came back from the high, I pushed into her with intent.

A muffled cry parted her lips, and I admired her beauty as she abandoned herself to me once again.

My movements became erratic. She wound her body around mine, holding me close and meeting me thrust for thrust. We were on the verge of combusting together, launched into another galaxy.

"Abby—" Her name sounded more like a prayer as it left my mouth.

She curled a hand around my neck to pull me down, and arching her back, she sought my mouth.

We moved in sync, kissing, holding on to each other. Maybe, like me, she didn't want this moment to end— afraid that letting go would make it end too soon.

An orgasm rippled through her, and any restraint I still possessed deserted me. My own climax followed, shattering me to pieces.

"Merry Christmas," I whispered once we caught our breaths, and I hauled her over me, her heart beating to the same rhythm as mine, our bodies steamy, and our hands unable to stop touching each other, our fire untamable.

"Do you want to shower together?"

I blinked and scanned the small room. "There's a shower here?"

She bobbed her head. "It's a VIP private suite. It's like a teeny-tiny hotel room."

"How are you—?"

Abby pressed her finger against my lips. "Shh. Don't."

I threaded my fingers through her hair and tugged her forward. "Then I'd love nothing more than to shower together. And I wanna love you again. Because if we only get one night with each other and this is your Christmas present, I want to make this night one to remember. Forever. I want it to be your best Christmas."

Her face lit up, and I kissed her some more. Abby tasted like whiskey and sugar. Addictive and forbidden. Sweet and spicy.

In the small shower, I lifted her up and circled her puckered nipples with my tongue as her legs locked around my waist.

My finger entered her moist heat, and her inner muscles contracted around me.

She whimpered, making me hard for her all over again.

In slow motion, I eased her back onto her feet and went down on her, sucking on her clit as I pushed another finger in and worked her toward a climax. She jerked her hips, her hand holding my head, seeking more friction. I increased the pace, entranced by her cries of pleasure, the rapture keeping us hostage. Her body convulsed around my digits, and she groaned my name in a whisper, the sound quivering through me. After she took several deep breaths, she tugged my hair with shaky fingers, tipped my head back, and searched my eyes. "Andy, I don't ever want you to stop. This is the best present ever."

Unable to hold myself back any longer, I walked out of the shower, carrying her in my arms, and after I toweled us off the best I could, I rolled another condom over my still hard-as-rock length and slid back inside her. Our bodies danced together as though we'd done this many times before. I glided in and out of her, taking my time. My mouth feasted on hers. Until my lips became sensitive. I kneaded her breasts, the pads of my thumbs toying with her pink nipples. Moving down, I sucked on her hard peaks, my tongue yearning to taste all of her again. I increased the pace of my hips.

Abby hooked her legs around my waist, keeping me close.

I swallowed all her whimpers, the sound drawing new waves of pleasure through me.

"Andy, it feels so good."

"I know," I said against her mouth. Sex with Abby was better than any sex I'd ever had. I was close. So damn close. It wasn't just sex. What we were experiencing together was a connection. Something deep and raw. Something that spoke not only to my body, but to my soul too. "Abby, look at me."

Her eyes popped open, and I lost myself in her crystal irises as I thrust deeper into her. Again and again. With purpose. Until I branded myself on her.

"Fuck, you're beautiful. Abby, if you were my girl, I'd tell you that all the time."

She let her breath slip through parted lips while I pounded into her one last time, both of us exploding in ecstasy.

I fell forward and rested my forehead against hers. The quick rise and fall of her chest matched mine.

A strangled sound escaped her mouth, and I leaned back to watch her.

My throat closed at the sight of a lone tear rolling down her cheek. I caught it with a kiss. "Hey, what's wrong? Talk to me."

She shook her head. "Nothing. That's the problem. It's perfect."

I sprinkled kisses on her eyelids, the tip of her nose, the corners of her mouth, understanding her emotions. Hoping she could sense everything I wanted to tell her, I claimed her lips in a searing kiss. What we had just done, what we'd just shared, felt like it had moved the planet off its axis, and I feared nothing would ever be the same.

Because how could something that barely existed feel so right?

Chapter 8
Abigail

ndy cherished my body as if I belonged to him. As if I mattered to him and was precious. Each swirl of his tongue and caress of his lips over my naked flesh brought me to a state of ecstasy. All my cells trembled when he touched me. I could barely breathe on my own, intoxicated by his scent and everything he was, my heart beating to the rhythm of his own. He lay on top of me, propped up on one elbow, his face hovering over mine.

A single tear traced a path down my cheek, and he kissed it away. "Hey, what's wrong? Talk to me."

"Nothing. That's the problem. It's perfect." What we just did—us, being together like that—had been so much more than what I had expected. I already knew we connected easily, but loving each other proved our connection ran much deeper than I'd thought.

Andy kissed each inch of my face before capturing my lips in a deep, heated kiss that made my toes curl.

Right then, I wished we never had to part or walk away from each other. What we shared couldn't be described in words. My body recognized the signs, though—like free-falling into something highly addictive.

Star-crossed lovers. We would never be anything beyond this night.

"Is it weird if I say I'll miss this? Us?" I asked once my heart rate settled down.

"Nah. Somehow, I feel closer to you right now than I've ever felt to most people I know… Even my friends, and I've known them for years…" He combed my hair back with his fingers, and I shivered under the delicate touch. "Can we do this again?"

"What? Sex?"

"Yes. But also, can we play that stupid game again? The one from earlier?"

"Which one?" I asked.

"Guess the lie."

"O-kay."

"One. I have a mole on my left butt cheek. Two. I never sleep naked. Three. I've never gone down on a girl before tonight. Four. I can't wait to be in Memphis."

Bracing myself on my arms, I pulled him down over me as I inspected his ass. "One is a truth." I kissed him. I followed the trail between his pectoral muscles and abs with a finger when he lifted himself back up, and I relished the shivers that spread through him.

Andy watched me with a raised eyebrow, waiting for me to answer. In that moment, he looked relaxed, even happy. "Which one is it?"

"Mm-hmm, I can't decide. Two or four is the lie. Give

me a hint. If number four is the lie I won't hold it against you, but number two confused me…"

"What about number three?"

I snorted. "Come on, I've experienced it firsthand. Don't downplay your talents. That wasn't a first-timer skill."

"I have skills? Tell me all about it."

I backhanded his chest. "You know you do. Brag about it all you want, I don't care. Which means, number two is the lie." *Which means you can't wait to be away from here…from me.* The thought stung. Sure, we hadn't known each other a long time, but still, I believed that what we shared tonight meant something. I just hoped it meant something to him too.

"Beginner's luck, baby."

I blinked a dozen times. "Don't sugarcoat it. I'm not some fragile princess you need to protect. It's okay if you've done this with other girls before me."

With a finger, Andy tilted my head up until we stared at each other. "I usually sleep in boxer briefs. And I really don't wanna go back to Memphis right now. Take a guess."

Oh, so he wasn't in a rush to leave either. A soothing calm settled over my heart at the realization. "Oh, you were not kidding?"

He shook his head, a pink hue covering his cheeks. He looked adorable. And boyish with his crooked smile. "Abby, you were my first. It never felt right with anyone else. Not that I possess an extensive list of conquests, but you're the only one."

I framed his face with both palms and kissed him, soft and deep, moaning as I did. "For your information, nobody has ever gone down on me before." I kissed him again. "And I'm not sure I want anybody else to ever do it if it won't be as good as with you."

"I was right when we first met and I thought you'll kill me by the end of the night. Keep saying things like that and neither of us is ever getting out of this room or boarding a plane anytime soon."

In a swift movement, he flipped me over until I straddled him, and with his hands cupping my ass and his upper body pressing against mine, Andy devoured my mouth, as if he needed my oxygen to breathe.

A heart-quake developed inside me.

ow could something so right last only a night? The thought that our story would be over in a couple of hours hurt more than it should.

Star-crossed lovers. Again, that was how this felt.

I kissed him back with everything I had.

Our tongues danced together. Our bodies molded to perfection. This was the most perfect Christmas gift a girl could ever ask for.

I was breathless and surfing a high I never knew could exist.

"Wanna get out of here?" I asked when we both leaned back to catch some air. "I'm famished."

"Not sure food is mandatory to survive anymore, don't you think? I bet we could last days by only sampling each other."

"But there wouldn't be any of you left afterward." I pouted. "And I kinda like having you here."

"Will I be allowed to hold your hand and kiss you if we go?"

I nodded.

"For the record, and please make the jury take notes, I'm never going back to that chair."

"Fine by me."

"Then I accept this deal." Andy peppered kisses over

my still-naked chest, and I squirmed, feeling ticklish "Don't move. I'm sealing this deal."

A loud laugh escaped my mouth at the sight of him being playful. I had done it. I had chased away his sulkiness. Happy Andy looked so much hotter than his grumpy counterpart. My heart did a victory dance. Warmth spread through me at the thought I had brought sunshine into his dark night.

We stood, and before I could start dressing up, he slapped my backside, and I gasped. "God, you have the most perfect ass. I noticed it the moment you walked into that café, you know."

I pushed his chest with both hands. "Such a pervert."

"Only for you."

"Rewind a sec. You noticed me first?"

"Yeah. Well before you looked my way. I was just too stubborn to talk to you or acknowledge your existence back then."

"Mm…so you were—"

Before I could say more, he pushed me into the wall and crashed his mouth back onto mine in a bruising kiss. As if Andy was marking his territory. Branding me as his. "I'm rectifying the situation right now."

I wound my arms around his neck and deepened the kiss, wanting to burn the moment into my memory.

"Girl, we better get out of here, or I'll eat you up all over again, and we'll never leave. Pancakes?"

"Nah. I want nachos. I spotted a Mexican joint earlier. This night has been nothing like I predicted, so we'd better end it on a high note and in an unpredictable manner."

Amusement played on his face. His dark hair was disheveled now and lips, a darker shade of pink. Andy looked thoroughly fucked, and I could only wish I looked the same. "Love how you think." He kissed me once more before picking up our discarded clothes from the floor and handing me mine.

———

Sitting next to each other, we sipped water as we waited for the server to bring our food. Andy's fingers were intertwined with mine and rested on my thigh.

"Any special plans for the holidays?" I asked, trying to sound more cheerful than I felt inside. My throat tightened as the seconds we had together slipped away.

"Christmas is usually spent only with Ma. Then I go out with my friends and we have a New Year's bash in a basement somewhere. Normally, we would drive to my aunt's on January second for a week—she lives in Mississippi—but since I have engagements back in New York, I'll miss it this year. I'll fly back instead. What about you?"

"There's this party I need to attend tonight. Then it will be mostly me and myself hanging together for two weeks before I return to my dorm. My parents aren't the festive types. They usually attend some dinners and church meetings I don't care about, and I spend my nights watching Christmas movies…or reading. Sometimes I wish I had a pet to keep me company when I spend time there."

"Whoa, that sucks. I hate that for you. I wish you could come home with me."

I snickered. "Yeah, like that wouldn't be awkward at all."

"Nah." Andy shook his head and grinned, then he glanced down. "Yeah…probably."

The server brought our food, interrupting our conversation.

"I'm starving." I was about to dip a tortilla chip into

the guacamole when Andy stopped me with his hand. "What?" I asked.

"Wait. Let me show you how to eat this."

I frowned. "What do you mean?"

He emptied the salsa, guacamole, and sour cream all over the chips and mixture of cheese, red pepper, tomato, and pulled pork and scrambled it all with a fork.

"*Nooo.* You're killing our dinner-breakfast." I pushed his hand back. "What are you doing? Stop murdering our food."

He offered me a satisfied smile. "Now taste it. You'll see. All the flavors will hit your tongue."

"But...but it looks kinda disgusting."

He smirked. "Then close your eyes, and you won't see it." He snickered. "Okay, do it and open your mouth. I'll feed you."

"No."

"C'mon. You blink, and it'll be over. I won't bite you during the ten point three seconds it will last."

I burst into a fit of laughter as he used my own words against me.

"And I won't steal your innocence in those few seconds," he said. "I swear."

I did as he asked and poked my tongue out. Lips I recognized too well brushed against mine in a languid kiss. Soon they were replaced by a mouthful of nachos-y mess.

My taste buds cheered as the mixed flavors hit exactly as Andy had described. "Ohmygod, this tastes amazing." My eyes popped open, I immediately went in for another bite. "What is it called?"

"Huh, nachos?"

"C'mon. It needs a more fitting name. What about Mixchos?"

Amusement played in his eyes. "Sounds right. Only you would wanna name a dish."

"Hey, it really is *that* good. And it's worth the mess."

"That's what she said," Andy said, his cockiness on full display now.

"You are terrible." I elbowed his side before taking another bite. "Be cocky all you want, though. I can take it. Once again, you deserve the recognition for this amazing dish."

He bowed next to me. "Thanks for recognizing my exceptional talent as a chef."

"You're very welcome. I wouldn't say it if I didn't mean it. You are a man of multiple talents, Andy. I can attest to that."

His phone rang, cutting short our heart-to-heart. He lifted a finger as if to say *Just a sec.*

A smile traced his lips when he brought the device to his ear. "Hey, Ma." He nodded, listening to what his mother was saying on the other end of the line. "Yeah, I'm still at the airport. My flight's been rescheduled for nine this morning." A pause. "Yes, I brought it with me." A longer pause. "No, I am fine. I can take care of myself." He shook his head. "Ma, I know you worry about me. You always do." His mouth tilted at the corner. "I swear I'm okay." He sighed. "I'm not alone… I…huh…I have a friend who's keeping me company. It's all good." A slight blush crept over his cheeks. "A *she*." His eyes met mine, and he leaned forward to plant a kiss on the tip of my nose. "I love you too, Ma. Go back to bed. I'll call you if there's a change. Otherwise, I'll see you later." The hue coloring his cheeks darkened. "Yeah, well…okay. I'll tell her. Bye now."

He hung up, and I watched him, blinking. "Your mom?"

"Yep. Sorry about that. She wanted to make sure I was

all right. I'm sure she barely slept knowing I'd be here overnight."

My hand moved to cup my heart. "That's so sweet."

Andy scratched the back of his neck. "Huh, she said *Hi* by the way."

I stared at him. "Your mom said *Hi* to me? You sure?"

"What can I say? She's glad I'm not stuck here on my own."

"Okay, wow. This is…wow. Your mom is something else."

He grinned. "She's the best."

"You're lucky to have her. Believe me, I'm speaking from experience."

His smile was filled with compassion. "I'll tell her. She'll be happy."

I rested my head on his shoulder and squeezed his forearm. "Thank you for being here. With me." Silence stretched between us. "See? I was right. I told you we'd be friends by the end of the night."

"One thing I forgot to tell you earlier," Andy said, his smile slipping away.

I braced myself for whatever would escape his lips and crush this perfect moment.

"Abby, you're a fucking incredible human being. Inside and outside. You are funny, smart, beautiful, caring, and hot as hell. Never let anyone tell you otherwise. Stand your ground. Always."

Fresh tears burned the back of my eyes at his words. I kissed his cheek, unable to tell him how much they meant to me and wishing he would understand.

He reached up to cradle my cheek. "You are magical."

"Thanks. You're pretty amazing too." I debated whether to tell him what weighed heavily on my shoulders, then decided to be honest. After everything we had shared tonight, it felt like the right thing to do. "I'm not sure I wanna go back to the real world." Warmth crept up my cheeks. "I kinda like this little bubble we've created for ourselves here."

His throat bobbed. "Me too. If skinny-dipping is your definition of freedom, well, this is mine. Be yourself, and let the consequences be damned. Do what feels right when it does feel right. Not sure if I make sense right now."

I squeezed the hand still holding mine under the table. "It does… To me."

Andy and I finished our meal, chatting about our musical preferences and all-time favorite bands.

Somehow, it felt like we'd known each other for more than just a few hours, and we were making up for lost time.

I wished I could press pause on some invisible remote so our time together would never end. Because just the thought of parting ways was enough to fill me with a sadness I'd never experienced before. And I knew deep down I'd never be ready to say goodbye.

Chapter 9

Anderson

At seven, Abby got ready to board her plane, and I pulled her in for another kiss. One last kiss. I tucked her hair behind her ear, framing her cheek with my palm, losing myself in the deep ocean of her eyes one last time. "Will you be all right?"

No matter how crazy it sounded, I had no idea how to let her go. I had experienced the best night of my life, and my insides coiled, knowing we only had minutes left.

She nodded, chewing on her bottom lip. By now, I knew it meant she was anxious about something—or uncomfortable. I wished I could reassure her that everything would be all right. That it wasn't the end. That we had more time. But it would all be a lie. I knew it. And she knew it too.

So instead of feeding her promises I wouldn't be able to keep, I pressed a kiss to her forehead. My lips lingered there for a long beat. How was I supposed to let her leave?

I laced my fingers with hers, unable to stop myself from touching her.

A long-distance relationship with someone I'd met only hours ago defied logic, no matter how intense our chemistry was. We both had our lives, our friends, and college. Relationships needed nurturing and commitment, something neither of us could pursue with hundreds of miles separating us. Our timing was all wrong. In another life, another time, maybe we could have made it work, but now, even if we tried, life would keep us apart. Neither of us needed the stress it would provide. And the truth was that we didn't know each other well, even though it felt like we did.

I fastened my arms around her body, and she buried her face in my chest. Entangled, we stood there, our hearts syncing, our silence speaking volumes, saying what we couldn't bring ourselves to voice aloud.

After what felt like just seconds, she leaned back from my embrace, a timid smile curling her lips, and lifted a finger. "Oh, wait. I forgot to give you your present."

"You got me something? I don't need a present, Abby. I didn't get you anything. Anyway, you already gave me more than a guy stranded in an airport could ask for. You brightened up my night. You made me smile. And you rocked my world. It's better than anything I could have ever hoped for."

Her expression softened, and she pressed a finger to my lips. "Andy, you gave me everything I wished for. You brought magic into my Christmas. It wouldn't have been special without you. Believe me, this will be the highlight of my winter break…or my year." She picked up a red box from the bag we'd been carrying around for the last few hours. "I asked the woman to double up on the bubble wrap. I hope it survived the night."

With repeated glances her way, I opened the package. Inside lay a snow globe. I flipped in over, and millions of glittery snowflakes fell over the couple frozen in time inside, kissing on a park bench between a white fir and a snowman.

My heart sizzled in my chest.

I blinked fast to dissipate the emotions strangling me. This girl. For a night, she had been my source of joy. My anchor. My everything. And in a moment, she would be nothing more than a memory from my past, a speck in my rearview mirror.

"Abby, wow. It's…it's beautiful… You sure you want me to have it?"

She bobbed her head, her eyes watery and her lower lip trembling. "Yes. I-I bought it for you. When I saw it earlier, it reminded me of you. Of the two of us."

"But… We didn't even know each other back then." My eyes searched hers.

"I feel like I've known you all along, Andy. Even before I came to talk to you in that café. I believe in destiny. And fate. And I'm confident we were meant to meet last night. That we were both there at the same time for a reason neither of us can explain."

"Kismet," I murmured.

"Maybe it's Christmas magic. Or fate….the universe… Maybe it's something else. But no matter what brought us together, I'll always cherish the hours we shared. Thank you for being my friend last night. And taking part in my silly challenge. And for loving me when I needed you to. It meant more than you'll ever imagine. I'm thankful. For every minute we spent together."

Her words hit me straight in the chest. My heart thrashed behind my ribs with a boatload of unfamiliar emotions.

When I opened my mouth, my words stuck to the tip of my tongue. There was so much I wanted to tell her, yet I had no idea how to express my deepest feelings. If love-struck was really something that could exist, I was sure it would look like us. But it was impossible. You couldn't feel this way about a stranger you'd only known for a few hours.

Before I could make a fool of myself and say things out loud that I should keep to myself, I turned the globe over, mesmerized by the magical display, and noticed a small inscription at the bottom.

Abby + Andy's Magical Night

More emotions choked me.

With the pad of my thumb, I wiped the tears streaming down Abby's cheeks. Her eyes looked bluer than before. Shiny ice crystals I refused to avoid.

"I love it. Abby, I can't promise you forever or that we'll ever meet again…but…but I can promise you I'll never forget you. That I swear." I cupped my thundering organ with one hand. "Meeting you has changed me. Forever. I'm the one who's thankful. And I wish this storm had lasted a very long time, so I wouldn't have to say goodbye to you so soon. Who knew being snowbound could be this amazing?"

I curled a hand around her neck and pulled her in. She rested her forehead against my chest, and we stood there, relishing the last few seconds we had with each other.

"This is the last boarding call for passengers on flight 217A to Nashville. Please proceed to gate three immediately…" a voice spoke through a microphone.

"It's my flight. I-I gotta go. Now," Abby said in a strangled voice. "I'm sorry."

She stepped back, and we stared at each other for what felt like an eternity, neither of us was brave enough to say goodbye. If we did, it would sound like finality, and I didn't want to be reminded it was over. Perhaps I could get her contacts, stay in touch, find a way to see her again. My chest swelled with possibilities.

"Abby—"

She pressed a finger to my lips, silencing me. "Thanks for making me feel special all night, Andy. And if you were my man, I would kiss you all the time. No promises, okay? We agreed it would be one magical night. Only one. It would hurt too much if we made promises to keep in touch and couldn't keep them." More tears pooled in her eyes, and she slung her bag over her shoulder, her fingers locked with mine until we were too far apart to touch. With one last look at me over her shoulder and a blown kiss, she disappeared.

Frozen, I stood there, feeling helpless, my heart shattering over a girl I barely knew.

I unfroze, and without thinking, I ran after her. Our story couldn't end like this. Whatever she said, we could fight for more. Or we could at least try.

I followed her steps, rushing toward the gate where she'd just disappeared. My heart sank in my chest as I came to a halt, breathless, like the world had tilted without warning. I was too late. The gate had already closed behind her, sealing her away from me. Our story would always feel incomplete. I had that certainty now.

I tugged at my hair until the roots burned. I was too fucking late. I had lost her. Forever. "I'm sorry, Abby. I should have asked for your full name when I had a chance." I stuffed my hands into the pockets of my jeans, my feet nailed to the floor as I watched her plane fly away, taking a piece of my heart with her. A piece I would never get back.

A fat tear slipped from my eye. I had no memory of ever crying over a girl before, or of the last time I had cried for no reason at all. But something told me I would regret not holding on to her. She had just left, and already I felt like my whole world had collapsed around me. It was as if the air had thinned, and I couldn't breathe.

I shook my head.

This didn't make sense. Nothing did.

It was just a holiday hookup. Nothing more.

How could it feel like so much more than that?

I should put the entire night behind me and forget all about it. That was the sensible thing to do. Regrets would lead me nowhere. I couldn't spend my time pining over a one-night fling.

Sitting on a chair, waiting for my plane to take off, my heart in shambles and my guitar in hand, I wrote a song for the girl I would never see again.

Chapter 10
Abigail

"Hey, what's wrong?" my roommate Ellie asked as I exited the stall where I emptied my stomach after we got dismissed from our music branding class.

At the sink, I splashed cold water over my face. "Stomach bug. It's been going all around campus for the last week. I'm its latest victim. Jessica and Shana have been locked in their dorm room for the last two days, eating chicken and noodle soup and watching reruns of a sitcom I shall not name, or the jingle will stick with me for the next decade." I turned the faucet off and dabbed my face with a paper towel. "Ellie, you should stay away. Sleep at Tom's or something. Until I feel better."

My friend shook her head. "Nah, I'm fine." She flexed her biceps. "Super extraordinary immune system here. Stomach bugs don't scare me easily, girl. And who will take care of you if you get a fever in the middle of the night? Or go on a painkiller run if you develop a stomachache?"

I raised my hands before me. "Fine. You win. But if you get sick, don't blame me. You've been warned."

"Nah, I won't." She snaked her arm through mine. "Let's go. Or we will be late for our next class, and I really wanna grab a chai latte on the way there."

Just the name of her favorite drink upset my stomach again.

I rushed to the closest stall, emptying my stomach for the third time since I woke up.

Minutes later, I splashed more water over my face and rinsed my mouth, trying to get rid of the putrid taste.

Ellie inched closer and lifted herself on the countertop next to the sink. "Abby, no offense, but you look like shit. I'll take notes. You need rest. And to hydrate yourself if you wanna fight this fucker. Go back to bed."

As if agreeing with her, a yawn left my mouth. My eyes brimmed with tears. I hated missing classes. I hated being sick. I hated feeling like hell. But Ellie was right. I felt so weak at the moment, and my bed was calling my name.

"Enough. Abigail Peña, get your ass moving. Bed. Now."

I slouched my shoulders forward and nodded. "Fine, Mom. But if I'm feeling better later, we're going to that fiesta happy hour at the Mexican place we've been dying to try, okay? I really don't wanna miss it."

"Deal," she said. "Can you believe it's been two weeks already since we came back from Winter Break? Time flies, and I'm scared we will miss all the fun stuff because we're always too busy. If we're not careful, soon we'll graduate and become real adults. I'm not ready for all the responsibilities." She shook her head, her platinum blonde hair sweeping her upper back, her shoulders dipping. "I'd love to surf the late teenager wave a bit longer. Screw up and experiment while I still have the chance."

"Yeah, well, you're lucky your parents are paying for all your extravaganzas. Some of us need to work to afford college tuition. If it weren't for that academic scholarship, I'd be attending garden parties and dating the heir of a powerful family, being molded into a future politician's perfect stay-at-home wife. My parents are stuck in their own beliefs. They still don't understand why I wanna work in the music industry. If they had to decide my future, I'd be a trophy wife. Because this is the only career path viable for women like me who have parents more skilled at parading their wealth than caring for their offspring's well-being and happiness." A long sigh left my mouth. "I'm so tired of hearing the same bullshit every time I'm back home. My mother used to be different a long time ago when I was little. She was a flight attendant, and she used to laugh and have fun. Her smile was more genuine than the plastic one she's stuck with nowadays. She used to thrive." I grabbed my phone to look at the time. "Ellie, you should go, or you'll be late. I'm sorry. Now you won't be able to get that drink before class. Leave. I'll be okay."

My friend flipped her wrist. "Nah, no worries. I have Tom on speed dial. He'll break a leg for me if it means making me happy...and satisfied. Talking about satisfied, he learned a new tongue trick. *Gurrrl*, I'm telling you, you gotta experience it before you die. It's kinda miraculous. I thought I went to heaven and was resuscitated. No kidding."

I pushed her upper arm. "Please no tongue trick four-one-one today. Wait until I feel better to gimme all the details, okay? I wish I had time for a boyfriend." I shrugged. "One day..."

"Don't lie to yourself. Even if you had, you'd still be

hung up on that guy you met at the airport. Give it time. There are other perfectly fine male specimens out there."

"I guess… He was special. We connected. It's harder than I thought to get over him." A wave of nausea filled my mouth, and I placed a hand over my lips until it settled down. "Sorry."

Ellie touched my forehead. "No fever. But you're as pale as the wall. Go to bed. It's a roommate order. I've got you covered." She jumped from the counter and kissed my cheek. "Sleep it off."

"Thanks. For always having my back." We walked out together toward her next class. "Bye," I said as we parted ways in front of the brick dining hall building.

"See you later," she called out over her shoulder, laughing, as she sauntered away.

Ellie and I had formed an instant friendship when we shared a dorm room during our freshman year. We hit it off right away. She was the bubbly, oversharing friend. I was the more introvert one. Together, we balanced each other. Ellie had grown up in a family resembling mine. Super strict, wealthy, and very old school. Both of us only children, we saw our college years as an opportunity to shine on our own, to experiment, and to live a life we were both shielded from in the past. The only difference was that my friend's parents paid for all her expenses, even the ones they didn't approve of, while mine only helped when it suited their own ambitions. College wasn't their aspiration for me. As long as I stayed enrolled, they agreed to cover what my scholarship didn't, as long as I paid for everything else myself.

A guy from my management class waved at me when we crossed paths, and I returned the gesture.

My stomach made a funny sound, and I closed my

eyes, counting to ten, begging it to stay still until I reached my dorm, a ten-minute walk away.

"Hey, are you okay?" he asked, nearing me.

I swallowed. "Yes. Stomach bug or something. You shouldn't get too close to me."

He sighed. "Not you too? You're the third person I've met today who's sick." He took a step back and lifted his hands in surrender. "I'm sorry, but I don't wanna catch it."

"It's fine. Going back to bed anyway."

"Good luck, Abby."

After he left, I adjusted my knitted cream beanie and padded away, thankful for the crisp winter air as it cooled my feverish self, my hands holding my jacket tight around me.

Sitting in a booth, a few hours later, I nursed my second glass of icy water, watching my roommate dirty dancing with Tom. They had been friends with benefits for a long time, but I could see they were in love, even if they pretended otherwise. Tom had his hands all over her as he whispered what I assumed to be filthy promises, seeing the way she was flustered every time his mouth neared her ear.

The Mexican eatery slash bar had opened a few weeks ago, and Ellie and I had been dying to try it out. Famous for their salsa music and homemade guacamole, they had become a popular hangout spot for college students since their opening. Lime green walls, terracotta tiled floors, ceramic topped table, this place was a chaos of colors. For some reason, here the visual overload worked. Somehow.

Amelia, a girl from my leadership and ethics class, slid into the seat opposite me.

"Hey there." Dressed in all black, with dirty blonde hair and thick kohl lines framing her deep-green eyes, she took a sip from the oversized margarita in her hand. "Where's Ellie?"

With my chin, I pointed to the dance floor behind her.

"Oh," she said, turning her head in my roommate's direction. "Damn, I would kill for a guy like Tom."

I sighed. Because I would too. My friend kept repeating to everyone, all the time, they were just friends enjoying each other's company and having amazing sex. But the way they were joined at the hip and all lovey-dovey, they didn't fool any of us.

With my elbow propped up on the table and my chin resting on my open palm, I watched my friend. She looked happy. And carefree. After dating a possessive jerk last year, I was glad she had ended up with a good guy this time. Ellie deserved the happiness.

My stomach rumbled, and I splayed a hand over my abdomen, trying to calm the waves rocking my insides.

Taking slow, deep breaths, I tried to regain my composure, but the chaos inside me refused to ease, and I cupped my mouth with my hand as I rushed toward the restroom. Again.

After my four-hour nap this afternoon, I really thought I was well enough to spend a night out with my friends. Yeah, the joke was on me.

Pearls of sweat lined my back as I exited the stall after emptying the contents of my stomach. On wobbly legs, I splashed cold water on my face and rinsed my mouth, then made my way back to our table.

Dropping onto the seat, I pressed the glass of icy water against my cheeks.

"Girl, you look like hell," Amelia said, chewing olives from the plate set in the middle of the table.

A new surge of nausea swirled in my stomach. "Oh God. I can't be in here right now." Standing, I picked up my bag, ready to bolt out of the restaurant.

"You're leaving?"

"Yeah, well, I thought I was feeling better. Not the case…clearly. Can you tell Ellie I had to go, please?" My eyes drifted to my roommate, still in her little love bubble with her boyfriend. Yes, those two weren't fooling me. "I'm calling it a night and going back to bed."

Amelia offered me a thumbs-up, bringing her drink to her lips and licking the salty rim. Just the sight of it made my stomach churn.

"Go before I get sick." She shooed me away with a wave of her hand. "If you're contagious, stay away from me." Her fingers circled my wrist before I could leave, and a wrinkle etched her forehead. "Abby, wait. You look like you're about to faint. Are you okay to go back by yourself?"

"I'll halt a cab. Or walk. Don't worry for me."

My legs trembled as I reached the sidewalk. Trying to ease my agitated stomach, I took a huge breath in.

For the second time today, I enjoyed the cold air as it made its way to my lungs. After buttoning my jacket, I decided to walk to my dorm, afraid the vibrations of the car would mess with the calm that had now settled inside me.

———

"*Gurrrl,* it's been three days. Are you sure you don't have anything serious?" Ellie asked as she removed her coat and discarded it on her bed. She opened the paper bag in her hand and offered me a bowl.

"What is it?" I asked, bracing myself on my forearms, my blanket billowing out around my waist.

"Soup. Thought you'd like that. It's from your favorite place on campus."

"Ellie, you're a lifesaver. I've dreamed about this soup all day."

Cross-legged on my bed, I pushed the fluffy blanket away and dug into the chicken noodles delicacy. "Mmm-hmm, this is so good," I said between mouthfuls. "You want some?"

My friend raised a hand between us. "No, thanks. I might be super germ-resistant, but I won't tempt fate." She paused to study me. "I know I already asked, but you never answered. You sure it's viral?"

I shrugged. "Yeah. What else could it be? I heard the girls in room four-zero-six, had been down for almost a week. It's been half of that, so don't panic just yet."

She shook her head. "Fine. If you say so." She peeled her jeans down her long legs and slid them into a pair of sweatpants before turning around. "Up for a movie? There's a new Amanda Stephenson blockbuster that has just come out. I heard it's pretty great. And swoony. The actor is a British hunk with corded forearms, a nice set of abs, and dark stubble. I'm certain you'll heal just by watching him. I saw the trailer… There's an ocean skinny-dipping scene. Drop-dead-gorgeous." She stretched the *S* and fanned herself. "Trust me."

I scooted over on my bed and placed a pillow behind my back before patting the mattress beside me. "C'mon over, I slept all day. I'm due for some steamy rom-com action. And I love scruffy hunks."

My roommate tilted her head back and let out a loud laugh before fetching a beer can from the mini fridge we shared. "That's my girl. Want one?"

A chill passed through me. "Ugh, no. Thanks. It'll be a miracle if I can keep this soup down for more than an hour or two."

Our dorm room wasn't big but included two of everything: single beds, desks, and closets. Ellie and I each had a side that mirrored the other. The beds framed the door, and our desks lined the large rectangular window on the opposite wall. In between them were a small refrigerator and a microwave. Powder-blue walls, wooden trims, and a deep-blue carpeted floor, it was nothing fancy, but it was ours to share.

Side by side, we watched the movie on her laptop until my eyelids grew heavy and I finally gave in to sleep, lowering myself onto the bed. Soon, I fell into a deep slumber and dreamed about the guy with the scruffy jaw who wasn't British but could sing and play the guitar like a god.

The next morning, I woke up early, feeling rested—and a whole lot better. My first class wasn't before nine, so I decided to shower before getting ready. The hot water helped relax my shoulders and upper back. Yeah, the virus seemed to have decided living in my body wasn't fun enough and had left. Or so I believed.

Three girls from my floor entered the common bathroom, and one of them wore an overpowering coconut scent that triggered my nausea. Abandoning my shower caddy and stuff on the floor, I rushed to a stall just in time, and heaved, my mostly empty stomach protesting.

My eyes watered. I wanted to go back to class. I loved it. Even the boring lessons were still entertaining when you were studying what you had dreamed of since childhood, back when the sky had no limits. My hands shook with tremors. I felt hot and sweaty. How would I survive six hours of class in this state?

A knock on the door startled me.

"Hey, are you okay?" a girl asked.

I wiped my mouth with toilet paper and moved to my feet. "Yeah…sure. All good."

I inhaled, rolled my shoulders back, and exited the stall, only to come face to face with her.

I forced my lips into a tiny curve and rounded her to get to the sinks.

"Are you pregnant?" she asked from behind me.

I blinked, tipped my chin up, and met her gaze in the mirror. "What?"

"I said, are you pregnant?"

"Huh, no. It's the flu. Or something else. It's been running around campus. I'm its latest victim."

She furrowed her eyebrows and crossed her arms over her chest. "You sure?"

"Yes," I said with as much conviction and attitude as I could muster.

"If you say so..." She gave me a slow once-over that left me feeling self-conscious.

Why wouldn't she let it go? I was sick, not about to be a mother. I hated when people couldn't mind their own business. And meddled in mine instead.

"Last semester, my roommate barfed for nothing, and she was three months pregnant. Her jackass of a boyfriend ran away, and she was left dealing with everything by herself. You remind me of her."

"Well, I'm not her."

She shrugged. "Believe whatever you want." She pivoted on her heels, motioning to her friends. "Come on, girls, we'll be late if we don't hurry up. I'm working all day at the free clinic."

The three of them left me in the bathroom by myself, not offering me another glance.

"Me? Pregnant? Yeah, right," I said out loud once the door clicked after them.

After I brushed my teeth and applied a little makeup, I felt more like myself than I had in days.

"Oh, you look better," Ellie greeted me, perched on her bed, applying flashy blue nail polish to her toes. "That green mask you've been wearing in the last few days is mostly gone. Rosy cheeks are a better look on you."

I sighed. "I thought I was doing fine. Until I got sick minutes ago and a girl asked me if I was pregnant."

Ellie blinked. And blinked again. "Wait. She did? How bold."

"Yep. And she told me about her roommate who got knocked up. When I replied she was wrong about me, she eyed me like I was an idiot and left. The nerve."

"*Gurrrl*, you would tell me if you were pregnant, right?"

I slouched on my bed facing her, my towel still wrapped around me. "Ellie, how can you believe such nonsense? You've been here every day since I caught that bug. You've seen Jessica and Shana unable to go to class either. Come on, don't jump on the rumor wagon. The three of us aren't all magically pregnant at the same time. Fake news is so last year."

She exhaled heavily. "I had to ask. As your best friend, it's my duty. In case you have doubts."

I tossed a pillow at her, and she raised her hands in front of her to block it, the nail polish cap still lodged between her teeth.

"Okay, you're forgiven since you had my best interests at heart." I wiggled my finger in her direction. "Finish your art thingy. I'll get dressed. Maybe you could paint my nails next. I'm feeling almost back to normal. Today is the day I'm returning to class."

She arched a brow. "You sure?"

"Yes. Stop worrying about me. I'll be all right. Even Mr. Matthews's boring class sounds amazing right now."

"Okay then."

I rummaged through my closet for something to wear.

In my head, the gears started running. Even though I tried to brush it off, the girl's question haunted my thoughts. *Are you pregnant?*

Yeah, right. Me, the girl without a boyfriend and still hung up on Andy, the guy I'd met days before Christmas, whom I'd never see again. His tousled dark hair and the scruff on his jaw. The build of his shoulders or the way he held on to me as if I mattered to him. His kisses. His permanent scowl that vanished when he looked at me, like really looked at me. We had shared our souls for a night, and I could have gotten lost in the depths of his eyes. They were so mesmerizing, like he could see me. The real me. Oh God. Just the memories of that night were enough to send a swirl of heat to my lower belly. And those hours we'd spent together, I knew they would stick with me forever. A sad smile stretched my lips at the idea we would never cross paths again. I didn't know his full name, and we hadn't exchanged contact info. I had to forget about him. The sooner, the better.

Easier said than done. Flashbacks of our time together still invaded my waking hours. Perhaps forgetting him wouldn't be as easy as I'd thought. So far, it had proved almost impossible.

Weeks later, reminiscing about how special, beautiful, and desired he had made me feel still sent my heart into overdrive. Melancholy filled me. I had replayed that night multiple times in my head since we went our separate ways, and it still wasn't enough. When I'd boarded the plane that took me away from him, I'd bawled my eyes out. For what could have been. And what I had lost. Even though, in all honesty, I never really had him. But, for a few hours, it felt like I had. Thinking about Andy always messed with my feelings. Tears prickled the back of my eyes. Sucking a breath to erase the emotional turmoil taking over me, I picked up a pair of jeans and my favorite sweater, hoping the comfort would ease my internal storm.

Being sick and feverish could explain why the thought of him was sending me into an emotional spiral. My entire self was weak from the virus I'd been battling. It had nothing to do with the man to whom my heart belonged for a night of harmless fun.

This was ridiculous. I was being ridiculous.

For some reason, I couldn't push away the words that girl spoke as I finished gathering my stuff and Ellie colored my toenails in a peachy-pink hue. We walked to our first class of the morning, and the crisp air did nothing to cool down my complicated emotions this time.

If only it could stop my mind from spinning and put my doubts to rest.

Chapter 11

Anderson

"Are you coming tonight?" my friend Joe asked just as I was sending the piece of music I'd been working on for the last month. It was due for an assignment in four days, but I was confident it was already as perfect as it could ever be. Nothing like submitting schoolwork early and gaining some free time in the process—I had a gig scheduled for tomorrow night and a wedding in two days.

Joe and I were sharing a small apartment in Brooklyn in a building owned by his uncle. He had agreed to lease us the space at a cheap price—way below market rent for New York City—in exchange for us acting as superintendents, keeping the place clean, and doing some handiwork for him from time to time. Once a month, I also performed at the club he owned. I wasn't paid for my time, but I got to keep the tips, which usually added up to a few hundred bucks. The monthly gig alone was enough to get my heart pumping, because it brought me closer to my dream. Another step in the right direction, as my mother would say.

She wasn't super ecstatic about the idea of my pursuing a professional music career. After all, she had dated a guy who was famous and got her pregnant with me, and when she thought they would settle down together, he had returned to his wife and never looked back.

I got it. She got burned by love. In more ways than I could ever imagine.

But aside from sharing half his genes, I wasn't him.

Never would I be the kind of guy who lived a double life and hurt the people he cared about by doing so. Never would I abandon my own child, no matter what it implied. See? My sperm donor and I weren't wired the same. My mother had to realize that. She couldn't blame my choices and dreams on the jackass who had knocked her up.

"So, are you coming?" Joe repeated.

I blinked to reboot my brain. This had been happening a lot lately. My zoning out. Losing myself in my thoughts. Most of the time, they involved Abby. The girl I'd sworn to myself I would forget but couldn't seem to.

"Nah, I think I'll stay in… Write." Since the night I'd spent with Abby a while back, I'd been really inspired. I couldn't stop writing every time I had some free time. Soon, I would have two full albums worth of new material if I kept going at this rhythm.

Our place was not big by any means. White walls and simple furniture, it was everything we needed and nothing more. A vintage oak dining table set that used to belong to Joe's grandmother, a black leather couch we bought at a garage sale when we'd first moved in, and a dark-wood coffee table that doubled as an ottoman. Posters from our favorite movies decorated the walls on each side of the television, just above a chipped, red-painted console that hosted video games, an array of liquor bottles, and a bunch of music-related magazines. My mother had sewn the charcoal curtains framing the patio door and kitchen windows, and two matching cushions that gave the living room a homey feel, as she'd said.

Joe slouched on the couch beside me. "Man, what happened to you during the holidays? You were dedicated before, but you still had time to mingle. Now you're acting like a hermit. You refuse every opportunity to go out and meet people. Seriously, you need a pussy. Someone to snap you out of this funk. Your Abby-girl is long gone. You can't pine for her forever. At some point, you'll have to move on. I thought we'd already agreed on that. And the best way to get over a girl is to get under another, you know the saying."

"It's a guy. Not girl."

Confusion painted his face, and his eyebrows bunched together.

"The saying. The best way to get over a guy is to get under another. See? It's *guy*, not girl."

He studied me for a long second before shrugging. "Whatever. Sounds alike. Same principle. If it works for girls, it should work for you too, no?"

"That's the thing. I don't wanna forget about her. My short time with her had triggered my creative side. When I think about her, I can't stop writing music. Good music. Amazing stuff. Wait until you hear it. You'll be flabbergasted. I'm telling you. Who knows… If I forget her, maybe it will shut down the creative juices… Trust me, I'm not ready to find out."

"If I didn't know you like I do, I would believe you were in love."

I elbowed his side. "Stop starting rumors. We had a

great time. She was nice...amazing. We had fun. And now the memories of her are serving my purpose. Don't put too much thought into it."

He eyed me, and I bet he could read through my bullshit. It'd been a little over six weeks since Abby and I had parted ways, and every night, I still dreamed about our short time together. And every day, I sang to her as I wrote new material. She had taken a permanent place in my mind, and I had no idea why or how, but I wasn't ready to chase away the only memory I had left of her. That and the snow globe she'd gifted me. Set on the bookshelf by my bed, I stared at it every morning, wondering what she was up to. Then I'd shake my head, call myself silly, and move on with my day.

It'd been over a month of the same shit. Whatever. At this point, I didn't question the process anymore. I just rolled with it.

"Man, you sure you're staying here?" Joe asked once more as he moved to his feet, ready to leave to attend another frat party, after preening in the mirror.

Going to a party. Dressing up to look sharp. Two things I hadn't done in a while. These days, my everyday outfit consisted of a pair of washed-out jeans and a plaid shirt rolled up at the elbows. Sometimes, I spiced up my look by wearing an unbuttoned shirt over a plain T-shirt. A leather cuff around my wrist and some biker boots completed the outfit. Simple, casual, and comfy.

"Yep. I am. See you later."

He waved and disappeared as my eyes stayed locked on the front door for some time. As if I expected someone to walk in. A petite girl with jet-black hair and piercing blue eyes.

With a shake of my head, I pushed the thoughts away

and grabbed my guitar. She and I would be up all night. I could already tell.

————

"Oh. My. Goodness. You were so good up there. Hot. Hot. Hot. So much that your singing gave me a heatstroke. And…and the way you played your guitar. I could die listening to you. I wish you would play my body like that. I bet those fingers have skills with the hours of practice you probably put in. Andy, I am so wet for you." Liliana, the bride's little sister, had been clinging to my arm for the last fifteen minutes, fangirling over my performance while her father watched closely from across the room.

For the umpteenth time, tried to peel the fingers embedded in my biceps away one by one, but in vain. The girl was like Velcro. At this point, she was practically permanently attached to my arm. I faked a smile, and her eyes practically shot sparks. Long blonde hair spilled over her shoulders, thick—probably fake—lashes framing her eyes, and dark red lipstick painted across her lips. She was beautiful. In another life, I might have taken her up on her offer. Yeah, she'd been propositioning me for hours. But not tonight. I couldn't bring myself to go along with it. Because if I did, would it dull the memory of Abby? Would I lose what fueled my music, the raw ache her absence had carved into my songs? Sex with a beautiful girl wasn't enough for me to risk it all. Nah, I preferred my celibacy. For now.

Liliana moved to her tiptoes and murmured into my ear, "I have a hotel suite. To myself. With a hot tub. Meet me there in thirty minutes. I'll order champagne." She pushed a plastic keycard into my hand, her lips dancing over the stubble of my jaw. "Room forty-six-twenty-seven.

I'll wait for you, *Anderson*." She started to walk away, swaying her hips, before she appeared to remember something and returned to my side. Her lips brushed the shell of my ear as she added, "Clothes are optional." She flashed me a grin and disappeared into the crowd filling the dance floor.

My gaze trailed her movement until I couldn't see her anymore.

I scanned the space around me, ready to bolt. From the opposite side of the ballroom, her daddy dearest's eyes locked onto mine, and he sent me his best menacing glare, that said *Touch my daughter and I'll kill you.*

With a small shake of my head and a lopsided smile, I brought the bottle of beer to my lips and dragged my other hand down my face.

Tonight, I'd go to bed alone.

After finishing my drink, I met the groom to collect my payment, shook hands with the band now entertaining the crowd, and gathered my guitar. When I passed Lilliana's daddy, I pushed the keycard into his chest. His fingers connected with the plastic rectangle as he watched me with rounded eyes. "Night, sir," I said before leaving.

New York City's cold breeze tingled the tip of my nose. I buttoned up my jacket and opened an app on my phone to book a cab.

While I waited, I people-watched everyone entering and exiting the posh hotel. Businessmen, families, couples. Two people caught my attention: a guy about my age arguing with his—what I assumed was his—girlfriend. Both gestured wildly, clearly not agreeing on something. The girl shook her head, about to retort, when the guy leaned forward, cupped her face, and kissed her. Hard. She steeled against him for a second before melting in his arms and kissing him back, the fight forgotten.

Feeling like a voyeur, I averted my eyes and checked the time on my phone instead.

Perhaps I should have accepted Liliana's offer. I sighed. Who was I kidding? Based on how my last experience had gone and its aftermath, I knew I wasn't cut out for no-strings-attached sex. I preferred relationships. Always had. And the idea of wetting my dick in anyone else felt like I was cheating on a girl whose full name I didn't even know.

How pathetic had I become?

Before I could chastise myself, a car pulled up, and my phone chimed, notifying me that my ride had arrived. I slid my guitar case in and hauled myself into the backseat.

"Good evening, sir," the driver said before pulling away.

I returned his greeting with a sharp nod and let my eyes drift over the glittering Manhattan skyline I could see through the window, *what-ifs* swirling in my head. Another melody played in my mind, and I drummed my fingertips on my thigh as the lyrics took shape. I jotted notes on my phone so I wouldn't forget, then relaxed against the seat, eyes closed, a hint of a smile tugging at my lips as the song looped in my head.

In that instant, I made a promise to myself—and the girl inspiring all my music. "I'll never stop looking for you. Please, look for me too."

Chapter 12

Abigail

"What's wrong?" Ellie asked, sitting on her bed. "You haven't been yourself lately. You're silent, you go to bed early, you don't join me when I go out. I'm getting worried. Are you still sick? It's been over two weeks. You should feel better by now."

Could I tell her what was on my mind? If someone could understand, it was her.

I sighed and fidgeted with the hem of my shirt, avoiding her eyes in case she could read the thoughts that had been polluting my mind feed for the last sixteen days, six hours, and forty-five minutes.

"*Gurrrl*, tell me. Now."

"It's about… You know…huh…that morning."

She moved to sit next to me, crossing her legs and forcing me to face her. "That morning…?" She tapped her finger on her chin. "Hmmm, morning is a daily occurrence. Care to be more specific?"

I swallowed the lump forming in my throat as it swelled to the size of a boulder.

Ellie grabbed my hands in hers. "Whatever it is, spill it. You know you can trust me. No matter what, I won't judge you. All I'll do is try to help you. I swear."

I freed my hands and pushed my hair back, then met her eyes. "I know…" My voice had lost all conviction, sounding tiny and unfamiliar to my own ears. "It's just… You'll think I'm being stupid. I'm sure I am worrying for nothing."

"Abby, stop with the mental gymnastics and say it."

"No."

"Yes."

I breathed out. "What if I really was pregnant?"

My friend's eyes widened, scanning my face with a single raised brow. "Huh. How? You said it was impossible two weeks ago when we talked about it."

"It—it's been nagging at me ever since that girl mentioned it. I have no reason to believe I am, but—"

"But? Abby, what are you not telling me?"

"I checked my calendar. My last period was before Winter Break."

Ellie counted on her fingers before bringing her attention back to me. "Fuck, you're like what, six weeks late? And you didn't realize it sooner?"

"I'm…I'm often late. Nothing unusual. I often skip one or two cycles. With the new semester and being sick, I got so caught up that I kinda forgot about it. Until…until I did the math sixteen days ago. My cycles have always been irregular and all over the place, so I really have no reason to freak out, but… I don't know. Something is different this time. I can tell. For the past two weeks, I've been trying to explain away all the symptoms I've been feeling. Nothing makes sense except…"

"Are you sure?"

"What else could it be? I need to find out. It's turning into an obsession. It's all I think about, and and it's slowly driving me insane."

Ellie enveloped me in her arms. "Why didn't you confide in me sooner? You shouldn't freak out about it on your own."

"I thought it was all in my head. You know how it is when you Google your symptoms, convince yourself you have some incurable disease, and then suddenly notice new symptoms that seem to confirm your pseudo-diagnosis? Well, I thought I had a case of hypochondria."

"Okay, now you're being silly. Since when do *you* make up diseases in your mind?"

I shrugged.

"See? You're not being yourself. Let's find out." She pulled away and jumped to her feet. "I'll be right back."

I hooked my fingers onto her forearm before she could get too far. "What are you doing? Where are you going? Don't leave me alone with my thoughts."

"Getting pregnancy tests. So, you can put this silly idea to rest once and for all."

I ran a hand over my face. "Huh… I've already bought tests. They're in the bag on the floor under my desk. I've been too chickenshit to take them on my own." My lips trembled, a wave of sadness rising in my core and sweeping through me.

"Oh, Abby, I'm right here. I'm not going anywhere."

A sob from my chest. "Ellie, what if I *am* pregnant? That would be a disaster. Everything I've been working for… My independence… All my dreams…" I hiccupped. "My parents would never forgive me. They still think you'll burn in hell if you have sex before marriage. And that a woman's place is at home with her children, looking pretty on her husband's arm. It would be a nightmare."

My friend wrapped an arm around my heaving shoulders and pressed a kiss to my temple. "Let's find out first, then panic later, okay? No matter what, you've got options. It's not too late."

I nodded, wiping my teary eyes with the sleeve of my dust-blue SSB sweatshirt. "Okay."

My roommate fetched the drugstore bag I'd discarded three days ago. "Oh-fucking-God, how many tests did you buy?" she asked, waving a box of two in my face and shaking the bag.

"Seven. I heard about false positives… And false negatives. I'm not taking any chances. I bought four different brands."

She sat back next to me. "Question, though. How could it be? You're always the smart one. Tom and I aren't even officially dating, and we skip protection most of the time. I'm allergic to latex, and no way am I asking him to wear those lambskin condoms when he fucks me." She shivered. "Dis-gus-ting. We're exclusive. We both got tested before we got together and I'm on the pill and he always pulls out. But still, it sounds more like something that would happen to me."

I exhaled a long and painful breath. "Elles, that's a lot of information I didn't need. You know there are other options for you too, right?" I repeated her own words.

Ellie waved a hand as if to refuse to acknowledge what I'd just said.

I buried my face in my hands. "We used a condom. Condoms. Plural. I swear we did. My first time hooking up with a stranger and see where it has gotten me? I've never had a one-nighter in my life before that. I slept with two guys in total. This can't be the end of my sex life. Gosh, I should have been on the pill."

Tears filled my eyes, prickling at the rawness that had developed there in the last hour.

With my hands still over my face, I hid myself from the world—and hoped the world couldn't see me either. All I required was a break, and someplace to lick my wounds in peace.

Ellie scooted closer and rubbed my back. "I'm sure it's nothing. Don't worry, okay? Whatever it says, it's gonna be all right. We'll figure it out."

I snorted. "All right, yeah. As if being pregnant in college with no way to ever get a hold of the guy whose DNA might be inside of me will ever be fine."

"You're Abigail Peña. You're resourceful. Strong and badass. You'll manage. I have faith in you."

I sagged my shoulders. "Well, right now I have none."

"Let's find out first before making plans and assuming the worst."

"Ellie, I'm not sure I wanna know. If it's positive, nothing will ever be the same… Life as it is now will be over."

My heart sank in my chest, ripped open.

No matter what my friend said, I would be on my own. And Andy would never know how the best night of my life had turned into a sour memory. He would never be part of our baby's life.

I dried my teary face with my sleeve and grabbed the collection of unwrapped tests Ellie handed me.

In two minutes, my life could change forever.

I swallowed the bile rising in my throat, pushed my shoulders back, and left our dorm room for the bathroom, the weight of the world pressing on my delicate shoulders.

Chapter 13
Anderson

"Okay, enough. You gotta get out of here. And I'm not taking no for an answer. The semester is over, and you're going back to Tennessee soon for two weeks. No way am I letting you miss out on college opportunities anymore. I've been patient since we got back from Winter Break, but that patience ends now."

My attention drifted away from my laptop and rested on my best friend.

Joe pointed at his chest with his thumb, his annoyed frown fully in place.

"I don't feel like partying," I said, hoping I was convincing enough. "I prefer staying in and writing music."

"No. Lie. You prefer moping on your own. I checked your browser history. It's pathetic, Andy. For the last ninety days, all you've searched for are Abbis, Abis, Abbys,

Abbies, Abigails, Abbeys, and any other names beginning with an *A* and a *B*. I'm pretty sure that's what you're doing right now."

If looks could kill, Joe would have been dead. Turned into a pile of ashes. Instead of giving myself away, I rolled my eyes and pretended to be unaffected by his—rightful—accusations. "Not your problem," I said when his gaze fixed on me without another word.

"That's where you're wrong. I miss my best friend. My wingman. Even when I bring girls over, I'm scared it will affect your romantic predispositions and you'll go back to isolating yourself from the rest of the world. The only times you get out are when you have a show or to go to class." He tipped a brow as if to dare me to disagree. I couldn't. Joe spoke the truth. I barely went out anymore, still hung up on a girl I couldn't get over after months apart. I had become…lame. My friend was right, but I'd never tell him that.

"So?" I tapped the floor with my right foot. I was so ready for him to run off and attend whatever end-of-semester party he had planned, leaving me to my own devices.

"So? This is over. No more being on your own and reminiscing about a night that will never happen again. And a girl you should have forgotten by now. Sure, she made an impact on you. Good. I understand. But it's over, Andy. She's gone. Rearview mirror. You gotta put yourself back on the market. Start living again."

Anger rose inside me. "What if I don't want to? She was the best thing that has ever happened to me. I-I let her go… I didn't fucking fight for her. The memories of that night are still fresh in my mind. Even my brain refuses to forget all about it."

He stood up, turned on his heel, and disappeared into the kitchen only to return a second later with a bottle of whiskey.

"What for?" I asked when he handed it to me after uncapping it and taking a long gulp.

"Musician's bitter poison. Drink it."

I shook my head and made no motion to grab the bottle. "Thanks, but I'm fine."

"Take the liquor, Andy. Or I'll make you."

I sighed. "What is it? Threat two-o-one?"

"Nah. More like *Let's get you drunk tonight and fix the loose screw in your head* kinda intervention."

"Not interested."

Joe pushed the bottle into my chest, so I had no other choice but to take it. "No isn't an option. Drink. Believe me, it'll heal your sensitive heart. And bring my best friend back at the same time."

"Geez, I'm not dead, man."

"Maybe not, but the result is the same. You've abandoned me, Andy. You prefer your solitude to my company. You are lucky I'm not easily offended."

What if he was right and I was just wasting all this time chasing a shadow? It had been months, and I had looked everywhere I could. So far, no trace of Abby anywhere. I was tired. Last month, in a moment of desperation, I even considered camping on Silverville School of Business's front lawn in case she happened to walk by. The risk of getting arrested for being a creep kept me from doing anything stupid.

One afternoon, I even called their administration office and pretended to be a long-lost relative who had some bad news to announce, but they didn't fall for the lie. I tried again, weeks later, going for the truth this time, but they refused to disclose their students' names. A classmate of mine suggested I hire a hacker to go through SSB's database, but I wasn't willing to risk getting caught if it backfired. It could damage my career if it ever came out sometime in the future. I wasn't seasoned enough in the clandestine side of the internet to trust that nobody would ever find out.

Joe's eyes pleaded with me to trust him.

Would a night out without obsessing about things I had no control over do me good?

I brought the bottle to my lips and took a hefty swallow. "Happy now?"

My best friend's wide grin reached both ears. He inched closer and clapped my shoulder. "Yep. Finally. Now change and let's get the hell out of here. We'll grab a bite with the guys and go to a party on campus afterward. A sorority house. Bethany will be there. Who knows? The timing could be right for you two this time."

"Not interested."

Joe drew me into a hug. "Keep telling yourself that, man. Trust your best friend. I have your back. Always will."

I leaned away and dragged a hand over my face. This was such a bad idea. Whenever Joe got involved in my love life, it always backfired.

"Hurry up. The clock is ticking." He smirked, and I knew he wouldn't let go until I agreed.

"Fine. Gimme fifteen minutes, I need to shower."

He pumped his fist and let out a loud cheer. "My man is back."

I shook my head and exhaled loudly. "Whatever." I locked myself in the bathroom and shut down all the voices in my head, the ones nagging me to scour the internet and social media feeds in case I caught a glimpse of Abby.

Joe's words rang true, though. I had become a pathetic version of myself this semester. It was about time I shook myself out of this state and got on with my life—or I'd be miserable forever.

———

Joe, a bunch of guys from our vocal training class, and I walked into the party at Delta Phi Epsilon. A small, two-story white cottage with royal-blue shutters near campus.

Loud music blasted through the speakers and deafened me as soon as we entered the place. At full capacity, there were half-dressed bodies showing curves and cleavages everywhere. Some girls were busy mixing drinks in the kitchen while two guys fixed a keg by the side door. The overpowering scent of sweat and a mix of aftershaves and perfumes made me dizzy.

A girl I recognized as Camille, Bethany's roommate, walked over with a handful of beer cans, handing me one and the rest to the guys. She folded her now empty arms under her chest, pushing her tits up on purpose. "Oh wow, Anderson Ford has decided to join us. I thought you were dead. No one has seen you in months." She batted her eyelashes at me. When I didn't give her pushed-up chest any attention, she anchored herself to my arm, pressing her soft breasts into my side. "We missed you. *I* missed you."

From beside me, Joe cleared his throat, and I threw daggers at him when our eyes connected. He elbowed me in the ribs as he walked past and muttered under his breath, "You deserve this, man. Some harmless fun. And a blowjob. Live a little for once." He turned and followed a girl with a pink pixie cut, who beckoned him with a finger.

"Really, man?"

He watched me over his shoulder and shrugged. *Best therapy to get you back in the game*, he mouthed, unable to tame his shit-eating grin.

I returned my attention to the girl, still attached to my arm. "Is Beth here tonight?" Camille was too clingy, and I had no intention of ever pursuing anything with her.

Her lips transformed into a pout. "Why? You don't wanna spend time with me?"

"Maybe later." Later meant never. I wasn't the kind of guy who pushed people away without a second thought. And the last thing I wished for was hurting her feelings. While Camille was clingy, whiny, and always on the lookout for a good time, Bethany was more level-headed, introvert, and focused. She was studying ballet and just like me, wasn't sleeping around for the sake of it. Last fall, at the beginning of the semester, we went on a few dates that never led anywhere, since she was still hurting from the damage her cheating ex had caused. One night in December, she knocked on my apartment door and told me she was ready to commit to a relationship if that was what I wanted too. We had talked a few times and made plans to go out in January, once we both returned to class. After my airport fling, I wasn't in the mood to spend time with another girl, so I never returned her multiple calls when classes resumed in mid-January. After a while, she stopped trying to reach me, and I stopped feeling guilty about ignoring her.

Bethany had always been honest with me, and she deserved some explanation as to why I had ghosted her all semester.

Camille's face fell. "She's on the back deck. Not sure she wants to see you, though. You flushed her from your life without an explanation. She's mad at you, Andy. You've been warned."

I yanked away from her grip and shoved my hands into my pockets. "Well, I'll deal with it. Thanks, Cam." I finished my beer and dropped the empty can in the recycle bin, looking for the girl I had to apologize to. Even though I'd told Joe earlier I wasn't interested in rekindling anything with Bethany, now that I was here, the idea didn't repulse me as much. I was tired of chasing a ghost. And maybe I really had to dust myself off and move on.

With her long chestnut hair braided into a sophisticated updo and deep brown eyes, Bethany was sitting in an Adirondack chair when I reached the back deck, chatting with a group of people and holding a red cup in one hand.

With determined steps, I neared her. A girl standing next to her nudged her side when she saw me closing in on them.

"Hey, Beth," I said when her eyes met mine. "Can we talk?" I rocked on my heels, my hands buried deep in my pockets, feeling all eyes on me.

She looked away, ignoring me. Seconds later, her stance relaxed, and she angled herself to face me. "What do you want, Anderson? Until now, I thought you were dead."

I offered her a half-shrug. "To talk to you."

"Not interested."

"Please. There are things I need to tell you."

She huffed and nodded. "Fine. You have five minutes." She turned to her friend. "Save my seat. I'll be right back."

We wove through a group of our drunk classmates, looking for an empty corner where we could talk privately, and ended up in the laundry room. This would have to do.

Bethany crossed her arms over her chest, her posture strained. "Talk. You have four minutes left."

"Huh…listen. Long story short. I met someone on the day I flew home for the holidays. There was a storm, and we got snowbound at the airport for a night. We didn't exchange contact info. I've been trying to find her for weeks now… Without success. I didn't wanna ghost you. You…you did nothing wrong. It's all on me. I'm done chasing someone I can't find. Here, this is the whole truth. It wasn't a *you* but a *me* thing."

Her brown eyes widened. "Not you but me. Wow. Classic excuse." She snorted and glanced at me with an unimpressed glare. "Couldn't you come up with something more original?"

I lifted both arms in surrender. "I swear. It messed with my mind. It's the truth."

"Is it?"

"Yep. All true. We clicked. But it was a one-night kind of thing. It's over. It's about time I get my life back on track and forget about it." *Not forget,* my mind nagged me, *but move on.* "I'm sorry about everything. Ghosting you wasn't my intention."

"Are you?"

I cocked one brow in question.

"Ready to move on?"

"Yeah. It makes no sense to hang on to something so fleeting that I sometimes wonder whether I imagined the whole thing." Until I closed my eyes at night and the images of our silly challenges filled my dreams. Or in the morning when I caught sight of the snow globe sitting on my bookshelf. But Bethany didn't need to hear that.

Her dark eyes pierced mine, searching for answers. "What does it mean for us?"

I closed some of the distance between us with a step and molded my hands to her hips.

She relaxed under my touch.

"I don't know. Are you over what your ex did to you?"

"Yeah… I went to therapy for a while. He moved back to Seattle. We talked, and we got the closure we both deserved. He won't be a problem anymore." A small smile grazed her lips. "I'd like to see where this thing between us goes. But I'm not playing second fiddle to your mystery hookup."

I nodded. "It's fair. Are you going home for the summer?"

"I'll be in Maine for two weeks visiting my father, then Washington for a month to spend time with my mom. I'm leaving in five days. If we're still willing to give this a chance, let's talk when we're both back on campus. No promises until we return to New York and have had time to think it through. Any plan to go to Memphis?"

"Short-term. Then I'm back in town because I have gigs scheduled all summer, and I'm working for Joe's uncle during the day."

Bethany pressed her palms to my chest. "I'm glad we chatted."

I mirrored her soft smile. "Me too." A small voice in my head asked whether I could really do this—put Abby in the rearview mirror, as Joe had said, and be in a relationship with Bethany.

Before my mind could take over, Bethany's lips teased mine. I stilled, not sure I was ready for all that the kiss implied tonight.

She must have sensed my hesitation because she leaned back and put some distance between us. "Sorry," she said, a red hue creeping up her cheeks.

I swallowed. "Don't be. It took me by surprise." With a step back, I added more space between us and scratched the back of my neck.

Bethany blinked, hurt flashing across her features.

Before she could make a big deal about it and leave, I reached forward and circled her wrists with my fingers.

"Once we're back on campus, we'll get together and see where we're at, okay?"

She averted her eyes for a longssecond before bringing them back to mine. "Are you sure you're over her?"

I offered her a one-shoulder shrug and steeled my back. "Yeah. It's over. It never even started."

She inched closer and rose onto her tiptoes to press a kiss to my cheek. "Good. I'll text you when I'm back in town."

Side by side, we sat on the washer and dryer for the next hour, catching up. The music and chatter from the party were muffled by the closed door, and I savored the calm it offered.

"I heard the song you played at the end-of-year show-case, Andy. It was beautiful."

A smile broke free on my lips, and it felt good to just be for a night and not worry about things I had no control over. "Thanks. It's one of my new compositions. I was testing how it sounded."

"Amazing. That's the only word that came to mind when I heard it. You're talented. No surprise you won."

Each year, at the end of the winter semester, New York Arts and Music Academy hosted a showcase featuring their students and awarded three of them ten-thousand-dollar prizes. One for each department: dance, music, and perfor-mance. This year, I'd won the music one. I had deposited the check in a savings account I was keeping for later, to help me launch my music career once I graduated.

"Thanks. It was very personal to me."

"You deserved it. I swear."

When we left the room and rejoined the party soon after, Bethany squeezed my forearm and spun to face me. "Don't leave without saying goodbye."

"Not my intention," I said, tracing my knuckles along her cheekbone. "See you later."

Joe draped his arm over my shoulders and smirked at me seconds after Bethany returned to her group of friends. "Andy, my man. You did it. You broke the curse. Any action in there?" He pointed to the room Bethany and I had just vacated with his thumb while stabbing his tongue into his cheek over and over.

"What are you? Six?"

He tapped my upper arm. "Twelve. Because that's the age when I turned into a horny little shit."

"Man…"

"So, did Bethany reward you for going out tonight?"

I pressed a finger over my mouth. "My lips are sealed. Sorry."

"Come on, man. I'm your best friend. And the one you should thank for getting you back in the game."

He turned, grabbed two beers, and pushed one into my hand.

I scoffed. "Want me to send you flowers?" He bobbed his head, and I punched his shoulder. "In your dreams. We talked. Made peace. And we'll see how things go. No pressure."

We both opened the cans, and my friend clinked his with mine. "Glad to have you back. Now let's get wasted because we won't be seeing each other for five weeks, and I wanna make sure you have the best time before I go to Nebraska for that internship."

The rest of the night passed in a blur, and it felt good to enjoy myself for a change. To let my brain rest and not overthink everything. Yeah, I could go back to being responsible in the morning.

Joe came to me around two in the morning, a girl wrapped under his arm, her hands all over him as she busied herself licking his neck, giggling. "Going home. Wanna share a ride?" he asked, stealing a kiss as the girl moaned somethings against his lips.

"Nah. I promised Beth I'd find her *beforrre* leaving." I squinted, my vision blurry, trying to get some focus back. Fuck, I couldn't remember the last time I'd been this drunk. "Don't wait for *meee*. I might stay here a little bit longer or grab a bite before coming home so I don't have to hear *youuu* guys screaming for hours. I can do without the trauma."

My friend shook his head, a full smirk on display. "Suit yourself. Or we can share. Your call." He winked.

I wasn't drunk enough to forget he said that. "Not my style. Thanks for the offer, but I'll pass."

"Your loss. Hey, before I forget. Brunch at Jamieson's place tomorrow at ten. Don't be late." He spun to leave but hesitated and turned to face me. "Have fun. You deserve it."

The sorority house was half-empty. I had to thread through slumped bodies far too drunk to be coherent to reach Bethany on the back deck, chatting with the same group of people as earlier.

"You leaving?" she asked, moving to her feet to meet me.

"Soon. Do you have a ride? I can walk you to your place."

"Oh, that'd be fantastic. Camille was supposed to go back with me, but she left with a water polo player an hour ago."

"Well, I know how you hate to walk by yourself at night after what happened last year to those girls."

A chill traversed her as she scooted closer and snaked her arm through mine. "No need to remind me of that rapist. I hope he rots in jail."

"Me too. Let's get out of here."

I exchanged handshakes and half-hugs with three guys I knew before we finally stepped onto the sidewalk, welcomed by the thick, humid spring air. I tilted my head back, enjoying the breeze brushing against my skin.

Looking upward, I narrowed my eyes. The glow of the city made it impossible to see the stars shining above.

"You good?" Bethany asked.

I sighed. "Yes." I grabbed her hand and led her forward.

We remained silent for most of the mile-long stroll, her head pressed against my shoulder and her hand nestled in mine.

"That girl," she said, once we reached her dorm building, "she really made an impression on you, didn't she?"

"I don't wanna talk about it. It's in the past anyway. Nothing worth discussing right now." How I wished my words rang true to my own ears.

She snuggled against my chest, and I looped my arms around her. Angling her head back, she studied me. "Wanna spend the night?" She kissed the corner of my mouth and the contours of my jaw, trailing down my neck.

Warmth washed through me as she cupped my junk and stirred sensations in me I had forgotten all about over the last few months.

"Huh…not sure it's a good idea. We said we'd wait." We broke apart when I took a step back.

Why was I pushing her away? What was wrong with me? The booze had fried my brain cells. Bethany was nice, smart, and funny. She was pretty, and she cared about me. I should've been a willing participant in whatever we were doing.

"Listen, you can sleep on the couch. Or you can go back to your place and have Joe entertain you all night with the girl he brought home… What do you say?" Her eyes were pleading with me to say yes. From the pink hue on her cheeks and glossy eyes, I could tell Bethany was tipsy but not drunk. She rarely drank alcohol, so a glass or two had this effect on her. It loosened her up.

I shut my eyes for an instant, trying to make up my mind. The beer and shots I'd been drinking all night were slowing my thought process. Why was it so hard right now to decide what to do? If I agreed to this and ended up in her bed—which would erase Abby from my thoughts—I had to be willing to accept the risk that it could affect my creativity. And my body. Like withdrawal from the only thing that had ever made me feel alive. For months, I had wanted no one but her. But if I never found her, would I be willing to live a celibate life in case moving forward affected my music? Would I be okay being alone forever? Nah.

On the other end, the last thing I wanted was to be privy to Joe's sexfest.

"Andy," Bethany whispered. "Stop overprocessing everything in that head of yours. I'm here. I'm not a ghost from your past. And it's just a couch, not a marriage proposal."

I blinked at her, still unsure what to do, because a stupid part of me felt like a cheater if I agreed to go upstairs. How screwed-up was that?

I was being ridiculous. How could it be cheating if I had only known someone for a night? Joe was right. I needed to break the cycle. Get my life back on track. Chase my dreams. Work toward my future. And it started tonight. I was done being a sad puppy.

"Yeah, I'm staying." My voice sounded rougher than usual. Anderson Ford had gotten lost during the last semester. And I had to bring him back.

I had one life to live and was free to make the most of it the way I intended to. Once I was out of college, I'd have responsibilities and be forced to be an adult. For now, I could be a little selfish and think about myself for the time it lasted.

I didn't wanna forget Abby…but what other choice did I have?

Chapter 14
Abigail

"Nothing fits me anymore." I fell on my back on the bed, bringing both palms over my eyes, on the verge of tears. "I can't change my wardrobe every month. I'll go broke in no time."

"Let me help you out," Ellie said, rummaging through the clothes I'd spread all over our room. "I have leggings you can borrow. And Tom gave me a few sweatshirts that are too big for me. You can have them."

"The ones with the university and football team logos on them?"

"Yes. Those. You'll look like you're invested in the school spirit." She pumped her fist. "Go, Pirates."

"Is this what I have come down to? Seriously?" I had no idea if I should laugh or curl up into a ball and bawl my eyes out.

"*Gurrrl*, you look fantastic. Don't do this to yourself, okay? Be happy and proud."

"It's…I-I can…" I blew out a long breath, reeling in the cocktail of emotions swirling inside me that I had no idea how to tackle. "Everyone will be able to tell I'm getting fatter by the day." A fresh batch of tears burned the back of my eyes. Every little detail turned me into a crying mess these days.

Ellie wrapped her arms around me and caressed my hair with her fingers. "But a very beautiful and pregnant fat lady," she teased.

"How did this happen? How did I turn into this?" I asked, pointing to my stomach.

"Well, if you want the specifics, it started with a penis and a vagina, two people attracted to each other, and a lot of kisses…"

I pulled free from her embrace, sat on my bed, and threw a pillow at her face. I couldn't help but laugh at her antics. "Elles. Stop."

"Want me to mimic how it really happens? I can draw it too if you prefer." She paused. "I think we may need to circle back to the birds-and-the-bees talk. Maybe you missed a lesson."

A loud chuckle burst free. "Geez. You are incorrigible."

She sat next to me. "But I make you laugh. And this is worth a lot. I miss Happy Abby. You've been hiding here since the day we found out you were indeed pregnant. You don't go out anymore. You either work or go to classes or sleep. And that smile of yours is never reaching both ears anymore. We need to get her back before she's lost under a pile of dirty diapers and feeding bottles and gone forever."

Tears flooded my vision at her words. I loved my friend. She was my anchor. And the one person I could always count on. Pulling her into a tight hug, I hoped she could feel how much she meant to me too.

"I love you," I said before releasing her. "I'm sorry for

not being a good friend lately… It's just…it's just a lot to process."

She squeezed my hand between hers. "I know. It's okay. I just don't want you to turn into a ghost. You have nothing to be ashamed of. This baby was created from love particles. Everything happens for a reason, and this little one will teach you something. Resilience maybe. Or how to slip on a onesie… No matter what it is, it will be all right."

I nodded, the words stuck in my throat. I wasn't ready to be a mother at nineteen. And I had no idea how to do this. Even if I wanted to, adoption wasn't an option. This baby was Andy's and mine. I already loved him or her so much that never could I consider giving our child away. Still, my fears were hard to kick to the curb.

"Elles, what am I going to do? For real? I didn't think this through. How is it supposed to work? I'm four months in, and I'm exhausted all the time and crying at the drop of a hat. At least I'm done with the morning sickness, or else I would go crazy."

"You should rest. And have fun. Enjoy the time you have left before you gotta care for that tiny human growing inside of you. Instead, you're overworking yourself. A forty-hour work week, in addition to the extra classes you took on last semester, is just too much for your pregnant self."

"This baby won't pay for itself. I must take the next semester off. Or else, once I give birth, I'll miss too many classes to be able to catch up and get good enough grades to keep my scholarship."

"I know. I have no idea what I'd do if I were in your shoes, but I'm confident you'll make it work. Still, you need the rest… And to enjoy time with your friends, where you don't have to obsess over your to-do list for a few hours and can just be."

"Yeah, well, if I don't want my life to go to hell, I've gotta put as much money as possible into my savings account for the days when I won't be able to work. Babies are expensive."

"If you spread yourself thin, you'll crack. A lot is going on in your life. Go easy on yourself."

"I'll try. In the meantime, I have to meet with the advisor to discuss my scholarship for next year. See how it'd work out since I gotta skip a semester due to reasons I have no control over anymore."

"You haven't already?" my friend asked with a tipped brow.

"Nah. I wasn't ready for the world to know I got knocked up. And… Imagine if they revoke it? What will I do if that's the case? I can't pay the tuition fees on my own. And you know my parents won't help me out. My appointment is tomorrow afternoon, so we'll see."

"No matter what, I'm here. I'll help you out. We can place a crib between our beds…and switch night shifts. You won't be alone."

I snickered. "Thanks. But not sure I'll be allowed to have a baby sleeping in the dorm." I paused, my heart heavy in my chest. "I'll have to find an apartment. It's another expense I can't afford right now. What am I going to do?"

For the first time, my friend remained silent.

I got myself into this mess, I would have to get myself out of it. On my own.

"Let's go somewhere to eat, away from this campus. I'm buying," Ellie said after a beat. "You need a balanced diet and can't survive and grow a healthy baby on instant noodles and grilled cheese."

"But I like grilled cheese. My baby requests them."

Ellie roared with laughter. "Keep telling yourself that.

In the meantime, we're having tacos and guacamole. Who knows, maybe your baby will crave that too from now on and start dancing the salsa in your belly."

"Tacos…right." Any mention of Mexican food now reminded me of Andy. The memory pricked my heart like tiny needles every single time.

Ellie moved to her side of the room and tossed me a pair of black leggings and a Silverville School of Business sweatshirt that fell to my mid-thighs, oblivious to my mental struggles. "See? Nobody will be able to tell you're pregnant."

I got up and pulled my friend into a hug. "Thanks for having my back, Elles."

"Always."

In front of the full-length mirror attached to the closet door, I dressed and studied my reflection from every angle, making sure my stomach was concealed. Once I was confident no one could notice my new figure, I breathed out a sigh of relief. "Ready," I said.

"Yay, let's go stuff our faces."

I shrugged. "I might get Mixchos instead."

"What?"

"Never mind. Let's go."

With our arms linked together, we exited our room.

"Have you decided when you'll tell your parents?"

I shook my head. "No. They can't know. Not until I have no other choice. Trust me, the longer I hide the truth from them, the better it is for everyone."

"Are you still trying to find your baby's daddy?"

I nodded. "Andrew is a common name. Since I don't know his last name, it's pretty impossible to locate him. When I go home next week, I'll drive to Memphis. If I'm lucky and the stars align themselves, perhaps I'll enter a coffee shop and walk in on him. Who knows? Destiny should be on my side on this one, no?"

Ellie tightened her grip on my arm. "You deserve the best, Abby. Never doubt it. No matter the shitty situations life throws your way." She paused. "For now, let's celebrate the end of this semester. Oh, and I just got an idea. I'll try to get my parents to pay for a small apartment for next fall. I'll tell them I need to get out of the dorm. They won't question it. You could come to live with me. Rent-free. Nobody would know. Until we figure out a better option."

I halted and enveloped my best friend in a bone-crushing hug. "Thank you. For everything." My chest swelled with a new surge of overwhelming emotions I couldn't contain. Ellie was truly the best friend a girl could ever ask for.

"Hey, don't cry."

Leaning back, I wiped my face with my sleeve. "Better get used to it. I'll be pregnant for another five months."

———

"We're sorry, Ms. Peña. There's nothing we can do. Our hands are tied here. The conditions of your scholarship stipulate that you must maintain a 3.7 GPA and graduate within four years. If you finish your classes four months later than planned by taking summer courses after your peers graduate, then you're failing that condition."

Tears pooled in my eyes, and my heart hammered in my chest. This was a nightmare. "There must be something you can do?" My voice quivered with each word exiting my mouth. "I have a three-point-nine GPA. It must count for something, no? I'll work my butt off. I would take summer classes this year, but I need to work and make some money, and most of my classes are not available during the summer semester."

"I'm sorry," the advisor said.

I slouched in my chair, sobs shaking my body. "Wh-what am I gonna do?" I sniffled. "I...I...I need that scholarship. I worked extra hard to get it."

"You can reapply next year, but I can't assure you it'll still be available. There are other students on the waitlist who fill the conditions." The advisor pushed a box of tissues across her mahogany desk. "I know it's not what you wanted to hear. Call my office when you're ready to come back, and we'll see if there are options available then. Scholarships are rarely given to third-year students. We could set up a payment plan for you." She moved to stand, letting me know the meeting was over. "Good luck with everything," she said as she opened the door and showed me out.

Ellie, who was waiting for me in the small, adjacent room, sprung to her feet when I neared her, pulling me into her arms. "Ohmygod. What did she say? Why are you crying?"

I hiccupped. "I-I... There's nothing they... There's nothing they can do. It's over, Ellie. My dream is—" I breathed in a shaky gulp of air. "My dream is over. I'll never be a...a...music executive." With a protective hand, I cradled my belly. It wasn't my baby's fault. I wasn't even mad at Andy either. Just at the circumstances. And the rigid, archaic system that had never been designed for women in the first place. Guys too had babies in college, but they were never forced to take time off or abandon their education to give birth to them or care for them. It wasn't fair. I was a dedicated student. A good student. At the top of my classes. If I had been sick instead of pregnant, they would have made an exception. The supervisor had told me. Having cancer treatment would have been okay but not having a baby. In what twisted world were we living in?

As we walked back to the dorm, I held on to my best friend, while emptying—once again—my tear well. Being sad was exhausting.

Around eight that night, I zipped up my suitcase and announced, "I'm done. I finished packing."

"You sure you won't appeal the decision?" Ellie asked, watching me from her bed.

"Nah. It's too many emotions. I can't deal with that right now. Stress isn't good for either of us. The nurse told me at my last appointment. I need some time off to assess my options."

"The apartment offer is still standing."

"Thanks. I think I wanna go home for a while. Find my bearings."

"What about your parents? They're not the most welcoming people on Earth. Their views are pretty narrow-minded."

"They are my parents. I'm sure once the shock passes and they see I'm fully invested in making this work, they'll be more than happy to give me a hand. What else can they do? Not talk to me until the baby is eighteen? It makes no sense. I believe they still have a heart in there somewhere. Anyway, that room over the garage, it's small, but it could make a great apartment. For now. I just need to find some courage inside me to face them."

A voice in my head told me convincing my parents wouldn't be as easy as I let my friend believe, but I didn't want her to worry about me. She had done more than her share ever since all seven pregnancy tests came back positive.

"Whatever you do, Abby, you'll do amazing. Just don't

give up on all your ambitions because, down the road, you'll be bitter if you do."

"Elles, I don't wanna abandon all my dreams, but I have this little one to think of first." I inhaled, trying to keep a new flood of tears at bay. "One day, I'll make it. No matter how long it takes, I will not stop until I get there. I promise."

"I'm proud of you." She paused. "What about Andy? Are you still gonna try to find him?"

I nodded. "He has a right to know. I have faith that one day we'll meet again. Until then, I'll do my best to make up for his absence."

"What time is your flight?"

"Eight-fifteen tomorrow morning."

"I'll drive you to the airport."

"No need. I can grab a cab. You don't have to wake up early for me."

Ellie sat beside me and rested her hand on my thigh. "I insist. Told you already. I'll do everything I can to help you out. I'll miss you like crazy next year. I can't believe how close-minded and outdated this college is."

"You know the worst part? She had a framed picture of her three daughters on her desk. I don't get it. She's a mother. She should know better and fight for our rights."

"This is unfair. And misogynistic. They're making a big mistake."

My friend wasn't an overly emotional person, so I hugged her when I saw moisture shining in her eyes. "Thank you for being you." I kissed her cheek, and after we both got ready for bed, we slid under her comforter and watched a movie on her laptop for the very last time in my too-short college life.

Chapter 15
Abigail

In the driveway of my parents' home, with two pieces of luggage at my feet, I took the biggest breath my lungs could hold. This was it. The day I would tell my parents all about the new developments in my life. Deep down, I prayed they would hug me and promise me everything would be all right. That they would help me find a solution so I could finish my degree while being a single mother. I only had two years left before graduating. I didn't want to have to choose between my baby and my education. Women were entitled to have both. I did too.

My gaze moved along the freshly painted white siding to the red front door. The immaculate flowerbeds and hedges that looked like they were featured in a photo spread of a home decor magazine. And the shiny new SUV with chrome wheels sitting before the three-door garage.

My mother spent all her time at home, cooking and

cleaning, even though they had a maid who came twice a week to help her out. When I was little, she had a career of her own. My father came from money and ran for Congress when I turned fourteen. The jovial, happy man I had known from my childhood was gone from that day, as he tried to impress the political scene with outdated ideas that made no sense in the real world. Ideas that sent us, as a society, sixty years into the past and mostly targeted women's rights. Ideas that made me wonder if he had joined a cult, so far had they drifted from his former way of thinking. For reasons I never understood, my mother stopped fighting for her own rights—and mine—and stood by his side, embracing his political ambitions no matter the cost. She had traded her flight attendant career for a stay-at-home slash trophy-wife role. And the genuine, warm curl of her lips for a plastic smile devoid of any human emotion, becoming a shell of the woman she used to be.

I often wondered, over the years, how they could abandon everything they had once been for these new conservative ideologies. What had happened to them that made them become ghosts of themselves?

In the last five years, my parents had started hanging out with similar refractory people who didn't believe in higher education for women and felt religion should rule the world with doctrines of the past.

My friends from high school all came from families who adhered to my parents' beliefs. Over the years, I'd become a loner. In between the required appearance at church and other obligations my parents thrust on me, I spent most of my time on my own, reading and dreaming about my life outside of here. My parents would always complain about my taste in music, art, and fiction reading.

With my big dreams and ambitions, I was the loose cannon in their perfectly planned existence.

No matter what, I would never settle for less than what I deserved and earned.

They knew it.

If their cult-like lives pleased them, fine by me, but I wanted more for myself.

Even though we didn't agree on it, I was nineteen years old and allowed to make my own choices. As long as they didn't interfere with my father's political vision or my parents' picture-perfect, made-up existence that they showcased to their peers.

Here I was, standing in their driveway, four months pregnant, a single mother-to-be, and a college dropout. For now.

Everything that would kill them to acknowledge.

Before the school advisor crushed all my hopes, I had made plans to spend my summer in Silverville, working full-time. Not coming to Nashville to face what would be my parents' wrath. And utter disappointment in me.

At this instant, I yearned for some love and compassion. For strong arms to wrap around me and a deep voice to promise me that things would right themselves. That it would be all okay in the end.

And my parents' acceptance.

With a straight back and chin held high, I knocked on the front door, fidgeting with the hem of my sweater as I waited for my mother to open the door. If I entered the house on my own, I'd get scolded. The day I'd moved to college was the day I became a guest in their house, according to them. I had called yesterday to tell them I would visit for some time, and it had taken them two full minutes to agree. You would think that, being their only child, they would be excited to have me back after four months away, but no. That wasn't how the Peña household rolled.

No surprise arrival. And mostly, not coming home without prior announcement.

The door unlocked after my mother peeked through the lace curtain covering the window panel.

"Oh, it's you," she greeted me when she opened the door. As if she'd expected someone else.

A lot of my happy childhood memories involved my grandparents, who were all deceased now. My granddad had taught me how to ride a bike. My grandma had cooked with me on the weekends or driven me to school. When I was little, my father had been busy, but he still made time for me in his tight schedule. Now, not so much. Unless I made an appointment with his secretary weeks in advance.

I fixed a curl to my lips. "Hey, Mother," I replied as I carried my suitcases inside. I leaned in and kissed her cheek. This was the most affection my parents were comfortable with these days. Even though it killed me inside not to be able to hug them like I used to. In that instant, I missed my grandparents. Because even though I had no idea how my parents would react to my pregnancy news, my grandparents, on the other hand, would have welcomed me and my baby with open arms and even wider smiles. Their hearts had been so big.

Thanks to Tom's sweatshirts, that Ellie had gifted me, I was able to conceal the tiny bump my stomach had grown into.

"You should go and change. Into a dress," my mother said, giving me a slow, disapproving once-over, her short dark hair coiffed in perfect curls and held in place with a silver vintage hair brooch. The same way she'd been wearing it for years now. "Something more appropriate for a young lady like you." In her mind, she only imagined me wearing floral-patterned demure dresses under hand-knit

cardigans, covering my shoulders, chest, and ankles. All at
once. "Don't become a temptation," she had once said
when I'd turned sixteen. Since I was a bit of a tomboy
back in the day, I mostly wore shorts and T-shirts, to her
great despair.

The carefree mother wearing denim cut-offs and a tank
top over a bikini with her hair pulled into a long ponytail
hadn't been around for a long time.

Without another word, she dismissed me with a flick
of her hand and returned to her place behind the gas
stove, as she did every afternoon, as if I weren't even there.
Right now, I wished I could have a drink. Or that there
was booze in this house. Or that I had a sibling. To fight
alongside me when I needed to be heard. Because I had
no idea how I'd even survive dinner time once my father
got here.

Wasting time in my bedroom to avoid the inevitable for
as long as I could, I sent Ellie a text message. Even though
I wanted to help prep dinner or set the table, my mother
wouldn't want me near her. She would tell me to go and
freshen up.

ME

Home. Safe for now.

ELLIE

Have you told them yet?

ME

Negative. My mother is not the show-your-
emotions type. She barely said two words
to me since I got here. The last time I
visited, I got lectured for days about God's
vow to punish me for cutting my hair
shorter than my shoulders, so imagine the
shock later.

ELLIE

Maybe they'll surprise you this time. And be happy for you. After all, they'll be grandparents. That must count for something, right?

ME

We'll see.

I heard the front door open and the distinctive sounds of my father's footsteps. Which meant dinner was served, not a care in the world that it was only five-thirty.

ME

Wish me luck. My father just arrived.

ELLIE

Call me later, okay? I wanna know how it went down.

ME

Yeah. If I'm still alive. Later xx

"Abigail," my father greeted me when I entered the dining room, already seated at the end of the table, looking like a king about to rule his kingdom. His jacket had been discarded on the backrest of an empty chair, and his sleeves rolled up to his elbows, displaying the expensive golden watch around his wrist. His burgundy tie was swept to the side, a cloth napkin covering the front of his button-down shirt.

My mother looked just as perfectly put together in her white blouse, pearl necklace, and mid-shin black pencil skirt.

Standing at the other end of the room in a pair of leggings, which used to belong to Ellie, and her boyfriend's sweatshirt, I didn't look the part.

Again, I was a big contradiction in their existence.

The smell of beef and potatoes made my stomach roll, and I placed a protective palm over my belly as I breathed in to calm the swell of nausea hitting me.

My father's eyes cut to my figure, disapproval clear in his expression. Under his scrutiny, I felt like a little girl about to be chastised for being late for dinner after spending a day playing outside or for having rested my elbows on the table.

"Why haven't you changed into a lady's proper attire?" my mother asked, scowling at me. "I told you so earlier."

I took a seat opposite her and tugged at the sleeves of my sweatshirt, trying to be invisible as judgment poured out from both of them when they exchanged a quick disapproving glance and a sigh.

My father cleared his throat. "It's not lady-like to wear such awful clothes at the dinner table. What would people think if they saw you dressed like this? Abigail, where are your manners? What has this college of yours been teaching you all year?"

I swallowed the uneasiness clogging my airways. "I'm sorry." I bit my inner cheek, trying to summon the courage I lacked to confide in them. "There's something I gotta tell you both," I began, laying the cloth napkin over my lap, twisting a corner as if it were a lifeline.

"Whatever it is," my mother said, "it can wait after dinner."

I nodded and fidgeted with the napkin under the table the entire time. Dinner time in the Peña household was spent in silence. No one shared stories about their day or made small talk anymore. Only the clinking of cutlery against porcelain plates could be heard.

After dinner was served and eaten and more jitters filled me, I attempted once more to open the discussion.

"Can we have that talk now?" I asked, not meeting their eyes to avoid the censure I was sure to read there.

My parents both gave a stiff nod.

"Mother. Father." Mama and Daddy or even Mom and Dad weren't terms I was allowed to use anymore. Yep, my parents had put so much distance between us that sometimes they felt like strangers. I inhaled a cleansing breath. I could do this. Unable to find the right words, I stood and pushed my chair aside and lifted the front of my sweatshirt to expose my pregnant figure.

I heard "Ahhs," and a few God-related curses. Then I met my parents' gazes. Their complexions were now a ghostly shade of white. My mother's fingers trembled around the gold cross hanging around her neck, a permanent fixture as far as I could remember. As if she were preparing herself for a catastrophe.

My father whispered, his hands clasped in prayer, acting as if I'd just announced I had married the devil himself.

In the slowest motion ever, they returned their attention to me, their stares empty and their lips twisted in disdain. Sitting back down, I wished I could melt into my chair—and be as far away from here as possible.

"You're pregnant?" My mother's eyes stayed locked on my abdomen. "With a baby?"

I was tempted to reply *What else?* then thought better of it and only said a stern "Yes."

"Did someone do that to you?"

I blinked at my father. He had to be kidding me. As if there were any other way to make babies. I shrugged instead of mouthing the sarcastic retort tingling the tip of my tongue.

He leaned forward and lifted my left hand, studying my

ring finger. "Where's the ring? And why didn't we get invited to the wedding?"

Wedding. I should have guessed that was what they would obsess with.

I swallowed the discomfort strangling me and straightened my back, ready to answer their questions and refute their accusations. I wouldn't let my own parents belittle me or my baby. Nor Andy. I agreed this whole situation was a clusterfuck of epic proportions, but once the shock had subsided, I wasn't so scared anymore. Other than the fact I had no idea how I'd finish my degree and raise a child on my own. But that was a conversation for another time.

"Let me explain. Huh… It was a one-time thing. We used protection. Still, it happened. Nobody is getting married. And also, I-I can't contact the father. I swear he's a nice guy, so it's not his fault." There. I said it all. Well, the important parts at least.

My mother's blue eyes, the same shade as mine, rounded. "You did the act before your nuptials? How come?"

I snorted under my breath. She couldn't even say the word *sex.* "Because I met an amazing guy and it felt right."

My mother delivered the first punch. "Abigail, you're a shame to this family. We thought we raised you better than this. We're so disappointed in you right now. I'll pray for your soul. It's lost. I knew college was a bad idea. And you just proved it."

My father held her hand in a comforting gesture. My parents, no matter how much they didn't understand me and lived in another era where the television, internet, and electricity were the evils of the world, loved each other. This was clear, even after all these years.

"A baby?" My father's words cut through me, and his features settled into the politician's fake mask he wore for everyone he met. "We'll send you away. Until it's born. Pretend you're doing some charitable work overseas. Shantel did that when her daughter got pregnant in high school. The pastor of our church can help set it all up. We'll give it for adoption. No one has to know."

It took me a fraction of a second to register his words. My fist hit the table, the sound reverberating through the room. I rarely confronted them and their opinions. Except this time, it concerned not only me, but also my baby. Only I decided my baby's future. No one else. "No. I'm not getting rid of the baby. Never. He or she is a part of me. Of us. Andy and me. And it's not an *it* either. This is a human being, not something you can simply discard as you please."

"You don't even know how to reach this unworthy man. There's no *us*, Abigail. How are you gonna provide for this… ? For…for him or her? You're a college student and have no job. And most importantly, you're not married or to be wed anytime soon."

"I've been working all semester. I have savings. And I'll pile on two jobs this summer if I must. I'm resourceful. No matter what, I'll find a way to make it work."

"And how do you expect to afford everything this child will need? You're delusional. Or deeply sick." She closed her eyes for a second before glaring at me. "Dream again. If you're keeping the baby, you must marry a man. And fast. No child is born outside a marital union. It's not our God's wish." My mother was ruthless. If she knew me just a bit, she'd be aware I'd never agree to this.

My heart sunk in my chest. "I am not. You can't force me to get married. This is so wrong. It's not nineteen-thirty anymore. Doesn't my happiness mean more than your morals or values?"

My father looked at me as if I were the biggest mistake

he'd ever encountered in his life. "You are a child of our God, Abigail. And we're not going to disrespect him because you were reckless for a night and let your desire rule your better judgment. You should know yielding to the temptation of flesh is a sin." They exchanged a glance. "We'll give you a choice. Here and now. Either you do it our way—like God intended you to live your life—or you're not welcome in this house anymore, and we're cutting all ties with you. Our God will deny you as one of his children, and we won't be accomplices in your depravity and lack of respect for the core values we've taught you all your life. I can't preach his values if my own daughter can't keep her legs crossed. What would your mother and I look like? It will discredit us in everyone's eyes. We would appear weak. The citizens of this town, this state, and this country look up to us. If our own daughter can't set a good example for the youngsters out there, it leaves us with no choice. You and that bastard won't ruin the political career I've worked so hard to achieve."

Not sure I heard him right, I stuttered when I asked, "Wh-what?" What era did my parents think we were living in?

"If you marry a nice man or give the baby away for adoption, we'll help you through this. If you don't, then you're on your own. And you're no longer part of this family."

"Wait, you would disavow me because you're ashamed I got knocked up by a decent guy?"

My mother gasped. "Language. You're not knocked up, you're with child."

Chills traversed my entire body. This was worse than any scenario I had imagined every time I thought about how this episode of my life would go down.

My mother pressed the back of her hand against her forehead like she was about to faint. "I still can't believe this is happening. We're being punished. All of us. For your indiscretion. How could you betray us like that?"

"No decent man would ever turn away from his responsibilities."

This was a prank. It had to be.

"You should find him if you're so sure he's deserving of you. Perhaps he'll do the right thing by you and this child."

"I can't… I-I tried." Shame grew in me as I admitted the ugly truth. "I don't know… I don't know his last name. I have no way of contacting him. I've been looking for him, but this country has over three hundred million people."

"Abigail, I can't believe you let a man trick you and steal your virginity. There's a special place in hell for such men."

"I'm not… I…I wasn't—"

My mother lifted her hand to silence my protests. "Stop. We've heard enough. What will it be, Abigail?"

"I'm…I'm not giving up my baby. Forget it. And I'm not exiling myself to Europe either."

Her stare turned glacial. "Then you know what to do. You must be gone by Wednesday night."

"How? Where? Can I at least get some time to find a place to live? And a job?"

"Sorry. You made your choice, young lady. We won't tolerate your behavior for another minute. We shouldn't be punished for your wrongdoings. The sooner you leave, the lower the risk of anyone finding out about your sin."

"What about college? Since I can't attend next semester, they revoked my scholarship. I can't continue without financial help…"

"Right now, you're choosing to go on with the consequences of your acts, which means, we're no longer supporting you or your education and will not pay for your tuition fees. We disagreed with the idea of attending college from the very beginning, and you just proved us right. Once again."

"They corrupted your soul, young lady."

My eyes brimmed with tears, and my heart lodged in my throat. "You serious?"

"Yes. We are. As your mother just said, we won't be accomplices in your sinful life."

As if I never mattered in their lives, my parents cast another disappointed glance at me before my father went to his study to read, and my mother cleared the table—the same way they did every night.

I neared her by the stove. "Mother. Can we talk about this?"

She remained mute.

Tears streamed down my cheeks. "Mother. Please. I'm your daughter. Your only daughter… It must count for something."

No words. Only an icy silence wrapped around us.

I tugged at her sleeve, hoping for a reaction. Something. Anything. "Please." My voice was a breathless plea. "I need you. How am I supposed to do this all on my own?"

She whirled around and met my gaze. Her eyes were cold, devoid of warmth. With her lips pressed into a firm line, her gaze swept over me—without an ounce of love.

"Mother?"

The sound of her palm connecting with my cheek filled the heavy silence, and I jumped back at the contact. The sting drew new tears from my eyes.

"You are no longer my daughter, Abigail. I'm done

with you. Now stay in your room. I've seen enough of you tonight."

My lips quivered. My heart fractured behind my ribcage.

I was aware my parents wouldn't be happy with the news, but never did I imagine their throwing me out and disowning me.

With a step back, I put distance between us. I was numb. My head spun. My insides hurt. I couldn't process anything, too shocked. My hand rested on my left cheek, easing the burn on my sensitive flesh. I looked around. In all the years I'd lived here, my childhood house had never appeared so cold and uninviting. Impeccably polished wooden floors covered every room. Crucifixes, crosses, and other religious symbols filled the beige, almost yellow walls and bourbon-colored tables.

My mother returned to her stove, and erected an ice wall between us. Her action severed the last thread of love tying us together.

I rushed out of the kitchen, blinking the fresh batch of tears building in my eyes.

Locked in the bathroom, I took in the matching set of green bathtub, sink, and toilet. The lid covered in a piece of ugly pink rug. The same color as the rectangular one spread over the mocha tiled floor—as depressing as the rest of the house. A contrast to its pristine and updated exterior.

No one would ever guess my parents were wealthy just by touring the house.

Splashing cold water over my face, I tried to come to terms with my new reality as I admired the red mark spread across my cheek. I was nineteen years old, preg-nant, single, and about to live on the street if I didn't find a shelter or a cheap apartment soon. Not the life I'd ever imagined for myself, or my unborn child.

My red-rimmed eyes were glossy and void of my usual optimism. "Please, Andy. If somehow you can hear me, I need you. Even if it's just for moral support...or...or a hug. I'll never ask anything from you, but I could really use some cheering up right now. I'm all alone in this world. And I'm...I'm scared. I-I have no idea what I'm doing. Perhaps you don't even remember me, but I have a hunch our story isn't over yet. I'm sorry... Ohmygod, I'm so sorry I left without exchanging numbers. If we never cross paths again, this will always be my biggest regret. Not because of the baby, but because there was something powerful between us, and I'll forever wonder if we were meant to... if we were meant to be. We're now linked for life, and you have no idea. How ironic."

The reality of the last hour sank in.

No way would I ever be able to finish my degree. Not without a scholarship or my parents helping me out, even in the form of a loan.

The thought of it sent my heart plummeting further down my chest.

My palms cradled the little bundle of joy growing inside me. "We'll be okay. You and I. I-I promise. I'll do whatever I can to make this work and see to it that you never lack for anything. I might require a little time, but keep faith in me, okay? We'll do this. Together. We're a team now. You are my family."

When I stared at my reflection in the mirror, I promised myself one thing: I wouldn't give up on my dreams. No matter how hard it got or how tired it made me, I would get there. Even if I had to take night classes while breastfeeding a newborn, I would get my degree.

And climb the ladder until I became a music executive.

I clamped the sink tight with both hands and nodded at my reflection. "Girl, you can do this. Alone or not, you're stronger than you realize. You *are* a superstar, and you *are* gonna shine."

With one last nod, I exited the bathroom and reached my bedroom, ready to box whatever I had that I could bring along. I would create my own life.

The way I saw it.

The way I liked it.

No matter what it took.

Chapter 16
Anderson

"Anderson. I've missed you so much. Come, hug your mama." My mother pulled me into a warm embrace the moment I stepped through the front door.

She lived in a white ranch-style house with black trim, doors, and shutters on a half-acre property. Colorful flowerbeds and a well-manicured lawn—both of which she spent several hours a week tending—covered the front and back yards. A large wooden back deck connected to the living room through a set of garden doors and overlooked an old white oak where my gramps had hung a tire swing when I was just a kid. A small pond, where I'd spent countless hours playing when I was little, separated the property from the neighbor's. A few miles from downtown Memphis, my childhood home reminded me of summer days and endless fun with my friends, and it always smelled of trees and fresh-cut grass. It was calm and quiet, far away from the city's commotion and busy streets. My own slice of paradise for as long as I could remember, until I'd left for college.

I dropped my bag and guitar case at my feet and wound my arms around her. I loved my independence and my life in New York City, but I missed my mother—and my home—too. Growing up, it had always been just the two of us.

"Hey, Ma." I planted a kiss on her cheek. "Glad to be home."

"Not as much as I am. I baked chocolate chip cookies for you. They're still warm and cooling off on a rack in the kitchen." She tugged at my hand, pulling me further into the house. "Oh, and I made lemonade too. Let's sit and catch up." She stopped in the hallway leading to the kitchen and turned to look at me. She caressed my cheek with her soft hand, a smile curving her lips. "Why does it always seem like you've grown up since the last time I saw you?"

A chuckle left my mouth. "Ma, you know I'm nineteen and my growth spurt is over, right? I was the same height when I came home for the holidays four months ago."

She shrugged. "I guess. It's good to have you home. I wish you were in town for the whole summer. Soon, you'll have your own life and won't visit much. You've grown up too fast. I swear, it was yesterday that you were a toddler in a diaper, emptying kitchen cupboards and making music with anything you could get your hands on."

I snickered. "I guess. You said cookies a minute ago, right?"

"Follow me."

I draped an arm around her shoulders and motioned her closer. My mother wasn't a tiny woman, but next to my six-foot-two frame, she looked small.

We chatted about everything and nothing for a while until she asked, "What's going on with you, Anderson? You smile, but it doesn't reach your eyes. Something's bothering you. Talk to me."

Over the years, my mother had always been more of a friend to me, and I had a hard time keeping anything from her.

I propped my elbow up on the table and ran one palm over my face. "It's nothing. Really."

"Anderson Curtis Ford. Didn't anybody ever tell you that you were a bad liar? You have that face. Talk. Now."

I averted my eyes for a long second before bringing my attention back to her, my chin resting on my fists. "Huh…I need a break from my own life. Remember the girl I told you about? The one from the airport?"

She nodded.

"I've been trying to find her. For months. In vain. She has unlocked something inside me, and I've been writing my best music since I met her. I'm scared that if I forget about her, it will impact my creativity."

"Then don't. Don't forget her. Keep her alive in your music."

"That's the other thing… I'm haunted by the memory of her. Not sure if it's as simple as it seems." I sighed. "Remember Bethany? The one I went on a few dates with last fall?"

"The one who had gotten out of a toxic relationship at the time?"

"Yeah. So…we've been talking. She wants us to get together next semester. For real this time."

My mother leaned forward and grabbed one of my hands between hers. "Is that what you want? Date Bethany?"

"I suppose… She's smart and nice."

"Why do I sense a *but?*" She tipped one eyebrow, waiting for me to explain. My mother possessed a sixth sense when it came to me.

"How can I be invested in a relationship with a girl when in my head, I spend every waking minute writing songs about someone else? It's kinda sick. I'd be cheating on her with the memory of another girl…" I lifted my eyes to meet hers. "Do you get what I mean?" I inhaled. "Gosh. Just hearing myself say it out loud makes me sound lame."

"Oh, I see."

"What should I do? It's so fucked up. I can't be in love with a girl I only met once. Still, the time we spent together, it felt more real than any other relationship I've ever been in before."

"Anderson, I wish I possessed magical powers that would make it all okay. But I don't. You're here for two weeks. Take the time to unwind, think about other stuff. Enjoy this vacation and clear your head. Go out with your friends. Maybe when you go back to New York, things won't be so messy."

"You think?"

"Time makes things better. It's not just a saying. It helps you see the situation from a different angle. I'm not telling you it'll be easy, but maybe give it a try."

I hung my head. "I will. Thanks, Ma."

With a pile of cookies in front of me, I reflected on my mother's words of wisdom. Could I really do that, think about other things?

I surveyed the house. From where I sat, I could see most of the main floor. Blond wooden floors, sage-green walls, large windows opening onto the lush green landscape of the backyard, and a faint scent of citrus that I knew came from the essential oil diffuser set on the fireplace mantel.

A painting on the living room wall caught my attention. "Is this new?" I asked, my focus back on my mother.

"Yes. Painted it last month. It's yours when you have your own place."

My attention was drawn back to the piece of art. A man with tousled dark hair with a woman straddling him, their foreheads pressed together. The man's hands cradled her cheeks, and she had hers planted on his chest. A guitar rested against the side of the chair. It was a mixture of dark and neutral colors except for the woman's lipstick which was a deep shade of red. Even though their faces weren't defined due to coarse brush strokes, I could sense the love pouring out from them. My gaze lingered on the painting. It was mesmerizing. It spoke to my heart in a raw way, sending a wave of nostalgia through me.

"How did you—" I found it impossible to put my thoughts into words, too many feelings surging inside me at once.

My mother nodded. "You inspired it. That song you sent me back in February. I played it on repeat and sat before my easel and couldn't stop."

"It's about her."

My mother nodded. "I guessed it."

I pinched the bridge of my nose and glanced down, my emotions getting the better of me.

After a beat, I said, "I love it. It's perfect." How could my mother, who'd never met Abby or seen her picture, portray her with such accuracy? A shiver worked up my spine, and I looked away.

"Anderson, your new music is good. More mature. More emotional." She enveloped my hand with hers. "I'm proud of you. Always have been."

We exchanged small smiles. "Thanks. It means a lot."

Her words reinforced the idea Abby had changed me and my art. For the better.

My mother's soft voice interrupted my train of thought. "Now go settle into your room and relax because you and I are going out tonight. No way is my only son in town and we're not celebrating the end of his second year of college."

Back in my old bedroom, I sat on the edge of the mattress and scanned the space. Royal-blue walls and white trims. A stuffed frog sitting on the bookshelf amongst old textbooks and fiction novels. My high school talent show ribbons were pinned on the bulletin board, surrounded by pictures of my teen years. Of me and my mom. Me and my friends. The first concert I'd performed when I was twelve. My high school graduation. Scotty, my late black Labrador, who had been my confidant and roommate all through childhood.

I bent forward and grabbed my guitar from its case as a new song took form in my head. I could hear the melody clearly. I hummed it, trying to fit words around the notes.

That night I was angry and
  alone
The storm was raging outside
And soft music was playing on
  the radio
Everything around me was
  dark (and sad)
Colors had left my life. Black
  and white was my theme
And then you came my way,
  and I got hypnotized by you

**Blue is the color of the sky in
    summer
Blue is the shade of the ocean
    on a sunny day
Blue is my mood when you're
    not around
But blue is also the color of
    your eyes
The light in my darkness
The iced crystals shining
    across the room
Little beacons showing me
    the way
My heart is yours, my home
    is you
And all I see now is blue**

A soft knock on my door brought me out of my creative process. My mother's head peeked through the ajar door. "You wrote this?"

I nodded. "Just about now."

"It's beautiful. I miss listening to you play and coming up with melodies. Any title?"

I offered her a half-shrug. "Blue?" It sounded more like a question than a statement.

"It's perfect. Keep going. Will you play it for me later?"

"Sure."

She started to leave but halted mid-motion. "Anderson… I'm sorry if I ever tried to convince you to choose another career path. You're where you belong. Don't listen to anyone who tells you otherwise."

A smile tilted my lips up. "Thanks, Ma. I'm glad you recognize it."

"You're my pride and joy, Anderson. I love you."

The door closed behind her with a low click, and I returned to the song, writing down the lyrics in the old notebook I kept on the bedside table.

———

"Man, does my old man know you're in town?" Rufus, one of my childhood best friends said when we met for a base-ball game two days later. His father owned a brewery slash bar downtown, and he had believed in my musical talent early on, ever since he saw me perform at a middle school recital.

Whenever I was home, he always tried to book me to play for a night or two. "I sent him a text earlier. He said he'd call me tomorrow to discuss dates."

"He sings your praise all the fucking time. I swear he's your biggest fan."

I clinked my soda can to his. "We all need a first. How is Stan's mama doing?" My friend's mother had just completed her last round of chemotherapy for an aggres-sive case of breast cancer. She was our third-grade teacher and the sweetest woman in the world.

"I saw her last week. She's a ghost of herself, man. She can barely walk on her own. All her hair is gone, and her skin is a greenish-gray hue. They don't know yet if the treatments were successful."

I shook my head. "Wow, I gotta see her while I'm here." The last time I was in town, I'd spent an hour singing to her by her bedside after she said it soothed her soul.

Rufus and I talked through the rest of the game. My friend had forfeited a college education for a job at his uncle's construction business as a carpenter.

Hours later, we made our way back to our parked

pickup trucks.

"Are you coming to Round and Round later?" he asked. "The guys will be there. Claire and Josie too. It's trivia night. They're having game nights all summer. Then we'll hit one of the clubs on the outskirts of town and dance the night away. Are you in?"

"Sure. I don't have anything scheduled." I had no plans whatsoever, and I was trying to let go and have a great time while I was here, like I'd assured my mother I would.

"Meet us there at eight."

We bumped fists the same manner we'd been doing since we were little kids and parted ways.

Around eight, my friends and I sat in a booth at Round and Round. After forming teams, we listened as the guy at the front explained the rules of trivia night. My attention drifted to a girl exiting the ladies' room. For a split second, I believed I saw Abby. The girl looped her arm through her friend's, and I shook my head. *Now my brain is conjuring images of her. Great.* My Abby couldn't be here. In Memphis, in a bar, on trivia night. *My Abby.* Could she really be here, of all places? I was hallucinating…or maybe just going nuts. I stood up to check if it was really her.

Josh, sitting next to me, followed my line of vision. "Who's this?"

The girl turned, and she wasn't the one I expected to see. I sank back into my seat, feeling ridiculous. "No one."

He let out a loud chuckle, pointing at me. "Man, tell that to your face."

I sighed. "Someone from my past. Or not." I shook my head. "Not sure. It's…it's nothing."

Someone tapped my shoulder, snapping me out of it, and I found Josie watching me with a concerned expression. "Everything okay? You look like you've seen a ghost."

Back in high school, we dated for six months before we realized we were way better as friends. She had been my first kiss.

"I thought I saw someone I know." I shrugged and brought my drink to my lips to avoid talking about it.

Fuck, now my mind was imagining things. How screwed was I?

Rufus bumped my fist from the opposite side of the booth. "Ready to annihilate every other team, Ford? 'Cause we all know you're the smartest one amongst us."

A loud laugh tumbled out of my mouth. "Said the guy who secured a perfect score on his SAT."

Our entire group of friends joined in.

"Well, I might be book-smart, but you, my friend, are street-smart. And in the jungle, you'd be the one still standing in the end if things got wild."

"True," Coop agreed.

All our friends agreed too.

I smirked. "Let's see who's gonna end up kicking whose ass tonight."

We ended trivia night in second place, thanks to my musical knowledge—no thanks to my political know-how.

Sometime later, Coop, Josh, and I were standing around a high table in a club while the others were dancing under the stream of violet and blue laser beams and pounding beats. I took a sip of cherry soda, my foot tapping along to the rhythm on the sticky, worn floor.

Claire tugged at my sleeve, and I turned to face her. "Dance with me, Andy."

I winced. "Not my scene. I'll pass."

"C'mon. We haven't seen you in months. And you look like a guy who needs some fun in his life. When did you get so stuck up?"

I shrugged. "I'm not… It's just—"

If Joe were here, he would tell me to let go. Were all my friends in on this *Let's get Anderson to loosen up* thing? Had they all been seeing something about me that I'd overlooked until now?

Claire batted her eyelashes, doing her best *Please do it for me* face, and I gave in. "Fine. One dance."

She clapped her hands, doing a little victory jig. "Deal." She whisked me to the middle of the dance floor before I could add anything else, the music deafening and the lights blinding.

Even though I tried to stay in the moment, my eyes swept across everything around me. Somehow, my mind was still reeling from seeing that girl earlier, the one reminding me of Abby.

Why did I keep expecting her to appear wherever I was?

"Andy, where did you go?" Claire asked.

My attention shifted to her. "I'm right here."

"Nah. You were far away from here." Amusement played on her face. "Did something happen in New York?"

I stopped moving and frowned. "No. Why would you ask that?"

"All night, you've kept scanning the room, as if expecting someone who isn't here."

"I'm here all right. No need to make things up."

She sighed and gave her head a small shake. "We've been friends since what…fourth grade? I can tell when you're bullshitting me. But suit yourself if it makes you feel better."

"Sorry, okay? I'm here now. Guess I owe you another song."

"You bet you do." She smirked and looped her arms

around my neck, and I ended up spending the rest of my night drinking and dancing with my friends.

————

A few nights later, I was taking a break, sitting at a picnic table in the alley—transformed into an extension of the establishment—soaking in the humid summer air. A faint smell of barbecue and something sweet lingered in the air every time the breeze swept my way.

Tonight was my set at Rock 'n' Country, the bar Rufus's father owned.

Scrolling through my phone, I opened the pictures my mom had sent an hour ago. A bunch of shots from my early days until now. My lips tilted up at the sight of the tiny version of me holding my first guitar and another one of me dressed in a cowboy outfit for Halloween. Back when I dreamed of being a rancher.

I sent her a text message.

ME

> Wow, I was such a tiny human. Feeling nostalgic?

She replied within a minute.

MOM

> Time flies. I remember each one of them like it was yesterday. Was going through your picture albums. You've grown into a fine young man, Anderson. I'm proud of you. Always.

ME

> I know, Ma. Gotta go. The second part of my set begins in a few minutes. Love you.

MOM

I love you too, son xx

Something didn't feel right. My mother wasn't one for reminiscing or getting all teary-eyed. Sometimes, I wondered if my absence made her feel lonely. Through the years, she had never brought a man home. I knew she went on dates—on occasion—but they never seemed to turn into something more. Or perhaps she was dating and not letting me know.

Whatever. It wasn't my business. Still, I wanted to see my mother happy, to know she had someone special in her life. I wanted her days not to be spent all alone now that I no longer lived at home full time.

Trying to shove my thoughts aside for the rest of the night, I went back inside. The second half of my set flew by—an hour and a half that felt more like twenty minutes.

Rufus joined me for a drink afterward, and we sat on the deck outside. Bordered by a wooden fence and sparkling with fairy lights above, the newly renovated beer garden looked amazing. Picnic tables, metallic-blue outdoor couch sets, and small high-standing tables were peppered all over the space. We could hear the music playing inside on the speakers attached to the exterior wall of the main building. A mouth-watering scent permeated the air, thanks to a food truck serving a variety of tacos, nachos, and other Mexican food.

"I love the new setup. Your dad did a great job," I told my friend as he sat opposite me with a full plate of food to share. "It's a far cry from the plastic chairs and tables that used to be here."

"Yeah. It looks great. My old man worked hard to make sure it would open on time."

"Well, he did amazing. I love the vibe he created here."

I picked a taco and devoured it in three bites, then started crushing the plate of nachos in front of me with a fork, pouring salsa and sour cream over it and mixing it all together.

"Geez, you're still doing that?" my friend asked. "Murdering your food?"

"I've never stopped. They're called Mixchos now."

Memories of my last few hours spent with Abby flashed like a movie in my mind, but I kept them at bay.

"Mixchos? What the hell, man."

"Nothing. It's stupid. Forget it." I gestured around me with a hand. "I've missed this. Southern vibe. New York is fine, I guess, but it'll never be home."

"I'll try to visit you next semester. We could catch a game together. Could be fun."

I wiped my mouth with the back of my hand and sipped my drink. "Joe's uncle has contacts. I'm sure he'd be able to get us good tickets at a decent price."

With a mouthful, my friend lifted his drink and clinked it to mine. "Deal."

When I got home two hours later, I tiptoed toward my bedroom, but my mother stopped me before I could reach it.

"Anderson, wait."

I surveyed the dim-lit hallway, where framed pictures of us lined the cream walls. My attention landed on one from the first concert I'd ever played, and my lips curled up at the memory. "Why are you still up? Were you waiting for me?"

She nodded. "Listen, we gotta talk."

"Can it wait till the morning?" I fished my phone out of my back pocket. "It's almost two in the morning, and I'm drained."

She shook her head. "Not sure I'll be able to sleep until we sit down and I come clean about some stuff."

I frowned. "Come clean? What are you talking about?"

She avoided my eyes. "Can we sit? I'll make tea."

I dragged a hand over my face, the exhaustion from my earlier performance catching up with me. "O-okay."

She bobbed her head, fidgeting with the bracelet around her wrist while motioning toward the kitchen, her gait tense and her back straight. I studied her demeanor. Something was wrong. I could tell. My mother was usually an endless well of contagious cheerfulness. Not tonight. I couldn't recall ever seeing her act this anxious.

"Does it have to do with your earlier travel down memory lane?"

Keeping her back to me, she shrugged.

I closed the distance and clasped her shoulders from behind. "Ma, talk to me. What's going on?" The air around us became charged. My hair stood on end on my arms, and something twisted in my stomach. "Are you sick?"

She twirled around and cradled my face with her small hands. "No. Nothing like that, I swear."

I huffed out the breath I was holding in. From up close, I noticed the redness in her eyes when they met mine. "You're not acting like yourself. What's going on?"

"Sit down. I'll bring tea. Gimme a minute, and I'll explain everything."

Minutes later, she took the chair next to mine at the kitchen table after placing a steamy mug in front of me on the wooden surface.

Fiddling with her mug's handle, my mother focused all her attention on the tea bag floating in the hot water.

"So…huh… About that… The thing is… When you left to play your set tonight, I did… I just…"

I covered her hand with mine. "Ma, get to the point."

She bobbed her head. "Sure." She swallowed and watched me for a moment. "First, let me repeat how proud I am of you and the man you are becoming and the artist you are. Never doubt it."

"I never did."

"Good. It's good. Earlier, I was going through your photo albums, trying to convince myself to reach out to your father."

"My father? The man who abandoned you when you got pregnant with me? The jerk who chose his other family over us because he couldn't care less about you? And me?" Anger boiled in my bloodstream at the mention of my sperm donor, the most selfish man walking the surface of this Earth. "That guy? Why would you want to talk to him after everything he did…or didn't?"

"We gotta talk about this, you and I. It's important."

I jumped to my feet, my chair scraping against the floor as I pushed it back. "No thanks. Not interested."

My mother's head snapped up, and she gripped my wrist before I could make it to my room. "Anderson, wait." Her soft tone quieted my raging thoughts. The ones that had taken over my mind in the last minute or so. "I'm not done."

"Well, I am."

My mother moved to stand, not letting go of me, her face more serious than it had ever been. "Sit. Now."

"Ma."

"Don't Ma me." She pointed to the chair I'd just vacated. "Sit."

Before I could even think about all I wanted to say, the words exited my mouth on their own. "No." I folded my arms over my chest, and she had to let go of me. "I'm not having this talk. Anything concerning that dickhead, I don't wanna hear about it. After nineteen years, you think I'm interested in stuff related to him? Think again."

"Anderson, he could help you with your music career."

"Not. Interested. I don't care if he's the president. He's nothing to me."

"Anderson, we had a deal. And you've been keeping your end. I know I haven't been supportive so far of your music career… I really wanted you to get a college degree first. But I've seen the videos you've sent me…and Rufus's father sent me one tonight too." The corner of her mouth lifted in a smile, and she placed her hand over her heart. "You are so talented. I think you are ready for more. Your father is very well connected in the business. He could coach you. Make sure you have a mentor, someone you can trust in the industry. It's a shark's world. When you graduate and you decide to pursue a musical career, at least you'll know what to expect and which doors to knock on. Who to trust and who not to trust."

I blinked a million times. She was fucking high. How could my mother believe for one second I'd agree to this? "Did you fucking smoke crack?"

Confusion washed over her face before she caught up with what I was saying. "Language, Anderson. Can you be a grown-up for a few minutes? Hear me out and then you can decide whether you like the idea or not." She blew out a breath as if I were being difficult. "Sit."

"We can have this conversation while we're standing. I'm not sitting down and pretending everything is fine when it's not. Anyway, I'm not sure I trust you—or your judgment—right now. You're lucky I'm even listening to you."

"Talk to me with respect."

"What do you want me to say? Congratulations, you're

about to reach out to the man whose only great achievement in his life has been to empty his testicles inside you."

Her palm hit my cheek before I could react.

I rubbed the throbbing flesh with my hand, trying to diffuse the sting.

"Sorry," I said, hanging my head low. "I…I went too far."

"Yeah, you did." Her tone left no room for arguments. "Now you'll drink that tea with me and hear what I gotta tell you."

We sat down, and I pushed my chair to the left, adding distance between us. My mother hid her trembling hands under the table. Her shoulders sagged before she inhaled, straightened her posture, and stared at me with more conviction than I'd seen all night.

"Quick questions," I said, "before we begin. Did you actually talk to him?"

"Yes."

"Did he remember you after all these years?"

"Hmm… We had dinner together the other day."

"What? This is a joke. Tell me you're messing with me right now. How can you still talk to him? After everything? After he abandoned you? After he abandoned *us*?" I shut my eyes and breathed in and out, trying to quiet the tsunami rising in the depths of me. My mother didn't deserve my wrath—but she also did. She'd met with my father and had never told me. I thought honesty was our thing. I guess I was wrong the entire time. And this? It was a hard pill to swallow. She was supposed to be on *my* side. She'd always told me it was us against the world when I was little, and I had asked her why I didn't have a daddy like all my friends did.

Yeah, well, now the joke was on me.

"Anderson. Your father and I talk from time to time."

"He's not a stranger like you've always pretended? What do you mean you two *talk*? Why did he never talk to me then?" With my elbows propped on the table, I leaned forward and ran my hands through my hair, despair and confusion clinging to every fiber of my being. I breathed out and risked a look at her. "Has he ever asked about me?"

"All the time." Her voice broke as the truth flashed in her eyes. Neon lights telling me all along I'd been the fool.

"Why doesn't he want to see me now? Why wasn't he around all my life? What was so defective about me that he refused to have a relationship with me?"

"I…I kept him away. It's all on me. Not him."

Chills traversed my back. I had heard enough. My heart lurched in my throat. Nothing added up. This was a nightmare. Nothing else could explain the conversation we were having.

My words were clipped when I asked, "Why? Why now?"

"Because. Like I said, I recognize how talented you are. Anderson, you possess a rare gift. I know it because your father has the same one…" Her voice shook. "I thought he could help you reach for your dreams. I wanna send him your videos… Only if you agree. I want him to hear you play, and since you're in town only for a short time, he could come and meet you. He's not the villain in the story I've always portrayed him to be. He just wants to be part of your life."

My eyes widened in confusion. "Nothing you say makes sense. He wants to be part of my life? First, you're having dinner with him and now this? Are you messing with me for fun? He had nineteen years to show up on our doorstep and make up for his lack of parental presence, and he chose now? What a joke. I'm so over it."

She extended her arm to touch mine, but I jerked away from her touch. "Anderson, you don't know the entire story." Sobs shook her body.

I'd never seen my mother so broken before.

It took all my will not to pull her into my arms and promise her we'd be fine.

"Your father has always wanted to be part of your life. I-I'm sorry...so sorry...for everything." Tears streamed down her cheeks, and she stared at me as if to ask for my forgiveness.

I turned my head, meeting her teary eyes. A slice of my heart cracked. I hated witnessing the sadness in her features. Seeing my mother heartbroken was a hard sight. One I wasn't used to. Keeping quiet, I waited for her to explain herself because if I spoke, no doubt I would explode and say things I would regret later.

I clenched and unclenched my hands, trying to calm myself down.

My words were harsh when I spoke. "Why? He never showed up. Not for the holidays, not for my birthdays, not for any show I ever gave. He wasn't there when I lost my first tooth or graduated high school. And he wasn't there when I needed him growing up. Not a single time. When I yearned for a daddy. A man to teach me some stuff mothers can't. So don't make excuses for him. I was there...the entire time he wasn't."

She coughed and looked away. "All along, I was the one who asked him to stay away. I thought I was doing the right thing."

"You what?" I widened my eyes so big my eyeballs were practically at risk of popping out. "Care to repeat that? You kept my father away from me? On purpose? All this time?"

She huffed a long breath, pleading with her eyes for me

to listen. "It's not as simple as it sounds. Ask me your questions, and I'll answer them all. It's about time we have that conversation."

My insides coiled in knots. I tried to speak, but no words came out. My mother, the one person I loved and respected the most, had lied to me my whole life. She had kept the one person I'd longed for my whole life away from me, fully aware of what she was doing. This was a freaking joke. How could any of this be real?

"Anderson." Her voice brought me out of my drowning thoughts. "I wanna explain everything to you. Your brother…well, half-brother…is also a big name on the music scene."

"I have a brother?"

"Yes. You probably have heard of him. His name is…"

I shook my head with enough velocity to unscrew it from my neck. "No. *No, no, no.* Stop. It's too much. I can't talk to you right now. I just can't do this with you." Hot tears prickled the back of my eyes. "I'm out of here. Going back to New York. I need fresh air. Away from you. All my life I thought my father was the villain and you were the victim of his Machiavellian ways. How wrong have I been."

I kicked my chair back and hurried to my bedroom, shut the door, and started packing all my belongings in the sole bag I'd brought with me.

My mother's broken voice resonated from the other side. "I understand you are mad, Anderson. I hope one day you'll be able to forgive me and give me a chance to explain. When you are ready. You're old enough now that we can talk about it. Like adults do. I-I'm not perfect. Your father isn't…and neither are you.But he's a…he's a good man, and you're at the age where you can decide for yourself if you want a relationship with him. Please don't leave."

Her steps faltered away, and I heard her bedroom door close. With one long exhale, I let go of the breath I was holding in, tears blurring my vision. My shoulders slumped, and I crashed onto my bed, feeling played. And defeated.

Minutes later, with one last look around me, I picked up my guitar case, shouldered my duffel bag ,and made my way outside. Piling my stuff on the backseat of my pickup truck, I decided to drive. I usually flew back and forth to college. In New York, I would have to find a place to park my truck, but right now it was an insignificant detail. The long hours by myself would help calm me down and, hopefully, let me see the whole thing in a different light.

What a fucking joke.

Three hours later, I pulled into the empty parking lot of a grocery store in Nashville. Sprawled across the backseat, using a balled-up hoodie as a pillow, I tried to find a comfortable position to fall asleep—a difficult mission given my size. The night had been long, and I craved the rest. Being here, in this town, I felt closer to the girl I missed a little less each day but who still owned my heart. No matter how crazy or farfetched it sounded.

I had no doubt that if she were here right now, she'd find a way to comfort me. And make it all better. Just by gluing a smile to my face with her silly challenges and happy demeanor.

Restless, with my heart crushed by an invisible vise, I tossed and turned for what appeared to be hours. My body was a jittery mess, and my mind refused to turn off. In the dark, I drummed a melody on my jean-clad thighs, unable to match the lyrics to my current state of mind.

On my back, with a folded arm under my head, I

made myself comfortable and counted my breaths, keeping the thoughts of my parents' fuck-ups away.

My brain finally shut off, and I surrendered myself to sleep in the early morning light, praying the night had been a nightmare I would wake up from. Or that I could go back in time to December, the last time I was truly happy, and have a do-over.

If given the chance, I'd do things right this time. Or at least do the wrong things the right way.

Chapter 17

Abigail

The grocery store parking lot was empty at this early hour. Aside from a few employees' vehicles, an RV, and a black pickup truck parked along the outer edge, it was just me. A cold drizzle fell from the dark sky, fitting my current mood. I'd been awake all night, too many thoughts crowding my mind. My emotions were all over the place. Today was moving day. The last day of life as I'd known it and the first of a new chapter whose pages hadn't been written yet.

With a carton of orange juice and a pack of store-bought chocolate chip cookies—my craving these days—I sat on the curb, soaking in the mist clinging to my skin as I looked skyward. A faint floral scent permeated the air, tingling my nostrils. These days, everything smelled different. I had no idea whether it was the pregnancy hormones playing tricks on my brain or if I'd simply become more attuned to everything around me as I tried to make sense of my life after losing so much in such a short time.

My focus drifted to the two vehicles parked at the other end of the lot, and I found myself imagining the stories of their occupants. The RV people probably had sold all their belongings and were traveling the world, one city at a time. The RV had become their home, and they were content with their nomadic way of living, wanting nothing more than their independence.

The guy in the pickup truck—for some reason, I'd decided he was a *he*—had been kicked out of his house just like me and was trying to make sense of his new reality. He had no money, no place to live, and his truck was his best option right now. Soon, he would find a job and an apartment and give his existence a new direction.

If he could do this and take back control of his life, why couldn't I do it too?

I downed half my juice to wash away the dry cookie crumbs stuck in my teeth before checking my phone. Seven twelve. A red car pulled up near the entrance, and a woman in her early thirties with a crying baby nestled in her arms rushed inside.

My eyes followed her until she disappeared.

That would be me. Soon.

My hand found my rounded belly and stayed there. My baby kicked as if to remind me he—or she—was real. For some reason, I believed he was a *he* too. A mini version of Andy growing inside me. I caressed my taut skin with my palm. "Morning, you. I was having a craving," I said. Anybody who walked by would think I was talking to myself. My abdomen was concealed under one of Tom's large SSB sweatshirts, and it was impossible to tell I was pregnant. "Even though I'm an emotional mess, please don't worry about me, okay? Today will be hard on me, but I'll figure it out. I swear. No matter where we end up, it will be temporary. I just require some time to get my act together. I'm not always like this… Disorganized and scared. It's just… It's… Let's just say nothing has been going as planned, and it's unnerving. But you are safe in there. I'll make sure of it."

Another kick. Was that his way of telling me he trusted me? I chose to believe it was.

"Remember when I told you your daddy dared me to dance on a chair in front of a bunch of strangers the night we met? I thought I wouldn't be able to go through with it. I was afraid of what people would think, and deep down, I didn't want to humiliate myself. It turned out I did it, and it filled me with pride because I did something I wouldn't have done otherwise. All that to say I'm still young and clueless, and I have no home or defined future, but we have each other. And even though I'm freaking out about the unknown, I learned a big lesson that night when I did the dare. If I put my mind to something, there's nothing I can't do. No matter how uncomfortable it might feel at first, I'll go through with it until we are settled. It's a promise."

With my eyes shut, I inhaled and exhaled, trying to be zen about the predicament I was in.

With as much resolve as I could muster right now, I stood up and crossed the parking lot, beginning the two-mile walk back to my parents' house. When I neared the black pickup truck, I caught movement inside and spotted a silhouette in the backseat. Maybe my backup story about the truck's owner wasn't that far-fetched after all—someone really had slept in there. Increasing my pace, I put distance between us, not wanting the occupant to believe I was spying on him. A foreign sensation buzzed through me. As if I was being observed. This was ridiculous. I glanced over my shoulder one last time, scanning the empty lot. No one was there. My imagination was playing tricks on me.

Tucking my hands into my sweatshirt sleeves, as if I could disappear into them, I kept walking, my mind wandering far away from here…to a world where I was safe, loved, and not about to be all alone.

Ellie arrived a little after ten in the morning. She had rented an SUV from the airport car rental agency and parked in the driveway, while I sat on the front steps of my parents' house, still wearing the sweatshirt and leggings I'd worn earlier. The drizzle had stopped, and the sun beat down hard. Thick humidity permeated the air, and I was suffocating underneath these clothes, but what other choice did I have? I wasn't allowed to parade—as my father had called it—around the house in anything that would bring attention to my abdomen. Since I told them about the pregnancy, they had barely looked at me and refused to engage with me. Each night, my dinner was left on my bedside table, a sign I wasn't welcome to share a meal with them. They had cast me out. Rejected me when I needed them the most.

I was now invisible, and a part of me couldn't wait to be out of here.

The other half was freaking out because I had found no place to live. Most apartments required proof of employment or my parents' endorsement, neither of which was an option.

In less than an hour, I would officially be homeless.

A *dropout*, homeless pregnant teenager. A walking cliché.

"What are you doing out here by yourself dressed as if it's wintertime?" my friend asked as she hopped out of the rental and hurried to wrap me in her arms. The only protective embrace I'd known for months.

"Waiting for you actually. I can't believe you're here. It's way too generous of you to help me move out, but I really appreciate it." A lone tear rolled down my cheek, and I wiped it off with my sleeve. "You have no idea what it means to me."

"You kidding? I wouldn't wanna be anywhere else. This is some crazy shit your parents are putting you through. Did you talk to them again?" She pushed away from me, clamping my upper arms and studying my face.

"It's like I'm dead to them. They won't look at me or talk to me or acknowledge I exist. Each night, I eat by myself in my room since I'm not allowed to sit at the dinner table with them. I could have murdered someone, and I think they would have been more accepting of my killer status than they are now."

"This is wrong. On so many levels."

"I'm nineteen and technically an adult. I can't force them to accept me."

"Still, they are *your parents*. Your flesh and blood. How can they be so cruel?"

"I did this to myself , so I guess it's earned."

"Nah. Did you trick Andy? Nah. Did you get knocked up on purpose? Nah. These things happen. No matter what, you don't deserve to be thrown out on the street like some piece of garbage by parents who are supposed to love you unconditionally." She surveyed the house behind me. "And excuse me, but it's not like your folks don't have the means or space to help you find your bearings and get your life back on track."

I sighed.

"You and this baby should matter more than some beliefs, elections, or popular votes. Any idea where you'll move to?"

I hid my hands in the sleeves of my sweatshirt—a new

habit of mine these days—and fidgeted with my fingers, casting a gaze down and looking at anything but my friend. "There is…" I inhaled some air and courage. "There is a women's shelter a few miles from here. Huh, I called… yesterday… They can take me in for a little while. I'll have a safe place to stay until I figure out my next move."

"A shelter? Are you sure?"

Angry tears burned the back of my eyes. "That's the only option, Elles… So far. If I stay at the hotel, I'll go through all my savings in no time."

"Or you could come back to Silverville and I could get that apartment and we could be roommates. You wouldn't be alone."

"Thanks." My voice quivered as the single word left my mouth.

Ellie was the only person still standing in my corner. The only one rooting for me. It meant something to me.

"I gotta stay here. Since I can't go back to college, I'll try to find a job in the city and work my way up. It's not the best-case scenario, but right now, it's the only thing I can hold on to. Nashville is the best place to find a job in the music industry. I don't want to give up on all my dreams so soon…you know, just in case." I swallowed the mass growing in my throat. "I've been looking into remote classes at the community college, and the lady is supposed to call me back next week. I could maybe take a few random business classes during the fall semester and enroll full-time next winter. Or part-time because I need a steady, well-paying job too. And a newborn won't gimme much time out of the house anyway."

Ellie's face softened. "It's a good plan, Abby. I'm sure it will all work out." She paused. "Since I'm in town till Sunday, let's grab your stuff and get out of here. I've got a room at The Row, the hotel downtown, and you're staying with me. It will be just like the dorm once again but fancier and with nicer, comfier beds. We'll visit that…huh…shelter…together and decide if it's good and safe enough for my girl. Also, since I've never been to Tennessee before, you'll give me a tour. By the way, tomorrow, we're driving to Memphis."

"Why?"

"Because I've never been. And perhaps, if fate is on our side, we could bump into you-know-who. It's worth trying. You're the one who had planned to go, remember?"

"Yeah, but then I decided against it. Memphis is big enough that we may never find him."

She shrugged. "We'll be able to say we at least tried. Now show me the way to your bedroom. We're having lunch afterward. I haven't eaten anything since last night."

Hand in hand, we walked through the front door. My mother was at the oven, bent over a pan.

"Hi, Mrs. Peña," my friend greeted her.

My mother glanced at us and grimaced, not even returning my friend's greeting. How rude. I clenched my jaw, gritting my teeth to avoid saying something I would regret. This was so humiliating. They were free to hate me, but disrespecting my best friend crossed a line. It was a new low, even for them.

Once in my bedroom, I closed the door behind us.

"Whoa, you were not joking. That's more than a cold shoulder you've got there. I could feel the icicles she was throwing at us." As if she sensed I needed some love, Ellie drew me into her arms. "Don't let them get to you. You deserve more than this. I won't let you down. Ever."

I nodded against her shoulders, more tears building in my eyes.

A stifled shriek of pain passed my lips.

"Shhh. It'll be okay." Ellie's arms tightened around me.

"One day at a time." She leaned back and dried my tears with her fingertips. "When is your next appointment with the OB-GYN?"

I sniffled. "Fr-Friday afternoon."

"I'll come with you. Can't wait to see that baby on a screen."

"You would?"

She bobbed her head. "Yeah. And then we'll have dinner together and do something fun."

"I've missed you," I told her. "I wish we were still roommates, and everything didn't have to change."

"I know." She looked around. "Is this all you have to stuff into the car?"

Three boxes, two suitcases, and a backpack contained all my possessions.

"That's all I own."

"Then let's do this. The sooner we're out of here, the easier it will be to make plans."

Fifteen minutes later, the car was packed, and we high-fived. My mood had improved since my friend parked in my driveway less than thirty minutes ago. Straightening my back and trying to look more confident than I felt, I went back inside. I cast one last glance around my empty bedroom. It was now void of any personal touch. Only the furniture remained. Somehow, it felt like I had never lived between those walls. Nostalgia, fear of the unknown, and anger mixed inside me. This was the end of a major chapter of my life—one I was forced to abandon despite myself. But I hoped it would be for the best in the end, that I had a different journey ahead of me. I took a deep breath, stepped out, and shut the door behind me, as ready as I could be for what would come next.

In the kitchen, my mother was still there, prepping

food, not glancing in my direction even after I cleared my throat.

"Well, all my stuff is in the car, so I'll get going." My voice sounded broken and so low I bet she had a hard time hearing me. Still, I had to get it off my chest. "No matter what, I've always loved you. It hurts that you think I'm not enough for you to love me back. I committed no crime. I just loved someone for a short while and this"—I said cradling my belly—"happened. I'm sorry you feel that punishing me and casting me out is your only option…and that treating me like a stranger is okay. Because it's not. You were pregnant with me once… How would you have felt if the people you were supposed to trust the most had kicked you out like you never meant anything to them?" My voice trembled, but I breathed in and rubbed my damp hands against my leggings, trying to stay calm and keep my emotions in check. "I'm still your child. No matter what you choose to believe or convince yourself of. The… the sad part is that I will get over it…over you. One day, I'll probably even forgive you." I gave her a stiff nod. "Not for you, but…but for me. Because I don't wanna live with a heart made of stone and bad memories. One thing is sure, though, you'll never get to know my baby…your only grandchild… This is the real shame. That's what breaks my heart the most. I know I'll get back on my feet—one day soon—but you'll forever have to live with the fact that you threw me out when I needed your love and acceptance the most. A parent's job isn't only to handle the beautiful parts of life. Sometimes life gets messy, but it's part of the deal… I'm not someone you should be ashamed of. I'm a great person. I have good values. I'm a hard worker. I'm honest and funny. And I choose to believe that good things happen to good people."

I paused, praying my mother would tell me she had

made a mistake or that she didn't want our relationship to end on a sad note, but she remained silent, her posture rigid and her gaze fixed ahead.

"You used to be fun, you know. Back when I was a child, you were full of energy and always smiling. I'm sorry you lost yourself along the way…your essence. It's never too late to get that part of you back, but it might be too late to rekindle whatever we once had. I wish you well and hope you are happy. Goodbye, Mother."

For a split second, I thought I saw a tear roll down her cheek, but she turned away from me, shutting me out. When she returned to her prep, her face was blank.

She still refused to look at me, and after a long minute of awful silence, I spun on my heel and left the only house I'd ever known as home in my short life.

After we finished stacking all my possessions in a corner of our hotel room, Ellie and I decided to freshen up before going out to grab a bite and stroll around town.

I was exiting the shower when my friend knocked on the bathroom door. "Abby, don't dress up just yet. I got you something."

Curious, I secured a towel around me and went to meet her by the bed. "What? You're already doing plenty. You don't have to."

"Don't be ridiculous. You can't spend your summer dressed in sweatshirts and leggings. You'll faint from heatstroke. Not good for the baby. Here." She handed me a shopping bag.

I lifted a brow before emptying the contents on the bed. Two summer dresses, four T-shirts, two tops, a pair of shorts, a pair of jeans, and a skirt. My eyes brimmed with emotions. "Ellie… Wow… Y-you didn't have to but thank you," I said, pulling her into my arms and squeezing her so tightly she had to beg me to let go.

She offered me a half-shrug and a wide grin. "I thought you deserved to look cute this summer."

"I'll never be able to repay you for everything."

"It's a gift. Be grateful. Say thank you and try it on. The lady at the maternity store said it should fit you even when your figure changes through the months."

I couldn't hide the smile spreading across my face. I chose a dress for tonight—an A-line sky-blue number with fluttery sleeves.

Feeling better than I had in a long while, I took the time to add a coat of shimmery lip gloss and mascara. Admiring myself in the mirror, I spun on the balls of my feet. For once, I felt like myself again—and even pretty.

Ellie clasped her hands when I exited the bathroom. "*Gurrrl*, you look perfect." She linked her arm with mine. "Let's go eat. I'm famished."

We sat on the terrace of a small eatery, enjoying the last of the sunshine. Unable to resist anything—I could have sworn she was the pregnant one—Ellie ordered far too much food for the two of us. We chatted for the next hour like we hadn't seen each other in months when, in fact, it had only been a few days.

"You sure your parents are okay with your spending money on me?"

She let out a loud laugh. "Kidding, right? As long as I'm not messing with their perfect lives, they much prefer me to have a field trip with their credit card. You're aware I'm nothing like the daughter they pictured when I was a child. I'm way too wild and free-spirited for them. If I were the one pregnant, they would fund the apartment, the nanny, and everything I might need, just to make sure I stayed away. In many ways, they're not much different from your parents in their old, outdated ideas of how women should live their lives. The main difference between us is that mine accept my craziness, as long as it doesn't affect them. They want me to thrive."

"Well, I wish I had that. Parents who accepted me." I downed my glass of water. "Were you serious when you said you'd visit the shelter with me? It kinda makes me nervous to go there on my own."

"Hell yes. No way are you living there without my approval."

"Thanks." The ice cubes clicked together as I swirled my glass. "Think it will all work out in the end?"

Her smile faded, and she nodded, seriousness flashing in her eyes. "I do. Hang in there, okay? Just a bit longer. You'll see, everything will fall into place when the timing is right."

"I'll try." Reality hit me. Like a ton of bricks straight to my chest. I was on my own. Ellie would leave in a couple of days, and I would have no one else to rely on. The thought scared the shit out of me, and I tried to mask my fears with a small smile, so my best friend wouldn't abandon her own life to fix mine. Because Ellie was *that* selfless and she would sacrifice her own dreams if she thought I couldn't manage on my own.

Her voice snapped me out of my drowning thoughts. "Tomorrow we'll drive to Memphis, sleep there, and come back in time for your appointment on Friday afternoon. How does it sound?"

"Great."

"I heard Round and Round is the place to be on Thursday nights during the summer. They have trivia nights every week. And we, girl, rock at those. Wanna go?"

I nodded. "Yes. Could be fun. To be young and carefree for a night."

She raised her glass to clink my empty one. "To us."

"To us," I repeated. At that moment, I chose to lock all my fears down and enjoy the time we had left together before facing the reality check waiting for me in a couple of days.

———

"This will be your room," Martha, the supervisor of the Baby and Me shelter said, opening the door to a small bedroom with a single bed, a crib, a sink, and a closet. "I know it's not much but for the time you are here, it is yours."

She had short brown hair sprinkled with gray strands, and her eyes were a deep shade of brown. She was a petite woman with broad shoulders and a soft expression on her face, reminding me of my late grandmother.

I surveyed the space. My lower lip quivered, and I bit down on it, determined not to let my emotions get the better of me. The room was simple: white walls that needed a fresh coat of paint, a steel bed frame with a mattress that looked clean enough, a rectangular birch crib with baby-yellow sheets and blankets, mocha-colored carpet, and a padded rocking chair tucked into the corner beside a window framed by dark curtains that still let the sunlight in.

"It-it's perfect," I murmured.

Beside me, Ellie squeezed my hand in hers. "You sure, Abby?"

I nodded, casting another glance around the room. "Yeah. Huh…I'll take it."

"Awesome," Martha said, pressing a protective hand on

my forearm. "Most girls here have been through a lot. Many fled abusive relationships or ended up homeless. A few were using hard drugs and are now trying to get clean and sober. We have an alarm system and cameras all over the property. Breakfast is served between seven and eight, and dinner between six and seven. Lunch is your responsibility. We have a nurse who comes once a week for health checkups. And workshops every Tuesday." She lifted a hand and began counting things off on her fingers. *"Healthy habits for a healthy pregnancy. What to expect when in labor. How to care for a newborn. Breastfeeding. Juggling responsibilities as a new mother."*

"Okay."

"We encourage you to find a job and save money so you can afford your own place within six months. If your stay is to be longer, we'll sit together and talk about your options. We won't throw you out onto the street without resources, but we do expect you to put in the work to regain your independence. We have a used clothes store next door that is run by our residents. You can pick a few shifts there, if you like, based on their availabilities. And you can also work in the kitchen if you can't find a job outside of here or if your security is at risk. We'll talk about all of this once you move in."

She offered me a warm smile that I returned the best I could. All this seemed surreal. Like I was stuck in a dream I had no way of waking up from.

"Abigail, do you have any questions?"

I shook my head. "Huh…no. Not for now. I think you covered it all."

"Oh," Martha exclaimed as if she had forgotten something. "Bathrooms are down the hall. You don't have your own, but there are six shower stalls, and they're kept clean.

There's even a baby station with a bathtub, a changing table, and everything you might need."

"O-okay."

"When are you due?"

I swallowed. Nobody except my doctor and Ellie had ever asked or taken an interest in my pregnancy. "September sixteen."

"You'll have enough time to get familiar with the installations until then. So, I'll see you on Monday morning?"

I bowed my head and forced a smile out. Tears flowed down my cheeks. I couldn't comprehend why a perfect stranger would help me out and show me acceptance when my own parents had refused to.

Martha hugged me. She was in her late fifties and had a motherly look and gentleness spread across her features. "It's okay, sweetie. I know what it's like. I was in your situation once. You'll do great. I can tell. All you need is to get back on your feet to feel in control. And I'm here for you. Always. My bedroom is on the second floor. You can knock on the door night and day. The best reward for me is when I see my girls thriving after they leave this place. It's normal to feel overwhelmed and emotional. Those damn pregnancy hormones are the real deal, and your life has been uprooted, but you'll get there, I swear."

"Th…thanks."

"Anytime. Let me show you around. Come on, follow me."

In the hallway, Ellie and I kept a short distance from Martha.

"Hey, are you sure you are fine with moving here?" my friend asked. "We can find another place if you're not."

"Yeah. I've never pictured myself living in a shelter… and depending on other people to get through my life. It's a lot to take in." I inhaled a cleansing breath, trying to hold myself together.

"The lady is right, though. Give yourself some time, and you'll be back to being the fearless Abby I know. You call me if it's not working, and we'll figure out something else."

I squeezed her hand, not sure I could let go anytime soon. Once I did, everything would become real—and I'd be alone. "Thanks."

Chapter 18

We arrived in Memphis the next day around noon. Sitting on the deck of Roasted, a bistro on Beale Street, Ellie and I scanned every male about our age passing by. The vibe here reminded me of my hometown. Restaurants, bars, and shops lined both sides of the busy street. Tourists and locals filled the side-walks. Music poured out from the open windows, a mix of country, jazz, blues, and rock 'n' roll. The breeze carried the scent of barbecue and burgers, while the red awning over the deck provided much-needed shade from the scorching sun above.

The server neared our table, a pad and pencil in her hand. She tipped a hip forward, chewing gum as if her life depended on it. "Can I get you two anything to drink?" she asked in a cold, nonchalant tone.

"Iced tea," Ellie said.

"Lemonade for me," I added.

Before she turned around, Ellie asked her the same question she'd been asking everyone we'd come face to face with since arriving in town. "Excuse me. Would you happen to know anyone around twenty years old named Andy? Dark hair, tall, broody, musician."

The woman seemed to think for a minute, blowing a bubble with her gum. "Does he have a last name?"

My best friend and I shook our heads.

"Sorry. I can't think of anyone."

"Thanks," I murmured, another thread of hope in me breaking as she padded away.

For the rest of the afternoon, we visited all bars close to downtown and stopped groups of people our age who appeared to be locals and asked them the same question. In vain.

Without a picture to show them or a last name, it was of no use.

After we booked a hotel room and dropped our luggage, Ellie and I made our way to Round and Round, ready for trivia night. She had fixed my hair in a half up-do and convinced me to wear the pair of jeans she'd gotten me and a black lacy top. For a second when I admired my reflection in the bathroom mirror, I felt young and sexy again. Not pregnant.

My heels dug into the worn wooden floor, and I gasped as we neared the front door. The place was jam-packed, and the aroma of beer and chicken wings hit me the second we walked in.

The lights were dimmed just enough to give the place a warm, welcoming atmosphere.

Ellie leaned against me and nudged my side. "Told you it was the place to be," she whispered in my ear. "So many people. Let's hope BD is here."

"BD?" I asked, my eyebrows bunching together.

"Baby Daddy. That's our codename for tonight."

"Oh."

I looked around, enjoying the lively ambiance of the crowded bar as my gaze glided over every guy's face. Country music played on the speakers embedded in the ceiling. Black leather booths were arranged in a semicircle, surrounding wooden tables and facing a small stage. Behind the bar, a beer-and-snack menu written in neon-colored chalk covered the black wall.

A guy with heavily tattooed arms and wearing dark skinny jeans and a sleeveless plaid shirt met us, a pile of menus under his arm. "How many?"

"Two," I answered. "We're here for trivia night."

His eyes trailed down my body, and I saw the surprise flashing in his eyes when he noticed I was pregnant. For an instant, I wanted to leave, crawl back into my skin, unsure how to act when people eyed me with curiosity. But then Ellie elbowed me, and I remembered I was growing a human being, not dealing drugs, and straightened my posture. I had nothing to be ashamed of. I was done feeling guilty about my situation. The guy smiled at me, and my reservations melted away. I caught a glint in his eye before he turned his gaze back to me. Good, he wasn't judging me. "A team must have between six and eight players to participate. Are you meeting anyone else?"

A guy with tousled blond hair, about our age, put a hand on both Ellie's and my shoulders.

"How is it going, Jonah?" the tattooed server asked.

"Great." Jonah's attention returned to Ellie and me. "Girls, today is your lucky day. My friends and I are a party of four tonight. If you wanna join us, we're one of the teams to beat." He pointed to the all-star board on our left. "The Clumsy Starfish. That's us. See? We're second in the best overall scores so far this year. Why would you wanna play with anyone else?" He cocked a brow, a smug smirk taking over his face, but in a kind of charming way.

"Whoa, you guys are good." Ellie hissed. "You'll be better with us. We are your secret weapon. We're in."

A minute later, we followed Jonah to his booth and sat down at the table as he introduced us to everyone.

"Luke, you're in charge of checking the chronometer. Ritz, you get the last word and vote when we don't agree. Abby, you're the designated secretary," he said, pointing at me from across the table. This guy was running a serious business here. No doubt that explained why they were at the top of the board. "Girls, you'd better bring your A-game. I hope you're ready to crush the Rock 'n' Tomatoes. They don't stand a chance with our two new special-weapon players." He winked at Ellie and me, and I realized I was right in my earlier assessment, and that trivia night was the real deal for these guys. They played to win.

I nodded. "Oh. Huh, okay. No pressure at all."

He offered us a mischievous grin. "You girls were the ones who said we'd be better with you."

The golf pencil he pushed across the table rolled over the surface and slipped into the gap between the seat cushion and the backrest. "Oops. Sorry, Abby."

I waved him off. "No biggie." I pushed my hand into the space and felt something metallic as my fingers closed around the pencil. "What's that?" I asked no one but myself.

The coin looked like a regular quarter, but upon closer inspection, it was fake. It was adorned with the image of a green frog on one side, and the word *Luck* was engraved on the other. My pulse increased as I turned the coin between my fingers. Even though it sounded silly, it reminded me of Andy. Being here, in this town, in a bar he might or might not have ever frequented, and the frog icon. A rush of memories from the night we'd shared back then resurfaced.

"Hey, are you okay?" Ellie asked from beside me as Jonah kept giving instructions.

I bobbed my head and swallowed. "Yeah. Sure." My fist closed around the small object, and I forced a curl on my lips. "Let's do this."

She touched my arm and pulled me closer. "I'm glad we're doing this. Together. You deserve some fun."

"Me too. Thanks for coming, Elles."

"Always."

I placed the coin in my pocket. Not sure why, but somehow, I felt like I had to hold on to it. Like it would mean something. One day. A treasure someone had lost and I was lucky enough to find.

———

Eating a late snack in our hotel room, Ellie and I lay in bed, talking, with the television playing in the background. My friend reached for my hand and squeezed it between hers. "I know my timing sucks, but I want you to know the truth."

I turned to face her, my hand frozen midair with a handful of popcorn, waiting for her to explain.

"Tom and I are dating. Officially."

A high-pitched shriek left my mouth, and I jumped to my knees to hugged my best friend. "Ohmygod, I knew it. That whole friends-with-benefits thing you've got going on was just a shitty excuse to avoid putting a label on your relationship. I'm so excited for you."

She cleared her throat, pulling away, and studied my face for a long second. "You're okay with it?"

"Why wouldn't I be? It's the best news. You guys have

been dating for a while, and you were the only two who didn't realize it."

She tilted her head back and laughed. "No, we weren't."

I joined in her laughter. "Yes, you were. Stop denying it. The guy is head over heels in love with you. That much is evident."

Her laughter died down. "You think?"

"Oh, Ellie, you're even more blind than I thought. And I know for a fact you love him too. It's written all over your face when you talk about him."

Her cheeks turned crimson. "Well, I don't... I... It's just... Okay, fine. I love him."

I pumped my fist and did a little victory dance before sitting back down. "Knew it. Have you told him yet?"

"Nah. I'm not one to disclose my feelings first. I'll wait until he says it, then I'll reciprocate."

"Suit yourself. Anyway, I'm so happy for you. You guys just fit together."

She blushed darker. "Thanks."

I was truly happy for my friend. If someone deserved love and happiness, it was her. She was the most selfless person I knew, often putting everyone else's needs before her own.

For the rest of the night, we chatted like we used to when we were roommates in college and fell asleep beside each other. Even though our stay in Memphis didn't go as planned—and by that I meant, we didn't cross paths with Andy—we still had a good time, and I was thankful for having my best friend along with me for the ride.

The next day, after we ate breakfast on the deck of a little restaurant downtown, scanning each male about our age walking by for one last time, Ellie and I made our way back to Nashville.

I napped during the second half of the drive and woke up to the mouthwatering smell of burgers Ellie had grabbed from a takeout joint.

We arrived in town just in time for my sonogram appointment.

"It's okay, right? If I come in?" Ellie asked when the nurse called my name.

"Yes. Please."

"Cool." She looked nervous, her hand crushing mine, as she walked next to me toward the exam room. "Can we know the sex?"

"It's possible…huh…I think. According to the motherhood book I'm reading, it should be."

"You wanna find out?"

I debated the idea in my head. "Not sure. Everything has been a surprise so far. And learning the sex is something I would have wanted to share with Andy. If he were here." My shoulders sagged forward as if I carried the weight of the world. "Somehow it feels wrong to know it while he's not aware of anything."

"I get it."

"I have a hunch it's a boy, but let's not find out today."

The nurse took my vitals and some blood work before I met with the doctor, and he asked a bunch of questions. The entire time, my heart pounded in my chest. He looked relieved when I admitted I would be moving into the Baby and Me shelter, and Martha would look after me.

After he handed me packs of vitamins and other supplements, he led us to the sonogram room, where I lay on my back and lifted my shirt to expose my stomach. With a towel protecting my clothes, the doctor applied some blue jelly to my skin and talked us through the images on the black-and-white screen.

Ellie's grip on my hand tightened when we heard the baby's heartbeat.

We looked at each other, both of us crying as we watched tiny feet and arms waving on the screen while the doctor took some measurements.

"This is so amazing," my friend said, her jaw hanging open.

"Do you wanna know the sex?" the doctor asked as he handed me a series of printed images of my baby.

I inhaled a deep breath and shook my head. "Nah. I think I'll wait."

Ellie and I exchanged a watery smile. "Can I have a picture too?" she asked.

After I nodded at the doctor, he printed her a copy.

"I'll be the best auntie in the entire world, I swear."

I laughed through my tears. "I have no doubt."

We hugged after the doctor left, and I fixed myself up before meeting him in his office for a final conversation.

———

"We need to celebrate," Ellie said as we returned to our hotel.

"Celebrate? What occasion?" I gestured around me with my hand. "My new living arrangements? My emancipation?"

"No, silly. We saw your baby today. And it was the most magical thing I've ever witnessed. Also, we went on a road trip together and our team won trivia night. We're also celebrating the beginning of this new chapter of your life. It may not seem like what you want right now, but believe me when I say it might be what you need."

I halted and pivoted to face her. "What do you mean?"

"Like a blessing disguised as a warped situation. Something you need to go through in order to get where you gotta be. Does it make sense?"

I assessed her words in my head for a beat. "Yeah. Kinda." I squeezed her hand. "I hope you're right."

"When was the last time I was wrong?" She cocked a brow, and we both burst out laughing. "So, celebration?"

"Yes. And I know just the place."

An hour later, we sat facing each other at Wild and Country, one of the most popular venues on Broadway. No matter how much time I'd spent away, every time I came back to town, I remembered why Nashville was my favorite place to be. It wasn't just about the music or the food, but also the energy, the people, the vibe. I loved everything about my hometown.

"What are we having?" Ellie asked.

"I swear, everything is good here. We could take a few dishes and share. What do you think?"

"All in."

We raised our glasses full of bubbly, alcohol-free cider.

"To us," Ellie said. "And you. And that baby you're growing inside that belly of yours. To new beginnings, new adventures, and being brave." She scratched her temple with the fingers of her free hand. "Did I miss something?"

I nodded. "To you. My best friend in the entire world. Thanks for sticking by my side when no one else did. Thanks for making me believe I can do this, and that I'm strong enough to go through it on my own. And cheers to making your relationship with Tom official. I love you."

"Forever."

We clinked our glasses, and I blinked to chase the tears forming in my eyes.

The live band playing on the small stage at the front of the bar-slash-restaurant was led by a woman in her early thirties with blue hair. I had never heard of her before. Old Abby would have known everyone who played here before they even set foot on that stage.

The new Abby was so busy with everything else, trying to figure her life out, that she couldn't keep up with everything happening in the music scene. I missed that part of my life. Sitting here, listening to her soulful melody, I promised myself I wouldn't lose that side of me. Sure, I could put her aside for the time being, but as soon as things settled down, I would dust her off and get back into the game.

"She's good," Ellie said, swaying on her chair as she sipped her drink.

"Yep. I love her sound. It's like a tragic love story. It gives me goose bumps." A loud yawn slipped past my lips, and I stifled it with a palm over my mouth.

"Wanna stay for the main act?" my friend asked. "It was supposed to be a band, but I heard some girl in the restroom earlier say they canceled at the last minute. It's supposed to be new talent."

Music was my passion. What made my soul vibrate.

But the tiny peanut growing inside me had become my main purpose. Right now, as it kicked around, a wave of exhaustion washed over me.

"I wish. I'm so tired. It's like the pressure of the last few days is finally catching up to me." I looked around, watching people eating and chatting, as the girl kept delivering her soul through her lyrics on the stage. "Would you hate me if we went back to our room?"

Ellie stretched her arm over the table and enveloped my hand with hers. "Never. It's been a crazy week. I would be drained too if I were you." She began to stand. "Let me pay the check, and we can go."

"Elles, you don't have to."

The smile that said *Don't argue with me, it's a waste of time* flashed on her face. The one I'd come to know well over the last few months."My treat."

"Thanks." I winced. "Shoot. Gimme a sec, this baby is pressing on my bladder. I'll be right back." Before she could add a word, I was hurrying toward the back of the bar to relieve myself for the third time in the last hour.

I still couldn't believe this had become my life.

When I returned, Ellie waved at me and gestured to meet her by the exit.

With our arms linked together, we walked back to our hotel.

Ellie pressed her cheek against my shoulder. "*Gurrrl*, it's too bad you're not on the market right now because I saw a guy when I went to pay the check, who was totally your type. He was eating by himself. Under any other circumstances, I would have played matchmaker."

I sighed. "One day, Elles. One day, I'll go back to dating." I paused, a million questions swirling in my head. "Do you think guys will wanna go out with me? I'll be a single mother… Isn't that a turn-off for most people?"

My friend's grip on my arm tightened. "Abby, look at you. You are smart, gorgeous, strong. You are a total catch. Any guy in his right mind would want to date you… The one you're supposed to be with won't care if you are a single mom. He'll see it as your strength, not your weakness. He'll love you, no matter what. If he doesn't, then he's not the one for you. And he's a jerk, and I'll kick his ass."

A loud laugh bubbled out of my throat. "What would I ever do without you?"

"You'd do just fine, *gurrrl*."

Her words played on a loop in my head for the rest of the walk to our hotel.

Chapter 19

Anderson

I changed my plans. Instead of driving straight to New York City, like I had decided when I had left my mother's house in a hurry, I stayed in Nashville for three days. I had even secured a gig on Broadway for Friday night. Turns out I went to a bar-slash-restaurant for lunch and ended up talking with the owner. Tucker Philips. A Chicago transplant who had gone from hedge fund banking to owning a country music bar. He part-owned Wild and Country with his wife and some other guy.

I was sold in no time. The food was delicious, and the atmosphere was everything I loved about a joint in Nashville. From time to time, he even had big names in country music playing on his stage.

"My main act for the night just canceled on me. Think you have what it takes to replace them?"

I flashed him my biggest grin. "Yep. I totally do. Wanna hear some of my stuff?"

"Sure."

He took the stool to my left, and I showed him clips of my last three performances on my phone.

"Okay, you are *that* good. I was wondering if you were just cocky."

"Never, man. So, is it a yes for tonight?"

"Absolutely. The stage is yours, kid. Be here at seven. You'll start at eight."

"Sounds great."

He clapped my shoulder and left me to my burger.

For the rest of the afternoon, I strolled around town. I loved everything about this city. The music, the people, the food, the ambiance, the bars. Sitting on a bench overlooking the Cumberland River, I tried to sort through my chaotic thoughts and find my calm. The idea of playing on Broadway tonight was the biggest adrenaline rush I'd had in forever. A dream of mine. Half of me wanted to say screw it to my college education and jump-start my musical career right now. But I had made a promise to my mother that I would be free to pursue any career I wanted, as long as I had a degree. I had two years of college left to hold up my end of the bargain. Still, I couldn't wait to be done with it and live my dream.

I returned to Wild and Country around six, in time to grab a bite before my set. Indulging in the best Southern chicken fries I'd ever had, I watched the live band led by a blue-haired girl singing her heart out. The lyrics that came out of her mouth sounded as if they were coming straight from her soul.

The band that had taken the stage earlier, when I'd first come here for lunch, was good, but they only played cover songs. When I performed, I always played my own compositions in between well-known songs the crowd could sing along to.

I loved the fact that the band right now was only playing original material. Just from the way their lead singer sang, I could tell she had probably written every single one of their songs—that they spoke to her and were a part of her.

I focused on the food on my plate when my skin prickled with awareness.

My spine tingled, and my senses went on high alert.

It had never happened before. Well, it had. Only once. The night Abby and I met last winter. When she had walked into that café, I had felt an unfamiliar sensation trail down my back. And when she had touched my hand, my pulse had quickened in a way it never had before.

With a roll of my shoulders, I tried to erase the feeling. No matter what I did, it stayed with me. Perhaps it was the idea of playing here. In a town I loved like my own and a stage that sometimes hosted some of my idols.

Still, a warm flush traveled along my core.

Looking around, I tried to spot anyone I might know. A figure that stood out in the crowd. Someone my soul recognized. Most people having dinner looked like they had just gotten off from work. A few tables were occupied by couples or friends enjoying happy hour.

My gaze settled on a girl about my age with platinum blonde hair swaying on her chair by herself and watching the band perform. Two half-eaten plates of food rested in front of her. She had company. I felt like a creep and brought my focus back to my own meal.

Scrolling through my phone, I killed time before it was my turn to shine onstage.

The girl I'd spied on earlier walked by my table as she followed a server to the bar. I watched her pay the check. Our eyes met, and a lopsided smile tilted her lips. She was pretty, but I felt no connection whatsoever as I stared at her for a fraction of a second.

She nodded in my direction, waved at someone, and moved toward the door, her night here over.

The air surrounding me eased. Whoever that girl was, I had no idea why my body had reacted to her presence. It didn't add up. If we were destined to meet, wouldn't I have felt attracted to her the moment our gazes met? Or felt some kind of connection? Love was confusing sometimes.

I gave my head a little shake. I was being silly and not making much sense.

Pushing the thought away, I shoved a hand into my pocket, searching for my lucky penny. The one that had followed me around for as long as I could remember. I'd always put it in my guitar case whenever I played a show.

When my fingers didn't connect with the familiar coin, I recalled I had misplaced it. Somehow. Somewhere. When I was in Memphis. I had no idea when it went missing exactly, but I'd realized it disappeared the night I played my set at Rock 'n' Country, the bar Rufus's dad owned.

I remembered everything went to hell when I couldn't find it. Yep, it was the night I got into that fight with my mother over my father. Fucking great.

Deciding to put that episode behind me, I finished my plate, and with minutes to spare before seven, I met Tucker in his office.

I knocked on the ajar door, and he invited me in. "Come on in. Ready, kid, or are you having cold feet?"

"As ready as I'll ever be. I wanted to thank you for the opportunity. It's a big deal for me to play here, and I'm grateful."

"You're welcome. Entertain my crowd and give a great show, and I'll call you back when I have openings."

"Huh…well. I live in New York City right now. I'm just here for a few days."

"College?"

"Yeah. Two years to go. Degree in music."

He nodded. "Wow. Love it. Proves you are serious." He sat back in his chair, one leg crossed over the other, his ankle resting on his knee. The man radiated effervescent energy, and for a second, I could picture him in a suit as a restless banker.

I sighed. "Yeah, but I'd much prefer to be here and play music every day instead."

"I can tell you have talent. Why not get a degree? It's never wasted. And who knows? It could turn out to be useful down the road."

"Why did you move here? If it's not too personal?"

"I fell in love. She liked it here. Sold everything, quit my job, and made a life for myself in town. I've never looked back."

I chuckled. "There's always a girl, right?"

He returned my laughter. "Yep. Always. When you find the one, never let her go. I almost lost mine once… Biggest mistake of my life." He turned around the picture frame set on his desk to show me his family. His wife was beautiful. Blonde hair and blue eyes so sparkling it reminded me of a girl with jet-black hair. A contrast to his dark skin, black crew-cut hair, and brown eyes. Their kids had mocha skin and curly brown hair and were a perfect mix of both their parents.

"They are beautiful. Seems like you rectified that mistake."

He nodded, staring at the picture, a smile drawing on his lips, clearly lost in some old memories. "Yeah. They are my entire world. It hasn't always been easy, and we've been through some really tough times, but in the end, it was all worth it." His attention returned to me. He stood and circled his desk, gesturing to the door. "Come with me. Let's get you set up."

Excitement bubbled inside me, and I had a hard time not grinning like a fool as we neared the back of the stage. Perhaps later I'd have to pinch myself to make sure I'd really performed here.

The night passed in a blur. Everything felt surreal, almost dreamlike. I played for nearly two hours. The crowd was ecstatic, and the more I strummed my guitar and sang, the more my mood improved, and the easier it became to push my parents' lies to the back of my mind.

Mid-set, Tucker met me onstage and handed me a bottle of water. "Man, you are more than talented. Fuck, I wish you lived in the city full-time. Whenever you're around, let me know. I'll find a spot for you. We exchanged a handshake, and he pointed to the bar at the back of the room. "Grab a snack or a drink when you're done. Whatever you want. It's on the house."

"Thanks. I appreciate it."

The rest of the night was electric, and I kept a thirty-minute slot open for special requests. I was so riled up I could have played for hours. I wasn't tired, but energized, as I strummed the first chords of the last song of the night.

People clapped and cheered, and it filled me with uncontainable joy.

"You're Anderson?" a man I recognized as Riley Burns, Nashville's most sought-after music manager, neared me while I was storing my guitar in its case after my set. Yes, I would really have to pinch myself later.

"Yes."

He held out his hand, and I shook it. "It's an honor to meet you, sir. Anderson Ford."

"Riley Burns. Don't sir me, man. I'm not my father." And, at that instant, I realized the man standing before me was none other than the son of Curtis Burns, a country music legend and one of my all-time idols. "That show you gave was incredible. I would love to talk to you when you have some time." He pushed a business card into my hand. "Call my assistant first thing Monday morning, and she'll schedule a meeting."

I swallowed my nervousness. "Huh, I-I won't be in town next week."

"No problem. She'll work with your schedule."

I scratched the nape of my neck. "The thing is that I don't live here... I'm studying in New York. Actually, I'm on my way there because I have gigs booked for the next couple of months and a job I need to return to."

Riley watched me with a frown and blinked. "You serious?"

"Totally. I promised my mother I'd finish my degree before pursuing a music career." I sighed. "Two years to go. As soon as I graduate, I'm free to do whatever I want. Until then, I have to focus on my studies. I only play for fun... Weddings. Receptions. Bars. Office parties."

"You know who I am, right?"

"You're the man behind Carter Hills's success. You are the best in the business."

"And yet, you prefer to finish your degree in—"

"Music."

He nodded and shoved his hands into his pockets. "Interesting. I respect you, kid. You have some spine. Let's make a deal here and now."

I bobbed my head. Riley Burns, manager extraordinaire, was showing an interest in me. This alone was like winning the lottery.

"Two years. As soon as you get your diploma, you call

my office, and we'll schedule that meeting. How does it sound? You have raw talent, man. And I can take you to the top if we work together."

"Thank you, si—Riley."

He turned to leave but stopped and lifted two fingers in my direction. "Two years, man. Find me or I'll come find you."

"Met Burns?" Tucker asked when I went to collect my pay. "The guy is the best in the business, and he was really impressed by your talent."

I swallowed down the emotions clogging my airways. I still couldn't believe Riley Burns had shown interest in me and I'd turned him down. "Yeah. He's like a superstar in the business."

"He sees a lot of emerging talent, but between you and me, he always says they all sound the same. You have that *je-ne-sais-quoi* that makes you unique. The guy is always looking for that little something that makes you different from the rest of the crowd. You'd be a fool not to call him. Just sayin'." We exchanged one last handshake. "Anyway, whenever you're in town and you wanna play, reach out."

"Sure thing. Thanks again. For giving me a chance."

On the sidewalk, I took a deep inhale of the night air. It was thick with humidity and carried a faint scent of barbecue and summer.

With nowhere to go and too exhausted to drive, now that the adrenaline had worn off, I decided to spend the night at a hotel. With the amount Wild and Country had paid me and the hefty tips I'd received tonight, I had made a generous sum of money, and I deserved a little reward. Aka, a hot shower and a real bed.

Within walking distance, I booked a room at The Row, a hotel with decent room prices and an industrial vibe.

Under the covers, I replayed the night in my mind. I couldn't believe I might have been signed to a major label soon—and I'd turned it down.

What a fucking joke.

Chapter 20
Abigail

Sunday came too early, and I bawled my eyes out when Ellie left after dinner. I drove her to the airport and kept the rental until the morning. Earlier, we had moved all my possessions to the shelter, but she'd insisted on keeping the hotel room for one more night so I could, as she put it, "indulge." I had one last night at the hotel, all by myself, in this little bubble my best friend had created before the next chapter of my life truly began.

In the comfort of the queen bed, dressed in nothing but a white terrycloth robe, I watched a movie on TV, eating my weight in room service. Ellie had ordered me a buffet of chicken and pasta, dumplings, and chocolate cake with a side of ice cream.

My eyes landed on the small, square black-and-white picture I'd put in a frame that rested on the bedside table.

With a hand over my belly, I spoke to my baby. Something I did more and more often these days. Somehow, I felt less alone, knowing I had someone to talk to.

"Your auntie Ellie left earlier. It's just the two of us now. I-I hope you can hear me. The truth is…I'm still scared about this whole thing, and I know I'll make mistakes along the way, but hang in there, okay? Things will get better. Not sure how, but I have faith. Tonight, we can still pretend everything is going according to plan, because tomorrow is unknown. I…I have… I have no clue what to expect."

I felt the baby fluttering in my stomach, and it brought a tilt to my lips.

"Tomorrow, we'll have a new home, you and I. A temporary home. Until I find a job and we can get our own place. Let's make the most of our last night here, okay? I need the rest. And soon we'll live with other people, so things might not be as calm as they are now."

After I brushed my teeth, I slid under the comforter, and in no time, sleep claimed me.

———

My first day at the shelter wasn't that bad. I met Lucinda and Chloe. Lucinda was twenty-four and had a one-year-old little boy and a three-year-old daughter. She had escaped an abusive relationship three months ago. Chloe was sixteen and seven and a half months pregnant. She had run away from home at fourteen and lived in the street and crossed the country, jumping from one train wagon to the other for the last year. She'd been raped one night while high in an alley. Since moving here four months ago, she told me she had stayed clean. Chloe worked ten hours a week at the used clothes store in the lobby of the building next door, and her goal was to get her high school diploma after giving birth. Her baby would be placed for adoption. She had already chosen a nice family and couldn't wait to get out of here. Both of them had taken me under their wings the moment I walked in.

Perhaps if I had friends while staying here, things wouldn't be so bad.

Now, in the privacy of my own room, I was curled up in a ball under the covers. Everything about this place felt foreign, and for the first time since I had left my parents' house, sadness hit me, and I couldn't keep the tears at bay any longer.

For the longest time, I was a sobbing mess, clutching the blanket around me, wishing I could teleport myself anywhere else. I hated being here on my own. It reminded me of the time I went to summer camp when I was nine and couldn't sleep because I felt like I didn't belong.

My entire body shook as more sobs rocked me.

Six months ago, I had my life all planned. My ducks were in a row. I was a girl with a goal. Now I was lost. My inner child felt rejected. My teenage self felt unworthy. All I wished for was some parental love. A hand to hold on to. Support. Acceptance.

"How did my life turn into this?" I asked no one. "How did I go from the kickass girl I used to be to sleeping in a women shelter?"

The injustice of losing my college scholarship hurt more now than it did before.

Anger at Andy for not being here ate me up inside. I usually found excuses not to blame him for my situation, but right now I was upset. He did this to me and didn't have to deal with any of the consequences.

He'd thrive while I would have to put all my own ambitions on the back burner to raise *our* child. The one we'd made together. Why was *I* the only one dealing with it then?

Tears blurred my vision. My entire self ached at the thought I had no one.

I didn't wanna be here. For an instant, I fought with the urge to pack all my shit up and leave. Where would I go? Back to Silverville and live with Ellie? She had her boyfriend, her life, and school. And I had none of those. She would feel obligated to care for me and the baby, no matter how it impacted her own life.

No, I wasn't selfish. Ellie already had done enough to help me. I wouldn't burden her with my mistakes.

This was it. Loneliness had never felt so lonely before.

With my arms around me, I rocked back and forth, trying to soothe myself and bring some comfort to my pain.

By the time my tears subsided a little, my eyes burned, and exhaustion wrapped itself tightly around me. I fisted the covers harder, praying sleep would claim me and bring me a little peace, even if only for now.

All day, I had watched my phone, longing for a miracle. My parents pleading with me to come back home. Or for Andy to have found me.

No, at this late hour, my hopes were dead.

My sobs resumed and choked me as I recalled everything I had left behind. Doubts crippled me.

I was just a kid.

How could I become a mother? I had no real-life experiences. And I had no idea where I was going. I was desperate for someone to love me. And even though I had never admitted it out loud, the idea of giving birth freaked me out. Already, my changing body wasn't easy to accept. Since I had ditched the baggy clothes, I couldn't hide the truth anymore. I couldn't pretend the pregnancy wasn't happening when I was out and about.

To add to my new insecurities, I had noticed how people were watching me when I went to the pharmacy or when Ellie and I strolled through town. Some showed sympathy while others judged me, without knowing anything about my situation.

My gaze trailed around the dark bedroom. I hated everything this place represented. My heartbeats increased. My fingers clenched the covers tighter. In the darkness, everything appeared worse. I craved sunlight. And a bedroom I was acquainted with. Light. Colors.

Hours passed, and I had no idea when I'd finally abandoned myself to sleep.

When I woke up the next morning, I took in my swollen eyes and the redness of my cheeks in the mirror over the sink.

Once I joined everyone else for breakfast, they would be able to tell I'd been crying most of the night.

Dressed in the jeans Ellie had gotten me and Tom's sweatshirt because it was the one piece of clothing that felt comforting right now, I slipped my feet into a pair of flip-flops. With careful steps, I climbed down the stairs after locking my bedroom door.

"Good morning," said a woman with dark skin whom I hadn't met yet. "I'm Desiree, the nurse. Are you Abigail?"

I nodded. "Abby." My voice sounded low and shaky, my throat still sensitive after all the tears I'd cried last night.

"We'll find some time to meet after breakfast," she said.

"Oh, huh…okay."

I hid my hands in the sleeves of my shirt, unsure of what to do. Around the table sat four women and three children all aged under five, their plates filled with pancakes, scrambled eggs, and pieces of buttery toast.

Desiree must have sensed my queasiness because she motioned me toward the breakfast buffet with one hand between my shoulder blades. "Here, honey. Grab a plate and some food. You need those vitamins and all the energy you can get."

She poured orange juice into a glass and handed it to me. "Drink this."

"Th-thanks."

Once again, I nodded and followed her instructions. I returned to the table, and a little boy pointed to the empty chair beside him. "You can sit with me," he said. "I'm Lukas. Who are you?"

I sat down and slid my chair forward. "Abby." I focused on my plate, shy to meet all the residents' curious gazes set on me.

An elbow nudged my side, and when I looked to my left, a wide grin lit up the boy's face. Keeping my head low, I ate while listening to the conversations around the table.

A woman opposite me caught my attention when she offered me a lopsided smile. "Don't worry, you'll get the hang of it quickly. We're family here. Welcome."

The corners of my lips lifted in what I hoped looked like an almost smile.

"My name is Miranda."

My gaze drifted to her pregnant figure.

"I'm five months along. If you need anything, come see me. My bedroom is next to yours. I've been living here for fifteen weeks. I know all there is to know around here."

"Huh, thank you." Why did my voice sound so frail? When did I become so shy that I had trouble holding a conversation?

"You know, I heard you last night," Miranda continued. "It's normal to feel helpless at first. And lost. We all go through this phase. It gets better. With time."

Right now, I wished she was speaking the truth.

After my meeting with Desiree, I spent most of the morning trying to make my bedroom mine by putting a few decor items from my boxes here and there. I placed the framed black and white sonogram picture of my baby by the bed, next to the stuffed frog I'd gotten after I learned I was pregnant. Satisfied with the result, I sent a picture to Ellie.

For lunch, I made myself a sandwich from the food I found in the refrigerator, and sauntered through town once I was done, looking for a job. Wearing one of the sundresses Ellie had gifted me and black ballerina shoes, I spent four hours going from business to business to drop off my resume. I was either not experienced enough or too pregnant or too young for all the places where they were hiring.

Defeated and about to get into another crying fest, I returned to the shelter. After three days of unsuccessful job hunting, I decided I needed a better strategy. I wouldn't give up. If I wanted a better life for me and my baby, I had to up my game somehow.

Miranda came to me the moment I entered the house. "Abby, where have you been?" she asked. "You looked sadder than you did a few days ago. How is that even possible?"

I was about to go to my room to avoid this conversation when she tugged at my arm. "Come on. I made pastry and tea. I was on kitchen duty today. Let's chat."

I swallowed. "I'm not really in the mood for a talk right now."

"No getting out of this. I'm sure I can help you."

Too tired to protest, I followed her to the kitchen. She

made me a plate and poured me some tea before we sat on old wooden stools beside each other at the kitchen counter. The cupboards had been painted a soothing teal hue. The black and white checker floor gave the room a retro vibe. A large window opening to the backyard let a lot of light in. The faint scent of lemon floated in the air, bringing a touch of freshness to the entire house, reminding me of cold lemonade on summer days.

"Still looking for a job?" Miranda asked.

I sighed, and my shoulders sagged forward. "Yeah. Nobody wants to hire a pregnant nineteen-year-old college dropout."

She squeezed my hand. "Been there. I was twenty-three, but I get it. Ever thought of working from home?"

"What do you mean?"

"Virtual assistant. It's like a personal assistant job, but you do it remotely. You can take as many clients as you wish, as many hours as you want, and fit your schedules around your obligations."

"Can I make enough money to afford an apartment and stuff?"

"Yes. As I said, you choose what works best for you. One of my clients, a food truck owner, is looking to add hours and I'm overbooked. I can't take any more. I could give him your name if you want. The salary is decent, and all you gotta do is update his social media feeds every day, sometimes three times a day, reply to his emails, and answer customers' inquiries. Once a week, you fill out orders with his suppliers. He has just bought two more trucks, so he needs all the help he can get during the day, as he's busy cooking and dealing with all the accounting stuff and employees."

"You serious? You would refer me?"

"Totally. You look like a girl with a head on her shoulders who needs a break. To make some money to get out of here, you gotta be organized, efficient, and reliable. And the more clients you get, the more money you make."

"Wow. When can I start?"

"Let me talk to him. Since I already work for him, I could help with the transition. I'm sure you could be fully set by next Monday."

I clasped my hands together under my chin, and for the first time since I'd moved here, something resembling happiness clung to me. And the sky—and my future— didn't look so dark anymore. "Thank you. It means a lot to me. Can I hug you?" I asked, unable to contain my joy at the prospect I could have a job and start making my own money soon.

"Girl, you can hug me anytime you feel like it."

I jumped to my feet and wrapped my arms around her.

She returned the embrace. "I'm glad I could help you. Want to give me a hand in the kitchen tonight? We're making lasagna. This way you'll meet everyone. It's much easier when we help each other out around here."

"I'd be happy to."

"All set then. Meet me back here at four. I gotta go now. I have work hours to put in."

As soon as I got back to my room, I shot Ellie a text message.

ME

Elles, I may have gotten a job. Virtual assistant. If it all works out, I should start Monday.

ELLIE

Yay. I'm so happy for you. I was about to set a foundation in your name and convince my parents to put money into it and pretend it was to save the squirrels in the Amazonian Forest.

ME

You think there are squirrels in the Amazonian Forest?

ELLIE

No, but who cares? They would have done it just to make me happy.

Can we talk later when I get back from work? The internship is not as much fun as I thought it would be, and I am dreading every second of it.

ME

Sure. I need a nap, or I'll faint. Sleep has been rough since I moved here.

ELLIE

Take care of yourself and my niece or nephew.

ME

I'm on kitchen duty tonight so maybe with the time difference, call me at like eight or nine your time.

ELLIE

It's a date. Talk later.

Before I even had time to think about my—fingers crossed—new job, my head hit the pillow and I drifted off to sleep. For once, I let go and enjoyed the rest it provided.

———

"Did you hear the commotion last night?" Rosie, the newcomer, asked.

Rosie's husband had left her with two-year-old twin boys after he emptied all their savings and disappeared with another woman somewhere in Asia. Rosie got evicted, and with no money left in her bank account and one of her children being sick and requiring long stays in the hospital, she had to move in here until she could turn her life around. Her timing was perfect since Chloe had just vacated her room after she gave birth and left town. Chloe and I had been getting closer over the six weeks I'd been here. Perhaps it was our age or our common interest in music, but since she'd left, I missed having her around.

We were sitting on the back deck having lunch. I only had fifteen minutes to spare before going back to my laptop for another five-hour work session.

Rosie continued before I could add a word. "The cops came. It was total chaos for at least an hour."

I was sure I looked like a deer caught in headlights because I had no idea what she was talking about. "What happened?"

"Lucinda's husband. He found her. They had to move her elsewhere in the middle of the night. For her protection. She left with the cops, and they drove her to another shelter."

"What?" I didn't even get a chance to say goodbye. Just like with Chloe, the women I considered friends here were coming and going from my life at such a fast pace I had a hard time keeping up with everything.

During the days, I spent my time locked in my bedroom, working as a virtual assistant. And, after dinner, I usually returned to my room to study. The advisor from Nashville State Community College had agreed to let me enroll in three summer classes I could do remotely so I would get a lighter workload next semester.

It wasn't as fancy as being enrolled at SSB, but at least she thought I could finish my degree remotely in a reasonable time if I put in the hard work. I would have to take a couple of summer classes to compensate for the part-time schedule, but I could do this. Since I was going to be a mother, I was allowed to apply for a scholarship and loan program, which meant all the costs would be covered as long as I was enrolled in school.

For a moment, I thought about applying for a scholarship and loan to go back to SSB, but after I talked with my advisor, she told me most scholarships weren't offered to third-year students, and since I would be studying part-time next semester, I'd be ineligible anyway. If I found one, the scholarship and loans would cover the tuition fees and maybe a bit of living expenses. But other than the apartment—babies weren't allowed in the dorms—food and textbooks fees, I would have to add baby supplies to my growing list of monthly expenses. Diapers and clothes, daycare, and other financial burdens I hadn't thought of. It would leave me with a pretty sum to pay out of my pocket, and I would never be able to go back without bankrupting myself in the process.

Community college was my best bet if I hoped for a degree.

"Gone. Poof. Just like that." Rosie snapped her fingers, and my attention returned to her. "Oh, and she left something for you."

"For me?" My thumb pointed to my chest. "You sure?"

"Yes. Gimme a sec. I'll get it for you." She entered the house, and the door clicked after her. Alone on the deck, I used the few minutes to close my eyes and tilt my head back so the sunrays could warm my face. I could hear birds chirping in the trees surrounding the property and a car's horn somewhere in the distance, reminding me the city was just a few miles away.

The backyard wasn't big, but it was surrounded by a fence and a thick hedge, offering much-required privacy.

The view of the immaculate blue sky eased me and gave me hope that it would all get better.

"Here," Rosie announced when she came back and placed a box on the little wooden table between our loungers.

"What is it?"

She shrugged. "No idea. She just told me to give it to you. Said it would be like having a baby shower early on."

I placed the box on my lap and opened it slowly, peeking inside. Onesies, pajamas, blankets, and other tiny baby clothes and accessories filled it. The sight of all those brought a wave of gratitude mixed with sadness to my eyes.

"Oh," Rosie said, bringing me back to the present. "And she also left a stroller, a car seat, and a pack and play for you in the basement. They are practically new. She didn't have enough room to take them along and left in such a hurry that she only gathered the necessities."

"Wow, this is nice of her. And generous. But it also saddens me she had to go like that and leave all her stuff behind. The circumstances suck."

"Well, it's yours now." She moved to her feet. "Gotta go. The kids will be up from their naps in no time. See you later, Abby."

"Yeah, I need to get back to work anyway. Thanks for all this."

Once in my bedroom, I sat on the bed and hugged my belly as I looked in the distance.

"Hey baby. There's something I haven't told you yet.

Something I've been keeping to myself." I inhaled a shaky breath. This was big news. "If I keep up with this job, as I've been doing for the last five weeks, and with my savings, we should be able to move to our own place very soon. I have a new client for a short-term contract, so I'll have to put in more hours next month, but the pay is amazing. And it will make us enough money to buy you a second-hand crib, a bed for me, and other stuff we might need. Remember Lucinda? She left the shelter last night and has gifted us baby stuff. Lots of it. I think we'll be okay, you and I. I have a great feeling about it. So, I'll start looking at apartments. What do you think? Are you on board with this plan?"

The baby pushed through the wall of my stomach with either a knee or an elbow, and I pushed it back gently. We did this dance three more times.

I laughed my heart out. "I guess it's a yes."

———

Facing the door, I rolled my shoulders back and exhaled. This was it. The moment I hoped my life would make sense again. I wrapped a shaky hand around the doorknob, and using the key I'd gotten earlier, I unlocked the door. Frozen on the threshold, I took it all at once. My new apartment was tiny—the only size I could afford in this city—but it was home. All mine. The place came simply furnished with a two-person round table, black appliances, a brown suede couch, a rectangular coffee table, a TV mounted over a console, a bookshelf, and bed frames in the bedrooms along with nightstands and dressers. A small electric fireplace with a wooden mantle was set in one corner of the living room, next to a window that let in enough daylight to light up the entire place.

I cradled my seven-month-pregnant belly with both hands while I spoke to my baby as I toured the place. "I can't wait for you to see that we have a home. It's not a castle, but it's perfect for us. You'll have your own bedroom. We'll make it ours. I have a few decor ideas for the nursery that I'm sure you're going to love."

My fingertips traced the walls as I entered and exited every room and looked around, unable to tame the smile taking over my face. With my arms stretched out on either side of me, I twirled on myself as I returned to the living room, laughing so much, my face hurt.

"You hear that, baby? This is me. Being happy. And hopeful."

With a pep in my step, I went outside to grab my stuff from the car I'd rented for the day. As I unlocked the doors with the key fob, two hands covered my eyes from behind. I yelped in surprise. A chuckle echoed behind me—one I'd recognize anywhere.

Turning around, I hugged Ellie as much as I could with the baby in the way. "Elles, what are you doing here?"

She mirrored my grin. "First, you look like you're about to burst any second, but you are beautiful, *gurrrl*." She pushed my hair away from my face and studied my expression for a beat. "You look tired but happy. Second, did you really think I would let you move in all by yourself while you are seven months pregnant?"

I blinked. "How… When… What?"

"Martha. I called the shelter. She told me when you were moving out. I wanted to surprise you."

Emotions welled up in my eyes. "You've done it."

I enveloped her in my arms again. "Ohmygod, I missed you so much, you have no idea."

She squeezed me tight. "Me too. So much to tell you.

Sorry I was busy the last couple of weeks. I'm done with that internship now, and I'm all yours."

"How long are you staying?" Now that she was here, the thought of Ellie leaving to go back to college stung.

"A week."

"You're staying with me, right?"

"*Gurrrl*, I wouldn't wanna be anywhere else."

She let go of me and pivoted to open the car's back door, lifting a box labeled *Bedroom* into her arms. I tried to do the same, but she nudged the door shut with her hip before I could grab anything.

"Hey," I protested.

"You are pregnant. Let me do the heavy lifting."

"Nothing is heavy, I swear. I can do this."

"Nope. The only thing you're allowed to do is open the food delivery app on your phone and order us lunch while I bring everything inside."

"But—"

She put her best *Don't argue with me* face on.

"Fine. We'll do it your way. This time only, though."

She smirked. And padded toward the front door of the building as I hurried after her. After a dozen trips to and from the rental car, Ellie slouched on the couch just as the delivery guy rang the buzzer to announce the pizza had arrived.

"Hungry?" I asked my friend.

"Starving."

We set the pizza box on the coffee table in the living room, and with our legs stretched out across it, we grabbed a slice each.

"This is home," I said, grinning like a fool.

"I'm so proud of you right now. Like a mother bird watching her babies fly out of the nest. You did it. I knew you were resilient, and it would pay off."

"Yes." I breathed out. "I did it." Not enough words existed to express the pride waltzing through me. I was still a nineteen-year-old mother-to-be, but I wasn't homeless or a college dropout anymore.

"I was thinking," Ellie swallowed a mouthful before continuing, "while I'm here, we could set up the nursery and everything that needs to be done. And I could also give you a haircut because once you give birth, you won't have time to pamper yourself. I've read you'll lose lots of hair, so better be ready for it. Also, we could go shopping for all the baby stuff you haven't gotten yet so you won't have to do it all on your own when the time comes...or if the baby comes early. What do you think?"

"Elles, this is very nice of you, but you're here on vacation. You don't have to."

"Forget it. I want to. When the semester starts, I won't be able to fly here as often as I'd like. You should take advantage of me while I'm here. Since we have a rental, it will be easier to come and go." She offered me a pointed look. "Accept the help, Abby. And say thank you."

"Okay." I sighed. "Thank you. For everything. It's hard for me to accept your generosity, but even when I freak out about it, I'm still grateful."

She snickered. "See? It wasn't that hard."

I joined in, and we clinked our bottles of water.

"Your timing is quite good, you know?"

Ellie waited for me to explain.

"I have a doctor's appointment in three days. Wanna come along?"

"I wouldn't miss it for the world. After all, I'm the baby's favorite auntie."

We chatted the rest of the afternoon away as we emptied some of the boxes meant for my bedroom, the kitchen, and the bathroom. After I told my best friend about my idea for the nursery, she agreed and promised we'd go to the hardware store in the morning to get started.

"I gotta grab some kitchen stuff and go grocery shopping," I said while we tried to make plans for the night. "The cupboards and drawers are stocked with pots and pans, and plates, cutlery, and glasses, but I still need to get food and basic supplies."

"Let's make a list."

A strange sensation tightened my stomach, and I doubled over, massaging the tight skin of my abdomen to soothe the pain. "Ellie—"

She neared me and kneeled between my legs. "Abby, what's going on?" I could hear the fear lacing her words. "Is it the baby?"

Sweat lined my forehead as the cramp intensified. "No idea, but it hurts." Tears burned the back of my eyes. "Ohmygod, I'm not ready for the baby to come yet. It's too early. Make it stop."

Leading me to a chair, Ellie sat me down. "Don't move. I'll call the doctor."

"Please, baby, stay in there." My words came out as a weak plea.

The contractions eased, but the tears wouldn't stop.

Soon—too soon—I'd have to give birth.

I wasn't ready.

There was no way out of this.

What was I going to do?

Chapter 21

"**M**an, this is heaven," I said when Joe passed me another beer once I emerged from the pool and dropped my ass on a lounger.

The start of the fall semester of our junior year had been one giant party after the other. Since the day I'd left Memphis after the blowout with my mother, I had only spoken to her twice. Things had been strained between us ever since she dropped that bombshell on me. I had no idea how to get over this one. All my life, I had trusted her to make the best decisions for me. But this time, she'd really messed things up. Months later, I still wasn't over it, and my anger hadn't eased. Bethany and I had gone out on a couple of dates, even though I wasn't convinced I wanted to pursue an actual relationship. A few days ago, she'd complained that I wasn't making an effort to spend real time with her. The last thing I needed was to be attached to someone. Once upon a time, I might have thought we could make it work. These days, not so much.

Deep down, I was trying to be invested, but the hurt from my mother's news ran deeper than I had anticipated and affected my emotions.

Our family was a fucking joke. I didn't want to repeat the mistakes my parents had made, so I'd built walls around myself to get through my last two years of college without the burden of caring too much about someone else.

Instead of throwing myself a pity party, I'd decided to act out. Never had I done that before, so it was about time I tried something new. Anyway, none of my previous ways of doing things had worked so far. Being a straight-A student with a good head on my shoulders hadn't served me so far. I'd lost a potential record deal—and the girl I wanted to be with. And maybe I'd lost my soul too somewhere along the way. Nothing was going as planned, and now I did my best not to give a shit about all the things I had no control over.

That was how bad things had gotten.

I, the guy who always looked for serious, long-term commitment and despised one-night stands, was enjoying the bachelor life a bit too much. Abby was still haunting my dreams from time to time, but I had decided not to let her screw with my mind during the day. At night, it was another story, though. Me and my fist often let ourselves get carried away while in the shower or the comfort of my bed when thinking about her and the night we'd shared.

I sighed and scanned the scene around me, letting the sun warm my skin, enjoying the moment. I closed my eyes for a second, and thoughts of my parents came back at full force. They always did. It was a new normal for me. Their mistakes were always at the forefront of my mind.

My entire childhood was a fucking lie. A big fat joke.

And since love and trust had taken a brand-new meaning lately, I had no intention of letting another human being dictate my actions. At twenty years old, I was now reevaluating everything I knew about life. I wouldn't let anyone who hadn't proven they were worth my time get too close.

Even my music had gone darker in the last few months —and sadder.

Gone were the lustful ballads and full of angst melodies.

I was angry, and it showed. My words were cruel and my voice, haunted.

Anderson Ford two-point-zero had taken over, and I had no idea how to send him back to where he belonged.

Today, a bunch of my friends and I were lounging around a pool at the house of a girl from one of our classes whose parents had made it big in the pharmaceutical industry.

All the girls in tiny bikinis, revealing almost everything, paraded around the backyard, sipping expensive champagne and eating their weight in caviar and other appetizers that barely tasted like real food.

I lowered the shades over my eyes, letting my gaze drift to the people around us. Someone had roasted sausages on the back deck minutes ago, and the scent still lingered in the air, mixed with the chlorine that clung to my skin. I pushed a hand through my hair and confirmed it was tousled and still damp. I shook my head, and my bare chest glistened with droplets of water.

Taking a sip of my beer, I enjoyed the cold liquid sliding down my throat—a contrast to the sun beating down on me.

"Well, that's what happens when yours truly fucks the

wealthiest girl in school. Thank you very much." Joe's mischievous grin lit up his face.

"I should start living my life according to your standards," I said with a smirk. "One day at a time. No promises. No second dates. I bet life would be much simpler."

My friend straightened in his lounger and studied me over the rim of his sunglasses with a frown. "You serious right now?"

I shrugged. "Maybe. I've been doing great lately. Might as well make it a permanent habit."

"Don't say things like that, man. It gives me false hopes." He shook his head. "Even though I'm wishing for it to be true, this new persona you've got going on is nothing like you. You're not a no-kissing, just-fucking kind of guy. You know it. I know it. You're the good one. The one girls want to take to Sunday dinner with their parents. The one making plans for the future. The trustworthy guy. The one who gives a shit."

"Well, I don't want to anymore."

He snickered. "Sorry to tell you that it doesn't work like that." He swung his legs over the edge of the chair and leaned toward me, tapping my shoulder. "I'm sorry, man. I wish it was easier, and you could flip a switch, but no chance. Ten or twenty years from now, you'll still be the good guy."

I dragged a hand over my scruffy jaw. "We'll see."

Joe clinked his bottle against mine. "To you, Andy. You're the best amongst us."

"Look where it's brought me."

"It's all gonna work out. Get out of this funk and be happy. Live your life. And please, stop with the sad, angry songs. Go back to your lover-boy hits. I miss them."

I flung both arms into the air. "You're the one who

wanted me to stop thinking about Abby and get into partying and stuff instead. And now that I'm over it…over her…you want me to go back to being that guy?"

He tipped his head back with a chuckle. "Let's drink and forget I said anything."

"Impossible. I'm living my best life right now. I play music. I fuck when I want. I go out when I'm free. What more could I possibly wish for?"

My friend's laughter died down, and he watched me some more. I could feel the weight of his gaze even through the tinted lenses of his sunglasses. "The thing is— and for the record, I can't believe I'm saying this—you don't sound like yourself, man. You sure you're okay?"

I tipped the bottle to my lips and downed it in a long gulp. "Yeah. No worries. All fine."

He sighed. "Your lips say one thing, but your face says another. Believe me, I love the carefree *I don't give a fuck* thing you've got going on. It's better than your pussy-whipped, *I'm a sad puppy* attitude of last semester. But since we've both been back to New York, you're nothing like your old self."

I turned my head, trying to evade his heavy stare.

"Talk to me. We've been best friends for a long time. Something happened when you went back home. I can tell. You're turning into a jerk."

My head snapped back, and my eyes fixated on him, my jaw tensed and my posture straight, praying the emotional tsunami playing inside me wouldn't show on my face. "It's nothing. Forget about it." My gaze lingered on the people playing chicken in the pool. "Wanna join them? I bet you can't win against me."

He cursed under his breath. Joe would never be able to resist a hot, soaked girl perched on his shoulders, her inner thighs pressing against the back of his neck. I knew the guy better than I knew myself.

"Don't tease me." He gave his head a small shake. "We're staying right here. Don't change the subject, man. Come on, spill your guts. Uncle Joe is listening."

He leaned back into his lounge chair, linking his fingers together behind his head and spreading his arms wide.

"Are you playing shrink right now?" I asked.

"Isn't it evident?" He cocked one brow as if to say *Play along*.

Before he could get another word out, I pushed off from the chair, jumped to my feet, and dived headfirst into the deep end of the pool.

The last words I heard from somewhere behind me were, "Is that fucker serious?"

———

I adjusted the strap of my guitar around my neck and the microphone on the stand before me. "Good evening, folks."

The crowd grew silent.

"My name is Andy, and I'll be your entertainment tonight." I turned my attention toward an older couple. "Mr. and Mrs. Jackson, happy fortieth anniversary." I raised my champagne flute, and every guest did the same.

The Jacksons' children had given me a set list of songs their parents loved to play, and I had included some of my own in between.

I performed for one hour straight before taking a fifteen-minute break. I'd met Mrs. Jackson at her daughter-in-law's baby shower last April, and she'd booked me as the main act for her anniversary party this September.

People smiled and danced and sometimes sang along as

I strummed my guitar and delivered the lyrics about love and destiny, sorrows and forever.

Seeing the happy couple swaying to my music teased the old version of me into making a comeback. I put all my heart into the melody while I got lost in the contemplation of their love that had survived four decades.

Midnight rang, and like a modern-day Cinderella, I cashed my pay and headed home. In the last three hours, I'd received three different offers to spend the night in some random girl's bed. I couldn't see myself fucking a stranger tonight. No, thanks. Anyway, I wasn't in the mood.

What I hadn't told Joe last week, when we attended the pool party, was that sometimes, late at night, when I couldn't sleep, I still searched for Abby online. The infatuation I'd had with her had died down, but a part of me was curious. Call it a challenge—I couldn't believe she'd turned into a ghost.

The other thing I hadn't told Joe was that on my drive back to New York, after I'd left Memphis and camped in Nashville for a couple of nights, I went to Silverville. For almost a week, I acted like a stalker on the Silverville School of Business's campus. I knew the semester was over, but knowing Abby and the little enthusiasm she had showed to go back to her parents' for Winter Break last year—call it a hunch—I believed she'd be the girl enrolling in summer classes.

My search led nowhere. Nobody had heard of her, and nobody I talked to knew who I was referring to.

So now, once a week, I brought my stalker ways online. I just wanted to make sure she was okay. And happy. Nothing else. Or maybe that was how I justified it to myself. That it was all for her own good.

Lying on my bed, freshly showered, I stared at the ceiling, wondering about my life and how I'd ended up here.

I perused the space around me. In all the time I'd lived here, I never really took the time to make this bedroom mine. The white walls were bare, no color, no pieces of art or pictures. A mismatched nightstand and dresser that doubled as a desk, which I'd found at a garage sale when I moved here in my sophomore year, flanked the queen-sized mattress. A pile of old wooden cases in a corner served as both a bookshelf and a junk drawer. The snow globe Abby had gifted me that night was set atop. Against the wall, between the door and the closet, lay my guitar case over a suitcase filled with things I never used and hadn't had time to store elsewhere. Only then did I realize how depressing it looked.

I scrolled through the social media feeds on my phone with my thumb, my eyelids weighing heavier with each passing minute.

The low-battery warning popped on the screen, and I plugged the charger in, returning to my wandering thoughts.

At some point, I drifted to sleep before I could take the time to put on a pair of boxer briefs or slip under the covers.

The chime of a text notification woke me up the next morning. A loud groan escaped my mouth as I flipped to my side and stretched my arm to unplug the device on the bedside table. I blinked, trying to shake the sleep from my eyes and clear my vision.

MOM

Anderson. Enough with this. I wanna talk to you. Give me a call, or I'll show up at your apartment in NY and won't leave until you let me explain.

I snorted and tossed my phone onto the bed as I stood up, ready to get dressed and jump-start my day. Joe's uncle had scheduled me to repaint two walls in the lobby today.

Anyway, I had no intention of talking to my mother or seeing her if she wasn't bluffing and actually showed up at my door. I had much better things to do than hear her plead for my forgiveness. Nope. I wasn't ready to pretend everything was fine between us, as if she hadn't lied to me all my life.

Chapter 22
Abigail

Tears leaked from my eyes as I jolted awake and shifted, trying to find a position that would soothe me and make the pain go away. I checked the time on my phone, strangling the device in my fist. *Seven thirty-six.* It couldn't happen now. I wasn't ready. No, the baby had to wait. I needed more time. More preparation. More everything. *Dammit, how much more could I hurt right now?* Sweat pearled on my forehead. I dropped my phone on the bed and clenched my hands into fists, hard enough to draw blood.

Breathe in. Breathe out.

Pain radiated through my body. I shut my eyes, picturing myself on a remote island, far from here, where the contractions weren't real. Or lounging by a pool, with the water lapping at my feet and the sun shining down on me.

In vain.

The pain was real.

I sucked in a shallow breath, my whole body shaking with tremors.

Breathe in. Breathe out.

Those stupid breathing exercises were of no use.

In the past two months, I'd been dealing with Braxton Hicks contractions every few days. Right now, these felt nothing like those. The pain radiated through my back, abdomen, and legs. My belly was hard to the touch and felt heavier.

At that moment, I wished my mother were here, back to being the affectionate person she used to be when I was a small child. Or Ellie. She'd pull me into her arms and shield me from everything.

Breathe in. Breathe out.

Or I anyone, really, so I wouldn't be on my own.

"I don't wanna do this alone," I spoke through clenched teeth. "I don't wanna do it by myself." The words escaped my mouth between sobs. My face was drenched, my spirits crushed. I bent over, pleading with the contractions to stop. I still had two more weeks left in this pregnancy. It wasn't time. No, it couldn't be time. I didn't agree with it at all. Why would my body think I was ready?

"Please, baby. Hang in there for a bit longer." My voice shook as I begged through clenched teeth. "Please."

I should have never had sex. What was I thinking? How could I have been so clueless about the consequences? I should've listened to my parents when they told me sex outside of marriage was bad. What am I saying? I'm delusional. Since when did my parents' words ring true? If I'd listened to them, I'd be exiled to Europe right now, being shamed for having a baby. A baby? Ohmygod, I am about to become a mother. I haven't turned twenty yet. What was I thinking when I'd begged Andy to have sex with me? I could see now how wrong it had been. How wrong I had been.

Another contraction ripped through me.

Oh gosh. They are getting closer in time. How can I postpone this? There must be a way I can keep this baby inside of me, no? How am I supposed to deliver a baby with no one beside me to hold my hand? Can I go back in time? Change the last nine months? Ohmygod, it hurts so bad. Why does it have to hurt?

"No. *No, no, no.*"

Okay. This is not happening. I am deep asleep, and this is all a dream. I know because I have had many of them in the last month. And in my dreams, it has never ended well. Once, I gave birth to a goat. Another time, my baby had four legs. The last time, I died because the doctors cut me open, and my baby was an orphan because they had no way of reaching his daddy. He was crying, and I couldn't comfort him because I had turned into a ghost.

My abdomen strained with a new contraction. "Fuck, it hurts."

Sitting on the edge of the bed, I pressed my hands on each side of my rounded stomach, massaging the tension away.

Once the tautness disappeared, and realizing the contractions were really getting closer and not further apart, I grabbed my phone to call Ellie. The last time she was here, we'd packed a bag together and decided on a procedure for when labor started, which was right about ten minutes ago.

My fingers quivered as I pressed the call button.

"Hey *gurrrl*," she said, her usual cheerfulness on full display. "How is it going?"

I relaxed my jaw, forcing the words out. "Elles…it-it's happening to…today. Now." I breathed through the pain radiating to my back as another contraction worked through me. "Like *now* now." Hot tears flowed freely down my cheeks.

"What? Like this is it? You're in labor?"

I cursed under my breath. "Yes." It sounded more like a moaning scream than an actual one-word answer.

"Are you…are you sure?"

"Fucking positive."

"Oh shit. Okay, wait. Breathe. Relax. Oh, wow. I can't believe it's happening. My God, Abby. Are you all right?"

"Ellie," I said, with an edge to my tone. "Focus. I'm the one about to push a baby out of my vagina." I inhaled. "On the list you made, it said to call you when the contractions were less than ten minutes apart."

"Oh yes. Sorry. How long between them?"

I blew out through my mouth in quick gasps. "No idea. But it's way less than ten minutes." Tension squeezed my abdomen in a tight grip. "Ellie. Do something or I'll give birth on my bed."

"Breathe, Abby. I'll send a cab and inform the hospital you're on your way. Do you have your bag?"

I spotted it in the corner of my bedroom. "Yeah."

"Everything is in there. We followed the list the doctor gave you, so don't worry about it."

More sobs shook me.

"Hey, talk to me," my friend asked. "Are you in pain?"

"Yes. It hurts so bad, but—"

"What is it?"

"I'm scared, Elles. I'm so afraid of what's coming. I'm not ready." I wiped my tears with my sleeves, the river down my face intensifying. "I want it to stop. I…I don't wanna deliver a baby. I'm not even twenty yet. I-I'm way too young to be a mother. I…no…I'm not wired to care for another human being. What if I screw up? Sorry, but I can't do this. Why are girls the ones who deal with pregnancy? Andy is free to live his life without stressing about any of this. He's not… He's not about to have his body ripped in two." My voice rose, and my words were clipped when I added, "I. DIDN'T. MAKE. THIS. BABY. ON. MY. OWN."

My best friend's soft and reassuring voice calmed me down. "I'm aware. Life is unfair sometimes, but you're the bravest person I know. If someone can deliver a baby on her own, it's you. It's scary. And it will hurt. And I wish I could hold your hand through this. Or even take away your pain. But you can do this. You will do this. You hear me out, Abigail Peña, you're going to give birth to that baby. Life doesn't care if you are nineteen or thirty-three. You're gonna fucking do it. Like the warrior you are. And once you cradle that baby in your arms, you'll be so proud and happy you went through with it. You didn't endure months of shit and hard work to give up at the end of the race. So, plaster your game face on, grab the bag, and climb into the cab that will be at your place in"—she paused, probably to check on her app—"two minutes and twenty-seven seconds. Did I make myself clear?"

I nodded, even though she couldn't see me.

"Did I make myself clear?" she repeated.

"Yes," I whispered.

"*Gurrrl*, you can do better than this. Did I make myself clear?"

"Yes, you did."

"Good. Now don't hang up because I'll stay with you for as long as you need me. I put a phone charger in your bag, so you won't run out of battery."

"Thanks." I shouldered my bag and was about to exit my bedroom when my abdomen tensed with a new contraction. I balanced against the doorjamb until it passed. "Okay, let's do this."

"That's the spirit," Ellie's voice said on the other end of the line.

The drive to the hospital didn't quite register with me. Everything that went down since I'd called Ellie was a bit blurry. Like I was going through the motions without being conscious of it. She kept talking into my ear, reassuring me, whispering her encouragement, but I heard almost nothing she said.

A nurse waited for me with a wheelchair when I climbed out of the cab. She took my bag from the driver's hands, and I hadn't taken three steps toward her when a popping sound surprised me, and hot liquid ran down the inner sides of my legs, pooling on the pavement. I froze. Did I just pee myself? My heart constricted in my chest. Oh no. If I had, this was beyond mortifying. More liquid streamed down my thighs, and I tried to stop the flow, but the more I clenched, the more came out. "Oh no, what's happening? I-I'm sorry. I didn't...I didn't mean to pee on the sidewalk," I said, my voice laced with shame. "What is going on?"

"What's wrong?" Ellie said in my ear. "Talk to me. Are you safe?"

The nurse must have caught onto my mortification because she neared me and put a comforting palm between my shoulder blades. "Honey, it's all fine. Your water just broke."

"Oh."

"It's normal. Nothing unusual. Let's get you inside and changed so the doctor can examine you, okay?"

I nodded.

"Abby, say something," Ellie asked, her voice filled with worry, and I snapped out of the daze I had fallen into.

I swallowed as my belly grew rigid and stole my breath away for a moment.

My voice shuddered when I said, "I'm fine. My-my water broke. For a second, I thought I had peed myself. Ellie—" Tears I hadn't shed in the last twenty minutes returned with a vengeance, and now that the dam had burst, I had no idea how to stop the flow. Feeling helpless, I did nothing to wipe them as they clouded my vision. I sat in the wheelchair and cried in silence. Nobody could understand how scary this episode of my life was.

"Don't cry," Ellie's low voice repeated in my ear. "You're not alone. Don't cry. Please. I'm right here with you. Let's get that baby out of you, okay?"

I sniffled. "O…o-okay."

"That's right."

She comforted me through every procedure and exam I went through before being wheeled to the delivery room.

Bigger than a regular hospital room, it had a small glass crib next to the bed. A newborn station, consisting of a heated bassinet beneath a warming lamp, stood in one corner beside a rocking chair. The walls were painted a soft shade of yellow. A colorful mural of cartoon characters covered the wall opposite the window. Buttons, monitors, and tubes were mounted behind the bed's headrest. Stainless steel counters and cupboards lined the fourth wall.

The room looked calming and inviting—nothing like the sterile one I'd imagined when I thought about this day, or the ones they showed in movies. After changing into a steel-blue hospital gown decorated with tiny snowflakes, I settled into bed. IV lines were taped to my arm, and a belt around my belly tracked each contraction on some kind of graph printer. Despite everything, I relaxed a little.

Remembering my best friend was still on the line, I switched the call to video chat.

"How is it going?" she asked. Judging by the dark

circles under her eyes and her reddened cheeks, I would've thought she was the one about to give birth.

"I-I'm still freaked out. But being here makes me feel a little calmer…huh…and more secure."

The doctor entered the room to check up on me. "At this rate, this baby will be born before dinner time." He tapped my folded knee over the cover. "Hang in there, Abby. I'll come back to check on you soon. In the meantime, try to catch some rest?"

I blinked. Fast. "Like sleep? How is that even possible? I'm in pain every two minutes."

"Sleep or not, but please rest. You'll soon need all the energy you can get. You're doing great. The nurse will be back with you in a minute."

"Abby, he's right," Ellie chimed in. "Put me on the table next to the bed. I won't go anywhere, I swear, but you need all your strength. I'll watch over you."

The next few hours were a mix of calm periods followed by great pain as if my insides were being torn apart. Over and over again.

I didn't fall asleep, but between contractions, I managed to close my eyes. I hadn't even started pushing yet, and I was already exhausted, as if I'd run a marathon. It was a weird mix, because the adrenaline and fear of the unknown were also keeping me on my toes.

The doctor returned to examine me, and by then I was a bit out of it. My entire body felt foreign, as if I weren't living my own life, but someone else's. "Ten centimeters. Fully dilated. We'll reposition the bed so you can start pushing."

That did the trick. I sprang into a semi-seated position. "No. *No, no, no.* I don't want to. I'm not ready to push. I'm fine staying like this for a while."

Jessie, the nurse who had been by my side all day,

inched closer and took my hand in hers. "Abby, you can do this. We've gone over the whole procedure multiple times already. Your baby is ready, and so is your body. I swear."

I swallowed. "No. It's too soon. I am *really* not ready for this."

"I understand, but this baby *is* ready to come," the doctor said, offering me a reassuring smile. "You'll do great. Don't worry. We're taking care of both of you."

My gaze drifted to Ellie's face filling my phone screen, and she nodded. "We're all here for you. It's time, *gurrrl.*"

Deep down, I wished she had been on my side and told me I could wait longer.

The labor lasted for hours, but it felt like only ten minutes had passed when the doctor asked me to push one last time, and Jessie placed my baby safely in my arms. "It's a boy." Wearing only a tiny powder-blue knitted hat, she placed his naked body against my bare chest. "It'll keep him warm, and the first skin-to-skin contact is very important."

I stared at him.

I couldn't speak. I couldn't move. Everything unfolded in the slowest motion. I was a mother. My mind struggled to register it. How had this happened? How had I created a human being?

His little fist curled around my finger as I caressed his tiny, delicate hand, and my heart melted in my chest. I examined his frail body, making sure he had all his fingers and toes. A wave of love I hadn't known I possessed washed over me.

My heart raced, emotions spilling over, making me jittery.

This little human was my son. This tiny, pink-fleshed creature with dark hair was my baby. The one I'd carried around for the last thirty-eight weeks. The one Andy and I made together that night. He was here because of a snow-storm—and because of a bunch of silly challenges after the guy I'd found both mesmerizing and intriguing back then had caught my eye.

He was the result of the wildest, most amazing night of my life.

Tears pooled in my eyes, and my heart swelled in my chest.

I wasn't tired anymore. I was in awe. And in love.

"Hi, baby. I'm your mama," I said, my voice quivering under the weight of emotion. *Mama.* I was a mother. No matter how many times I repeated it in my head, my brain still couldn't compute it. I would need to get used to this term while referring to myself.

With a finger, I caressed his cheek, his skin warm and soft. His eyelids fluttered, and I was entranced by every small movement. He had just been born, yet already he moved like a real person. I knew he was a real baby, but it filled me with awe—how the moment he took his first breath, his body was already fully functioning. His heart-shaped lips pursed, and he pressed closer against my bare chest. How could he look so perfect?

I had done it. I had given birth to the most beautiful little boy. He was my early—and best—birthday gift.

"Abby?" Ellie's voice pulled me out of my admiration.

Staring at the little bundle of love in my arms, I smiled before turning my attention to her. I shifted the phone so she could get a better view of my son. *My son.* It sounded almost surreal. "*Gurrrl.* You did amazing." Her own eyes brimmed with tears. Her palms connected together under her chin. "Wow, he's absolute perfection. I'm so proud of you. Do you have a name? You've never told me."

"Alexi." *Abby. Andy. Alexi. Yes, it felt right.* And it gave the three of us a sense of unity. Of family.

She clasped her hands. "I love it. Andy would be so proud. I know he has no idea, but from what you've told me, he would be here if he could. And would agree."

I nodded twice. "One day, I'll find him, Elles. I have no idea how or when. I'll even hire a P.I. if I need to. But one day, he'll meet his son, no matter what it takes."

Chapter 23
Anderson

I met Joe and some of our friends at a small brewery near campus.

"How did it go?" my best friend and roommate asked.

I shrugged. "About as well as you'd expect." I took a seat at the rectangular table. The aroma of chicken wings, fresh garlic bread, and stall beer filled my nose. I grabbed the wooden slate menu, held together by a large silicone band, and read through the page. "What are we having?"

"I've already ordered a pitcher," said Thomas, a senior old enough to buy us beer.

"And they should bring three mix platters until we're ready to order," Mike, a guy in one of my classes, added. "Wings, bruschetta, potato skins, cheese sticks, and a bunch of other stuff. I think we're covered for a while."

Joe kicked my foot under the table while I sank back into my chair and asked, "What happened?"

"Oh, that? Yeah…well… She wasn't happy about it. Said I was acting like chickenshit and she had agreed to our little arrangement all semester because she thought I would get tired of it and return to my senses."

"Harsh."

With a dismissive shake of my head, I continued. "I've been acting like a jerk. Bethany has been nothing but patient, and I kept pushing her away. I wouldn't have been happy with myself either if I were her. Anyway, it's over."

Joe offered me a small smile. "Sorry, man."

"Don't be. It's all on me. It was about time I cut her loose. Since the fall semester is over and she's going home for Winter Break, I hope she realizes she's better off without me."

"Did my dad contact you for his office party?"

"About the change of venue and date?"

He nodded.

"Yeah. It's a bit last minute, but since I hadn't booked anything else for that weekend, it's all good. It's just—"

My friend studied my reaction. As if he could read my mind. "How do you feel about it?"

I flicked my wrist to brush him off, hoping he wouldn't push the subject.

"Andy. Be real. How do you feel about going back there?"

"It's fine." I swallowed hard. "Don't make a big deal out of it, and I won't."

He lifted his hands in surrender. "Okay then. Did you change your mind about going home for the holidays?"

"I talked to my mom last night and told her I'd come home for a few days. It doesn't mean I've gotten over the lies and fuck-ups my parents have fed me over the years. It's just that I can't stand the idea of her being all alone at this time of the year."

"I'm sure Mama Ford meant no harm. You should let her explain. Could be beneficial for both of you."

"One day. When I'm ready. She promised that he wouldn't pay us a surprise visit, so we'll see. Can we change the topic? That last test was a bitch, and I'm starving."

As if summoned by my growling stomach, the server returned with our beer and food. For the rest of the night, the conversation stayed clear of my personal business as the guys chatted about the night's party, the upcoming vacations, and the girls they had hooked up with in the last few weeks. A more than welcome distraction.

———

Sitting in the same airport café I'd sat in a year ago, I studied each passenger coming and going through the terminal. Nobody knew I had planned to spend two days in the airport before boarding a plane to Tennessee. I'd come up with the idea during Thanksgiving, when I chose to stay in New York City instead of flying back home. Drunk and alone in the living room watching reruns of reality shows I had no interest in, I had chastised myself for not flying to Silverville and camping out in the airport in case some girl with jet-black hair and the bluest eyes I'd ever seen had the same idea.

That was the night I'd also decided I should break up with Bethany.I just had to wait a little until she was done with her finals, because there was no way I was going to mess with focus by dumping her. The last thing I wanted was to add more anxiety to her life. I knew how stressful a dance degree could be.

Here I was, three days before Christmas, ready to

spend my night running on too much caffeine just in case Abby happened to be here too.

If she wasn't, I promised myself I would forget her this time around. No relapses. I'd let go of her in my mind. The last time I'd tried, that newfound resolve had only lasted a short while. Not this time, though. I had to move on, or I'd go stir-crazy.

I lingered on a bench near the departure gate, my guitar in hand, trying out a new song that had been nagging at me all night. The memories of being here last year had awakened the creative part of my brain, and lyrics and melodies battled in my head for release.

A middle-aged man sat next to me. "How is it going?" he asked.

Lost in my creative flow, I didn't want to be disturbed. I removed the pen I'd been squeezing between my teeth and noted the new arrangement in the notebook I always kept with me.

"Good." I returned my focus to my guitar, hoping he would get the message that I wanted to be on my own. The only person allowed to interrupt me tonight hadn't shown up yet. If she ever would.

The man listened to my playing for a long beat before moving to his feet. "You are very talented. No doubt you'll make it big someday. Good luck."

I nodded a *Thank you* as he spun on his heel and left.

Taking a break and sipping what must have been my sixth cup of coffee, I people-watched everyone who passed in front of me. A family of four, the kids sporting huge smiles and hopping around, barely listening to the directions their father had repeated at least three times. Even I, who had been distracted, could recite them. A couple in their early twenties was laughing. Wearing a Santa hat, the girl sat on a luggage caddy while her boyfriend pushed her around. At some point, he stopped and pulled her to him, kissing her senseless. The girl smiled against his lips and when she leaned back, stars lit up in her gaze.

My heart frizzled in my chest.

Loads of memories crashed through me.

Why was I here? This was beyond stupid. One year had gone by since Abby and I shared a night. One night. Not months, years, or a lifetime, but a single night.

Why couldn't I let it go even after all this time? Why was I still hooked on this—on her—a year later? Was my life so lame I had nothing better to do?

After playing at Joe's father's Christmas office party, I should have asked to stay at their place for the night instead of being here, searching for a ghost. I had no idea if she would even remember my sorry ass.

Picking up my bag and guitar case, I was about to move to the waiting area when I spotted a girl with black hair in the distance. My heartbeat went ballistic. Sweat gathered in my armpits. My throat itched, my mouth dry.

Could it really be…? Could it be her?

I stayed frozen in place, waiting. My hands shook with anticipation, and I dropped my luggage at my feet.

From where I stood, I couldn't tell if it was her.

My skin prickled as I stood there, barely able to breathe. The guy blocking her from my sight sidestepped, and she turned around.

Oxygen failed to reach my brain as I braced myself for any eventuality.

Chapter 24
Abigail

My hands shook as I uncapped the pen and stared at the blank page, not knowing what to write, but trying to let my heart do the talking.

Dear Mother and Father,

Merry Christmas to you both. This is Alexi, your grandson. He and I wish you a happy holiday season and send love your way.

We haven't talked in a long time, and I feel that since the holidays are a chance to start fresh, there are things I need to tell you.

I'm sorry I'm not the child you wished me to be and that our relationship ended the way it did. It was never my intention to upset you, but you have to understand this is my life, my baby, and my body, and I was the only one allowed to make a decision about any of this. I'm sorry you couldn't give me time to figure my life out and were too ashamed of me to see I needed your help, your support, and your love more than anything else. I'm sorry I believed I was the most important person in your life and that you would want me to be happy instead of lost and sad. And alone.

You know what? I'm done making excuses for the decisions I've made, for who I am, and for the person I'm becoming. I shouldn't have to justify my choices and my actions to you or anyone else.

I'm an honest, brilliant, and talented woman, and I'm making the most of a situation I haven't planned for but wouldn't change. No, it's not always easy and sometimes I'm tired, but Alexi and I, we are thriving. We are happy.

As much as I love you, I will never shy away from who I am to please you anymore. I'm a grown-up woman and proved it many times over. From now on, I'm done feeling like I don't belong or like I'm not good enough.

I AM good enough. And I'm even more than good enough. I'll be the best in what I choose to do with my life. And I'll prove it to you. Well, I'll prove it to myself. And my son. Because he deserves the best version of me. I'll work nights and days, and I won't stop until I reach the top. If it doesn't please you, you have no obligation to be part of our lives, but if you feel like you could accept me the way I am, maybe we can make it work down the line. Maybe one day.

No matter what you decide, just be aware that I'm done dimming my light so you don't get offended by my glow. I'm a shining star, and I love how bright I radiate. I love how I shine because it's my special power. I'm my own superhero. In my life, all I've ever tried to do is to please you and everyone else, always putting myself last. I wanted to be part of your world so bad, but no matter how hard I tried, I just never fit in. I was always the outsider. I've been for a long time. I know it now. I can see it.

The thing is, I'm not mad at you anymore. Not

really. My only wish is that you accept me how I am, with my strengths and flaws, my ups and downs, like I do with you. In the past, I've always felt like it wasn't enough. Perhaps this could change if you'd like to get to know the real me, not the one I've always had to pretend to be. Being a mother made me realize being a parent is a difficult job.

There is no right or wrong way to do it, but you gotta give it your best. Every second of every day. You gotta show up and do the work because no one else will do it for you. I also realized that loving your child, as he or she is, shouldn't be a chore; it should come naturally. It should be straightforward. Nobody is perfect after all.

I love Alexi with every fiber of my being. My son is my pride and joy. The best thing that has ever happened to me. His smiles fix bullet holes in my heart and his hugs chase the gray storms of my life away. I wish you could experience it yourself because nothing else equals the pure and raw happiness he gives me in this world.

If you ever want to meet us, my phone number hasn't changed.

I wish you the best, and I hope you are happy.

I'm not ready to forgive you today, but I'm deciding now I'd like to one day.

With love,
Abigail

My heart banged in my chest as I folded the paper into thirds after rereading the letter, placed it in an envelope with a picture of Alexi and me dressed in our best holiday attire, and sealed it. I had done it. One step toward forgiveness…or reconciliation. If they wished for it too. The ball was in their camp now.

At least, even if they refused to meet with us, I'd know in my heart that I tried.

Tomorrow, I would mail the letter.

And I'd pray for some Christmas miracle to happen."

Chapter 25

Abigail

The bottle dropped from my grip before I could secure its lid. Breast milk—and an hour of pumping—gone to waste. Alexi's cries intensified. "I'm coming, I'm coming." I bet he didn't believe me anymore because I'd been repeating the same words for the last five minutes.

Tears drenched my cheeks. I was trying, doing my best. Sometimes, though, I felt like I couldn't do it all. I sucked a deep breath in and firmed my back. No time to throw myself a pity party. No matter how inexperienced or how young I was, so far, I had managed the whole baby thing by myself. It wasn't perfect. *I* wasn't perfect, but I did my best. Each day, I showed up and did the work. Unless I collapsed from exhaustion, I would continue to do so until Alexi and I figured it out. Found our rhythm. And what worked for us.

Tossing a dishcloth over the mess on the floor, I hurried

to the infant swing, a gift from Ellie's parents, and picked up my fussy baby. Who would have thought babies were so loud? Not me. They were all tiny and cute but could pierce your eardrums when they got upset.

I pressed his flushed body against me, stepping back and forth in some sort of dance that usually did the trick to soothe him while I murmured "Shhh" in his ear, kissing the crown of his head. "I'm here. It's okay. I'm aware you are hungry, but I kinda ruined your dinner. I'll need a few more minutes to fix you another bottle."

After weeks of trying to breastfeed him with the help of a lactation specialist after his birth, I gave up and decided to pump and bottle-feed him instead. In a way, I preferred that. It might sound weird, or maybe it was my age talking, but I preferred my baby suckling on a bottle nipple rather than on my breast. Perhaps if I had some kind of *Mommy and Me* group or female figures in my life, I'd feel different. I did not have enough time to attend the first one, and the second one was nonexistent. When I'd asked the nurse at the hospital, she'd assured me there were no right or wrong ways of feeding a baby and that as long as Alexi got the required nutrients, I could use a bottle without shame.

His soft baby hair tickled my nostrils as I peppered more kisses on the top of his head and took a big whiff of his baby scent. Serenity spread through me, and he appeared to sense it because he relaxed against my chest.

Once he stopped screaming, I laid my son in the crook of my arm and offered him his pacifier. While he sucked on it with determination, I carefully stepped over the spilled milk mess and warmed up another pouch of baby nectar. It took twice the amount of time since I had only one free hand, but in the end, I managed.

Together we sat on the couch. Soft Christmas music

played on a speaker set on the fireplace mantel. With all the commotion of the last ten minutes, I had totally forgotten it was on. Alexi's fingers curled around one of mine, and he held on to me tight as if he feared I would leave him. Or vanish. His big eyes, now a midnight shade of blue and framed by thick dark lashes that any woman would envy, were fixed on mine. "It's good?" I asked.

A sound resembling a grunt passed his lips, and I decided it meant *yes*.

I tucked a pillow under my arm and sank back against the backrest. His eyelids seemed to weigh heavy, and soon his eyes closed, his mouth still sucking every drop of milk from the bottle and his fingers never releasing mine.

I surveyed the room around me. In early November, as soon as Halloween was over, I'd decorated a small Christmas tree with white lights and silver and blue ornaments. I'd pinned stockings with our initials to the mantel. It wasn't much, but it gave the place a festive feel. The holidays would consist of only the two of us this year. No one-nighter with a stranger, no family dinner, no Winter Break. I had work scheduled every day and had even opened a few extra hours on my calendar for clients whose assistants were taking some time off. The slots had filled up in no time. The extra cash would come in handy once I took on a fuller course load next semester.

The community college had agreed to let me finish my degree remotely and at my own pace. Sure, it wasn't the best option for a social life, but for me, who had one goal in mind and a newborn to care for, it was the perfect opportunity to multitask. I'd sent in my two final papers three days ago and was now done with school for almost a month.

From where I sat on the couch, I spotted the overflowing hamper by Alexi's bedroom door. Things got intense quickly around here, and I was often overwhelmed by all the chores on top of everything else. Tomorrow morning, I would do some laundry. Not tonight, though. Tonight, I was done. I had to rest and recharge my batteries because I was running on empty.

It didn't help that Alexi had been waking up every three hours for the last week. So far, he had been getting better at sleeping for longer stretches of time, but these past few days he had been hungrier and crankier than usual. 'Growth spurt,' the nurse at the pediatrician's office had concluded when I called, worried something might be wrong.

My head fell forward as exhaustion won the battle. I removed the bottle from between my son's lips and watched his mouth continue to suckle even though there was nothing to suck on. I swooned at the sight. My little guy was, for now, the one true love of my life.

Once changed and dressed in a very adorable one-piece bunny pajama, I laid him in the pack and play I kept in my bedroom. His soft snoring sent a curl to my lips. I hadn't succeeded at letting him spend an entire night in his crib yet. During the day, I could do it, let him sleep in his own bedroom, but at night, I feared I'd be too sound asleep to hear him if he woke up.

With a palm over his chest, I made sure he was breathing and that his heart was still beating.

Once satisfied with its steady rhythm, and without even taking the time to undress or shower, I wrapped myself in a blanket and collapsed onto the mattress. Sleep claimed me before I had time to catch up with it.

———

In an attempt to add some holiday spirit to our days, Alexi and I spent a week dressed in PJs. I drank far too much hot chocolate, piled high with whipped cream, ate Mixchos—the only way I ate nachos nowadays—and sang too many Christmas carols. Even though he was only three months old and wouldn't remember any of this, it was important to me to create some traditions.

Sitting on the living room floor with my baby on his back on a fluffy blanket, I tickled his little feet and belly once I'd finished changing his diaper. Today, he wore a red Santa hat and pajamas with elf feet, reminding me of the outfit his daddy had worn the night we met. Unable to resist, I took way too many pictures on my phone. His big, curious eyes followed the reindeer hand puppet I moved above him. Today was one of those perfect days. Alexi had slept five hours straight last night and had woken up with a smile, watching me as if I were his entire world—in a sense, I guess I was—and kept babbling the entire time I set him down.

The buzzer, announcing someone was at the door, broke our improvised photoshoot. Lifting my son in my arms, I pressed the intercom button. "Can I help you?"

"Delivery for Mr. and Ms. Peña."

Hearing the man calling Alexi *Mr. Peña* brought a smile to my lips. Only Ellie would do such a thing. "Come on in," I said, buzzing the delivery guy in.

Alexi's wet mouth connected with my cheek in what could only be described as soaked kisses. We stepped over the threshold and waited for the man to join us. When I turned Alexi around so he could see the stranger coming, he started waving his arms and kicking his legs. "Ba-ba-baba-ba."

"Hey you," the man told Alexi before bringing his gaze to me. "Here, for you." He placed the box on the floor at my feet and made a device appear from his pocket. "Please sign here."

Using my finger, I did as asked.

"Merry Christmas," he said.

"Thank you. Merry Christmas to you too."

After the man left, I made my way inside and placed Alexi on his mat, then brought the box in. As guessed, Ellie's name was written above the sender's address.

For a brief second, when the man buzzed at the door, I wished it were my parents. Three weeks ago, I had sent them that letter with a picture of Alexi and me wearing matching Santa hats that we'd taken when we visited Santa at the mall, but I never heard back. At least the envelope didn't bounce back, so I hoped they kept it and didn't throw it in the garbage.

The letter had been my attempt to offer them an olive branch, a hope that they would realize they had made a mistake and decide they wanted to be part of our lives.

Up until now, total silence. No news. Nothing.

It felt as if I had died—or they had died—and our relationship had never existed.

After dropping the box on the kitchen table, I picked up my son and settled him in the crook of my elbow while I got a pair of scissors. Wrapped in red and green silk paper were several Christmas-themed wagons along with a model railroad to assemble.

I opened the card.

Merry Christmas, you two
I wish I could be there with you to celebrate.
I'll try to fly in before the winter semester starts.

I found this at a garage sale and thought of you. The train works like a charm, and it can also play music. I believe Alexi—and you—will love it under your tree. It includes a tunnel you can put over a section of the railing so he'll see it disappear and reappear seconds later. Kids love playing peek-a-boo. Don't they? I think so.

I miss you guys.
Tom says hello.

Call me when you read it.

I love you, and I'm proud of you. And that Santa picture was amazing. I framed it, and it feels like you guys are here with me somehow.

Ellie xxx

After video chatting with Ellie and assembling the train, Alexi and I spent the rest of the day sprawled on the living room floor, admiring the wagons coming in and out of the tunnel, just like my friend had suggested.

When I put him to bed later, I squeezed in four hours of work before calling it a day and settling on the couch with a mug of hot chocolate and a movie—something I barely ever did nowadays because of my busy schedule.

No matter what I did tonight, the smile that had taken over my face earlier never faded.

For the first time in a long time, I felt like I had my life together. And it meant everything to me.

If only…

I chased the thought away as far as possible.
What-ifs could come back to haunt me another day.
Tonight, I wouldn't let them affect my mood.

Chapter 26
Anderson

TWO YEARS LATER

With my music degree in hand, I packed all my things into my pickup and hugged Joe after returning my apartment key. A new sensation coiled in my insides. I was excited about everything coming into my life, and yet also insecure about it.

Following through on his words, later today I had a meeting scheduled with Riley Burns at his office in Nashville.

We had met a few months ago when I flew there during Winter Break after Tucker Philips booked me for half a dozen concerts at Wild and Country over the holidays.

Then I'd driven to Memphis and spent a week home before flying back to New York City for the last semester of my college career.

Things had changed a lot for me in the past two years since I'd camped at the Silverville airport for forty-eight hours days before Christmas, hoping to catch sight of Abby if she was there too. I'd kept the promise I made to myself that night: I stopped pining for her and moved on with my life. I locked down Anderson 2.0 because I didn't like the person I was becoming. For almost a year after that, I had been in a serious relationship with a girl who lived in our building. We broke up six weeks ago when we realized we weren't meant to go the distance. We had fun while it lasted, but we both reached the same conclusion that there was no future for us after college.

Riley was impressed with the demo I'd sent last February, and we'd been in touch every other week since then.

Two nights ago, I'd received a notice that he would fly me to Nashville on the private jet of none other than my idol and one of the biggest stars in country music, Carter Hills. Who happened to be Riley's protégé and biggest client.

"Man, I'm just a phone call away," my best friend said. The same guy who never showed emotions because he thought it made him look weak had glossy eyes as we hugged a second time.

He and I had been living together for four years, and soon we'd be apart and never share an apartment or a dorm room ever again. A piano prodigy, Joe was studying to be a jazz and classical music performer in big productions. He had snatched a gig as a short-term Broadway pianist that would keep him in New York City for the summer. Afterward, he was aiming to stay either in New York or move to Los Angeles, which meant it was unlikely that our professional careers would ever tangle together.

"Call me when you get there," he said, clapping my back and not releasing me.

"Yes, Mom." I leaned back and winked at him. "Oh, come on, man. It's not like we'll never see each other again."

"It won't be the same. This Evan guy who's moving in next week is not you. And I'm sure his life will be much less entertaining than yours."

"I'll text you every day to keep you updated. And it will be like I never left."

He grimaced. "I'm opening my heart to you, and all you do is make fun of me."

"You know I love you, right?" I teased.

"Yes, well, you're moving away, so it's debatable."

"And, ladies and gentlemen, the guy who avoids clingy girls as if they're STD carriers is not willing to let me move out. How ironic."

He jerked his head back and burst out laughing. "*Touché.*"

"If—no, when. When my music career takes off, I'll travel all over the globe. And you may travel too. Let's promise each other that when we're in the same city, we'll find time to get together. Grab a drink or something. Deal?" I held out my hand, and he pressed his palm into it.

"Fine. Deal." He paused and scanned the room around us. "Do you have everything?"

I nodded.

"Quick question. Are you really gonna fly on your idol's jet?"

I shook my head as if to make sure it wasn't a joke. Yeah, even I had a hard time believing it. "Yep. Well, it's his manager's private jet, but it's mostly being used by Hills. It's like crazy."

"Agreed." Joe bent down, picked up the guitar case at

my feet, and handed it to me. "Here, get into that car waiting for you, and I'll grab the two boxes left in your room and carry them down."

"Thanks, man."

"You're already living the rich and famous lifestyle, and no one has heard of you yet. I'm proud of you."

"You will kill it on Broadway. They're lucky to have you."

His face lit up. "Seems like we'll both be taking Broadway by storm. Same street name. Different towns."

The entire length of the flight, I tried to forget I was riding like royalty and focused on my music. In vain.

A stewardess kept bringing me food and drinks, and no matter how cool I tried to play it, the truth was that I had freaking boarded a rock star's plane. It looked nothing like the commercial flights I was used to. If I had grown up with my supposedly big-shot father, this could have been my life. Maybe. Funny how things sometimes came full circle.

In Nashville, a black SUV was waiting for me. After two men unloaded my stuff from the plane and stored it in the trunk, the driver—a man in his late fifties, with salt and pepper hair—drove me to Riley Burns's office downtown.

Riley stood by the elevator when I reached his floor and exited the car, extending his arm to shake my hand. "Anderson, welcome. Usually, I would have picked you up in New York myself or met you at the airport, but I had an emergency that couldn't wait. Welcome back to Nashville. Follow me."

He steered me toward a hallway framed by a glass wall, and we passed a secretary sitting at a concrete-and-reclaimed-wood desk, busy typing something. The large windows offered the most beautiful view of Nashville's skyline. On our left was a small waiting area consisting of four chairs and a low concrete table filled with magazines, most covers featuring my music idols.

Enlarged black and white pictures of different artists performing onstage covered a section of the planked wood walls down the hallway leading to the offices and what I assumed to be a conference room. The flooring was concrete and the ceilings were open and spray-painted black, giving the entire place a semi-country, semi-industrial vibe.

When we entered Riley's office, located in one corner of the building, I froze. Two of the walls were floor-to-ceiling windows, offering a panoramic view of the city and miles of scenery beyond. Album covers and awards from music ceremonies were affixed to one of the other walls, just above a white leather couch. Two upholstered chairs and a large, slim rectangular coffee table—similar to the one in the waiting area—faced the couch, beside a bar stocked with what appeared to be expensive liquor bottles and crystal tumblers.

A concrete desk was positioned in front of the panoramic windows and was surrounded by three leather chairs. A tall cactus stood beside it, and a small door led to what I assumed was an en-suite bathroom.

"Wow. This is… Wow. I'm speechless right now."

Riley stepped aside as I followed him inside. "Grab a seat. Want anything to drink? Whiskey? Coffee? Water?"

I cleared my throat. "Water and whiskey would be great. Thanks."

When you met with the man who could change your life, you didn't refuse a drink even if it was still early in the afternoon.

While he busied himself pouring us drinks, I took a seat on the couch and studied him. Brown hair cut short on the side and longer on the top, bright eyes, he wore a dark suit but had discarded the jacket, and the sleeves of his pink shirt were rolled up to his elbows, revealing corded forearms and an expensive watch. He wore an I-mean-business expression, but I could tell from our first meeting that he wasn't as serious as he projected. I bet the guy had a playful side when he wasn't in business mode. Not much older than me and yet he was at the top of his game in the music industry. From what I'd heard, his success had nothing to do with his famous father. Riley Burns had made a name for himself on his own. From a very young age, he was determined to make it big. He had discovered Carter Hills Band when the guys were eighteen. Together, they had reached stardom, and he had never looked back. Managing only a handful of artists that he personally chose, he was both trusted and very much liked in the business. I had done my homework before agreeing to meet with him. And my many conversations with Tucker Philips at Wild and Country confirmed everything I had learned about the man.

Even though this meeting had been agreed upon almost two years ago, I still felt queasy. Being here seemed surreal, as if I could taste my dreams becoming reality.

Riley sat before me after placing the tumblers and bottles of water on the table between us. "Don't be nervous, kid."

"Yeah, well… Huh… It's hard not to be."

"Today is just a *Let's get to know each other* meeting. In the upcoming weeks, we'll go over your music catalog together. The songs you have recorded and the ones you haven't. We'll talk about what I want, but mostly about what you desire and where you see yourself in one, five, or fifteen years from now. At some point, we'll hit the studio to record some music before meeting with the executives of different record labels. I don't think you're ready to get an album out in the next six months… Twelve to eighteen months is much more realistic as a timeline. Between here and then, we'll work on your image and your technique, get you ready for tours, schedule shows, appearances, and photoshoots, and the whole nine yards. At first, you'll probably be someone's opening act until you gather enough publicity and a big enough fan base to lead your own tour. Nobody knows who Anderson Ford is, and it's a shame. I'll be beside you through all this. You have questions, you come to me. My team will be there only as support at the beginning. Slowly, they'll become more invested in you, and you'll learn to work with them as well. How does it sound?"

My heart hammered in my chest. My hands turned moist. Everything Riley had just said spoke to me, to the artist in me. Still, it looked too good to be real. "Whoa, it's a lot to process, to be honest, but I can't wait to get started." A nervous laugh left me. "Will I be able to perform until we put that album out?"

He nodded. "Yes. Absolutely. Until that album is ready to be launched, your schedule will be full. Think big, Anderson. You'll sing with Aisha Jones, Trevor McLachlan, Dylan Daughtry, Carter Hills, just to name a few. And other big names. Usually, I'd say Sam Stevens too, but he's taking some time off due to some family matter. As soon as he's back out there, I'll book you to perform with him too. There's another half-dozen artists I want you to make surprise appearances with—duets and all… Like I said, think big."

I opened and closed my mouth like a fish out of the water.

"Are you okay?" Riley asked, grinning and looking as calm as someone could ever be.

"Yeah. Sure. Where do I sign?"

He lifted his drink to his lips. "Love your enthusiasm, kid. My lawyer will draft a contract and send it to you. Have your lawyer review it. Once you approve it and we agree on any changes both parties want to make, we'll be good to go."

I nodded twice. "Great." I tried to act casual, but inside I was a firework show about to explode. I had no idea how to deal with all this. A contract. A world tour. Duets with my idols. The whole thing sounded far-fetched, and yet so real at the same time.

"I'll get a car to drive you to Memphis with all your stuff. You should receive the contract by registered mail within a week or two. When you are ready to meet again and talk about it, let me know. We'll schedule a meeting. Once all the paperwork is signed, I'll get you an apartment in town until you secure something more permanent. It'll be easier if you're in town while we work together."

"O-okay. That's very generous of you."

"My artists are super important to me. They are family. And family is something you cherish."

For the next hour, we chatted about a million things related to the music industry and other unrelated stuff. It turned out Riley and I both had a sweet spot for rom-coms and couldn't get enough of tomato jam, a taste we'd both inherited from our fathers it seemed. I wasn't ashamed to say that Riley Burns was a great man. With good values my mother would approve of and a strong sense of ethics. At some point, my mind drifted to Abby. She would be ecstatic right now if she knew I were here with him. After all, this man was one of her idols.

When we stood, ready to part ways, I shook his hand.

Twenty minutes later, unable to reel in the stupid grin shaping my lips, I sat in the little bar next door to grab a bite before being driven to my mother's house. The driver

Riley had booked for me was on speed dial, ready to go as soon as I was. My relationship with my mother had improved over the past year. I was still not over all the lies, but I had agreed to give her the benefit of the doubt and trusted that she had done what she did out of love for me. One day, I'd let her explain, but I still wasn't ready, scared of the emotional tsunami that would follow.

I ordered a salad and was texting Joe about the meeting when a man I had only seen on TV sat across from me.

"Fuck" was the single word that escaped my mouth. "Whoa, you are *the* Curtis Burns."

"Hey, Anderson."

Oh, he knew my name. Wait. What? How come?

"Can we have a chat? I'm a friend of your mother. She told me about your meeting."

"My mother? How do you—?" Realization hit me. Like a ton of bricks. Air had a hard time reaching my lungs. It couldn't be, could it? My own idol. "No. No, this isn't funny. Tell me you're not who I think you are. Please." *Anderson Curtis Ford.* A storm rose inside me. I balled my fists against my thighs. "Are you…? Oh God, please say that you're not."

He watched me, not saying anything. His throat worked. For a long beat, our eyes fixated on each other. I studied his features. Green eyes with golden rims, brown hair almost the same shade as mine, square jaw, and thick golden brows. In many ways, we looked very much alike.

A wave of discomfort spread through me, making me dizzy. The hair on my arms stood on end. He didn't have to admit it out loud. I already knew the truth that would soon leave his lips. And ruin my entire life. "C'mon, old man. Spill it already."

"Anderson, I'm your father."

A loud chuckle left me. "Oh wow, it sounds like a line from a movie."

His face was unreadable, his lips not even twitching as we stared at each other.

"Fuck, it's not a joke, right?"

"No, *son*."

The admission of my worst fears sent a surge of nausea to the back of my throat, and my laughter died out. All this time, I had idolized my own father. Hung posters of him on my wall as a young teenager. Sung his songs at school talent shows. Pretended to be him at award ceremonies when I was nine.

My mother never said a thing about it. She'd kept it a secret until now. The fragile progress in our relationship died in an instant.

My parents were delusional. Two sick bastards. Liars.

Curtis Burns didn't even blink when he'd confirmed my suspicion.

"Fuck, I was conceived by two crackheads. Were you high that night?" His lips parted, but before he could say something, I added, "Say nothing. I don't wanna know the details of your sexual encounter." I breathed hard. "Let's rewind and get back to the reason you're here." I stared into his eyes, searching for answers. Answers to what, I had no clue, but something that could justify his presence here on one of the most important days of my professional life. "What were you doing just before coming here and spoiling my day? Spying on me? Waiting in the shadow of the building, ready to ambush me the moment I was alone?"

He sighed. "Not exactly. Anyway, we gotta talk. It's important."

"Nope. I have nothing to say to you. I already told my mother that the last time she tried to tell me about you, years ago. I'm still not interested. Get lost. Forget I exist. You've been great at doing that all my life… Just keep pretending we never met."

His stance stiffened. I was quite tall, but Curtis Burns had broader shoulders and looked more imposing than I did. Perhaps it was his age or life experience, but he didn't seem like a man you'd want to butt heads with. "Today, you will listen. I won't take no for an answer. I'm not your mama. I've been in this business a long time. Tantrums and big egos don't impress me. Don't throw a fit, and we'll be fine. Are we clear, son?"

I could feel anger awakening deep within me. "Don't call me that. I'm not yours and never was. And never will be. Forget about me, old man. And I know you weren't present in my life all this time, but I'm not three anymore, in case you haven't noticed. I don't throw a fit when I don't get sweets."

I motioned to stand, but he leaned over and grabbed my arm, preventing my escape. "Anderson. Sit. Now."

My eyes widened. All my life, I had wished I could meet with my idol, but right now, Curtis Burns was the last man I wanted to spend time with. But when he said my name like that, I felt obligated to listen. And hated myself for doing so.

He let go of me once I sank back into my seat and folded my arms over my chest. "What is it? You have five minutes."

He scratched his throat, as if he were uncomfortable saying whatever was about to leave his mouth.

I lifted one brow. "Talk. Four minutes and forty-three seconds. The clock is ticking, *Curtis*."

He flinched when I said his name. If he thought *Daddy* would come out of my mouth, he was in for the longest ride of his life.

"You can't sign with Riley. Before I say what I have to say, just know he's the best in the industry, but he isn't right for you."

"Why?" I coughed. A strange sensation knotted my stomach. It felt as if all my dreams were about to crash and burn. "Says who?" I studied his expression. Tight lips, flushed cheeks, he was indeed not kidding. "Why? Tell me one reason why I should listen to you. You've been M.I.A. forever, and now you think you have the right to boss me around?"

He remained silent as if searching for his next words.

For the second time in as many minutes, reality hit me like a cold shower. Riley Burns, the man about to propel me to stardom, was my big brother. *Half-brother.* But still, we were related, sharing DNA.

"Fuck no." I hesitated between hurling my glass at the wall and crying. This couldn't be true. It had to be a mistake. A fucking joke. Was it another one of my nightmares?

"As I said, we need to talk." His deep baritone voice reverberated through me.

"You. Are. Sick. Aren't you done messing with both your sons' lives? Aren't you too old to play games? You can't be serious. We have a deal, he and I."

"If you could listen for two seconds, I'll explain everything."

"Not interested. I already heard that song. From my mother. Wasn't interested then, and not interested now."

"Anderson. Please…"

I released a breath full of anger and spotted the server returning with my meal over his shoulder. *Dammit.*

My father looked straight into my eyes. "Riley, he… huh…he doesn't know about you. For now, I'd like to keep it that way."

I buried my face in my hands, wishing I could remove myself from this encounter. "Stop. Shut up. Leave. Don't talk anymore. Just go."

"I'm sorry, Anderson, but you can't work with him."

A deep tear ripped through my chest, and I had to hold myself back from becoming a sobbing mess at his words.

I stared at him, wondering if I were imagining our conversation. He offered me a soft, apologetic smile that confirmed it was all real.

My heart plummeted ten stories in my chest, and I stayed frozen. I'd been right seconds ago. All my dreams were crumbling before my eyes, and I was unable to do anything about it.

Chapter 27

Abigail

"It's okay, baby. Shhh. I'm right here. It will be fine. We're going to see the doctor."

Alexi's little fingers fisted my shirt, his koala bear blanket pressed between us, as fat tears streamed down his reddened cheeks.

I blinked away the ones forming in my eyes, hoping to stay strong.

In the last year, my baby had been sick more than he should have been, and I had no idea how to make it better. Since he turned one, recurrent ear infections had been keeping us up too many nights to count and had brought us to the emergency room more times than I could remember. He wailed, his face pressed into my chest, and my heart fractured. My shoulders dropped, and I felt so powerless.

The cab halted before us on the sidewalk, and I fastened my arms around my son. The night air sent shivers through me. Shifting Alexi to my left hip, I fiddled with the cab door handle, trying not to drop my purse, which had slid down to my elbow.

His cries intensified, and he pressed his hands over his ears, jerking his head back with a sudden motion I wasn't prepared for.

I lost my footing and braced a hand against the steel frame of the vehicle to keep from falling into the street. My heart pounded in my head, and I let out a heavy sigh as I slouched into the backseat and pulled the door shut behind me.

"*Mammma.*" My baby's voice acted like a sword stabbing my heart. He lifted his watery eyes to me, and I could read all the suffering lingering in their midnight-blue depths. His dark brown hair was soaked and stuck to his forehead, and I pushed the soft curls back with my fingers. Alexi was a miniature version of Andy. Except for his blue irises, everything about my baby was a tiny replica of his father.

A pinch in my chest reminded me I was alone on this journey, and I shut my eyes to chase away the fresh surge of sadness twisting my insides and filling my heart with pain. On nights like this, I wished I had someone to rely on. Someone to tell me everything would be all right, to kiss me and wrap me in their arms, shielding me from the harsh truths of the world for an instant, to pick me up when I felt like I was falling apart.

I pressed a kiss to the top of my baby's head and wiped his teary face with a finger. "I love you, Alexi. I love you so much. And I-I'm sorry you are hurting." My voice cracked, and my eyes burned with my own tears. "I'm sorry that I can't take your pain away... That it hurts so bad."

The painkiller finally kicked in, and his eyelids fluttered close. He felt heavier in my arms, and the soft sound of his snoring mixed with the soothing sound of the tires rolling on the pavement. I blinked quickly to keep the new tears burning at the back of my eyes at bay, and with my arms wrapped protectively around him, I watched the scenery pass by through the window.

Alexi moaned and shifted in his sleep, nestling himself deeper in my arms.

Entangled together, we held on to each other for the rest of the ride.

Last year, after he had suffered four back-to-back ear infections, a lot of fluid had built up in his middle ear. The doctors had to insert tubes into his eardrums to drain the fluid and relieve the pressure and pain. But even nine months later, the infections were still coming back every couple of weeks. So here we were again, on our way to meet with the ENT late at night.

The car came to a stop, and, taking care not to wake my son, I slid across the backseat until my feet landed on the sidewalk. With one hand braced on the back of the seat, I pushed myself out of the cab and kicked the door shut behind me.

After I checked in with the nurse on duty, we were led to a room where I laid Alexi on the bed, covering him with his fluffy silver-gray koala blanket. I brushed his hair back with my fingers as I sat on the edge of the bed and watched him sleep peacefully. His face no longer carried the same painful expression as it had earlier, and I relaxed a little.

A voice in my head nagged at me. Telling me we weren't out of the storm. That I needed to find the strength within me for the challenges about to hit our lives.

After everything that had happened since the day my parents kicked me out of the house, I hadn't caught a break. Deep down, I was exhausted, but I had no time for a mental breakdown. I had to keep going. Keep pushing through. Until I made all my dreams come true.

The doctor met us, and after further examination, he prescribed another run of antibiotics. "Ms. Peña, we need to talk about Alexi's condition. We've tried everything, but the chronic infections are still coming back. I'm afraid there will be long-term side effects if this keeps happening."

I stood straight, waiting for him to explain himself. "Wh-what do you mean?"

"So many ear infections at this age can lead to speech and language difficulties. Delays that will need to be addressed as he grows older."

My eyes drifted to my little boy's sleeping form beneath his favorite blanket, and a mass grew in my chest. "What… Ohmygod… What do we do now?"

He unlocked the tablet in his hand and scrolled through it before lifting his eyes back to mine. "I can schedule you a follow-up appointment in ten days. We'll wait until the antibiotics have healed the current infection, and then we'll run some tests. How does it sound?"

I nodded, at a loss for words.

Dr. Philibert tapped my shoulder. "Don't get ahead of yourself, Ms. Peña. We won't jump to conclusions until we know more. Go back home, get some sleep, and take care of your little boy. My assistant will call you on Monday to schedule that follow-up appointment."

My emotions had deserted me, and I remained still, unsure how to process everything.

"Ms. Peña?"

I snapped out of it. "Yes. Sorry."

"It's late, and it's a lot to take in. You can rest assured we'll do everything in our power to make Alexi feel better. Any questions?"

I shook my head, unsure what to ask as I was still processing the news.

"Have a great night."

I swallowed. "Thank you. For seeing us tonight. I'll wait for your…huh…assistant's call."

Shouldering my purse, I gathered my son—still enveloped in his blanket—after booking a cab on my phone.

Sitting on a bench outside the hospital, I cradled him, rocking back and forth, wishing we were already home—or ten days later, when we'd know more about his condition, as Dr. Philibert had said earlier.

With my eyes closed and my head pressed against the brick wall behind me, I imagined a life where things would flow easily and wouldn't be so hard all the time.

———

The next morning, I woke up at six, after sleeping for about three hours. Alexi slept beside me, his dark locks spread across the pillow, his angelic face bringing a smile to my lips. One hour after we'd returned home last night, he woke up in his bed, screaming and pressing his palms to either side of his head, blinded by tears. The pain was back. After another dose of painkiller, I carried him to my bed, and we snuggled until the tears dried and sleep won the battle. For both of us.

Dressed in nothing but the long T-shirt I used to wear while I was pregnant and knee socks, with my hair knotted into a messy updo, I shuffled toward the kitchen, stifling a yawn. I poured myself a giant mug of coffee the minute the coffeemaker announced it was ready. Bringing the hot drink to my nose, I took a deep breath, hoping the aroma was strong enough to wake me up fully.

I had an eight-hour workload today that I could manage in five if everything went as planned, along with two readings and a paper due by tonight. Working and studying remotely at least allowed me to be there for my baby. Anyway, it wasn't like I could afford daycare right now. With medical expenses, the rent, groceries, and utilities, I was barely making ends meet. A third client had agreed to start working together next month. He'd pay me a generous amount for fifteen hours of work per week to manage his social media and newsletter. I had no idea how I'd be able to fit him into my busy schedule, but I needed the money, so I'd have to make time for him. If things went well, he said he would double my hours within three months. He would pay an hourly rate higher than my two other clients combined, so this was the perfect scenario. Fewer hours of work for a bigger pay, which meant more time to study and play or go to the park with Alexi during the day.

My gaze drifted around the room. The scattered wooden blocks in the living room brought a smile to my face.

While I prepped breakfast, I checked my emails and updated my calendar for the day. Yesterday had been cut short to care for my baby boy, and that had put me behind schedule. I would let him sleep in this morning since his night had been hectic. Through the partly open door of my bedroom, I checked on Alexi, making sure he was still deep asleep. Tiptoeing away, I grabbed my laptop and my breakfast and sat at the refurbished desk I had set in the hallway between our bedrooms. Painted in a happy shade of yellow, the old desk brought a touch of color to our apartment.

For three hours, I worked without interruption. My

phone vibrated next to me, and I returned to the kitchen to take the call, so it wouldn't wake up my son.

Ellie's face flashed on the screen. "Morning, *gurrrl*. How are you doing?" she greeted, her usual cheerful tone unconvincing.

"Hey you. Back from England?"

"Nah. I'm there for another week. You won't believe who I met in that little dive bar I visited last night."

"He or she?"

"He."

"Do I know him?"

"Of course. Come on, guess."

"Huh… Any clue?"

"Silverville."

"Tom?" My first guess was Ellie's college boyfriend. She was heartbroken when they split up after graduation because he'd accepted a job offer in Japan.

"Yep. The same."

"And?"

"*Gurrrl*, it was like no time had passed since we last saw each other. I don't know… A part of me still misses him."

"Did you talk to him?" I asked, now engrossed in the retelling of this encounter.

"Not at first. I sat in a corner and spied on him. He looked so handsome in his tailored suit and shorter hair. Like businessman hot. I swear, my ovaries cried. He was all alone, sitting at the bar, his tie loose around his neck and his elbows propped up on the counter. Somehow, he looked sad. And lonely."

"The same guy who was always in party mode and couldn't stay still for more than a minute in class?"

"Yep. My heart broke at the sight."

"Ellie. Come on, I have work to do and a pretty busy day. Just say it already."

She laughed, but it lacked her usual warmth. "I went to him. His eyes widened when he realized it was me standing next to him, and his lips transformed into a small smile. We didn't have to talk to each other. Our eyes said it all."

"Did you—?"

"We spent the night together. He took the first flight back to Japan this morning." Her voice quivered. "I'm sad now."

"Oh honey, I'm so sorry. I know he was the one who got away. I wish I could hug you right now."

"He-he said he was moving back here. Well, not here, but the US. Next year. Do you think it's like fate or something? Destiny giving us another chance?"

I weighed my words before asking, "Ellie, do you still love him?"

She remained silent for a long minute. "Last night, we didn't fuck. Does that answer your question?"

I huffed long breath. "Yes. What are you going to do?"

"No idea. He hasn't been in a relationship since we broke up. Me neither. I tried. Many times. Went on dates… But my heart is never into it. I wish I could take the next flight to Japan and be together with him."

"I know. It's funny when you think about what we all saw when you two were together back then and you kept denying you were nothing more than a fling. Sorry for asking, but did he say whether he could see you two picking things up where you left off?"

"When he was sitting by himself, all sad, he had heard our song on his way over, and he had written me a text. He just never sent it. He showed it to me. My hair stood on end on my arms when I read his words." She paused. "It's crazy to think we could have another chance… Or that my last boyfriend is my forever guy."

"Join the club," I said, my words tinted with a little humor.

"Enough talking about Tom. How's my man doing? If I wait another twenty years, think Alexi would date an older woman?"

"Ellie."

"Just joking. My heart is taken. I'm screwed. Seriously, how's my little guy?"

"Not so great. We spent the night at the ER."

"Again?"

"Yeah."

"His ears?" she asked, her voice gentle and filled with empathy now.

"Even the tubes have failed. I'm supposed to meet with his otolaryngologist again in ten days. They'll run some tests. They think it could eventually affect his speech and language."

"Oh, I'm so sorry, Abby. You guys don't need another hardship in your lives. Why can't you two catch a break for once?"

My shoulders slumped, and I sank into a kitchen chair. "Guess it's not in our immediate future."

"When I'm back in the country and have some free time, I'm flying in to see you. We'll eat junk food and binge-watch rom-coms and tearjerker movies for an entire weekend. And drink too much wine. And together cry about our love lives. And snuggle up against your little guy because he's the best, and I miss you two."

"We miss you too."

"I wish we were lovers, you and I. We could co-parent Alexi together, and life would be much simpler. Abigail Peña, would you marry me?"

"Any day, if that was even a possibility." I checked the time when the sound of little feet padding on the floor from my bedroom caught my attention. My face brightened when Alexi's face peeked through the ajar door, and his lips curled into a smile when his gaze landed on me. In that moment, I knew that no matter what life threw at us, we'd be fine. "Elles, I gotta go. Alexi is up, and I need to give him his medicine and prep his breakfast."

"Can I say hi first? Switch to video. I wanna see his baby face."

Seconds later, my best friend's face appeared on the screen.

"Oh, geez. You look terrible," I said before I could lock the words in.

"Yeah, well, I could say the same to you. Did you even get any sleep last night after your visit to the ER? At least my reasons were big and thick since I was busy orgasming around the best dick and tongue in town. You really need a break. Next time I have time off, I swear I'm ringing your doorbell."

I lifted my baby boy into my arms, and he grabbed the device from my grip. Before either Ellie or I could say something, he planted a kiss on the screen. "Lili," he singsonged in a small sleepy voice.

"Oh my goodness, I miss you so much, little guy. Auntie Lili will come visit you soon, okay?"

He bobbed his head a couple of times before pointing to his right ear. "Booboo."

"Your ear hurts?" Ellie asked.

Once again, Alexi bobbed his head. "Ouch."

"I know, sweetie. I'll leave you to your mama so she can take good care of you." Her attention switched to me. "If you need anything—money or for me to hire a babysitter —you'd tell me, right?" Her face bore no room for arguments.

"Yes. But I won't." Each month, since the day I'd

moved out of my parents' house, she had been asking me the same question. Every time, except once, I'd refused her help. I owed her five hundred bucks, and as soon as I had some savings, I would pay her back. She kept saying it wasn't a loan but a gift. Blame it on my pride, but I didn't like the idea of being a charity case. So one day, I'd pay my friend back. The entire amount. Plus interest.

"I don't know how you do it all on your own. Again, you're a superwoman, Abby, and my idol. I'm so proud of you."

Tears welled up in my eyes. I was exhausted. Both physically and mentally. "Thanks. It means a lot."

In my arms, Alexi rested his head in the crook of my neck and started moaning in pain. My lips lingered on the side of his head.

"Go, take care of him," Ellie said, her eyes full of concern.

"I'll be okay, I swear. Don't worry about me. Keep me updated about the developments in Tom's and your story. I'll live vicariously through you."

"I will. We're supposed to chat later. Try to take some time off for yourself. You really look like shi—you really look awful. Bye. Love you."

"Love you too."

After Alexi took his medicine and ate pieces of toast— grimacing when I tried to feed him watermelon, something he and his daddy had in common—we settled on the couch, and I rocked him in my arms. With my eyes closed, I sang to him. His little arms, which were holding me tight, relaxed around me, and his breathing slowed. Switching positions, I lay on my side and decided a nap would be beneficial for both of us. After I set the alarm on my phone, I drifted into a dreamless slumber.

———

"What do you mean?" I asked Dr. Philibert in a shaky voice as we sat in his office, a sterile room with bluish-white walls and chrome and glossy white Formica furniture. We weren't in his usual child-friendly office with lime-green walls and colorful accessories that Alexi and I had gotten to know over the last year. No, this room felt more like a *you have three months left to live* kinda room. here cancer patients received their final diagnosis.The first step toward the dark tunnel. The thought sent chills through me.

I fastened my cardigan before wrapping my arms around myself, trying to inject some warmth into my body. And much-needed comfort. Through a small window, I peeked at Alexi, busy playing with his toy cars with a nurse because Dr. Philibert had insisted we have an adult chat without interruption.

"As I was saying, according to all the tests we've run so far…"

His words hadn't even reached my ears the first time, so I'd asked him to repeat himself so I could process everything he'd said.

I nodded and made some unconvincing *Mmm-hmm* sounds while he scrolled through a tablet, showing me data and graphs I had no interest in.

"As you can see, Ms. Peña, we have options. We'll run more tests, and as Alexi grows older, we'll know more about the condition. Often, with a diagnosis like his, it gets better with age. As the body matures. But I don't want you to get your hopes up. As the pictures I showed you minutes ago demonstrate, his case is a tricky one. And these weren't the results I expected."

"Will…will he—?" I couldn't bring myself to ask the question out loud. As if asking it would make it true.

The doctor squeezed my hand over the desk for a brief second, as if trying to offer me some comfort…or keep me from feeling alone. "The truth?"

I bobbed my head a few times, staring into his eyes to make sure he wasn't bullshitting me.

He shook his head once and exhaled loudly. "We don't know. It's hard to tell without further testing a few years down the line. In two or three years…maybe."

My gaze drifted back to my baby playing in the other room, not aware of the burden of the news the ENT had delivered just now.

"I can refer you to support groups. Or other families who have gone through the same ordeal. We hold information sessions here at the hospital every other month. You won't be alone. We have an entire team who will support you in this transition…into this new reality."

My eyes stayed wide, as if I were blinded by headlights in the middle of the night on a dark street, unsure what to do. What was I supposed to say? What questions was I supposed to ask? My brain had fried—there was no other explanation. It felt as if I couldn't think or speak anymore. All the information I'd just received had piled up in my mind, and my brain couldn't process it, let alone analyze it.

"Do you have family who can help you out? Alexi's father perhaps. His grandparents?"

I stayed silent.

"Ms. Peña?"

Slowly, I moved my head from side to side. My mouth was parched. I closed my eyes for a second, trying to gather my thoughts. Something inside me felt like it was shaking loose…maybe a piece of my heart. When I returned my attention to the doctor, who was watching me closely, I drew in a shallow breath. "We're…we're all alone. We… we've always…we've always been."

He bowed his head. "Remember that we're here to help you through all of this."

We chatted a little longer, but I barely heard a word. All I wanted right now was to get my little boy and cuddle him until the storm passed. Until we knew more. Until I felt strong enough to face my reality head-on.

Once I got home, I went through the motions, feeding my son and putting him down for his nap. I stayed sitting on his bed next to him, combing his hair back with my fingertips, praying this day had never happened and I would get a do-over. With a different endgame.

My tears were stuck in my throat.

Even though I tried to cry—I wanted to cry—they wouldn't come.

At some point, I left his bedroom and went into the kitchen. It was as if I were living in a parallel universe and no longer in control. As if my body and soul were out of sync. A ghost in my own home, not sure what to think, what to feel, or what to do next.

After I poured myself a cup of tea and sat on the couch, I dialed Ellie. I had to talk to someone. To try to understand the weight of the news I'd received. To get it off my chest. And to rationalize it and move into solution mode…or something like that.

She picked up after the third ring. At the sound of her voice, something inside me broke, like a dam giving way. No matter how much I told myself to stop crying, I couldn't.

"What did the doctor say?" she asked. She knew about the appointment. We had talked over the phone last night about it, and she'd promised everything would be all right.

I sobbed, unable to get a grip on my emotions.

"Hey, talk to me." Her soft voice enveloped me. Like a hug.

Something I missed so badly these days. For some reason, I wished my parents were still in my life. Or that I had someone who could kiss it better. The former had never reached out, and the latter, well, I had no time for a love life.

"I can't—" My voice cracked. "It-it's bad. How am I going to survive another challenge?" More sobs shook my core. "I'm so exhausted…"

Tremors wracked my body. Curling up in a ball on the couch with my phone clasped in my hand and pressed to my ear, I cried until my throat felt raw. And my tear ducts had dried up.

Once I calmed down, my best friend said, "Abby, tell me everything the ENT said."

I sniffled. "Ellie, I'm not equipped to deal with this."

"You're Abigail Peña. Never underestimate yourself. You're the most extraordinary and resilient person I know. Whatever it is, don't let it set you back. It's okay to be defeated, but you gotta get up and ride the shit out of whatever news you have received. You hear me?"

I remained silent.

"You hear me?" she repeated. "Say it. Out loud. So I can hear you."

"I hear you."

"Louder. With more conviction."

"I hear you. I'm gonna ride the shit out of this news and move forward. Because I'm fucking Abigail Peña and I can do this."

"Great. Now switch the call to video chat and tell me everything."

I nodded and did as she asked, not in the mood to fight. I propped my device up on the armrest of the couch over a pillow and sat cross-legged, trying to explain everything I remembered from the doctor's visit earlier.

Once I put it out there, I saw the wet gloss shining in her eyes.

"Oh wow. This isn't what I expected either." She paused for a beat. "I'm sorry, Abby," she said after a moment. "But if someone can go through this, it's you. You're strong. And fierce. Alexi is lucky to have you in his life. What are the next steps?"

I shrugged and buried my face in my hands, helplessness and fear raging inside me. "If only I knew…"

———

Continue the story in **_Broken Link_**
emmanuellesnowshop.com/products/broken-link

Thank you for reading the first part of Abigail and Anderson's beautiful and emotional story.
emmanuellesnow.com

———

Carter Hills's story: Read **_False Promises_**
Riley Burns's story: Read **_Last Hope_**
Aisha Jones's story: Read **_Midnight Sparks_**
All available at emmanuellesnow.com

ACKNOWLEDGMENTS

From the moment Andy and Abby took shape in my mind, I knew I had to tell their story. Those two stole my heart from the first line. Two years ago, I wrote about their love in the form of a novella, and readers acclaimed the book. There had always been a little voice in my head telling me I should write their complete journey. The one with all the ups and downs, loves, fears, and hopes. The one where nothing went as planned, but love won in the end.

Andy and Abby's story is not a simple one. It's an emotional roller coaster that leaves you breathless most times and teary eyed on occasion. But it's also one of resilience, faith, and serendipity. But mostly, it's about true love.

I hope these two live in your heart for a long time, and I can't wait to bring the conclusion of their wild journey.

Thank you to my kids, because being an author is a family endeavor. They are my biggest supporters, the ones who are there on the good and bad days. I love you guys. Each time they ask a stranger if they know about my books, I can't help but smile at the innocence of their hearts.

Thank you to my husband, my partner in crime, who takes over my chores when I'm in a creative flow or on strict deadlines. You never complain, and I love you for being a hands-on dad and my best friend on this journey called life.

To my editor, Shalini. These stories wouldn't be the same without you adding your magical touch. Thank you for pushing me to always be the best author I can be.

To Virginie. Working together is one of the highlights of my months. You bring a sense of calm into my life and hope that everything will work out in the end.

To my Snowmates team, you guys are amazing. I love your excitement each time I announce a new release.

To the Bookstagrammers, YouTubers, TikTokers, bloggers, and everyone else who loves my books and helps spread the word, a big thank you. I can't tell you how happy it makes me to see you talk, share, and post reviews about my books. I wish I could hug you all.

To my readers. THANK YOU! I think it sums it all.

To everyone who believes they have been dealt a bad hand in life, remember when everything goes to hell, life comes through, bringing its own surprises, and often things get better when we least expect it. It sounds clichéd, but it's true.

Snowbound is a wrap. Thank you all for making this book even more special than it is.

With much love and gratitude,

Emmanuelle

WANT MORE EMOTIONAL LOVE STORIES?

WHICH COUPLE WILL YOU PICK NEXT?

False Promises

★★★★★ "The angst, the utter heartbreak, and protectiveness I felt for Carter during this book is unreal!"

★★★★★ "Emmanuelle Snow really knows how to tug at all of your emotions and does such a great job of bringing her characters to life!"

A gripping story of sizzling passion, lust, and the price of fame.
Start Carter Hills's story now

———

Sweet Agony

★★★★★ "If I could give more than 5 stars, I would."

★★★★★ "This is not a romance, it is a story about first love, first heartbreak and growing up."

A compelling tale of love, friendship, and self-discovery that will tug at your heartstrings.

Start Dahlia's story now

———

Cruel Destiny

★★★★★ "Wow. Just wow. If that could be my review, that is all I would write."

★★★★★ "Emmanuelle has done it yet again. She found a way to slip into my mind and heart with her words and the creation of characters you can't help but fall in love with."

★★★★★ "This book broke my heart in the first twenty five percent and sewed it back together."

A story of healing, second chances, and the risks of opening your heart to someone new. Can they trust each other with their hearts, or will their pasts keep them apart?

Read Nick and Dahlia's love story now

———

Wild Encounter

★★★★★ "This is by far one of the most well-written

book I've read this month. It is dynamic, intriguing, interesting, unafraid to go there and most of all touching."

★★★★★ "I personally wouldn't call this book JUST a romance novel because it's so much more. I 100% recommend it no doubt in mind."

A tale of passion and perseverance that will leave your heart racing and your spirit soaring.

Read Tucker and Addison's love story now

————

Last Hope

★★★★★ "This book was not only about the darkness but it was about pure love, hope, spice, family, and friendships on point with just the right amount without overpowering the storyline at all."

★★★★★ "Devon and Riley's story is a beautiful one with a lot of emotions. The subject matter is intense but it is handled very gently."

A tale of resilience and second chances in a world where love and danger intertwine.

Read Riley and Devon's love story now

————

Midnight Sparks

★★★★★ "The characters, the love, the humor, the steaminess, the emotions… it's everything I hoped and more."

★★★★★ "I think that is one Emmanuelle Snow's sexiest novels yet."

Welcome to the island where Holiday magic meets unexpected romance and a chance at a fresh start.

Read Gavin and Aisha's love story now

————

Fallen Legend

★★★★★ ""The love that grows, not only through tough angst but through unconditional moments had my heart. This is a spicy and riveting book"

★★★★★ "Emmanuelle Snow doesn't just tell a story, she creates an entire world."

A poignant and uplifting journey of hope, love, and the power of second chances.

Read Sam and Madison's love story now

————

Snowbound

★★★★★ "5 big stars from me for this amazing story. Absolutely loved it!"

★★★★★ "Emmanuelle Snow's stories are always full of angst, and Snowbound is no exception."

The intertwined lives of two strangers bound by fate in the midst of a snowstorm.

Read Anderson and Abigail's love story now

———

All available at emmanuellesnow.com

ABOUT THE AUTHOR

Soulfully Beautiful Love Stories

USA Today Bestselling Author Emmanuelle Snow is an author of contemporary YA and women's fiction love stories, who gives life to strong characters who'll fight with all they have to reach their life goals and find their own happiness. She loves her characters to be relatable and realistic.

Emmanuelle is in love with love. Especially complicated, deep, and passionate feelings that make a relationship extraordinary and complex all at the same time.

In her spare time, when she's not writing or reading, she likes to go on road trips—with her four kids and her own soulmate—watch movies, paint, or do some DIY, always with a cup of green tea in her hand and listening to country music.

She splits her time between beautiful Canada and the small US towns she adores.

Find all of Emmanuelle's books here:

emmanuellesnow.com

———

Want to connect with Emmanuelle online?
YOU CAN FIND HER HERE:

Website
emmanuellesnow.com

Author's bookstore and merch store
emmanuellesnow.com

Snow's VIP newsletter
emmanuellesnow.com

Readers' VIP group Snow's Soulmates
facebook.com/groups/snowvip

amazon.com/author/emmanuellesnow

goodreads.com/emmanuellesnow

bookbub.com/authors/emmanuelle-snow

facebook.com/esnowauthor

instagram.com/snowemmanuelle

x.com/snowemmanuelle

pinterest.com/snowemmanuelle

tiktok.com/@snowemmanuelle

ALSO BY THE AUTHOR

CARTER HILLS BAND UNIVERSE

(suggested reading order)

Carter Hills Band series

False Promises

HEART SONG DUET

Blindsided

Forevermore

Whiskey Melody series

Sweet Agony

SECOND TEAR DUET

Cruel Destiny

Beautiful Salvation

BREATHLESS DUET

Wild Encounter

Brittle Scars

Upon A Star Series

Last Hope

Midnight Sparks

Love Song For Two Series

EMMANUELLE
USA TODAY BESTSELLING AUTHOR
SNOW
LAST
HOPE
Upon a Star series - book one
LOVE
HOPE

LAST HOPE

RILEY

Our eyes met. Something passed between us. Attraction. Recognition. Yearning. Maybe a mix of all three. And much more. I brought the tumbler to my lips, relishing the burning sensation of the whiskey as it slid down my throat.

A gear shifted inside me.

My heart did one of its moves. The one where it got all bothered and excited.

I fastened my grip around the glass in my hand.

The woman pushed her long, curled blonde hair over one shoulder, giving me a perfect view of her lickable, slim neck. *Lickable?* Was that even a word? I pushed the thought away. I was a man on a mission.

The vampiric side of me—the one I hadn't known existed until now—emerged in full force.

I blinked.

The temptation to bite the soft flesh of her neck multiplied by the second.

The woman smiled, and all my restraints broke loose. They caught fire and burned to ashes in the dark night.

I gave her a subtle nod as I continued staring, hoping for a slight hint of encouragement from her.

Her red-painted lips pursed as she mouthed *Hey* in my direction.

Smoothing my palm over my trousers, I made a beeline for her, my steps light and focused, not allowing the sea of people to break our eye contact. The air around us heated up. We were outdoors, but it felt as if someone had cranked up the thermostat. Slowly, I raked my fingers through my brown hair, gelled to perfection tonight, doing my best not to mess it up. From an outsider's point of view, I bet I looked in control—the opposite of how I really felt. No one in the business needed to know how unruly my heart was behaving. Or the tremble that had started in my fingers. The flickers of excitement that burned in my core.

A server passed by, and I discarded my tumbler before grabbing two champagne flutes from his tray.

In two long strides, I reached the woman in the red lace dress. Her smile reached her eyes when I offered her the sparkling alcohol. "To a great night and even greater company," I said as we clinked our glasses. "I'm Riley." I held out my hand for her to shake. Our palms met, and a jolt of heat surged through me, setting my insides ablaze in a way no woman ever had. Her touch alone threatened to make me combust.

"I'm Devon."

I lifted our joined hands to my lips and kissed the back of hers.

Her soft chuckle resonated through me. "I can already tell you're a gentleman."

"My mama taught me well. So, what brings you here, Devon? I've never seen you at one of these country music parties before."

"Oh, you go to these a lot? This is my first time. It's

quite intimidating. A friend of mine invited me, but she's running late."

I followed her gaze across the rooftop bar. Country music singers, songwriters, and musicians counted for more than half of the patrons here, and together, they'd won enough awards to fill an entire room. Woven through them were music producers, managers, movie stars, and their dates. Yeah, to someone unfamiliar, the crowd could easily appear impressive.

My man, Carter Hills, waved at me when my eyes drifted to him. I raised my glass in his direction. He was not only one of the biggest artists here tonight, but also one of my protégés and closest friends. Over the years, we rose to the top of this industry together, our friendship growing stronger with each album. We had each other's backs. Always.

"All these people, they aren't as intimidating as they look once you get to know them. Most of them are pretty great actually. Down to earth, and genuinely nice. Don't let their success make you nervous. Looking great is part of their job description. But there's much more to them. Well, to some of them at least."

The woman snickered and clutched my elbow, balancing her weight on her four-inch nude stilettos. "You seem like the kind of man who knows a lot about the country music scene, am I right?"

I took another sip of my drink and shrugged, my eyes trained on her face, enjoying the tilt of her red lips. "You could say that. I've been around these folks my entire life, but an active part of their world for almost a decade."

Devon's gray-blue eyes flared. "You're a country singer? Ohmygod, I'm sorry if I didn't recognize you." A flush crept along her neck and cheeks. The same neck I was still dying to feast on.

"Nah. I'm not. Believe me, you don't want to hear me sing. It may burst your eardrums. No kidding."

She grinned at me, and my heart swelled in my chest. "Who are you then? What's your superpower?"

"I'm a manager." I pointed to Carter, now deep in a conversation with Rita L. Sterling, a music producer. "I manage this fellow's career, amongst others."

Devon moved closer and lowered her voice to a whisper as if she feared someone would hear her. Not a chance with the chatter and music surrounding us. "Is that Carter Hills? I'm sorry. I'm not a groupie, I swear, but I thought I recognized him earlier when I walked in."

"Yeah, that's him. I can introduce you later."

She shook her head, the blush on her cheeks darkening. "No, you don't have to. I-I'm nobody here. I'm not part of this world. This night is surreal, I—"

A waitress bumped into my side and lost her footing, sending an entire tray of red wine glasses crashing all over me.

Time seemed to slow. I blinked as my clothes absorbed every drop.

"Oh, shit. I'm...I'm so sorry. It's...oh gosh, it's my first night here. I'm so, so sorry. I-I messed up. Wh-what can I do?" she asked, her eyes glistening with tears as she righted the now-empty wine glasses on the splattered tray. "Ohmygod. I ruined your shirt, sir. This is...this is so unprofessional. I'll get fired over this. Wait here, I-I'll be right back. I will...I'll get my purse. Dry-cleaning is on me."

I wrapped my hand around her wrist before she could run away and leveled my eyes with hers. "Stop. Breathe. It's just a shirt. I own a dozen more just like it. You won't get fired because nobody will say anything to your boss. I might even have been the one who bumped into you. I should've stood on the side of the deck. See? I'm standing in the way."

The waitress raised her watery eyes, studying me as if there was a *but* about to come out of my lips. There wasn't.

"What's your name?"

"Daph…Daphne."

"Well, Daphne. Breathe in. Breathe out. It'll help to calm your nerves."

She filled her lungs with a deep inhale.

"Yeah, like this." Her shoulders dropped. "See? Much better. Listen, now you go back there," I pointed to the bar, "fill this tray up, smile, and get on with your night. Don't let this little incident affect you. You're doing a great job."

She blinked and swallowed hard, a quiver of a smile trembling over her lips. "How-how can you tell? You don't even know me, sir."

"It doesn't matter. I'd recognize a hard worker anywhere. I have a flair for finding good people. It's my superpower." I fished a business card out of the inner pocket of my now damp jacket. "If waitressing doesn't work out or you're ever looking out for a job, gimme a call. I might be able to put in a good word for you. Don't worry. The sun always comes out after the storm."

"Wow…huh…thank you. I… This… That's the nicest thing someone has ever said to me." She clutched my business card, pressed it against her chest as if I'd just promised her the world. With a shy smile, she turned and walked away, chin raised and back straight.

Warmth filled me. Daphne would be okay. She just needed a pep talk. And I happened to be good at those too. Perhaps I possessed more than just one superpower after all.

Devon leaned closer, and her eyes widened in stunned disbelief. Her perfume wrapped around me, tipping my senses into a dizzy haze. She smelled like spring and rain. Fresh and flowery. I burned the fragrance to my memory. Even my heart seemed to enjoy it as it expanded in my chest and drummed faster.

"Wow. That was… That was amazing. Most people would have screamed at the poor girl or threatened to get her fired. Instead, you boosted her self-confidence. That's very noble of you. You are a good man, Riley."

I looked down and pinched the fabric of my stained shirt to unglue it from my chest. "Thank you. It was just a clumsy mishap. Now, would you excuse me for a minute? I need to freshen up." I grimaced as she grinned at me, the gleam in her eyes captivating me.

Her smile grew wider, and she gave a gentle nod. "Go ahead. I can't wait to see how you manage to come back still dressed in these clothes. This should be interesting." She wrinkled her nose at my drenched state and said, "Yeah, very interesting."

I smiled. Like a fool. There was no way I could hold it back. Falling under this woman's charm felt like breathing. Easy. Natural. And imperative. "Wait and see. I may surprise you. I always find ways to turn impossible situations around."

Devon chuckled. "I'm sure you do. While you are in there cleaning up, I'll order us more drinks. Whiskey?"

"On the rocks," I said, holding back a grin. Did Devon notice what I was drinking earlier? If so, it made her even more attractive. I dreaded walking away from her, not ready to escape the magnetism that had settled between us. "I'll be quick."

We eye-fucked each other for a few seconds, my pulse spiking at the way her eyes brought her whole face to life.

Full lashes, high cheekbones, straight nose, heart-shaped lips. She was every shade of beautiful. With just one glance in my direction, this woman had captured my heart the moment I first saw her. It made no sense, but I wasn't about to overthink it.

So far, our encounter was the highlight of my night—of my day, maybe even my week.

With a sigh, I broke eye contact.

In a hurry to get back to her, I weaved through the bar crowd, my jacket now open, my soaked shirt sticking to my abs, and the front of my trousers molded to my thighs. Nothing about being wet and dressed up felt good. I was pretty sure even my socks were damp. I frowned at my predicament, wondering how I was supposed to get through the night in clothes soaked with red wine. It wasn't as if I had a change of clothes in my car or something. It wasn't as if I could just run home and change, even though I lived less than ten miles away. Tonight, I had no intention of letting Devon out of my sight, even for just a few minutes.

In the men's room, I peeled off my once-white shirt, gave it a disapproving look, and dropped it in the trash. A complete loss. I couldn't save it even if my life depended on it. After dabbing my trousers with paper towels, I turned the undershirt around and tucked it into my pants. I used more paper towels to soak up the excess wine from my jacket and put it back on. The look wasn't perfect, but in the dark bar, nobody would look too closely to notice.

I eyed myself in the mirror one last time, fixed my hair and the lapel of my jacket, and with determination in each step, made my way back into the night, looking for the woman in the red dress.

———

Read Riley and Devon's story,

Last Hope, now

emmanuellesnow.com/products/last-hope

Author's bookstore at emmanuellesnow.com

"Once again Emmanuelle Snow has created such amazing work. I went through an emotional journey with this story, I had happy tears, sad tears and laughter. It was just so heartfelt and pure. I couldn't put the book down." **(Goodreads)**

"I always love it when an author is able to make me feel all kinds of emotions. And with 'Hope and Country', Emmanuelle definitely managed that. This read was romantic, fun, sad, heartbreaking and wonderful." **(Goodreads)**

Read **Last Hope** now
Get your copy on the author's bookshop
emmanuellesnowshop.com/products/last-hope

BOARDING PASS
PENA / ABIGAIL
BOARDING PASS
FORD / ANDERSON
SILVERVILLE, PA
NASHVILLE, TN
ECONOMY
FORD / ANDERSON
SILVERVILLE, PA
MEMPHIS

www.ingramcontent.com/pod-product-compliance
Lightning Source LLC
Chambersburg PA
CBHW020227010826

48973CB00006B/1410